"You don't have to be strong. You don't even have to be strong for yourself all the time," John said. "We're a crew together, we help each other. Support each other."

"And what happens when we reach Cimarron Springs?" Moira asked.

"What do you mean?"

"What happens when I become dependent on you and then you're not there anymore?"

"Well, it'll be different, that's for sure. Town life is quite a bit different from trail life."

"It's not only that." She'd promised herself she'd remain aloft from the girls. The more time they spent together, the more difficult keeping her promise became. "Once we're back in town, everyone will go their separate ways."

"You can write letters."

"That'll never happen. Out of sight is out of mind for people. Once this is over, we'll never even think of each other again."

"Do you really think that?"

"Don't you?" She avoided his dark gaze. Lately she worried she'd miss the cowboy most of all.

Sherri Shackelford
and
Winnie Griggs

The Cattleman
Meets His Match
&
Second Chance Hero

LOVE INSPIRED
INSPIRATIONAL ROMANCE

Recycling programs
for this product may
not exist in your area.

LOVE INSPIRED®
INSPIRATIONAL ROMANCE

ISBN-13: 978-1-335-44879-8

The Cattleman Meets His Match & Second Chance Hero

Copyright © 2021 by Harlequin Books S.A.

The Cattleman Meets His Match
First published in 2014. This edition published in 2021.
Copyright © 2014 by Sherri Shackelford

Second Chance Hero
First published in 2015. This edition published in 2021.
Copyright © 2015 by Winnie Griggs

This edition published by arrangement with Harlequin Books S.A.

For questions and comments about the quality of this book, please contact us
at CustomerService@Harlequin.com.

Love Inspired
22 Adelaide St. West, 40th Floor
Toronto, Ontario M5H 4E3, Canada
www.Harlequin.com

Printed in U.S.A.

CONTENTS

Sherri Shackelford is an award-winning author of inspirational books featuring ordinary people discovering extraordinary love. A reformed pessimist, Sherri has a passion for storytelling. Her books are fast paced and heartfelt with a generous dose of humor. She loves to hear from readers at sherri@sherrishackelford.com. Visit her website at sherrishackelford.com.

Books by Sherri Shackelford

Love Inspired Suspense

No Safe Place
Killer Amnesia
Stolen Secrets
Arctic Christmas Ambush

Visit the Author Profile page
at Harlequin.com for more titles.

THE CATTLEMAN MEETS HIS MATCH

Sherri Shackelford

For which of you, intending to build a tower, sitteth not down first, and counteth the cost, whether he have sufficient to finish it?
—*Luke* 14:28

To Kristie Ryan, for knowing me better than anyone and liking me anyway.

To my mom, Bonnie, because I didn't acknowledge her in my last dedication. And she mentioned the oversight—a couple of times. Love you, Mom!

Chapter One

Fool's End, Indian Territory
September 1881

If John Elder hadn't been so furious with his mutinous crew of cattle hands, he might have noticed the woman dangling above his head sooner.

Except nothing had gone right since his arrival in the bustling cow town of Fool's End. Night had long since fallen by the time he'd discovered his four missing cowhands. Drunk. In a brothel. He'd fired them on the spot.

As John had circled behind the row of connected buildings, mud from a chilly autumn rain sucked at his boots and slowed his pace. Walking the alley at night wasn't the wisest choice, but he didn't have much time. He'd discovered the men's horses—*his horses*—at the livery earlier. He was taking back his property before his crew sobered up.

He kept the same rules as his father and his grandfather before him—no gambling, drinking or sporting women until the job was finished.

Moonlight glinted off broken bottles and the stench

of sour mash whiskey burned his nostrils. Propped open with a dented brass spittoon, the saloon's rear door released a dense cloud of cigar smoke. John skirted the hazy shaft of light with a grunt. He'd wasted half the day. For nothing.

A scuffle sounded behind him and he pivoted with his fists raised. Only inky darkness met his searching gaze. John dropped his arms. A man couldn't be too careful in this corrupt town.

The space behind the buildings wasn't as much an alley as an afterthought of the hastily constructed cow town. Dreamers and schemers had built Fool's End from one hundred people to five hundred practically overnight. The pains of rapid expansion had ravaged the city's grid work. Hope and despair fought a never-ending battle in the red soil, leaving behind an odd carnage. Buffalo hunters, cattle hands and fortune seekers had sprouted opportunity and corruption in equal measures.

A raucous piano ditty spilled from the nearest open saloon door and John's head throbbed in time with the grating tune. If any one of his six older brothers could see him now, he'd never live it down. Halfway from Paris, Texas, to his final destination of Cimarron Springs, Kansas, and he was spitting distance from failure. Again.

Sure, there'd been times in the past when his optimism had outpaced his good sense. But not this time.

John snorted at the irony. He shouldn't have let his temper get the better of him. Firing the men left him with only a cantankerous chuck wagon cook named Pops who was older than dirt and just as talkative, and eight hundred head of longhorn cattle he couldn't drive to Cimarron Springs alone. A small herd by most standards, but too large for two men alone.

It was imperative he reach the Kansas border or forfeit his dreams of starting his own cattle ranch. Fearful of Texas fever, a disease spread by longhorns to other livestock, the state was steadily moving the quarantine line farther west. He'd gambled the line would hold. Farmers and ranchers were filling the state, and their vote was bound to sway the legislature. Which gave John two weeks to cross into Kansas before the vote to close the borders took place.

Time enough for finding a new crew. But not much time.

The faint scuffing grew louder. Pausing, he glanced left and right, then lifted his chin and caught the first blow on his upturned cheek.

"Out of my way," a feminine voice called down.

The heel of her sturdy boot knocked him sideways. Staggering upright, John clutched his battered shoulder. A slender form dangled from a knotted bed sheet above his head.

His jaw dropped.

The girl craned her neck toward the ground, her face an alabaster oval against the darkness. A blur of pale petticoats covered by a dark skirt met his astonished gaze.

Her gaze snapped upward and her red hair shimmered in the moonlight like a wild, exotic halo. "Let out more rope. I'm still six feet from the ground," she hissed.

Her voice was mature. John craned his neck. The harder he looked, the more he realized this was a woman, not a girl. Her body twisted and his heart lurched.

He thrust out his arms and her flailing leg grazed his right hand. "Ouch."

Scooting aside, he reached with his left hand and she smacked that one too. "Take it easy!"

Retreating a safe distance, he assessed the situation. Either this was a dangerous prank or the woman was involved in something nefarious. *He didn't care.* He wasn't getting involved. No way. No how. Right now he had more problems than time.

"We haven't any more slack," a thin voice replied from the upper window. "That's all the sheets."

A dark-haired girl, no more than twelve years old, thrust her head into the shaft of light from the second-story window.

A blonde of the same age appeared at her right and stretched over the sill, her brilliant pale hair curtaining her face. "Maybe we should pull Moira up. This was a bad idea."

John rolled his bruised shoulder. "That's an understatement."

Their casual assessment of the situation confirmed his first instinct. This *was* some sort of childish prank. And the woman suspended above him was old enough to know better.

The girls chattered away, their heads bent together, complaining about the lack of decent bed sheets while completely ignoring both him and the dangling woman.

John shook his head. Of all the irrational sights he'd seen in this cow town over the past two days, this topped the list.

While yet another young lady joined the overlapping discussion, the woman above his head struggled for purchase on the rough clapboard walls. Her feet slipped up and down against the chipped paint as though she was running in midair.

John heaved a sigh. He had a singular way of sizing up a situation and predicting the outcome. Even his brothers grudgingly admired his innate ability.

He reached up and patted the woman's foot. "Let go and I'll catch you."

"Everything is quite under control," she replied primly.

"Lady, I don't know what kind of stunt you're pulling, but I see four girls in that window, and not a one of them realizes your arms are shaking and you're about to break an ankle. Or worse."

"This is none of your concern," she announced, her voice strained. "The plan is sound. I simply miscalculated the sheet length. I think it was the knots. Yes. That's it. The knots took up more slack than I expected."

"Either way, you're in a pickle."

The females in the window giggled.

"Be quiet up there," the woman ordered, a sense of urgency lacing her words. "If they catch us—"

She lost her grip and John dove forward. He grasped her around the waist and staggered, his feet held immobile in the mire. Keeping a tight hold on the squirming woman, he teetered backward and sat down. Hard. Icy water oozed through his canvas pants and chilled his backside.

The woman scrambled in his loose hold and her elbow cracked his ribs. John flinched. So much for playing the gentleman. She didn't appear at all grateful he'd taken the brunt of the fall—and soaked himself in the process. As she squirmed, her toe dug into his bent ankle.

He yelped and circled her waist with one arm. "Take it easy."

The woman whipped around, battling against his protective grasp. Her eyes widened. "Let go of me this instant or I'll scream. *Please.*"

Sensing her terror, John obliged. With her arms braced against his chest, his sudden release propelled her backward. She sprang from his embrace and landed flat on her back, sprawled in the oily puddle.

A chorus of titters sounded from above.

The blonde girl swung her leg over the sill in a flurry of white petticoats. "I'm going next."

John scrambled upright, slipping and sliding in the muck. "No. Wait."

While his gaze swung between the prone woman and the knotted rope, the second girl crawled out the window. She shimmied down the length until her feet swayed just out of reach.

John caught sight of a third girl straddling the ledge and his heartbeat quickened.

"Stop!" he ordered ineffectively.

The blonde dropped into his outstretched arms and he caught her slight weight against his chest.

As he set her on her feet, she tipped back her head and struck his jaw. John saw stars. He was going to be black-and-blue by the time this was over.

"Thanks." The girl sketched a wave and scurried aside. "I'm Sarah. I'll help Moira while you catch the others."

A pair of short boots descended into view, and John rubbed his sore chin.

He slanted a glance at the woman he'd rescued first. "Lady, please tell me someone up there has some sense."

"Don't count on it." She avoided his searching gaze and stretched her right hand toward Sarah. "And you may call me Miss O'Mara."

John hid a grin as Sarah awkwardly assisted *Miss O'Mara* onto unsteady legs. For a wild moment the two clung to each other like a couple of drunken sailors on a pitched deck. The moment the woman regained her footing, they sprang apart.

Miss O'Mara shook the mud from her back, then tugged her dark skirts lower. They were too short, showing a good bit of her worn boots and sliver of ankle. Together with her innocent face, it was easy to mistake her for an adolescent at first glance. On closer inspection, it was obvious she was in her late teens or early twenties.

"You'd better stand firm," the woman ordered, swiping the back of her hand over her mud-splattered face. "That's Darcy and she's the heaviest."

Distracted by the enticing smudge on Miss O'Mara's cheek, John didn't see the third escapee release her hold. His inattention cost him. A sharp elbow hammered his head and a boot scraped along his cheek. Blindly lifting his arms, he groaned beneath the girl's weight and managed to set her aside before another, much smaller, pair of boots descended into his vision.

A curly-haired child hugged the knotted sheets, her ankles crossed.

John reached out. "Let go. I've got you."

The youngster shook her head, her dark curls almost black against the moonlight.

Miss O'Mara stomped forward, her fisted hands planted on her slim hips. "Hazel, we haven't much time. Let go this instant."

The girl frantically shook her head. John rolled his eyes. Logic and orders weren't going to convince Hazel of safety.

Stepping back a pace, he caught the little girl's frightened gaze. "Almost there, Hazel. I'll catch you."

The frightened child sniffled. "Promise?"

"Promise."

John swiped his index finger in an *x* across his chest. The childish display of fealty captured Hazel's attention.

After a moment's hesitation, she tumbled free and he easily caught her slight form. The instant he set her safely on the ground, she giggled. "That was fun. Can I do it again?"

"No!" Moira and John shouted in unison.

The last girl descended the rope and waved him aside. "Don't need your help, mister."

Unlike the previous girls, she released her legs and worked her hands down the length until she was only a few feet above the ground. John crossed his arms and stepped back as she easily dropped the abbreviated distance.

Straightening from her crouch, the girl dusted her hands together. "Thanks for helping with Hazel. I'm Antonella. But everyone calls me Tony."

The girl pumped his hand once and stomped off.

John searched the empty window. A red velvet curtain flapped gently in the breeze. "Is that all of you?"

Miss O'Mara gathered her charges. "That's four. Darcy, Sarah, Tony and Hazel."

Scratching his head, John studied the motley gathering. "What are your ages, girls?"

Darcy boldly elbowed forward. "I'm fifteen next month."

"Thirteen," Sarah replied.

"Twelve and a half," Tony chimed in.

The littlest girl, Hazel, glanced up. "I'm ten."

John caught Miss O'Mara's gaze and lifted an eyebrow.

She pursed her lips. "My age is none of your concern."

Over twenty, he surmised immediately. Over twenty was about the age when a single woman ceased advertising her age. Little did she know. He'd give anything to be in his early twenties once more, when he'd still felt invincible.

Hazel tugged on his pant leg. "Are we safe now?"

The hairs on the back of John's neck stirred. Each building had a distinctive look from the front, but facing the alley, they blended together into one indistinguishable row. He counted the doors from the corner and his chest tightened.

"Hey," a slurred voice called from the open window. "Get back here."

The girls shrieked and spun away.

Summoned by the commotion, a bearded man stuck his head out the saloon door and spit into the mud. "What's goin' on?"

A clamor sounded from the far end of the alley.

Miss O'Mara ushered the girls deeper into the darkness without even a backward glance. John split his attention between the growing cacophony of voices and the escapees.

Indecision kept his feet immobile. The girls hadn't asked for his help. He could leave without an ounce of guilt. Considering they were obviously up to mischief, he'd already done more than most men would have.

"Hey, mister." The drunken man smacked his palms against the sill. "Stop them girls. They stole my money."

Of course. John mentally slapped his forehead. He should have known. He'd nearly been taken by a similar bunch in Buffalo Gap. Hastily stuffing his hands into his pockets, he breathed a sigh of relief. His fingers closed around the cool metal of his money clip. At least they'd rewarded his assistance by leaving him with the contents of his pockets intact.

Desperate children forced into desperate measures.

But what punishment did they deserve? John clenched his jaw. It wasn't for him to decide.

A flash of yellow caught his attention. Half immersed in the mire, a rag doll lay forgotten. He pinched its yellow yarn braid between two fingers and held it aloft in the moonlight.

Above him, the shouting man worked his way down the rope. The sheets held firm and a grudging admiration for Miss O'Mara filtered through John's annoyance. She tied knots like a trail boss.

"Well, mister," the man demanded, his breath a fog of alcohol fumes. "Where'd them little thieves go?"

What now? If his brothers were here, they'd shove John aside like a pesky obstacle. They'd take charge and assume he didn't have anything to offer. Like a herd of stampeding cattle, they'd wrestle all of the decisions—right or wrong—out of his hands. When his brothers were around, he never had to bother with taking responsibility.

John squinted into the darkened alley.

The inebriated man shoved him. "You deaf? I asked you a question."

John clenched his jaw. The sooner he put Miss O'Mara out of his thoughts, the sooner he could continue his journey. Heaven knew he hadn't even proved himself worthy of caring for a herd of cattle. A motley group of pickpocket orphans and a beautiful woman with fiery red hair were problems well beyond his limited resources.

Miss O'Mara and her charges were knee-deep in calamity and sinking fast. Moira required someone with the time, focus and connections to unravel her difficulties. Someone with the resources to steer her charges toward a respectable path. A hero. She'd gotten him instead. Maybe she'd have better luck down the road.

The drunken man took off in the direction Miss O'Mara and her charges had escaped. John snatched the man's arm and pointed the opposite way. "I'd check down there."

Moira heard the cowboy's betrayal and her heart lodged in her throat. She tugged on Hazel's arm and quickened her pace. With each pounding step her lungs burned and her vision blurred. What did speed matter when they were running blind? They'd be caught again for certain.

A hand tugged on her sleeve and tears of defeat sprang in her eyes. She yanked away. She wasn't giving up. Not yet. The fingers kept a brutal grip.

"Miss O'Mara," the cowboy spoke near her ear. "Let me carry Hazel. We'll make better time."

"No. You betrayed us."

Moira stumbled and the cowboy steadied her with a hand cupping her elbow.

"I didn't. Look around if you don't believe me."

At his calm reassurance, she slowed and glanced behind them. The alley was empty. No one pursued them.

While her exhausted brain grappled with the realization, the cowboy knelt. With childish faith, Hazel clambered onto his back. The little girl wrapped her legs around his waist and buried her face in his neck, effectively forcing Moira to follow. They ran another two blocks, her hand clasped in his solid grasp, before he halted.

The cowboy jerked his head toward a closed door. "In there."

Frightened and weak with hunger, Moira instinctively reacted to the innate authority in his tone. She tore open the door and guided the others inside.

The pungent aroma of animals assailed her senses. Her eyes gradually adjusted to the dim light and she noted Dutch doors lining either side of a cavernous center corridor. The cowboy had led them into the livery.

Horses stamped and snorted at the disturbance. The girls whispered together and Moira quickly shushed them. Their footsteps sounded like a stampede and their raspy, labored breathing chafed her taut nerves. She crept across the hay-strewn floor behind the cowboy, her index finger pressed against her lips for silence.

The cowboy gently lowered Hazel and propped an empty wooden saddle rack before the exit. Walking the aisle, he peered into each stall in turn, pausing before the third. He swung his arm in an arc, motioning them forward.

While the girls scurried inside the empty stall and huddled in the far corner, Moira bent and clutched the stitch in her side. In an effort to calm her rapid breathing, she dragged a deep breath into her tight lungs. The stall wasn't much of a hiding place, but at least they weren't out in the open anymore.

The cowboy returned a moment later with an enormous hay bale and tossed it onto the ground. He came back twice more in quick succession. Understanding his intent, Moira yanked on the bale wire, grimacing as it dug into her palms. Each bundle must weigh a hundred pounds, yet the cowboy showed no signs of strain.

He returned again with a stack of burlap feed sacks draped over his arm. "Cover yourselves with these and don't make a sound. If he searches the building, don't move, don't talk, don't even breathe."

"Wait," Moira called in a soft voice. "Why are you doing this?"

He hesitated and she sensed a war raging within him.

During their escape from the brothel, she'd noted his lean, muscular build and caught a glimpse of his square jaw. In the milky light of the stable, she made out the dark hair curling from beneath his hat and the raspy-looking whiskers darkening his jaw. He had an aristocratic face with deep-set eyes, a patrician nose, and lips that qualified as works of art.

He was, without a doubt, the most handsome man she'd ever laid eyes on. If only she had her sketch pad. He'd make a superb subject. Like a hero in a *penny awful* rescuing the damsel in distress, he had the sort of face that inspired romantic dreams.

Moira mentally shook the wayward thoughts from her head. Dreaming of a happily ever after was like building a house on a shifting sandbar. She'd seen too many people caught by the enticing trap, starting with her own mother. Over the years she'd guarded her heart well, and she wasn't about to weaken her resolve for a chiseled jaw.

A muscle worked in John's cheek. "Keep your head down. I may have to cause a distraction. Whatever you hear, stay out of sight unless I tell you to run."

His voice was rough and uneven and the look in his

eyes did nothing to reassure her. Moira had effectively trapped them in a corner.

She swallowed around the lump in her throat. She'd entrusted their lives to a stranger, albeit a handsome stranger. "What's your name?"

"John. John Elder."

Oddly comforted by the harmless name, she nodded. At least he hadn't replied with something like Deadly Dan or Killer Miller.

Searching for an innocuous rejoinder, she blurted, "I'm Moira."

He lifted the corner of his mouth in a half grin that sent her heart tripping. "Nice to meet you, *Miss* O'Mara."

Her cheeks burned beneath his reference to her earlier insistence on his use of her formal name. She might have been a touch rude, but there weren't exactly rules of etiquette for a brothel escape.

She cleared her throat. "You never answered my question. Why are you helping us?"

He stared into the distance. "Because it suits me for now."

"What happens when it doesn't suit you?"

"I guess we'll find out when that happens."

Her stomach dipped. For a moment she'd thought he was different. That he was actually helping them out of the kindness of his heart, out of Christian charity. Turned out he was like everyone else. He obviously had an ulterior motive. Maybe they were an amusement, maybe he was bored, maybe he'd flipped an imaginary coin and their predicament had come up tails. His motivation didn't really matter.

Whatever the reason, he'd cease helping once they

ceased serving whatever purpose he'd assigned them. People only cared when they needed something.

With a last appeal for silence, John stepped into the corridor and slid the door closed behind him.

Finally grasping the gravity of the situation, the girls remained unnaturally quiet. Moira flopped into position. Blood thumped rhythmically in her ears. She rubbed her damp hands against her thighs, then tugged her too-short skirts over her ankles. The dress was a castoff from the foster family she and her brother, Tommy, had lived with before Tommy ran away. Mrs. Gifford had recycled the expensive lace at the hem for her own purpose and left Moira with her ankles showing.

The cowboy probably thought… Moira fisted her hands. Why waste her energy worrying about what Mr. Elder thought of her clothing when they were still in peril? She'd heard Fool's End was dangerous, but every one-horse town she'd passed through had been dangerous.

She should have heeded the warnings this time.

Normally she'd never go out after dark, but she'd waited two hours for Mr. Grey, only to be told that he didn't know anything about her brother Tommy.

Tears pricked behind her eyes. Another dead end, another disappointment. After four years, she was certain this time she'd finally catch up with him. A maid from the Gifford house who remembered her fondly had discovered the charred bits of a telegram in the fireplace of Mr. Gifford's study. Piecing together what few words she could read, Moira had made out the names "Mr. Grey" and "Fool's End." The sender's name had been clear as well: Mr. Thomas O'Mara.

A name and a location weren't much to go on, but it

was all she had. Tommy must have forgiven her for the trouble she'd caused if he'd contacted her. She'd stolen Mr. Gifford's watch, and in her cowardice, she'd let her brother take the blame. He'd run away that same evening and she hadn't seen him since. There was no doubt in her mind the telegram had been for her. She doubted Mr. Gifford burned his own correspondence.

She'd considered posting a letter to Mr. Grey but then quickly dismissed the thought. Letters were impersonal and mail service unreliable. Instead, she'd set off almost immediately. Yet her arrival today had been too late. Tommy was nowhere to be found.

Mr. Grey had denied knowing anything about Tommy or the telegram, but something in his denial didn't sit right with her. On her way back to the hotel, not two blocks from her destination, some drunken fool had nabbed and locked her in that second-story room with four other girls.

Children.

She hadn't seen a one of them before that moment. Yet they'd formed an instant bond against a mutual enemy. Moira shuddered at the implication. She might be naive, but she knew a brothel when she saw one. If they were discovered, there'd be no escaping unscathed the next time.

Keeping her expression neutral, she passed each of the girls a sack. The less they picked up on her terror, the better. Being afraid didn't change anything anyway. It only made the waiting more excruciating.

Together they huddled silently in the deepest recess of the darkened stall, barely concealed behind the stack of hay bales. Hazel crawled onto her lap and Moira started. The frightened little girl had clung to her since her kidnapping. Had that been only a few hours ago? It seemed like an eternity. Hazel burrowed deeper. Unused to such open displays of affection, Moira awkwardly patted the child's back.

Tony took Hazel's cue and clustered on Moira's left side, Sarah on the other.

Darcy sat a distance apart, wrapping her arms around her bent legs and resting her chin on her knees. "This is stupid," she announced in a harsh whisper. "You should have waited until I thought of a better plan."

Moira pursed her lips. At fifteen, Darcy was the oldest of the girls—and the most sullen. The only words she'd uttered in the past two hours had been complaints or criticisms.

Darcy snarled another gripe beneath her breath.

Since they were all terrified and half-crazy with hunger, Moira bit back an angry retort. "We're here now and we'll have to make the best of it."

Darcy scowled but kept blessedly quiet.

For the next several minutes they waited in tense silence. As time ticked away, the air beneath the burlap sacks grew thick and hot. Sarah shifted and coughed. Footsteps sounded from the corridor and Moira hugged Hazel tighter.

"Can I help you, sir?" an unfamiliar voice spoke.

"I'm looking for a gang of thieves."

Moira immediately recognized the second man as her kidnapper. His raspy voice was etched on her soul.

"Five of them," the kidnapper continued. "A bunch of girls. One of them picked the wrong pocket this time. Stole Mr. Grey's gold watch."

"Why didn't he nab the little thief right then?" the

first man spoke, his voice tinted with an accent that might have been Norwegian or Swedish.

"Because he didn't notice his watch was missing right off."

"Then how does he know who done took his watch?" The Norwegian sounded dazed.

"Because we got three reports of the same kind of thing." The kidnapper's voice raised an octave. "An orphan girl comes in begging for change or food, and the next thing people know, their watches and money go missing."

"Well, I'm plum confused by the whole thing. Is it one girl you're after or five?" The Norwegian sputtered. "Did all five of them pick Mr. Grey's pocket? What'd she look like? Wait a second. What did *they* look like?"

"Well, let me see here. Mr. Grey seen a girl with red hair just before—" The kidnapper huffed. "Never mind. It ain't your business. Have you seen them or not?"

Moira's blood simmered. *Why that low-down, no good, drunken...*

Another thought jerked her upright. *A watch.* Four years ago a pocket watch had set off a chain of events that had changed her life forever. It was somehow fitting a timepiece had been at the center of this evening's troubles.

Would John Elder protect them if he thought they were thieves? Who else would help them if that vile man spread lies to cover his foul deeds?

"I ain't seen nobody," the Norwegian replied.

A scuff sounded, as though someone had opened a door.

"Now you'll have to leave," the Norwegian ordered. "That's a paying customer and you're not."

"Hey," the kidnapper snapped. "Ain't you the fellow from the alley?"

"Yep, that's me."

Moira started. John Elder was the "customer" who had come through the door. He must have escaped through the back and circled around front.

"The name is John," her rescuer answered, sounding bored and a touch annoyed. "And I already told you where to find the girls."

"Except I didn't find them, did I?" The kidnapper cackled. "Maybe you're saving them for yourself."

Moira's heart hammered so loudly and she feared they'd hear its drumbeat thumping through the slats in the stall door. She'd misjudged her reluctant rescuer once already tonight. Or had she?

"Look yourself," John replied, his annoyance apparent. "They're your problem, not mine."

The horse in the neighboring stall whinnied and bumped against the wall. Moira stuffed her fist against her mouth. Itchy hay poked through her clothing and she resisted the urge to scratch. A moment later the footsteps paused before their stall. The door scraped open. She held her breath and prayed.

An eternity passed before the door slid closed once more. Moira heaved a sigh of relief, then offered a silent prayer and a couple of promises concerning future atonement for good measure. Another few seconds and they'd be safe.

Sarah stifled a sneeze. The sound was faint and muffled, but it might as well have been a shotgun blast. The door scraped open once more.

"Hey," John called. "What did you just say to me?"

"Back off," the kidnapper snapped. "I didn't say nothing."

"I think you did."

Boots scuffed in the dirt and Moira winced at the sound of flesh hitting flesh. She whipped the bag from her head and sat erect, swiping her tangled and static hair from her eyes. From her vantage point, she watched as the cowboy spun the kidnapper around. John was obviously diverting the man's attention.

Setting Hazel aside, Moira leaped to her feet. She'd best spring into action before John Elder decided that rescuing a bunch of orphans no longer *suited* him. She snatched a pitchfork from the corner and charged, jabbing her kidnapper in the backside. Yelping, the man sprang upright, his hands clutching his back pockets.

The kidnapper whipped around with a snarl and her stomach clenched. Roaring in fury, he hurtled across the distance. Moira quickly sidestepped, then stumbled.

A glint of light reflected from a star on the kidnapper's lapel. Moira blanched.

Had her past finally caught up with her?

Chapter Two

Fear spiraled through Moira's stomach and shot to her knees, weakening her stance. She'd gone and done it now.

The cowboy was easily two paces behind the kidnapper. Feinting right, she swept the handle around and batted her attacker's legs. The man staggered and his arms windmilled. His left hand smashed against a hanging lantern. Glass shattered and sparks showered over the hay-strewn floor. Like a wild animal set loose, brilliant orange flames spread across the dry kindling. Astonished by the sudden destructive force, she staggered back a step.

In light of this new threat, Moira tossed aside the pitchfork and stomped on the rapidly spreading danger.

"Get back!" John hollered.

The kidnapper's face twisted into a contorted mask of rage.

He pointed at Moira through the growing wall of smoke separating them. "It's fitting you'll die in fire, you little hoyden."

With another shouted curse he pivoted toward the

exit. Midstride, his right foot caught the curved tongs of Moira's discarded pitchfork. The handle sprang upright and ricocheted off his forehead. The kidnapper's expression morphed into a comical mask of astonishment before going slack. He stumbled back a step, jerked and collapsed. A soft cloud of hay dust billowed around his motionless body.

Moira stifled a shocked peal of laughter.

The cowboy gaped. "You are a menace."

Her sudden burst of hysterics dissipated as quickly as it had appeared. Flames licked across the floor, belching black smoke in their wake.

Moira waved her hand before her face. "Stop bickering and help me put out the fire. I'll get, I'll…"

She stumbled over her words and her feet as she dashed back into the stall.

She lifted the sacks, revealing four flushed faces. "Fire! Everybody up. Help me beat out the flames."

The girls scrambled from their hiding place and dutifully rushed past, each of them snatching a sack in turn.

Using his coat, the cowboy had already doused two of the smaller fires. "Wet those sacks first!" he shouted.

Without needing instruction, Moira and Tony doused their sacks and joined him. Hazel tugged a heavy bucket of water from a nearby stall. Sarah met her halfway and together they hoisted it into the air and dumped the contents onto a pile of glowing embers. The water hissed and steamed over the scorched ground. Darcy flitted around the edges, snapping her damp sack and adding more fuel than help.

The horses whinnied and kicked at their stalls. Tony opened the enclosure nearest the fire, then covered the horse's eyes with a scrap of cloth.

A panicked shout announced the arrival of yet another man. He was old and grizzled, his back bent into a *c* and his arms no more than long, thin twigs jutting from his spare body. Judging by his muttered grumblings, Moira figured he was the Norwegian she'd heard earlier—the livery owner. He joined their efforts, stomping on the dying embers in a frantic jig.

Between the seven of them, they had the flames under control in short order. As the smoke dissipated, Moira kicked at the dusty floor, scraping away the top layer of ashes. The room went silent for a tense few minutes as they searched for hidden embers.

Once they determined the fire was well and truly extinguished, their forced camaraderie ceased.

The irate old man flailed his puny arms. "What in the world? You nearly burned down my barn. I ought to call the sheriff." He stilled and scratched the prickly gray patchwork of whiskers covering his chin. "Except Sunday is poker night. Maybe the new deputy is around. Haven't met that feller yet."

John dug into his pocket and pulled out a wad of bills. "This is feed and board for my horses." He added several more bills to the fat pile. "This is for the damage."

The wizened man accepted the money with one gnarled hand and rubbed the shiny bald spot on the back of his head with the other. "Suit yourself."

Moira wasn't certain the exact amount the cowboy had paid, but it was enough to send the livery owner away whistling a merry tune.

Gathering her scattered nerves, she folded her burlap sack into a neat square. Her eyes watered and her lungs burned from the grit she'd inhaled.

John paced back and forth before her, his face red.

After three passes, he halted and opened his mouth. No words came. Moira tilted her head.

"Are you crying?" he demanded at last.

"No. It's from the smoke."

"Good." The cowboy worked his hands in the air before her as though he was strangling some invisible apparition. "I gave you very specific instructions. What did you think you were doing?"

"Assisting you, of course. And you might have thanked me."

"I had everything under control. You, on the other hand, nearly burned down the barn. And us in the process."

"That's a bit of an exaggeration, don't you think?"

"If you had followed my *very* simple instructions, none of this would have happened. Give me some credit. I happen to know what I'm doing." The cowboy thrust his hands into his flap pockets and his expression turned incredulous. He lifted his jacket hem, revealing where his fingers poked through a charred hole. "You've ruined my best coat."

Moira stifled a grin at this outrage. He didn't appear in the mood to appreciate the absurdity of the situation. "You were the one who used it to beat out an open flame."

"I didn't want to *die*."

Moira's eyes widened. She'd never heard anyone enunciate that clearly with their teeth still clenched together.

And why on earth was he angry? She planted her hands on her hips. Judging by the mottled red creeping up his neck, he wasn't merely angry, he was furious. His searing glare would have melted a less hearty soul.

Moira straightened her spine. "You were hardly at risk of death."

"You don't know that. Your crazy stunt set this place ablaze."

"I beg to differ. My *crazy stunt* saved our hides. Not to mention I used this perfectly useful burlap sack and not my *best jacket*. You might have done the same."

"You could have trusted me. I haven't proven myself unworthy *yet*. You might have at least waited."

She cast him an annoyed glance. "What are you blathering on about now?"

"You are the most—"

"I haven't time to debate with you." Moira rubbed her eyes in tight circles with the heels of her hands. She instinctively knew their plight no longer suited John Elder's interest. He'd be gone in a flash for certain.

Moira smoothed her hair and adjusted her collar. For a moment she'd thought the kidnapper was sporting a silver star. The glimpse she'd seen must have been a trick of the light. Besides, St. Louis was a lifetime ago. If the Giffords hadn't looked for her after she'd left four years ago, they certainly weren't looking for her now.

Dismissing the cowboy, her reluctant rescuer, she faced the girls.

Her stomach roiled. *What now?*

She hadn't thought much past their immediate escape. Judging by their dazed expressions, neither had the others. Darcy had abandoned her indifferent sneer and Hazel's lower lip trembled. Tears brimmed in Hazel's wide brown eyes. Even Tony had lost her swagger.

"It's safe now," Moira announced and flapped her hands dismissively. "I believe our kidnapper will be indisposed for an extended period of time. You may all go home."

"I'm sorry I sneezed and gave away our hiding place." Sarah wrapped her arms around her slight body. "I can't go home."

"Of course you can," Moira urged. "Mr. Elder will walk you safely home, won't he?"

She lifted a meaningful eyebrow in his direction. Let him wiggle out of that one.

Sarah shook her head. "We haven't any place to go."

Moira caught sight of the safety pin, the number long-since faded, attached to the girl's pinafore. Nausea rose in the back of her throat. "You were on the orphan train?"

"I have an uncle." Tony cut in, her expression defiant. "He gave me a letter and everything. He said he'd come for me."

Darcy braced her legs apart and planted her hands on her hips. "Then where is he now? You can claim whatever you want, but you're no better off than the rest of us."

"The woman on the train took my letter." Tony lifted her chin. "She stole it while I was asleep. So I ran away. Folks don't want children. They want workers. We're free labor, plain and simple." Tony jabbed her thumb at her chest. "I'm worth more. I was doing fine on my own until I was caught." Her face blanched. "Until that man. Until tonight when we were…you know. I got sloppy, but it won't happen again."

"Don't worry." Moira patted her hand. "It's all over now."

The hollow platitudes stuck in the back of her throat. They were children. Alone. They'd never be safe. Her head spun with the implications of the impossible situation. Life for discarded children was ruthless and devoid of fairy-tale endings. At best they'd be neglected, at worst they'd be exploited. Driven into impossible choices.

The air sizzled with emotion and the girls crowded around her, speaking over each other, demanding her attention. She backed away from the onslaught and they crowded her against the stall door.

"I have a sister," Sarah announced with a nod. "She's older than me. She said she'd take care of me, but her husband didn't want me. They put me on the train anyway."

Moira swayed on her feet. The past came rushing back. She pictured her mother standing on the platform, her ever-present handkerchief pressed against her mouth as she coughed. Moira had held her brother's hand clasped in her own.

"I'll take care of you, Tommy."

She knew better than anyone did the perils of survival. She'd been tested herself. Tested, and failed.

"Miss O'Mara," John Elder's voice interrupted her memories. "What's going on here? Aren't you together?" He circled his arms and touched his fingertips together. "Aren't you a gang of little pickpockets?"

Her body stiffened in shock. "You'd believe a drunken kidnapper over a bunch of innocent children?"

She hadn't stolen anything in the four years since she'd left the Giffords'. Not even when she'd been near starving. He didn't know anything about her. He was making a blind guess, that's all.

A horse stuck its head from the stall door and nuzzled her ear. Moira absently scratched its muzzle.

Hazel tugged on her skirts. "What's a pickpocket?"

Guilt skittered across the cowboy's face. "I'm sorry," he spoke. "I'm not certain what's going on here. It's not that I don't have sympathy for your predicament, but I've got a herd of cattle." He motioned over his shoulder. "I can't leave them for much longer."

Moira ran her hand through her sweat-dampened hair. What was she going to do? She couldn't hide them all. "I'm renting a room at the hotel. It's the size of a water closet."

She was tired and hungry and bruised. The entire trip had been a waste of time and she was penniless. Stuck in this corrupt town unless she could find a respectable job. As much as she wanted to help, there wasn't much she could do. She could barely take care of herself.

The four girls cowered before her like penned animals who'd escaped their enclosure. They were wide-eyed and curious, frightened and hesitant. And lost. That was the thing about growing up in a caged environment, a person could always feel around the edges and find where the ground dropped off. Even being homeless was as much of a cage as anything else. When the basic needs of food and shelter consumed every waking moment, survival was a jail all its own. No time for dreams or hopes or plans of the future. The moment they'd found one another, the rules had altered. They were a team.

Moira vividly recalled her first year alone after leaving the Giffords—the fear, the uncertainty, the uneasy exhilaration of holding her own fate in her hands, unencumbered by the push and pull of others. A similar feeling was blossoming in the girls.

Having stretched beyond their solitary struggles, they showed the first trembling signs of hope. They'd discovered kindred spirits, and they were holding on tight, lashing together their brittle fellowship like a flimsy raft against troubled waters. Moira hadn't the heart to tell them they were better off alone. Sooner or later, everyone wound up alone.

Sarah hung her head. "No one picked me at the last stop," she spoke quietly. "I couldn't stand it anymore. It's like at recess when nobody picks you for a team. When the chaperones came for us at the hotel, I hid. I did what I had to do. I know I've done things wrong and I've prayed for forgiveness. After you helped us, I felt like my prayers were answered."

The room swayed and Moira's vision clouded. She knew the feeling of being passed around like a secondhand coat nobody wanted anymore. Though she feared the answer, she asked anyway, "Where have you been staying since then?"

"We all just sort of found each other and stuck together. There's an abandoned building near the edge of town." Sarah ducked her head. "That's where that man found us."

Darcy's expression remained defiant. "You all knew it couldn't last. You knew they'd catch us sooner or later. I was on my own for four years without getting caught." She noticed Moira's curious glance and her countenance faltered. "I was on my own for four years," she repeated.

Though Moira didn't want to hear any more, didn't want to know any more, she'd set her questions into motion and there was no going back.

She knelt before Hazel, the youngest. The little girl wore a faded blue calico dress, the grayed rickrack trim ripped and drooping below her hem. "Do you have a home?" Moira asked gently.

The littlest girl shook her head. "A family picked me, but I was bad and they took me back." Hazel sniffled. "I left the chicken coop open by accident and the dog got in. All the chickens died. Mrs. Vicky didn't want me any more after that. Then tonight I only wanted an apple... I would have worked for it. I would have."

Sarah rested a hand on her shoulder. "You don't have to say any more."

Moira gritted her teeth. They were just children and they'd been discarded like so much rubbish. She was sick of it. Sick of people thinking children didn't have thoughts or feelings. "How did you wind up in Indian Territory?"

"Because this is the end of the line," Darcy said.

There wasn't much between the Indian Territories and California. Moira supposed No Man's Land was as good a place as any to dump the unwanted children.

Ten years ago she'd been a rider on the orphan train. She and her brother, Tommy. She hadn't kept the promise she'd made to her mother. She hadn't taken care of Tommy.

Sometimes she felt as though she was being punished for her failure. She hadn't felt peace since that fateful day when she'd slipped Mr. Gifford's watch into her pocket. She'd known it was wrong. She'd known it was stealing. She couldn't help herself. She often wondered what kind of person she'd become. She wondered if there was any going back. If she'd slipped once, how much temptation did she need before she slipped again?

Mr. Gifford had blamed Tommy for the missing watch and she'd been too terrified to admit the truth. Mr. Gifford had promised retribution, but Tommy hadn't waited around for the punishment. By the following morning, he was gone. And he hadn't even said goodbye.

Once she found him, once she confessed what she'd done, this pain would end. She'd waited another year at the Giffords' even though staying had been near torture. She'd waited hoping Tommy would return so she could explain the truth and finally take the blame. Except he'd never come back.

After she'd left the Giffords', she'd remained in St. Louis, hoping against hope she'd glimpse him. It was crazy, but it was all she had. She'd kept in touch with anyone she thought she could trust, but most of the servants were too scared for their jobs to return the favor. Then she'd received the charred bits of the telegram from the maid with Tommy's name. Her prayers had finally been answered.

The girls stared at her, their faces expectant. Moira knew better than anyone what fate awaited the orphan girls, but there was nothing she could do. The system was too far broken for one lone person to fix. She glanced at the cowboy. He looked away. Mr. Elder wanted a crew, not a bunch of waifs.

Moira shook her head in denial. They didn't know her. They didn't know how she'd failed Tommy. How she'd fail them if they put their faith in her. They'd turn on her for certain if they knew how she'd betrayed her own brother.

Shame robbed the breath from her lungs. "I'm sorry, but I can't help you. Any of you."

The defeat in Moira's voice knocked John down a peg. For the past twenty minutes he'd been patting himself on the back, lauding his clever handling of the situation. While the rescue hadn't been particularly elegant, he'd accomplished his goal. He'd saved the girls from the dubious justice of a drunken vigilante and disabled the man in the process. What had his false pride netted him? He hadn't solved anything. He'd mined a heap of new problems instead.

One night, John told himself. He'd lost a whole day already, what was one more?

His brothers' words rang in his ears. *You'll never make it without our help.*

All his life they'd treated him as though he wasn't capable. Every bit of clothing he'd had growing up had been a hand-me-down. If he had an idea, they had a thousand reasons why it wouldn't work. If he wanted to try something new at the ranch, he had to ask permission like a child. At thirty-three years old, they still treated him as though he was a kid. Truth be told, he was the odd man out in his family. He'd always been more relaxed, more easygoing than the rest of his siblings.

His brothers attacked their responsibilities, no matter how minor, with all-consuming zeal and they expected him to do the same. John figured there were times when letting go was just as difficult as fighting. Yet he'd never once seen a monument erected in honor of a calculated retreat.

He and his brother Robert had fought the worst. Their last argument had divided the family, and John had realized it was time to set out on his own. If he stayed, one of them was bound to say something they couldn't take back. The only way they were going to get along was if one of them backed down. He'd demanded his share of the herd and declared his intention to take over the homestead his older brother Jack had abandoned when he'd married.

You'll never make it without our help.

Robert's words rang in his ears. John pulled out his watch and checked the time. Eleven o'clock. Too late for anything but sleeping. He'd quit tomorrow, when things were less complicated.

Hazel tugged on his pant leg. "I'm tired. Can we come home with you?"

"I don't have a home. Not here anyway." Weary resignation softened his voice. When had his simple goal become this complicated? "I'm driving a herd of cattle to Cimarron Springs, Kansas."

He felt another tug on his pant leg.

Hazel's liquid brown eyes stared up at him. "Do you have any food at your camp?"

John's throat tightened. His whole life he'd been surrounded by the suffocating pressure of family. But he'd never gone to bed hungry.

And he'd never been homeless. "When was the last time any of you ate?"

Hazel shrugged.

John studied each of the girls in turn, their personalities already forming in his mind. Sarah kept her face downcast, as though asking for help was an imposition. Tony met his questioning gaze straight on, challenging. Darcy remained hesitant, uncertain, caught between rebellion and desperation.

Moira's eyes haunted him most of all. A curious shade of pale blue-green, the color of the tinted glass of a mason jar, translucent and ethereal. *Hopeless.* The foreign emotion resonated in his heart. You couldn't mourn for something you'd never had. What had Moira hoped for, and lost? She hadn't hoped for someone like him, that much was certain. She'd made her disdain of him apparent. Yet the desolate look in her eyes was hauntingly familiar. He'd seen that look once before.

Years ago, Robert had lost his wife during a bank robbery gone sour. He'd never forget the agony his brother had suffered. The pain of loss his niece and nephew had worn from that moment on. The death of their mother had bent them like saplings in the wind. They'd survived the tragedy, but they were irrevocably changed.

Robert had changed, too. He'd been married and widowed young. A man who'd grown old before his time beneath the weight of tragedy. Four years separated the brothers in age, though it might as well have been forty. He couldn't bridge the chasm between them—because knowing why Robert had changed and getting along with him were different things. After their last fight over how to run the family ranch, John had known he could no longer stay without tearing the rest of the family apart.

He rubbed his forehead. He had enough food back at camp to feed four hungry crewmen. Certainly enough for a few scrawny females.

He was well and truly trapped by his own conscience.

One night, he repeated. What was the harm in sheltering the girls for one night? Yet the past two months had taken its toll on his endurance. Even the most basic problems had multiplied, popping up like wild mushrooms after a spring rain.

Impatient with his indecision, Hazel took his hand. "Why are you taking your cattle for a walk?"

"It's not a walk," John patiently explained. "It's called a drive. I'm driving them to Cimarron Springs."

"How come?"

"Because I was tired of trying to prove myself," John grumbled beneath his breath.

Hazel's innocent questions struck too close to the heart of the matter. He didn't have any strength left to pretend he didn't care. Feigned complacency took energy, and he was plum out of flippant answers. Everyone in a family had a role, and John's role had been determined before he'd toddled off the porch and cut his chin. A scar he still bore. A preconceived legacy he couldn't shake.

He was the one who dove in headfirst without heeding the dangers. He was the most impulsive of his family, the most easygoing, too, as far as he could tell. Which meant his brothers rarely took his ideas seriously. When he'd declared his intent to purchase his brother Jack's plot of land in Cimarron Springs and drive his share of the herd north before Kansas closed its borders against longhorns, Robert had scoffed.

You'll lose your shirt.

John hadn't lost yet.

He *did* have an idea how to stop the girls' incessant questions. "You can stay with me tonight." A body couldn't talk while eating. "I'm coming back to town tomorrow. We'll find help during the day. There's nothing else we can do this late."

The relief on their faces disgraced him. "Can any of you ride?"

Tony and Darcy nodded.

Moira shrugged. "Some."

He'd earlier judged Miss O'Mara's age as early twenties. Old enough for courting and pretty enough for dozens of marriage proposals. John pictured the girls back home with their giggles and coy smiles. Moira could easily pass for one of those girls. She had a sweet face, pale and round, with a natural dusting of pink on her cheeks. Her lips were full and rose colored, perfect for kissing. But despite the natural innocence nature had bestowed on her face, her eyes held a jarring, world-weary cynicism.

John plucked the hat he'd lost during the fight from the ground and dusted the brim. He slanted a glance at the prone man who lay where Moira's discarded pitch-fork had rendered him senseless. Their pursuer would come to soon enough, and he'd be spitting mad.

They didn't have much time. "I'll take you back to my camp. We'll figure out the rest in the morning."

Moira moved protectively before the girls. "Is there anyone at camp besides you?"

"Yes," John answered truthfully.

She pursed her full lips and he glanced away from the distraction.

Moira tsked. "Then the answer is no. I'll take care of the girls myself."

The return of her elusive temper buoyed his spirits. That was more like it. "I've got a cook. His name is Pops and I'm pretty sure he's as old as dirt. And ornery. But he makes good grub." John laughed drily. "Too bad you weren't a bunch of boys. I'd hire you on as my new crew and save myself another trip into town."

His joke fell on deaf ears. A myriad of emotions flitted across Moira's expressive face. Doubt, hope, fear. She wanted to trust him, she didn't have much other choice, but he sensed her lack of faith. Not for the first time he wondered about Miss O'Mara's background. What was her story? She was at once an innocent girl and a jaded woman, and he couldn't help but wonder what forces had shaped her.

"I've got five horses I need delivered back to camp," John continued. "You'd be helping me out."

Hazel appeared crestfallen. "If I can't ride, does that mean I can't go?"

His heart heavy, John knelt before the little girl. "Of course you can go. You can ride with me."

He marveled at their expressive personalities. Darcy was petulant and defiant—he'd keep an eye on that one. Sarah was meek, with a thread of steel behind her shy demeanor. Tony pressed her independence, but she wasn't as brave as she appeared. Nothing prevented Tony from leaving. She'd stayed instead. And Hazel. What kind of heartless person discarded a little girl because of a simple mistake?

John faced Moira, the unspoken leader. Her eyes drooped at the corners and he realized she'd reached the end of her rope.

He knew that feeling well enough. "Trust me."

Her eyes sparked with emotion. "For tonight," she replied, her voice a telling mixture of exhaustion and determination. "Just for tonight."

The kidnapper stirred and groaned. John crossed the distance and looped his arms beneath the prone man's shoulders. Heels dragging tracks through the dirt floor, he dragged the dead weight into an empty stall. A glint of silver on the man's coat caught his attention. John flipped the lapel aside and groaned. The silver star knocked the wind from his lungs. The words stamped into the metal flickered in the lamplight: Deputy Sheriff.

John staggered back a few feet and braced his hands on the slatted walls. *Hang it all.* He'd gone and decked a lawman. A burst of anger flared in his chest. None of this nonsense would have happened if the fool deputy had declared himself a lawman right out. The drunken man had never once identified himself. Pacing the narrow enclosure, John considered his options. He didn't know what any of this meant, but he knew well enough this situation had gone from bad to worse.

His stomach grumbled. Time enough tomorrow for facing the consequences. As hungry as he was, the girls must be ravenous. Sorting out the details when they were all exhausted and near starved would only make matters worse.

He briefly considered waking the deputy before he caught another whiff of the alcohol. Moira and her charges were too vulnerable for a man who was bound to wake up mean. Keeping his gaze averted, John slid shut the stall door and dropped the T-bar into place.

He motioned toward Moira. "Let's get this show on the road."

With no other choice but to move forward, John gathered his five horses and had them saddled and ready in short order. Growing wearier by the moment, the girls groggily followed his orders, stifling yawns behind patched-elbow sleeves. Their eyes blinked slower and slower.

While the horses stamped and snorted, he quickly emptied his men's saddlebags into a burlap sack. When that task was completed, he cinched a rope around the top and placed the belongings with the livery owner for safekeeping.

The elderly man jerked upright from his half doze and accepted the parcel. "Your men ain't gonna be too happy when they come back and find their mounts gone."

John braced his knuckles against the doorframe. "They can keep their gear and the pay they earned this far. The horses are mine. They're well aware of that."

"You don't have to convince me." The livery owner kicked back in his chair and closed his eyes.

John set his jaw. He'd been second-guessed his whole life by his own family, he wasn't paying a bunch of two-bit cowhands for the privilege.

As the girls clustered in the moonlit corral, John took stock of their attire. Each of the younger girls wore warm coats buttoned to their throats. Not Moira. She wore only her thin cotton dress with its too-short hem—a dress more suited for a sultry summer evening than a crisp fall night. How had she wound up crawling out the window of a brothel? Why had the deputy stashed the girls in such an unlikely place? Snippets of girls' conversation rattled around his brain.

I was doing fine on my own until I was caught...

I got sloppy...

I only wanted an apple...

He pinched the bridge of his nose. He was too weary for the answer. Too cowardly to face what his questions might uncover. Tomorrow would come soon enough. He'd get his answers then. None of them appeared injured, at least not physically, which meant any questions he had could wait. A good night's sleep would make the reckoning that much easier.

Moira blinked at his lengthy silence.

John tilted his head and considered Miss O'Mara. The more time he spent with her, the more he realized she wasn't like the girls back at home at all. She didn't fill the silence with chatter. She hadn't asked for anything. Not food or help or even money. Certainly money would solve their most pressing problems. The fact remained, she hadn't asked and he wouldn't offer. He'd accepted responsibility only for their safety, at least for this evening. A guarantee he planned on keeping.

A light mist gathered on Moira's eyelashes, sparkling like tears in the moonlight. A delicate shiver fluttered down her arms. He realized she'd been holding herself rigidly, hiding her discomfort.

Feeling like a first-rate heel for letting her suffer in the chill night air, John shrugged out of his jacket and tossed it to her. "Take this."

She caught the material against her chest with a shake of her head. "I mustn't," she protested, but he couldn't help but note how she clutched the material, her knuckles whitening. "Thank you."

"I've got a slicker in my saddlebags." Her obvious gratitude roughened his voice. "That'll be good enough."

She should have been chastising him, not thanking him. His mother had taught him better. No matter the surroundings or the circumstances, he'd been raised a gentleman.

Moira glanced up shyly, staring at him through the delicate fringe of her eyelashes. She fingered the charred hole in his pocket and a mischievous grin lit her face. "Are you certain you trust me with your best coat?"

Heartened by her teasing, he replied, "Just don't set it on fire. Again."

For a moment her guard slipped. She smiled at him, a wide grin that plumped her cheeks and lit her eyes. His heart sputtered, an irregular beat as though it was searching for a new rhythm. Miss O'Mara was beautiful, though not from the perfection of her features. Her lips were too full, her nose too pert for classic beauty—yet her smile was captivating and her eyes tipped and exotic. Her brilliant red hair shimmered in the moonlight, a ruckus of curls tumbling over her shoulders, torn free from its moorings by the night's activities. She was perfect in her imperfection, and his addled brain grappled with his unexpected fascination.

Worrying that he'd give himself away at any moment, John tore his gaze away and cleared his throat. "We should, uh, the night's not getting any younger and neither am I."

Her expression faltered at his abrupt dismissal. As she turned he reached out his arm, then let it drop. It was better she didn't see him as her rescuer. A misty haze of desolation surrounded her, unsettling his judgment. She'd seen more of the world than was meant for one so young. More of the darkness.

John shook his thoughts back to the task at hand.

Having studied the girls while they saddled the horses, he had a fair idea of their experience. All of his mounts were trained and relatively well mannered. He'd broken them himself. He'd always kept his own horses on the ranch, all of them raised from foals and trained by his own hand. A gentle touch resulted in the best mounts, a theory mocked by many of the ranch hands. He ignored their jeers because his results spoke for themselves. His horses were sought out from Illinois to Nevada. Through his brother Jack's contacts, he'd even provided trained mounts for the Texas Rangers.

As with all animals, each of them had a personality, and he matched the girls accordingly.

"Mount up," he ordered, watching them from the corner of his eye.

Tony, the most experienced of the group, effectively

scurried into the saddle. John swung up behind Hazel and found the other three standing uncertainly beside their horses.

"Mount up," he ordered again.

Sarah shifted and spread her hands. "Um. I don't think I can."

John paused and assessed the problem. The stirrup hit at her shoulder. Between the height of the saddle and her confining skirts, she was stuck. Why hadn't he noticed before? *Because I don't usually ride out of a livery at midnight with a bunch of girls, that's why,* he reminded himself. Men, he understood. He'd been raised on a ranch full of men. Women, not so much.

"I'll help." John swung off his mount. He touched Hazel's leg and met her questioning brown eyes. "Wait here and don't wiggle too much."

The little girl patted the horse's neck. "What's her name?"

"*His* name is Bullhead."

"How come?"

"Because he's bullheaded."

"I don't like that," Hazel scowled. "I'll call him Prince instead. I like that better." She leaned forward and one of the horse's ears swiveled in her direction. "You like that better, too, don't you?"

The horse nickered, as though in approval. Hazel grinned triumphantly. "See? He likes his new name much better, don't you, Prince?"

Another nicker. John rolled his eyes. "Whatever strikes your fancy."

Not like the name was going to stick. She could call the horse Pretty Britches for all he cared. By tomorrow evening, he'd have Bullhead back.

A half smile at Hazel's antics plastered on his face, he gave Darcy and Sarah a leg up, then paused before Moira. She'd reluctantly donned his coat, and the sleeves hung well below her fingertips. Her scent teased his senses and he searched for the elusive source. It was floral, and familiar, inspiring a sense of peace and well-being. He pictured a summer's day, white moths fluttering above a field of bluebells, a gentle breeze whispering through the grass.

Peonies. That's what had struck a chord. She smelled like peonies.

He lifted her hand and turned back the cuff, then repeated his action on the other side.

Keeping her eyes narrowed, she remained stubbornly quiet during his ministrations. John recalled what he'd stuffed in his pocket earlier. He reached out and Moira started. He stilled immediately, then moved more slowly, approaching her as he might a frightened animal—gradually, gently. She was as skittish as a newborn calf. Cautiously reaching into the pocket of his coat, he lifted his hand and revealed the rag doll he'd found earlier.

Moira's face lit up. "That's Hazel's doll! Where did you find it?"

"In the mud beneath the window."

She took the doll from him, cradling the soft material in her cupped hands. She glanced in the direction of Hazel and Bullhead—newly christened as Prince. The little girl murmured softly, petting its neck. Fascinated with the horse, she certainly wasn't missing her lost doll.

Moira thoughtfully stroked the braided yarn, absently fingering the hand-sewn stitches. Her fingers moved reverently, lovingly, as though the fabric was silk instead of muslin.

Her rapt interest gave him pause. "Did you have a doll like that growing up?"

He didn't know what had inspired his question, this wasn't exactly the time or place for casual conversation.

She shook her head, her face melancholy. "No. I never had anything as fine as this."

John choked off a laugh, certain she was fooling around. When her expression remained somber, he cleared his throat. "You should keep it safe. Until we're back at camp."

"She needs a bit of washing, that's all. A little scrubbing and she'll be good as new."

"Of course." He floundered. "She'll be as bright as a brass button."

Lost in a world he didn't understand, Moira carefully wrapped the doll in a faded red handkerchief and gingerly replaced the bundle in the pocket of his jacket. For a moment the ground tilted on its axis and the world turned topsy-turvy. With Moira, the feelings sputtering in his chest were foreign, tossing him out of his element. This wide-eyed sprite carried a mixed bag of reactions. One minute she was chastising him, the next moment she was teary-eyed over a battered rag doll.

John shook his head. He'd never understand women. Not if he lived to be one hundred and ten years old.

"You ready?" he asked.

She nodded, then swiveled her head left and right, uncertain. She'd said she was a rider. She'd lied. Near as he could tell, she wasn't sure which side to mount on—a basic skill of horsemanship. In deference to her novice ability, he grasped her around the waist and easily lifted her, surprised by her diminutive weight.

She was slight and delicate, vulnerable and threatening all at the same time. As she sheepishly attempted to cover her ankles, he averted his gaze. The self-conscious action sparked a burst of sorrow in his chest. Someone as proud and brave as Moira deserved a wardrobe full of new dresses that dusted the ground, like a well-heeled lady.

Quelling his wayward emotions, he turned away. To his enormous relief, the livery owner scuffled into the corral, splintering the tense moment.

The older man gestured toward the stables. "What am I supposed to do with that fellow in the stall?"

"Let him out when he wakes up," John called over his shoulder. "You don't know anything."

"True enough," the man replied. "True enough."

Moira adjusted her feet in the stirrups and stared down at John. She must have discovered the starch in her spine while his back had been turned. She sat up straighter, her face a stern mask of disapproval. "You better not double-cross us, mister."

The obvious rebuke in her voice triggered a long-forgotten memory. Years ago at a family wedding he'd joked with Ruth Ann, his on-again, off-again sweetheart, about getting married. She'd looked him straight in the eye, her disappointment in him painfully clear. *"You're too easygoing. I need someone who can take care of me."*

Ruth Ann had married his best friend instead. They had five kids and a pecan farm not far from the Elder ranch.

John had set out to prove himself, and so far he'd come up short. He couldn't even take care of a herd of cows, let alone this vulnerable woman with her sorrowful, wounded eyes.

"I won't double-cross you," he replied evenly.

Moira's fears weren't unwarranted, just misdirected. He wasn't a hero. There was no one riding to the rescue and the sooner he separated from this bunch the better. Before they found out they'd placed their fragile hopes on the wrong man.

There was something else going on here, and he wasn't the man to sort it out.

Chapter Three

A short time later Moira swung off her horse and pain lanced up her legs. She winced, hobbling a short distance. She'd ridden a handful of times before and understood the rudimentary skills, but she wasn't nearly as confident as she'd let on.

She'd thought she'd fooled John Elder. The sympathy in his perceptive eyes had exposed her mistake. He'd known she was a fraud, and he'd been too polite to voice his observation. She'd paid the price for her bravado. With each step, her untried muscles screamed in protest. She unwittingly sank deeper into John Elder's coat and inhaled its comforting scent.

Over the years she'd come to associate two smells with men—cloying, headache-inducing cologne and the pungent scent of exertion. John's coat smelled different, a combination of animal, man and smoldering wood. The unfamiliar mixture was strange and soothing. Despite the cool night, warmth spread through her limbs.

Shadows dotted the horizon, silhouetted against the moonlight. Restless cattle lowed at their arrival and Moira shivered. The glow of a fire marked the center of the camp. A wagon and three oatmeal-colored canvas tents were pitched in an arc around the cheery flames. The orderly sight was reassuring.

When she'd turned eighteen, she'd left the Giffords with little more than the clothes on her back. The gentleman who'd delivered their milk took pity on her and talked his brother-in-law into giving her a job. The brother-in-law owned a hotel and she cooked and cleaned for her room and board. She'd even kept in touch with the delivery boy from the grocer, and he'd promised to tell her if Tommy returned to the Giffords.

She'd never have considered it possible, but she'd traveled the West in style up until now. Moving from train depot to train depot, staying among people, clinging to the last vestiges of civilization, keeping her adventures urbane. Everything beyond the trampled town streets was wild and untapped.

While she drank in her new surroundings, John gathered the girls into a tight circle and spoke, "These cattle aren't easily spooked, but they're not used to your voices or your scents. They don't know you're a bunch of harmless girls. No loud noises or sudden moves. Stay within fifteen feet of the fire at all times. Once an animal that size stampedes, there's no stopping."

Hazel fiddled with the drooping rickrack on her hem. "Can we pet them?"

"Not now," the cowboy replied without a hint of impatience. "Maybe in the morning. It's for your own good. I'm keeping you safe."

Safe. Moira hugged her arms around her chest. They weren't safe. They'd simply turned down the flame. That didn't mean they were any better off than they were before. Well, except the odds were better and the doors weren't locked. They could run if they chose.

John whistled softly and a blur of white and brown padded into view. Moira took an involuntary step backward. A large gold-and-white collie appeared. The dog took its place at John's heel and tilted its head. The cowboy absently patted the animal's ears.

The four girls immediately rushed forward.

"He's so cute!"

"What kind of dog is he?"

"Can he sleep with us tonight?"

John held up his hands. "Easy there. This is a working dog. He's not real friendly."

Moira craned her neck for a better view. The "working" dog had rolled onto its back. Its pink tongue lolled out the side of its snout while four paws gently sawed the air.

Darcy snickered. "He looks pretty friendly to me."

Though the dog appeared harmless, Moira kept her distance. She'd been bitten once and the experience had left her wary. Dogs were unpredictable and temperamental. Best not to get too close.

Hazel rubbed her hand along the puff of fur of the dog's belly. "What's her name?"

"*His* name is Dog."

"He's far too handsome for such a plain name," Sarah declared, rubbing one furry ear between her thumb and forefinger. "I think we should call him Champion."

"Or Spot," Hazel added.

Darcy shook her head. "That's stupid. Why would we call him Spot? He doesn't have a single spot on him."

The cowboy pressed two fingers against his temple. "He doesn't need a name. He's already got a name."

"Dog is a silly name," Hazel grumbled. "Just like Bullhead is a silly name. You're not very good at naming pets."

John smothered a grin with one hand. "I've been accused of a lot of shortcomings, but I have to say that's a new one."

"Then we'll give him a better name." Hazel backed away several paces. "Come here, Champion."

The dog trotted over.

Though the cowboy's face remained impassive, Moira noted the rise and fall of his chest as he heaved an exasperated breath.

She grudgingly admired John's even temper. Weak with hunger, her mood swung between rage and despair at a moment's notice. Right now she'd give anything for a soft bed and a slice of pie. *Apple pie.* A thick cut of crispy crust. She pictured cinnamon-flecked filling oozing between the tines of her fork. Her mouth watered and she swayed on her feet.

"What's all this?" another voice called.

Moira snapped to attention. A squat man emerged from the farthest tent. As round as he was tall, his bowed legs were exactly half of his size. A shock of gray hair topped his perfectly round head and his plump face was smooth and cleanly shaven. He adjusted his belt and crossed his arms over his chest.

The cowboy tossed a log onto the fire, sending a shower of sparks drifting skyward. "I've brought you some mouths to feed."

"What happened to the fellows?"

"Gone."

The abrupt answer piqued Moira's curiosity.

"Good riddance, I say," the older man replied. "Not a decent one in the lot."

John grunted and motioned between the squat man and the girls. "This is Pops. Pops, this is Darcy, Tony, Sarah, and little Hazel. They'll be staying with us tonight. And they could all use some grub."

John motioned Moira forward. "And this is Miss O'Mara, she's in charge of the girls."

"Well, not exactly, I wouldn't say—" Moira stuttered over her scattered explanation.

She was the outsider.

No one ever put her in charge of anything, let alone *anyone*. Her vagabond life from orphan to foundling had shaped her into an expert at dealing with rejection. She spent her time hovering on the fringes, unnoticed. She came and went before anyone had a chance to know her.

Folks didn't trust loners. Which at times she found annoying, especially considering the people who'd betrayed her trust most egregiously were the ones she'd known best of all.

Pops extended his hand. "Pleased to meet you, Miss."

Moira offered a quick shake and a weak smile.

"You look fit to eat your shoe leather," the old man continued. "Let me fetch something that'll stick to your ribs."

"I'll help," Sarah offered quickly.

Moira blinked. As the most shy of the bunch, she hadn't expected Sarah to step forward.

The next twenty minutes passed in a blur. Moira and the girls ate quickly, devouring the simple stew with gusto. Their chattering gradually quieted and their shoulders drooped. Pops and John rustled up a stack of blankets and Moira arranged them inside the tent nearest the warming fire. Once all four girls had pulled the covers over their shoulders, she sat back on her heels.

The dog wove his way through the tent, sniffing each girl in turn before returning outside and lying before the closed tent flaps and resting its snout on outstretched paws.

With her hunger sated for the first time in days, Moira transformed from bone-weary exhaustion into a bundle of nerves. Not tired, but not quite awake either. She was anxious and uncertain. The evening had been a chaotic ride fraught with danger. There'd been a time when she would have lit a precious candle and read until her restlessness passed, but she hadn't either a book or a candle.

Emerging from the tent, she gingerly stepped over Champion before arching her back. John crouched before the fire, arranging the logs with the whittled point of a stick.

Moira glanced around. "Where's Pops?"

"Asleep." John relaxed against his cinched bedroll and stretched out his legs, crossing his ankles and lacing his hands behind his head. His hat sat low on his forehead, shadowing his eyes as the firelight danced over the planes of his face. "I've never seen Pops that agreeable. It's worth having you girls around to enjoy his rare good temper."

Moira scoffed. "You're pulling my leg." The grandfatherly man was as gentle as a spring lamb.

"Don't let him fool you. He's meaner than a sack full of rattlesnakes."

She shrugged out of John's coat and approached the cowboy. "Thanks for letting me borrow this."

"Keep it."

Too tired for arguing, Moira put it back on. Stretching her arms through the sleeves once more, she inhaled his reassuring scent. She sat cross-legged before the cheery blaze, her hands folded in her lap. Cocooned by darkness, she was content with the silence between them, comforted by the lowing cattle and the crackling fire. Gradually the tension in her sore muscles eased.

The flames danced in the breeze, orange and yellow with an occasional flash of blue at the base. A fire not contained by brick and mortar was foreign. More beautiful and compelling.

John glanced across the distance, shadows flickering across his face. "The girls okay?"

Moira nodded.

"Did anything happen back there?" He tipped back his hat, revealing his clear and sympathetic eyes. "Anything more?"

Moira knew what he was asking, and she answered as best she could. "I don't think so. We were all taken this evening and locked in together."

A sigh of relief lowered his shoulders. "Thank God."

He visibly relaxed, and she realized he'd been carrying the tension since he'd counted the windows. He hadn't known she was watching, but she'd observed his studied concentration, seen his face change when he'd recognized the brothel.

"Amen to that," she replied quietly.

The question had cost him, that much was clear, and Moira admired his courage. It was easier ignoring the evil in life, easier looking away than facing wicked truths. Most folks would rather skirt a puddle than fix the drain.

She replayed the events of the night in her head. What did she know about John Elder—other than he smelled like an autumn breeze and looked like he should be advertising frock coats on a sketched fashion plate. Not that looks and scent counted for much. She knew he was driving his cattle north because *he was trying to prove himself.* He didn't appear the sort of man who'd let someone else hold him back.

Unable to curtail her curiosity, she braced her hands against her bent knees. "Where is the rest of your crew?"

"They went bad on me. Or maybe I went bad on them. It's hard telling sometimes."

"Surely you can't drive the cattle alone?" Moira frowned. She didn't know much about cattle drives, but she didn't figure he could accomplish the task single-handedly. "What will you do now?"

"Go back into town. Start over." He shook his head in disgust. "I'll figure it out. I always do." John cracked a slender branch over his bent knee. "I guess I'll find a short crew. It's seventy-five miles to Fort Preble, and double that to Cimarron Springs. That's ten days with good weather. Only ten more days." He grunted.

"Where'd you start from?"

"Paris."

Moira bit off a laugh. "Paris? What's wrong with American cows?"

"Paris, Texas." A half grin slid across his face. "My family owns a cattle ranch there."

Her cheeks heated. She was obviously too exhausted for witty banter. "Are you driving the cattle to Cimarron Springs to sell?"

"Nope." The cowboy paused for a long moment and Moira let the silence hang between them. Finally he replied, "Starting over," he spoke so quietly she almost didn't hear him. "It's a small herd, but it'll grow. Times are changing. The big cattle drives are drying up. In ten years' time, you will hardly see a one."

Moira knew a lot about starting over. A man with roots and family shouldn't feel the need. "What about your kin?"

He stared at her as though she'd grown a second head. "It's a long story."

Moira nodded her understanding. "They treated you unkindly."

"Not, uh, not really. Not mean exactly."

"It must be really dreadful. I didn't mean to pry."

"It wasn't really bad, we just, uh, we just didn't get along, that's all. There's no deep dark secret." The cowboy plucked another handful of kindling from a pile at his elbow and tossed sticks onto the crackling flames. "What about you? Where's your family?"

Thrown off guard by the abrupt turn of the tables, Moira considered her answer carefully. She didn't share details about her past with strangers. She didn't want pity or judgment.

Yet something in the night air and the cowboy's affable, forthright eyes compelled her confidence. "I'm searching for my brother. We were separated as teenagers. Last month I received a telegram. Well, part of one. It's a long story. Anyway, I gathered what information I could and came straight out, hoping he hadn't gone far. Except I got here too late. He's already gone." She recalled the cowboy's previous comment. "What did you mean earlier? If we were boys, you'd take us on as your crew?"

A chuckle drifted across the campfire. "It was a story my father used to tell. Back in forty-nine you couldn't find any able-bodied men for work. They'd all been lured away by the gold rush. A local rancher, desperate for hands, hired him and ten other boys. They drove twelve-hundred head of cattle almost four hundred miles. None of them but the rancher and the cook was over the age of fifteen."

"That's amazing!"

"Yeah, but I'm not sure how much I believe." John scoffed. "The story got bigger each time he told it."

Moira braced her hands behind her and leaned back. For the first time in years, she'd lost her direction. She'd run up against dead ends before. For some inexplicable reason, this time felt different, more final…more devastating.

"Too bad about your brother," John said. "I have six of 'em and I'm the youngest. Never lost a one though. They were always around. Too much so."

Moira's eyes widened. "What a blessing, having all that family."

The cowboy kept his eyes heavenward. "I don't know if I'd put it that way."

She followed his gaze, astonished by the sheer number of stars blanketing the night sky. She couldn't recall the last time she'd stared at the moon. If she was out after dark, she kept her defenses up, watching for strangers and pickpockets, not staring at the twinkling stars. "What about your parents?"

"Both dead. My pa died first and I guess my ma couldn't imagine living without him. She died a short while later."

"I'm sorry to hear that," Moira murmured. "I guess you're an orphan, too."

"I never thought about it that way." A wrinkle deepened on his forehead. "Except I'm the youngest, and I sometimes feel like I have six fathers. My reasons for leaving seem small now, after talking with you, but I had to set out on my own. When our folks were alive, they had a way of making sure we all had a voice. Now it's as if we're all fighting to be heard, only no one is listening. It got to the point where we'd argue over something just for the sake of a good brawl. I figured if I didn't leave soon, all that fighting would turn into hate. And hate is a hard thing to come back from. I know my folks wouldn't have wanted that for us."

Moira plucked a handful of prairie grass and held it in her fisted hand. "I wouldn't know."

Her own father had run off the year Tommy had been born. Her mother had once been young and beautiful, but time and illness had stolen the bloom from her cheeks. The more she needed and the less she gave, the less her husband came home at night. Once she'd lost her usefulness, he'd run. He'd run from his wife and his children. His responsibilities. He hadn't run far enough. He'd been killed in a factory accident three months later.

Moira had been in charge of herself for as long as she could remember. Her mother had worked herself sick, and Moira had cared for her little brother. When her mother could no longer even care for herself, a woman from the Missouri State Charitable Trust and Foundling Society had arrived.

Never outlive your usefulness, her mother had said.

Moira had felt her mother's death somewhere along the way, although she'd never received proper notice. One day she'd finally accepted that no one was coming for her. The realization had hardened her heart and made her more determined than ever to prove her worth.

Shortly after the Charitable Trust had found them, she

and Tommy had been taken in by the Giffords. Mrs. Gifford had fancied herself a society lady, except Mr. Gifford had never made enough money to keep her in the style she figured she deserved. Moira had initially been humbled, awed by their fine house and brocaded furniture. She'd soon learned it was all superficial luxury.

From the beginning, the Giffords had treated them like hirelings. To her foster family, she was a servant. Mrs. Gifford took great pride in parading her *charity* before her friends. The truth was far less charitable. The Giffords had put them to work. The siblings rolled cigars for ten hours a day, sometimes more. Pacing and frowning, Mr. Gifford had timed them with his ever-present pocket watch. More cigars meant more income for the Giffords.

Making Moira work from sunup to sundown for nothing more than a roof over her head and a castoff dress each spring didn't place Mrs. Gifford in the annals of sainthood, though she acted as if it did. After Tommy ran away, Moira had marked off the days until her eighteenth birthday and left that morning.

Mr. and Mrs. Gifford had figured she'd be back in a week, begging for help. She'd never doubted her decision. Tommy hadn't returned and neither would she.

The cowboy stretched and yawned. "When did you see Tommy last?"

"Five years ago. He was fifteen and I was almost seventeen. He ran away. I, uh, I thought he'd come back. I'd given up ever seeing him again until I received the telegram. It was the sign I'd been searching for all along."

She'd find him and make things right. She'd apologize for taking the watch, for getting him in trouble. No one had loved her, truly loved her since that fateful day when she'd hidden Mr. Gifford's infuriating pocket watch behind a tin of crackers in the pantry and let Tommy take the blame.

She was supposed to take care of him, and she'd failed. She'd failed in the worst way possible. The cowboy dug his heels into the soft earth. "That's a long time to look for someone."

"Not very long when you love the person."

"Point taken."

"We'll be a family again."

The cowboy resumed his stargazing. "You're what, twenty-one, twenty-two? He's almost twenty? That's a long time apart. People change. Maybe you should think about starting a family of your own."

Moira shook her head. "Not until I find Tommy."

"Well, he's probably looking for you, too. I'm sure it'll all work out."

The cowboy's casual words buoyed her fragile hope. Would her brother accept her? He'd never returned to the Giffords. He must have known it was her fault. She'd have told the truth, except she'd been too much of a coward. By the time she'd screwed up her courage, Tommy was gone. She'd waited for him at the Giffords then stayed on working at the hotel in St. Louis, hoping to catch a glimpse of him.

If he'd been looking, surely he'd have found her. Yet this past month she'd finally been given proof, courtesy of the Gifford's maid, that he'd tried to contact her. His concession had to mean something. "Everything will be better when we're together as a family again."

He'd forgive her. If she found him, if she explained, he'd forgive her. Then she could finally be whole again.

They could finally be a family again. She'd have a purpose once more.

John stood and dusted his pant legs. "It's late. You should get some sleep." He held out his hand. "You did real well tonight. You tie knots like a trail boss. Those girls are lucky to have you."

As she took his proffered hand, her heart stalled beneath his unexpected compliment. "Why are you doing this? Why are you helping us?"

No one ever did anything without an ulterior motive.

"Didn't have much other choice," he answered easily.

Moira kept her own counsel. He'd want payment for his help. She only hoped the price wasn't too steep.

Either way, she hadn't the energy to sort out his motives. She'd find Tommy, she'd settle for nothing less. Lord knew she'd pave a street to his doorstep brick by brick with her bare hands if only she knew the way. There was an empty space inside her, and she wouldn't be whole again until they were family once more. This was merely a detour in her journey. She wouldn't be distracted by the handsome cowboy and his deceptively kind eyes. Not now. Not ever.

She'd never open up her heart to the disappointment her mother had faced. She wouldn't spend her life proving her worth just to be abandoned in the end. Sooner or later everybody left. The first year at the hotel she'd tried to make friends, but no one ever stayed long. One by one all the people who'd been important to her were plucked away. She'd learned her lesson well—she was better off alone.

Moira glanced around and realized John was heading for the horses and not the tents. "Where are you going?"

"Keeping watch. Checking the remuda."

Champion scrambled upright. John pointed a finger. "Stay. Keep watch over the camp."

The animal immediately lay down and rested its head on its paws.

Moira followed the cowboy's shuffling steps and her earlier animosity softened. His shoulders had slumped since she'd first seen him striding through the darkened alley. He must be exhausted. If he didn't find a crew tomorrow, what then?

Thoughtful, she gazed into the darkness. Those cattle sure didn't care if she was a boy or a girl. Why should anyone else? If a dozen boys could drive twelve hundred head of cattle, couldn't a few girls drive this bunch? If they were useful, maybe that would be enough payment.

Moira shook off the crazy thought. She'd find another way.

Alone.

The less time she spent in the company of John Elder, the better. She'd only known him a short while and already her resolve was weakening. His shoulders were strong, and it had been a long time since she'd had someone to lean on. She was exhausted, that was all. After a good night's rest she'd be stronger. And after tomorrow, she'd never see him again. She was used to being on her own. Life was easier that way. Lonelier, perhaps, but she'd rather be solitary than grow fond of someone who would only be in her life a short time.

As the lavender fingers of dawn branched out from the east, John braced his hands against the saddle horn and locked his elbows. A faint haze on the horizon showed the first signs of the morning sun. He'd kept watch all night, dozing off and on, and was so exhausted he could hardly think straight.

Outside of Texas, the terrain had leveled. John had never considered himself a sentimental man, yet the changing landscape left him melancholy.

His longhorns would thrive on the rich buffalo grass of the plains. Cities like Wichita were growing while Dodge City faded. Kansas was shutting out the Texas cattle, but folks still needed to be fed. If an army marched on its stomach, then nations flourished on a full belly.

Pops poured a cup of coffee and John reached for the steaming brew. Pops had been around the Elder family for as long as John could remember. He should be retired now, kicking back and relaxing. Instead he'd chosen a grueling cattle drive. Some men just weren't made for retirement.

John's horse sidestepped and he carefully balanced the hot liquid over the ground.

The older man poured another. "What's the story on them girls?"

"Hard to say," John replied. "Looks like the deputy sheriff was rounding them up. Searching for pickpockets. Put 'em up in a sportin' house while he sorted out the details."

Pops scoffed. "Why'd he take them to a sportin' house?"

John sipped his coffee and winced against the heat. "Didn't ask."

"What do you think?"

"I think something doesn't feel right."

They'd dropped out of the sky onto his head. Literally. Then Moira had inadvertently knocked the sheriff's deputy senseless. *It's fitting you'll die in fire,* the deputy had said. That threat felt personal. Had they encountered each other before? Had Moira had a previous brush with the law?

The girls were still sleeping which gave John time for thinking. Too much time. The law in town was rounding up pickpockets. And not just any pickpockets. They were specifically looking for young girls.

While Moira was definitely a woman, she could be mistaken for an adolescent with her girlish skirts, petite stature and fresh-faced smile. The gang he'd encountered in Buffalo Gap had worked as a team. One member distracted a fellow while another lifted his belongings.

Was one of his unlikely charges in possession of Mr. Grey's watch? John's thoughts immediately lit on Darcy. Of all the girls, she had the hardest edge. While John was tempted to speculate, he shook off any supposition. All he could do was place them in someone else's safekeeping.

Pops stood and stretched his fisted hands toward the sky. "What are you going to do?"

"I'll go into town this morning. See if I can get the lay of the land while I'm posting a notice for a new crew." *See if I'm a wanted man.* John didn't suppose assaulting the sheriff's deputy was a crime without punishment.

In the crisp light of dawn he couldn't easily dismiss the way Moira had looked at him last evening. As though he'd already disappointed her. Ruth Ann had looked at him that way once, when he'd playfully asked her to marry him and she'd declared him unfit. At least he'd given Ruth Ann a reason. What reason did Moira have for doubting him? Though her opinion shouldn't matter, it did. He didn't like her looking at him as if she'd sized him up and was waiting for him to show weakness. To fail.

John shook his head. It was better this way. He didn't need the distraction. And Miss Moira O'Mara was definitely a distraction.

"I'll watch the girls while you're gone," Pops spoke, interrupting John's reverie.

"Suit yourself." His head pounding, John gulped the last of his cooled coffee. "Be sure and hide the valuables."

There was a good chance he'd brought a gaggle of half-size pickpockets into camp. They couldn't get away with much, but better safe than sorry.

Pops didn't appear concerned at the prospect. "I'll take my chances."

"What would the boys do?" John asked, knowing Pops would understand the question better than anyone.

The older man considered his answer as he hooked the handle of his Dutch oven with an iron rod and hoisted it over the flames. "I don't suppose it matters what your brothers would do. They're not here, are they?"

"The one time I wouldn't mind a little help, and they're not around."

Pops grinned. "Never say God doesn't have a sense of humor."

John stifled a sigh. If Moira was guilty of a crime, then she'd have to answer to a higher power than him. No matter what the outcome, he needed some distance between them. He had an uneasy sensation the feelings stirring in his chest wouldn't change based on the outcome of her guilt or innocence. According to Ruth Ann, he wasn't the sort of man people pinned their hopes on.

John's horse sidestepped and he glanced up. Two riders appeared on the horizon. Judging by the dirt clods they kicked up in their wake, the men were coming fast. The one on the right was lanky and tall. Familiar. John groaned. Even from a distance he recognized the deputy sheriff.

He tightened his fist around the reins. "Pops, why don't you round up the girls. We've got trouble."

"What kind of trouble?"

John nodded toward the approaching riders. "The law has caught up with us. Looks like I don't need to go into town after all."

Pops threw up his arms. "What in the name of Sam Hill happened last night?" He eyed John, his speculation manifest in his watery gray eyes. "I'm guessing there's more to the story than what you told me."

"I might have assaulted the sheriff's deputy."

"Might have or *did?*"

"I hit him." John shot his cook a quelling glance. He'd hoped to avoid admitting that particular transgression. "It's a long story and I don't have time to tell it right now. I'll meet our company. Let the girls know we have visitors."

Pops shook his head. "I'll round 'em up. But you're on your own after that. I've got a stew to finish."

John glanced behind him at the quiet tent. One thing was for certain, he sure hoped Miss O'Mara unraveled knots as well as she tied them.

Chapter Four

Moira stumbled into the early morning light and held the tent flap aside for the other girls. She stretched and yawned, then pressed her hands into the small of her back and arched.

Tony rubbed her eyes, blinked and blinked again.

Following her gaze, Moira bolted upright. The kidnapper and another man stood before them.

"Well, well, well. If it isn't the orphan bunch," the kidnapper said with a smirk.

"Stay away from us or I'll fetch the sheriff," Moira said.

The second man rubbed the back of his neck. "That would be me."

Nausea rose in the back of her throat. Both men wore stars on their lapels. Though one was tarnished and dull; the other twinkled in the morning sunlight.

"Some of you have met already," the second man continued. "Perhaps more formal introductions are in order. My name is Sheriff Taylor. This is my deputy, Wendell Ervin."

Moira glared at the deputy sheriff. One shirttail hung

loose from his sagging, brown trousers while greasy stains from a long-forgotten meal interrupted the black-and-gray satin stripes lining his vest like jailhouse bars. He'd removed his hat revealing a crown of thinning, sandy-colored hair pressed into place by layers of dirt and grime. A goose-egg bruise stood out between his shaggy eyebrows and purple half moons flared from the inside corners of his eyes.

He leered at her, showing a yellowed nightmare of a gap-toothed smile. Suppressing a delicate shudder, Moira leaned away. His close proximity revealed the bloodshot whites of his faded blue eyes. He pointed a crooked finger at her. "You'll be spending the rest of your life in jail."

She might have felt a modicum of satisfaction from his self-inflicted injury if she wasn't terrified of his threat. Moira figured the situation could only degrade from there.

While the deputy swaggered and postulated, it was clear he wasn't in charge. The man who'd introduced himself as the sheriff managed to overshadow his deputy with nothing more than a dismissive glare. Unlike Wendell, there wasn't a speck of dirt marring the sheriff's impeccable black suit. A crisp white shirt with a starched collar glowed between the dark folds of his lapels and his silver star sparkled.

Moira had a sudden absurd image of the sheriff blowing a hot breath against the metal and polishing the tin against his tidy black sleeve before riding into camp.

Her four charges stomped and huffed, rubbing their hands against chill shoulders. Despite the deputy's blustering threat, their expressions were dull and uncomprehending. The girls blinked and yawned, wrinkled and blurry-eyed from sleep.

The sheriff smoothed his neat, dark coat into place and focused his attention on John. "Your name?"

"John Elder," the cowboy replied, his voice a low growl.

He kept his face averted from Moira. Come to think of it, John hadn't met her eyes once this morning. As though sensing her perusal, he turned, revealing his stark profile and the hard set of his jaw. There was nothing reassuring about his demeanor and her chest throbbed with something weighty and ragged.

The sheriff dusted his hat brim. "I knew an Elder once. From Texas. You a relation?"

"Probably."

Her kidnapper stepped forward and hitched his thumbs into his belt loops. Moira took an involuntary step back. He might be a deputy sheriff, but he wasn't getting any closer. He took another step and she matched her withdrawal. They repeated the odd dance twice more. John and the sheriff watched the display with curious detachment, waiting to see how the impasse would play out. Moira glared at their lack of interference. She'd back her way right into Kansas at this rate, but she didn't care.

Champion growled.

The sound spurred John into action. With only a slight tension in his jaw, he ambled over and edged his sizeable form between Moira and the deputy sheriff until the two men stood nose to nose. Moira leaned away for a better view and sucked in a breath. The deputy, Wendell, narrowed his eyes and scraped his hand through his hair, leaving gummed furrows in the strands.

Another menacing growl sounded from Champion.

Wendell's gaze flickered toward the animal and his mask of indifference slipped. He ran one finger around his collar and skittered away.

At the deputy's hasty retreat, John held out a hand toward the dog. "Down, boy."

Sensing he'd lost ground in the exchange, Wendell's thunderous expression darkened. He drew himself upright, straightening the curve in his spine. "That's the man who jumped me last night. I'm gonna arrest him."

"Arrest Mr. Elder? I think not." With the cowboy safely lodged between her and the deputy, Moira's courage returned full-steam. "You, sir, snatched me and four innocent girls off the street and tossed us into a brothel. Mr. Elder was rescuing *us*. From *you*."

The sheriff dusted his coat sleeve with the back of his hand. "Looks like I came into this poker game without all the cards." He tilted back his head and stared down his tapered nose. "You left out the best parts of your story, Wendell."

His deputy touched the bruise between his eyes. "Where was I supposed to put them? The jail was full of men. That wouldn't have been safe now, would it? I did the next best thing. It was Sunday, after all. That's the slowest night for business."

"You'd know, wouldn't you? And I suppose you took the opportunity to imbibe?"

With a thumb and forefinger, Wendell rubbed the inside corners of his bloodshot eyes "I did not imbibe. I had one drink. But I was definitely not imbibed."

The sheriff's expression fluctuated between resignation and disgust. "Never mind. I think we have a misunderstanding. One thing is for certain. Wendell is my deputy and you all broke the law."

A burst of chatter erupted from the girls. They peeled away from Moira, forming a tight circle. Huddled together, they spoke in frantic whispers. Snippets of the exchange drifted beyond the boundaries of their bent heads.

"What if they—"

"Don't even say it."

"Nobody's coming for you."

Hazel clutched her recently returned rag doll against her chest. "Are we going to jail?"

Moira scooted closer and draped her arm around Hazel's shoulder. She offered her most encouraging smile. "Don't worry. This is all a misunderstanding. Mr. Elder will sort out the whole thing."

The chatter fell silent.

A muscle ticked along John Elder's jaw. "*I'm* sorting this out, am I?"

He obviously hadn't slept much. Lines of fatigue feathered from his eyes and the edges of his mouth. His clothing was rumpled, his boots dusty. The added layer of grime lent him a patina of danger that had her heart thumping uncomfortably in her chest.

Moira shivered. "*We* shall sort out this misunderstanding."

John shrugged his shoulders and moved defensively before the frightened bunch of girls. "If Wendell is your deputy, what was he doing kidnapping young girls?"

"Yes," Moira added. "Please explain yourself."

John held her in place, his touch on her shoulder firm and somehow comforting. "Let the man speak, Moira. We need to hear what he has to say."

"Exactly, Mr. Elder." Sheriff Taylor offered a twitch of his lips that might have been a smile. "We have a very special band of pickpockets targeting Fool's End these days." He slid his considering gaze over each girl in turn. "They've become an inconvenience for me, and I don't like to be inconvenienced. One particular young girl swiped Mr. Grey's watch. He's one of our finest and most upstanding citizens. He's none too pleased."

The sheriff grimaced on the words *finest* and *most upstanding.*

A collective gasp erupted from the group. Tony stomped her foot. "It ain't one of us."

Moira fought John's protective grasp. "What proof do you have?" she demanded.

The sheriff lifted one shoulder in a negligent shrug. "I have enough circumstantial proof to make a case." He frowned at Moira. "You look familiar. Have we met?"

She instantly reversed her direction, leaning away from John. "We most certainly have not met."

The cowboy's grip tightened on Moira's sleeve and she shook off his fingers. He released her but held her gaze for a charged instant, his expression intense.

Wendell grunted. "This has gone beyond a bunch of pickpockets. That man attacked me. He assaulted an officer of the law. He's got to be punished."

The sheriff flipped back his jacket and rested his fingers on his slim hips. "Something's been gnawing at me all morning. I've seen a lot of fights in my time, but I don't ever recall an injury quite like that egg on your forehead. How exactly did that happen?"

"Well, uh." Wendell stuttered. "It don't matter. He should be in jail. That's all." The deputy sputtered into silence like a petulant child.

John splayed his arms. "We still haven't solved the first problem. You have no proof that any of these girls is a thief." He tossed a bitter glare toward the deputy. "And your law enforcement is shoddy at best."

Wendell reared back. "You gave me the orders yourself. Round up any of them girls that looked to be homeless. Mr. Grey even found me special last evening when I was leaving the saloon—I mean the post office. He was especially interested in a particular redhead. Musta had a good reason, I figure."

The deputy spat in the dirt at Moira's feet.

Champion barked and John lunged. The sheriff caught Wendell by the scruff of his coat and yanked him back.

Moira's stomach lurched. "I was minding my own business. And I'm not homeless or a young girl. I'm certainly not a pickpocket. What gives you the right to accost me simply because of the color of my hair?"

"Whoa, whoa, whoa." Wendell shook out of the sheriff's hold and swung his head from side to side. "Easy there."

Momentarily distracted, Moira stared in fascination at his enormous head. Not a single hair moved out of its pressed mold. Grease made a powerful pomade.

"I didn't *accost* you," the deputy jerked Moira's thoughts back to the task at hand. "I just put you in that place for safekeeping. Nothin' else happened. So don't be blabbering about people getting accosted and whatnot. That ain't right. I'm a deputy sheriff and all. I got an image to uphold."

Moira rolled her eyes. "You've exhausted your supply of big words, Wendell. I said accost, not rap—"

"Enough." John interrupted. "Do you have any proof that this particular *woman*," he emphasized the word and cast a meaningful look in Moira's direction. "Had anything to do with stealing Mr. Grey's watch?"

Wendell had the decency to look sheepish. "It was getting dark. I had my orders. A red-haired woman who dresses like a girl. That's what I was told to look for. No women I know wear their skirt above their ankles outside the saloon."

Moira flushed and kept her gaze pinned on a shrub tree in the distance. It was somehow fitting she'd be falsely accused of stealing a watch after letting Tommy take the blame for the same crime all those years ago.

Wendell postured. "Everything fit. I spotted you right off. I was doing my job and I did good. One of them girls is a thief and a liar. Maybe all of them."

The sheriff waved Wendell's ramblings to a halt. "It seems we have more than one misunderstanding. My deputy may have been a touch overzealous in his approach to law enforcement, but his intentions were sound. If a crime has been committed, he has the right to round up suspects. In this case, he assumed, quite logically, that the suspects were young girls without adult supervision. I believe each of you meets the criteria?"

The girls scuffed the ground and avoided his searching gaze.

"My point precisely. With the noted exception of Miss O'Mara, Wendell had every right to think you might have been the pickpockets he was seeking." His paused. "Then again, Miss O'Mara was the only one with an accurate description."

John rubbed his forehead. "I'd like to know what your witnesses were *imbibing* if these are your suspects." He pointed at Hazel. "A nine-year-old with curly black hair." He indicated Sarah. "A blonde with pale blue eyes.

A redhead. What's next? A trained bear with a yellow bow in its fur?"

Hazel giggled.

"Your conditions are far too broad and your temporary jail was a travesty," John said. "As far as I knew, these girls had been kidnapped. I was protecting them. If your drunken deputy had identified himself, things might have turned out different."

The sheriff flashed a toothy smile. "An honorable cowboy. What an oddity around these parts. And you bring up a good question. Why didn't you identify yourself, Wendell?"

"I forgot, that's all. I only been doing this job for a week." The deputy snorted. "Let's haul them all back into town and search 'em. We'll have this sorted out soon enough once we shake 'em and see what falls out."

Sarah drew in a sharp breath and Tony placed a secure arm around her shoulder. "You ain't taking us nowhere," Tony challenged.

The sheriff rubbed his chin. "As Wendell has so ably demonstrated, I don't have the facilities to house you while we sort which of you has sticky fingers."

"Then let's search the lot of them right here." Wendell declared, looking unaccountably proud of his inspired suggestion. "Search them right now."

"No!" Darcy shouted. "You have no right."

Agitated by the raised voices, Champion barked and bounced from side to side on his front paws. In a flash the scene spiraled out of control. The girls erupted into a noisy argument, shouting and gesturing. Darcy shoved Tony. Sarah grasped Tony's arm against retaliation. Sheriff Taylor paced around the fringes, his orders for calm lost in the fray. Wendell flapped his arms like a chicken that forgot it couldn't fly.

After a moment, the sheriff let out a shrill whistle. Champion sat back on his haunches and whimpered, then let out a defiant bark.

John remained motionless in the fray. "Enough. This is getting us nowhere. If you people don't stop whistling and waving your arms around, we're going to have a stampede on our hands."

His quiet announcement flummoxed the group and everyone fell silent.

Wendell recovered first. "I'm taking this one back to town no matter what." He snatched Moira's arm. "She's the ringleader. She's the one you want. You cut off the snake's head and the body will die."

Moira stumbled and fell hard on her knees. Pain shot up her legs. Wendell yanked her upright.

John charged. The sheriff threw his left shoulder into the cowboy, knocking him off balance. Using his momentary advantage, Sheriff Taylor whipped out his gun and aimed the barrel at John's chest. Moira blanched.

The sheriff shook a scruff of hair from his eyes. "Wendell, I'll be taking charge of the woman before you get us all killed." He gently extracted Moira from the deputy's hold while keeping a wary eye on John. "You've made your point. I'd suggest you not rile Mr. Elder any further."

Sick and tired of being manhandled, Moira rubbed her bruised shoulder.

"Him?" Wendell slapped his chest. "What about me? I'm the abused party. Why isn't anyone worried about getting me riled up?"

"Because you have a singular way of escalating even

the most benign situations into shambles." The sheriff holstered his gun and raked his hair back into one place before repositioning his hat.

"But," Wendell sputtered. "It's her. We got to take her."

John caught Moira's gaze. "Why her?" the cowboy asked. "You seem awfully fired up about Miss O'Mara. Is there something more you're not telling us?"

Moira wondered the same thing. Why single her out? The cowboy looked more confused than accusing, and for that she was grateful. He hadn't immediately taken Wendell's side. That had to mean something.

"Look what she done to me!" Wendell pointed at his face.

Moira blanched. His injury explained a lot. He'd gone and knocked himself out before a group of witnesses. His pride had been hurt as much as his head.

The sheriff tucked his chin to his chest and rocked back on his heels. "Explain your injury or I leave right now."

"She hit me with a pitchfork."

"I did not," Moira declared. "Well, not in the face… I mean, there was a pitchfork involved."

She let her voice trail off. The long version of the explanation didn't exactly help her cause. She *had* whacked him. Just not in the face. "I hit him in the backside with the pitchfork." She caught the deputy's warning glare. "He did the rest himself. And that's the truth."

"You gotta do better than that." The sheriff hoisted a dark eyebrow in question. "Why don't you tell me the whole story, Miss O'Mara?"

Hazel giggled. The other girls snickered.

"Well…" She cleared her throat. Humiliating the deputy didn't feel like the best way to advance her case. "You must understand that I was under the impression I had been kidnapped. Your deputy never identified himself as a lawman. It was quite understandable that I had the wrong impression."

"Yes, yes. I got that part."

"He chased us into the livery." She cast a sidelong glance at Wendell.

The deputy glowered.

The sheriff heaved a breath. "The scene of the crime, as it were."

"Events progressed from there." Moira studied her laced fingers. "There was a brief altercation. Then a small fire. Well, um, I dropped a pitchfork and he, um, stepped on the tongs. Knocked himself out cold."

The sheriff threw back his head and laughed. Gathering himself, he swiped at his forehead with a turkey-red bandanna. He then straightened his lapels and buttoned his jacket. "As much as I'd like to pursue this line of explanation further, it's a waste of time. All we're doing is talking in circles, and I have more important work. Last night there was a shoot-out over a land claim. One of the fellows was gut-shot and it doesn't look good. If that fellow dies, I'll have a murder on my hands. Do you have any idea how much paperwork comes with a murder?"

The sheriff ran his thumb and forefinger down the crease of his lapel. "Pages. I've gone through a whole box of pencils this month alone. Not to mention I don't have any love for Mr. Grey or his two-dollar watch." He paused. "Why don't we strike a bargain? As long as you and the girls stay out of town, there's not much I can do. You show your face, even once, and I'll be forced to take action."

Moira opened her mouth and John silenced her with a quick slice of his hand. "What if Mr. Grey doesn't agree?"

"I'll handle Mr. Grey. I'll even let you in on a little something." He lowered his voice. "I'm only the interim sheriff here. I'm just biding my time until the permanent man arrives. Which means I don't have to play nice with Mr. Grey. So do we have a deal?"

"Yes!" Moira shouted immediately. Right then, anything was better than putting herself at the mercy of Wendell Ervin.

"No." The cowboy spoke low.

Her knees buckled.

"It's important I go back into town." John paced before the girls who watched his back-and-forth movements like spectators at a quick draw. "I've got no crew and eight-hundred-head of range cattle. What am I supposed to do with a bunch of girls out in the middle of nowhere?"

"You got food?" Sheriff Taylor asked.

"Yep."

"Shelter?"

"Yep."

The sheriff shrugged. "Seems like you're doing fine to me."

"Fine? How is that fine? These girls have nothing but the clothes on their backs." John threw up his arms. "Well, I guess if you don't count a couple hundred head of cattle and an absent crew, then, yes, everything is just dandy. Couldn't be brighter if there were two suns in the sky."

"You had a crew coming into town. Not my fault you lost them on the way out."

The cowboy made a strangled sound in his throat. John clutched his head and muttered beneath his breath, "I should have walked the long way home last night. I was tired and angry and not thinking straight. I tried to take the easy way out, but there are no shortcuts in life. I know better. I shouldn't have let my temper get the best of me. Yep, that was my first mistake. My second mistake was looking up. Always keep your head down, my brother Jack told me. But did I listen? No. All the years he lectured me, who knew he'd be right someday?"

Tony's eyes widened. "Oh my, he's gone and lost his mind, hasn't he?"

"Yep." Sarah nodded. "The same thing happened to my Great-Aunt Sylvia. One day she was frying pork chops, the next thing she was babbling like she'd lost her wits."

Darcy frowned. "Did she ever get 'em back? You know, her wits."

Sarah scratched her temple. "Not that I know of. And my ma was terrified of pork chops after that. She'd get all white and shaky over frying bacon even."

The girls nodded and elbowed each other, each recalling stories they'd heard of people losing their minds at the drop of a hat. While John muttered, the sheriff and his deputy spoke in low, agitated tones.

The cowboy had gone half-loco, the deputy was an imbecile and the sheriff was the worst of the lot. The head of law enforcement in that corrupt cow town was abandoning them. By refusing to declare their innocence, he'd effectively declared their guilt—because he didn't want to whittle down another pencil over a person's life. A sharp pain throbbed behind her eyes.

She'd lost patience with the lot of them.

Moira crossed her arms over her chest. "We'll take care of ourselves."

The sheriff jerked around and snapped his fingers. "It's the voice. It's right there on the edge of my memory."

Moira stiffened and tugged at her hair. "I suppose your watch is missing, too? Well I didn't take that either. And the gentlemen of Fool's End should keep better track of their valuables instead of accusing anyone who happens to be walking down the street at sunset."

"It's not that." The sheriff circled around her, one hand on his chin, his gaze appraising.

Once again Moira caught John's intent gaze and her heart froze. She didn't like the way the cowboy kept looking at her. Studying her as though he expected stolen coins and jewelry to shower from her person.

She met his accusing glare with one of her own. "You'd like that, wouldn't you?"

John reared back.

"You'd like for me to be some sort of pickpocket. Then you could run away and pat yourself on the back at the same time."

The wrinkle between the cowboy's eyes deepened. "That doesn't even make sense."

"Uh-oh." Tony slapped her leather hat over her dark hair and adjusted the rawhide strap beneath her chin. "We've lost another one. Now they've both gone loco."

The girls each nodded in unison.

The sheriff squinted.

Moira squirmed.

"What's your name again?"

"Moira." She drew herself upright. She was tired of

cowering from all these oafish men. "My name is Miss Moira O'Mara. You may call me Miss O'Mara."

"Aha!" The sheriff clapped his hands. "That's the connection. I had a run-in with a fellow by that name not long ago. He spoke like he was all high-and-mighty, too. Like you did just now. *Call me Mr. O'Mara*." The sheriff rubbed his jaw with a thumb and forefinger. "His first name was Ted. Or Thomas, something like that."

"Tommy! Tommy O'Mara?" Her spirits soared. "That's my brother."

Chapter Five

Moira's animosity toward the sheriff evaporated immediately. He was doing his job, that was all. No hard feelings need come between them.

"Tommy O'Mara," the sheriff repeated, his voice thoughtful. "Sounds right. Red hair. Not real tall. You two look alike. Heard rumors he ran afoul of Mr. Grey."

A trickle of horror filtered through her stomach. "Tommy? Is he all right? What happened? Is he still living in Fool's End? Mr. Grey said he hadn't ever met him. But I had a feeling he was lying. Did something happen to Tommy?"

"Easy there, little lady." The sheriff flashed a charming grin.

Moira remained stoic.

When the sheriff realized his dime-store charisma was wasted on her, his smile faded. "Nah. Talk around town was that Mr. Grey's daughter had taken a shine to your brother."

A girl? Tommy was only…nineteen, well, almost twenty. But that was young. The sheriff must be mistaken.

He smoothed his sleeve. "Keeping a couple of love-birds out of trouble isn't part of my job."

Moira clutched the sheriff's forearm. "Do you know where he is?"

The sheriff glanced at his rumpled sleeve, only recently straightened. Moira released her hold and sprang backward. She mustn't antagonize the man any further. Not if she hoped for more information about her brother. Other than the telegram, the sheriff was the first person she'd met who knew Tommy by name.

"Can't say that I know what happened to him after he lit out." The sheriff brushed out the wrinkle on his elbow. "If I find something, I'll send word. Where can I reach you?"

"Let me follow you back into town." Moira clasped her hands together. "I'm not who you're looking for."

"Can't do that." The sheriff's expression turned sympathetic. "Where's your next stop, Mr. Elder?"

The cowboy ceased his pacing. "I *had* planned on going across the border up through Cimarron Springs," his voice dripped with sarcasm. "I'm not real sure anymore. At this rate, I may have to circle back to Texas."

"You're not quitting now, you're going north. Everyone gets funneled through Cimarron Springs at some point. If I remember something, I'll drop you a line. Ask for Jo Cain at the telegraph office. I've gone through her before. She's reliable." The sheriff mounted his horse, his silver spurs jingling. "Don't forget our deal. I'm dead serious. It's not safe for those girls in town." He cast a meaningful glance toward his deputy. "I can't protect them next time."

Moira's earlier generosity faded like morning dew. Events were moving too quickly. "You can't just leave us here. What makes you think we'll be traveling together? And what about my personal belongings? My bag. I was staying at the hotel."

The sheriff shook his head. "That's not part of the deal. If any of you return, I'll have you arrested and brought before Mr. Grey. If he identifies you as the pickpocket, you'll be in jail by this afternoon."

"That's not fair! I didn't do anything."

"Then you're welcome to come with us. Take your chances. It's quite a gamble, considering what *each* of you has to lose."

His subtle rebuke wasn't lost on her. She'd been momentarily distracted by the news of Tommy. She wasn't alone; she had the girls to consider. They could all wind up behind bars.

Moira studied the two lawmen. Her choices were thinning out by the moment. She sure didn't trust Wendell and she didn't have much faith in the sheriff either. Neither man was interested in justice or sorting out right from wrong. One wanted revenge for his humiliation and the other wanted an easy fix and an early lunch.

She turned and caught the cowboy's attention. Her courage faltered. They were a burden to him. An unfair burden considering all he'd done for them up to this point. If the sheriff left them, they were stuck in the middle of Indian Territory with no resources.

Worse than the middle of nowhere, they were stuck in No Man's Land.

"None of this is my fault." She hadn't done anything after all. "You can't steal my belongings."

"I'm not a man you want to threaten." The sheriff's voice hardened. "And that sounds an awful lot like a threat."

Her heart died in her chest. She'd mistaken the sheriff's easy charm for an easy nature. He was setting her straight.

The sheriff watched her capitulation and set his easy grin back in place. This time Moira wasn't fooled.

He pulled a silver dollar from his pocket and balanced the coin on the tip of his thumb. "Never say I'm not a generous man."

The sheriff flipped his coin into the air. It arced and caught the early morning light, glinting through its downward spiral.

An easy catch. Moira refused the insult. She wouldn't grovel in the dirt for his money. That's what he wanted, after all. He wanted to show her who had the power between them.

The coin landed with a thud. She'd considered begging for his help, the cowboy didn't deserve any more trouble, but that changed her mind. She'd rather set out on her own than endure the sheriff's disdain.

The sheriff winked. "I've got your Irish up now, don't I?" He leaned forward. "Mr. Grey didn't like your brother stirring up trouble. He's not going to like you either."

The whole undercurrent in the conversation instantly crystallized and Moira groaned. No wonder they'd snatched her! Mr. Grey didn't want her because he thought she'd stolen from him. He had a bone to pick with her brother and she'd waltzed into his offices and flaunted her name and her family connection. Then, on her way back to the boardinghouse, she'd been abducted. She didn't believe it was a coincidence. She'd left Mr. Grey all the information they needed to find her. The deputy said as much when he outlined Mr. Grey's instructions. Her capture hadn't been an accident.

If Mr. Grey wanted revenge for the trouble Tommy had caused, she was an easy target. If that awful man had been lying, if he knew where her brother had gone… Moira fought the play of emotions simmering in her chest. Tommy would come for her if he thought she was in trouble. Wouldn't he?

While the men talked, Moira tugged her lower lip between her teeth. *No.* She couldn't do it. As much as she wanted to find Tommy, she couldn't risk laying a trap for him. She'd betrayed him once already. Besides, there was no guarantee Mr. Grey had more information.

"I'll stay here," she grudgingly replied.

Atop his mount, the sheriff loomed over them, showing his strength. He leaned one elbow on his saddle horn, his voice no more than a whisper, "Too bad really. I think you and I could have gotten along real fine."

Moving so quickly that Moira had no warning, John Elder shoved Moira behind him, shielding her from the sheriff's view. "I don't like your tone."

The sheriff tipped his hat with a grin, appearing as though he'd just won some grand prize. "Good luck to you," he said. "I have a feeling our paths will cross again."

John gripped the reins of the sheriff's horse. "This is not a deal. We don't have a deal. We have a disaster. You can't just leave me out here with a bunch of girls. I don't have the resources. I've got a herd of cattle and no crew."

"Not my problem either. Maybe next time you won't fire your crew until you have another one in place." The sheriff chuckled. "I bet you won't make that mistake again."

John Elder's shoulders stiffened and fear shot through her heart. Though she couldn't see his face, she felt the tension radiating from his body. His throat worked and she sensed the battle within him once more. Just like the previous night when he'd ushered them into the empty stall. He was fighting something, an enemy only he could see. After a moment he appeared to make a decision.

She didn't know how she sensed that, but she did. Even in such a short time she'd become attuned to his changing moods. The cowboy sucked in a deep breath, his chest rising and falling with the effort. His shoulders dropped a notch, his stance widened.

The sheriff stared at the girls, his expression thoughtful. "There's a drummer from the mercantile in town. He's usually heading south this time of year, but I can send him your way. Those girls will need to be outfitted proper."

"What if he can't find us?"

The sheriff scoffed. "If you were moving any slower, you'd be going backward. There can't be many all-girl cattle drives this side of Fort Preble. I'll point the drummer toward the fly swarm and let him take his chances. His name is Swede and I'll give him an idea of what you'll need. He's good people."

"I don't like it. We're defenseless out here. You must at least see that. We're in Indian Territory."

"I'm aware of your situation, Mr. Elder. Have a little faith in my judgment. The Indians are too beat down to cause you much trouble. Stay on the trail. They won't come near the army forts."

Moira held up her hand. "Send my bag with him."

"I dunno," the sheriff picked at a spot of lint on his lapel. "That's not part of the deal."

John snorted, then motioned the sheriff farther away from the group of girls. "I need a word. Alone."

The sheriff furrowed his brow and dutifully reined his horse aside. The two bent their heads together in a hushed conversation.

Moira tensed. What on earth was he up to now?

Tony touched her shoulder. "What are they talking about? Can you hear anything?"

"Nope," Moira answered. She sidled closer. She didn't like this. She didn't like this one bit.

What was John Elder saying that he didn't want the girls hearing?

Hazel halted her progress by hugging her leg. "Are we going to jail? I stole some apples from the grocer. I was real hungry. I know I shouldn't have done it."

"Don't worry." The men immediately forgotten, Moira ran her hands over Hazel's soft curls. "Everything is going to be all right. You'll see."

Darcy snorted.

Tony stuck out her chest. "You got something you want to say? Then say it."

"Why don't I tell them why you're here?" Darcy challenged. "How about that?"

A flush of red crept up Tony's neck.

Moira shushed them. "It's not your fault. It's nobody's fault. We've been blamed for something we didn't do. We're being punished for crimes we didn't commit. It's unfair and it's unjust and we're stuck. He's got all the power and we've got nothing. Fighting among ourselves only makes it worse."

The cowboy pivoted from his conversation, keeping

his head down. From the set of his jaw, Moira figured the discussion hadn't gone too well.

Wendell crowded his horse closer. The deputy leered, a half grin on his face. Moira met his challenge. He fisted his hands around the reins, tugging on the bit and sending his horse sidestepping. "I'll say it again, Taylor. You're making a mistake, letting them go. I got nothing to do with this." The deputy dug his heels into his horse's sides and galloped off in a kick of dust.

John adjusted his hat low on his forehead.

The sheriff swiveled in the saddle and followed his deputy's hasty retreat. "You assaulted my deputy. While I'd like to give you a medal for that, I can't. You did ask me for a favor and I'm not completely heartless. I'll see what I can do."

John remained impassive.

"I saw the crew you fired." The sheriff watched for a reaction from the cowboy. "My elderly mother has more gumption than that bunch. Besides, looks to me like you've got plenty of help."

"What's that supposed to mean?"

"Figure it out." The sheriff tipped his hat.

At his exit, they all remained in confused silence, uncertain what to do next. John whirled and kicked the loose pile of kindling near the campfire, scattering the twigs.

Moira sucked in a breath and faced the girls. They cast worried glances between her and the cowboy. She pulled her lower lip between her teeth.

Tony lifted her head. "What are we going to do now?"

"I don't know."

"Well…" Darcy began. "Maybe we should ask the cowboy."

"He doesn't appear to be in a talkative mood," Moira stalled.

Tony punched one fisted hand into the opposite palm. "I'll get him talking. I'll talk some sense right into him."

"No, no," Moira quickly admonished. "I'll... I'll handle this. He's a touch upset. I think a more delicate approach might be in order."

As much as she dreaded the realization, John Elder held their fate in his hands. None of the girls had anything more than their shabby clothing and few coins in their pockets. She glanced at the silver dollar resting in the dirt and got a sour taste in her mouth.

"Suit yourself." Tony shrugged. "But if you need a *less delicate touch,* you let me know."

"I'll do that." Moira squared her shoulders and approached their dubious rescuer. He *did* need something from them, he just didn't know it yet. He didn't deserve to be saddled with a bunch of orphans, but when did anyone get what they deserved?

He didn't look up. Not a good sign. "What now, Mr. Elder?"

A grunt answered her question. Moira cleared her throat. Despite all that was happening, she kept thinking about the cattle. The rest of them had choices. The animals were entirely at the mercy of others. "What are you going to do with the cattle?"

"Nothing I can do." He stared into the distance, his expression resigned. "Leave 'em here, I guess. Once word gets out there's range cattle for the taking, they'll be gone soon enough."

"You'd just leave them?" The action struck her as callous. "For anyone?"

"What else am I going to do? I can't protect you girls and drive the herd at the same time."

Moira searched the desolate horizon. She wasn't spontaneous. She was careful. Deliberate. She folded her clothing in neat squares, she layered her hairbrush and mirror in the folds to avoid breaking them. She arrived at the train station two hours prior to departure. Acting on impulse wasn't her strong suit. Even her spur-of-the-moment trip out west had been meticulously planned—hastily planned, but carefully planned.

How did she make him see their value? She tipped her head to the sky. "That didn't go so bad, did it? Considering we assaulted and confined a deputy sheriff. I mean, after all, none of us is in jail."

Even without looking, she could tell her question had thrown the cowboy off guard. Good. That's what she wanted. If he was off guard she had a better chance.

He grunted. "At least in jail a fellow gets three squares."

"Don't you have any faith in a higher plan? In God's powers?"

"I'd have a lot more faith if He sent me a crew," John mumbled.

Moira stepped closer, crowding his space, forcing him to tip his head back and look at her.

She had one chance to convince him of the impossible. "He did."

Chapter Six

"Whatever idea you've got, it won't work," John spoke.

Moira retreated and he almost mourned her easy capitulation. He needed a fight he could win. Anything to make him feel as though he had a modicum of control over *something*.

John rubbed his face and stared at the ground. For the first time in his life, he was plum out of ideas. Always before he'd found a way, invented a solution, defied the problem. Not this time. This time he was stuck in the middle of nowhere with eight-hundred-head of cattle, four orphans and a woman whose doleful eyes had him wishing he could save the world.

No one could blame him for being out of ideas. No one, not even his brothers could fault him for giving up this time.

Champion lay at his feet and he absently scratched behind one raised ear. As much as it pained him to admit it, the dog seemed to like the name.

Moira had an idea. John guffawed. It wouldn't work. He didn't even know what she was thinking, but he already knew her plan was doomed. He knew because he'd considered everything and all his ideas ended in calamity.

A sound caught his attention and a pair of familiar, scuffed boots came into view. He lifted his head and met Moira's steady gaze. The eyes that had haunted his dreams the previous night. They weren't forlorn anymore. They were determined and that didn't bode well for either of them. Tension tightened around his shoulder muscles.

She knotted her arms over her chest. "You said you were crossing the border into Kansas and traveling on to Cimarron Springs. How far is that?"

"It's about seventy-five miles to Fort Preble. That's the closest thing to civilization between here and Kansas. And there's nothing in between Fort Preble and Cimarron Springs except for a couple of cow towns that aren't safe for women and children."

"How many miles can the cattle travel per day?"

"About fifteen."

Moira did a quick mental calculation. "That's only five days to Fort Preble. You can find another crew there."

"In terms of math, yes, it's five days." He bit off a curse. "Except math is just numbers. Out here it's wind and weather and rugged trail. You can't put that in an equation."

"We'll drive your cattle as far as Fort Preble."

"Who is 'we'?"

"The girls and I."

John barked out a laugh. "Thanks for the joke, but I'm not in the mood just yet."

"The way I see it, you don't have any choice."

"Oh, I have choices." He bluffed. "Lots of choices."

She tilted her head. "Name one."

"I'm still sorting out the details," John grumbled. So much for bluffing Miss Moira O'Mara.

"The older three can ride well enough," she continued. "Tony can rope. We're your best option."

"Do you know how much those cattle weigh?" He scoffed. "You'd be hurt or killed before you crossed the Snake River. And the Snake River is about twenty yards away. You'd be ground into dust by Fort Preble."

Her chin tilted up a notch and she braced her feet apart, planting her hands on her hips. "You said children drove twelve-hundred-head of cattle twice the distance. Why can't we?"

"Because you're not boys. You're girls."

"What's the difference?"

John stood and mirrored her implacable stance. He didn't relish the task, but she needed a lesson. Conjuring his most intimidating glare, he lowered his voice into a deep, frightening growl. "The difference between boys and girls is weight and strength."

She drew herself up another notch. "What we lack in size we make up for in brains. I've seen plenty of cowhands. They're not real smart."

She had him there. "The cows aren't real smart either. That's why you have to be strong."

"You think women aren't strong?" Her lips tightened. "Do you have any idea what we go through each day? Have you ever worn a corset?"

John raised his arms in supplication. "I think we're wandering off the topic."

"Have you ever had your hair curled with a flaming hot iron?"

"Can't say that I have."

"Look at this." She palmed a ringlet from her fore-head, revealing a faint raised scar. "That's from a curl-ing iron. And I've barely scratched the surface."

He studied the shimmering halo of brilliant red curls cascading over her shoulders. "You shouldn't be using an iron anyway. Nature has done a fine job already."

"My hair is not the issue," she spoke through gritted teeth. "Please stick to the subject."

John gaped. "Don't get mad at me. You brought it up."

"I was trying to explain the difficulties of being a woman."

"Truce?" he said. He'd never understood the com-plexities of a woman's beauty regime, and not one word of this conversation left him wanting more information. Which was the exact flaw in her argument.

He had her now. "Women can be strong. But you don't have women, you have girls." *Aha!* She couldn't dispute that. "And I'm not risking the lives of girls."

Let Miss Moira O'Mara argue his logic now.

Her expression turned incredulous. "Then you'll just let the cattle starve here waiting for someone to stumble upon their corpses?"

"Don't change the subject when I'm winning."

"This isn't about winning or losing. This is about honor and integrity."

His ears grew hot and his vision blurred in a haze of red. "Don't you lecture me on honor and integrity. I could have left you in that alley."

"You still wouldn't have a crew."

"I could have gone back into town. I could have got-ten my old crew back."

"Would you have taken them back? Really?"

He was many things, but he wasn't a liar. "No." He

kept his gaze averted. He recognized the accusation in her voice. This wasn't the first time he'd disappointed someone, and it wouldn't be last. Ruth Ann had accused him of being too easy going to be a good husband. His brothers thought he was too reckless to make a good cattleman.

For once in his life he was being thoughtful and cautious, and he'd found the one person who wanted him to return to his old ways. "I told you. I'll drive the cattle toward richer pasture. Eventually, word will spread that there's free cattle for the taking. The rest will take care of itself."

He'd rather keep Moira safe than win her approval. It was that simple.

"Then you're quitting?" she asked.

His hackles rose. "No. I'm not quitting. I'm walking away from an impossible situation while ensuring the best possible outcome."

"That's just a fancy way of saying you're quitting." Moira smirked.

A low growl lodged in the back of his throat. If John didn't know better, he'd have thought his brothers sent Miss Moira O'Mara to torture him. It was as though he was being lectured by all six of them except the view was better. Yep. She was all half dozen of his brothers rolled into one beautiful, infuriating, redheaded package.

John scrubbed his hands down his face. There was no way he was winning a verbal sparring match. He was outgunned and outflanked. The best choice was a calculated retreat. "I'm not playing word games with you. This conversation is over."

"Fine. Then you're abandoning your cattle to anyone who sees fit to take them."

"Yes. Exactly." He huffed.

Oh no.

John staggered a step and rubbed his chest. He was huffing. Men didn't huff. Only one day with the girls and already they were changing him. This was not a good sign at all. Squaring his shoulders, he refocused his thoughts.

He might have lost his dignity but at least Moira finally understood the bigger picture. "I'm leaving the cattle and taking you girls to Fort Preble. That about sums it up."

"Excellent." She pivoted on her heel and stalked toward the campsite, tossing a last triumphant glare over her shoulder.

John studied her ramrod-stiff back and a cacophony of alarm bells sounded in his head. She hadn't won. Which begged the question: Why was she acting as though she'd won? What kind of trick was that?

Pops, who'd kept himself hidden since the sheriff's arrival, chose that unfortunate moment to reappear. He sipped his coffee and followed her progress. "You should go into town more often. I don't recall a more exciting cattle drive. Nope. I do not. And that's saying something. I've been around a while."

"Don't you have a stew that needs stirring or something?" Feeling like he'd been picked up and dropped by a twister, John struggled for a reply. "What does she think she's doing?"

Before his suspicious gaze, Moira gathered her charges. Keeping her voice low, she talked and gestured. Champion barked and danced around the group. The girls shot him concerned looks every so often but mostly kept their attention focused on Moira. After a moment, a wave of nods rippled over their bent heads.

The roar of alarm bells in John's head grew deafening. They were most decidedly up to mischief. Judging from the determined looks on their deceptively innocent faces, a decision had been made. The last time they'd put together an idea as a group, they'd dropped onto his head and gotten him banned from Fool's End. Well, this time he was prepared. He'd defuse this round of dynamite before they got him blown out of Indian Territory altogether.

Her expression smug, Moira approached him once more. "We've reached a decision."

John crossed his arms over his chest. "About what?"

"You've abandoned your cattle, Mr. Elder. We hereby assume responsibility for the herd."

He leaned closer, turning his face and angling one ear in her direction. "Say again?"

"You heard me."

John reared back. "If you're thinking what I think you're thinking, you'd better think again."

"I'm thinking you've gotten too much sun today. You aren't making a lick of sense. Would you like to sit in the shade for a moment?"

"I'm making perfect sense." He needed sleep, that was all. After a good night's rest, everything would make sense again. "I don't need shade."

"You're also a touch cranky."

He ignored the trap. A denial only sounded petulant.

"If the herd is up for grabs," she said. "We're taking it."

John searched for an ally. "Pops. Help me out."

The older man didn't quite meet his gaze. "She makes a sound case."

Rocking back on his heels, John absorbed the blow of betrayal from his most trusted advisor. "Don't tell me you're on their side?"

"I'm not taking sides," Pops began in a conciliatory tone. "I admire the lady's gumption. And she has a sound point. If you're abandoning the herd, she's got just as much right to the cattle as anybody else."

While John mulled over the dubious logic, Moira stepped forward. Her cheeks were flushed and she appeared taller somehow. "There's another thing. We'd like to trade twenty head of cattle for five horses."

John touched his forehead. She was right about one thing, the sun had obviously baked his brain. He must be hallucinating because she couldn't possibly be suggesting what he thought she was suggesting. "They're my cattle. I can't trade *my* cattle for *my* horses."

"The way I see it, you and Pops can lead twenty head easy enough. You can sell them in Kansas."

She was definitely taller. Had she changed shoes? John checked her boots. Nope. They were the same ratty pair she'd been sporting. "I'll give you that. But why would I make a trade with my own horses?"

"Because I counted ten horses in the remuda." She explained as though the argument made perfect sense. "Without your men, you don't need that many."

Pops bobbed his head in agreement. "That's true."

"Stop!" John shouted then immediately lowered his voice. "Stop helping me."

"I'm not the problem here." Pops lifted both shoulders, sloshing coffee over the side of his mug. "Since

Moira and the girls have claimed the herd, the cattle are hers to trade."

"I... You..." How could the lunatic proposal make sense to one person, let alone two? And two people he had previously considered sane, no less. "You've both gone loco. They're my horses and my cattle."

"Not after today," Pops added, warming right up to the idea like a snake to an occupied sleeping bag. "The way I figure, it's a good deal. You won't get that trade in Cimarron Springs, that's for certain."

"I'm dreaming. I must be dreaming."

A sharp pain stabbed his arm. He glanced down as Hazel released her fingers.

"Nope," she said. "You're not dreaming. I pinched you."

John rubbed the spot on his arm. "Not you, too!"

The kid did have strength, he'd give her that. He'd have a bruise come morning.

Moira ignored his outburst and stared him down. "Do we have a deal or not? I'd like the ten horses for rotation, but I figure we can make do with five since we're girls. I figure we're lighter than men are and we'll set an easier pace. The horses will be under less strain."

"You can't possibly be serious." John considered his next words carefully. Since his first, logical reasons weren't working, he decided on another tactic. "What are you going to do with all those cattle if, and that's a big 'if,' you make it as far as Fort Preble?"

"We'll sell them, of course. The fort will have plenty of buyers. We'll split the money and start over. It's not the best solution, but it'll do for now."

For an agonizing moment he followed her logic and found her argument sound.

Then he remembered the whole idea was impossible. "It's true. You've all gone crazy. I'm the only one here making sense." He opened and closed his mouth a few times. "I hear myself talking, but no one is listening. You'll never make it across the Snake River."

"Say," Pops interrupted John's rant. "Can I take my ten head of cattle and add them to the girls? I think I'll hitch a ride with the herd."

John felt like he'd been gut-shot. "Quit fooling around."

"The way I figure it," Pops babbled on. "Six of us make better odds than five. And I know the way. We'll point the cattle north and take our chances. What do we have to lose? The herd has come this far already. They're trail broke by now. Seasoned. All the fight is out of them. Northern Indian Territory into Kansas is the easiest stretch. The terrain is flat, the grass is holding out and there's plenty of water holes."

"I… You… But…" When had he lost control of the situation? John eyed the source of his problems. He'd lost control the moment Miss O'Mara had kicked him in the head. She must have shaken loose his brain. "You still don't see the point. You can't trade cattle that don't belong to you."

"They don't belong to you either."

"Yes. They do."

"Then what are you going to do with them?"

"Well I'm not handing them over to a bunch of girls. Children. Greenhorns no less."

Pops glared. "I'm not a greenhorn and I'm certainly not a child. I'm experienced. I'll take the cattle. I'll even keep the same deal. You can drive your share, the ten head, all the way if you want. Start over in Cimarron Springs. We'll keep the extra horses."

"I didn't make a deal," John's voice cracked beneath the strain of his disbelief. "There was no deal. That's the whole point."

Moira shook her head. "You're talking in circles again, Mr. Elder. And wasting daylight in the process. I've got a busy day teaching these girls the rudimentary skills and then we've got a stream to cross."

"It's a river."

"It's two feet deep in most places with more sandbars than water. It's not exactly the Missouri."

"There are places that drop off to five or six feet. And you don't even know the rudimentary skills yourself. How are you going to teach them to somebody else?"

"She's got good instincts." Pops tossed his coffee dredges onto the red earth and tugged on his suspenders. "I'll pack up camp." He stuck out an elbow. "Join me, Miss O'Mara?"

Behaving as though John wasn't an active participant in the conversation, Pops and Moira linked elbows and walked away.

The other four girls shifted on their feet and eyed him as though he was a stick of dynamite with a lit fuse. He recognized the emotions flitting across their faces—curiosity, doubt, fear, and worst of all, excitement. They were wary yet fascinated all at the same time.

He clutched his throbbing head. "What just happened?"

Tony chucked him on the shoulder. "You just got outwitted."

John rubbed his shoulder, still bruised from his rescue the previous evening and Hazel's pinch. "I did not get outwitted. You can't reason with crazy. Therefore, you cannot be outwitted by it."

The dark-haired girl scratched her head. "I know you think you're making sense, but I understood Moira a lot better."

John blew out a breath. He'd ceased understanding his own reasoning somewhere around the time he'd traded his own horses for his own cattle and lost his cook in the process. "I can't convince Moira, but you've got some cattle experience, Tony. I could tell by the way you rode yesterday. You know the dangers."

Her expression hardened and raw pain flickered in her dark eyes. "I did grow up on a ranch. My pa was a hand and my ma was a cook in the big house. Then the influenza came. My whole family got sick, but only I survived. The owner said I lived because I was special. He said I was so special, someone would surely pick me from the orphan train. But I knew he was lying, see? Because if I was such a great kid, why didn't they let me stay on the ranch? That was the only home I'd ever known. But I wasn't special. I was just another orphan."

John imagined Tony losing one family member after another and then being displaced from the only home she'd ever known. "You are special. He was a fool for not seeing that."

"I know that. My uncle said he'd come for me once he had money saved. Except the chaperone on the train stole my letter. That was my last chance at having a real family. At least that's what I thought. I have another chance. That's a good feeling and I'm not letting it go."

"This isn't the solution."

"I also know what I've left behind," she continued. "I'm not sure you do."

She turned away, leaving him in uneasy silence. He knew what they had to lose. He knew all too well. They were risking their very lives. That's why he couldn't let this cattle drive go forward.

"Are we going to jail?" Hazel asked. "Darcy says we're going to jail."

"Darcy is wrong." Moira cast a surreptitious glance over her shoulder.

John and Pops were engaged in a heated conversation. Well, more specifically, John was involved in a heated conversation. Pops kept his head down, carefully packing the chuck wagon. He offered the occasional nod, never looking up, never speaking.

Moira pulled a wad of bills from her pocket and let the folded edges unfurl in her hand. The meager offering represented everything she owned in the world. All of her possessions. She'd left everything else behind in a town that didn't even have a proper name as far as she could tell. Who named a town Fool's End, anyway?

Her scarred leather valise remained in her room at the hotel. A change of clothes, a few toiletries, her sketchbook. It hadn't seemed like much at the time. Except it was more than she had now. Nearly twenty-one years old and she had nothing to show for her life. *Nothing.* Hardly any money, no possessions, no sketches, no family.

Her mother's brush and mirror were in that bag. Moira tamped down the flood of sorrow.

Sucking in a fortifying breath, she took the sight of the peacefully grazing cattle. She might not have anything of substance, but she had a plan. And that counted for something.

She tipped back her head and offered up a quick

prayer for guidance. She wasn't a leader. She wasn't anything. Yet the girls looked to her as though she was the answer to *their* prayers.

She was just Moira O'Mara. Unfortunately, that *didn't* count for much. "We're not going to jail, but we can't go back to town."

"Good riddance, I say," Tony declared. "That town was full of nothing but thieves and criminals."

"You'd know," Darcy sneered.

"Hey!"

Sarah brushed the hair from her forehead. "Leaving is fine by me. But what happens after we reach our destination?"

"You heard her," Tony spoke. "We're gonna sell the herd and start over."

Darcy shook her head. "Impossible. We don't know what we're doing."

Sarah shrugged a shoulder. "It's not complicated. Like Moira says, we just have to be smarter than the cattle."

Tony snorted. "Yeah. You think you can manage that, Darcy?"

The older girl lunged and Moira snatched her by the collar. "This will never work if we waste our energy fighting. All we have right now is each other."

"If all we have to count on is each other, then this whole idea is doomed," Darcy grumbled.

"Goodbye, then." Tony sketched a wave. "Those cattle are dollar signs for all of us. We've got nothing but our wits right now. With money I can find my uncle. I'm sure he's looking for me now. We'll start over."

Hazel stuck out her lower lip. "This doesn't feel right. We can't steal Mr. Elder's cows. Not after everything he's done for us already. He found Miss Molly." She displayed her mud-splattered rag doll with its wilted yarn braids. "What's he going to do without his cows?"

Moira clenched her jaw. Mr. Elder had made his choice. Losing his cattle wasn't her fault. She hadn't asked to be kidnapped and she hadn't asked to be rescued. She'd been minding her own business and now she was good and trapped. If Mr. Elder was too pigheaded to do the same, it wasn't her problem. He had a willing and able crew camped out right beneath his nose, and he'd ignored their offer. He'd rather sacrifice his future than trust them, and that was his own downfall.

They were useful. Someday maybe he'd see that.

She leaned in and lowered her voice. The girls huddled closer. "Mr. Elder has made his choice. It's not our responsibility to make that choice more palatable to him."

Hazel frowned. "What's palatable?"

"It means tasty," Tony cut in.

Moira sighed. "Close enough. We don't have to make his decisions tasty for him. He might have helped us out last night, sure. I'm grateful. Things have gotten complicated, though. He's done helping us now. We're on our own."

"I still think it's stealing," Hazel grumbled.

Tony rubbed her chin. "Those cattle are worth a lot of money if we sell them."

Moira's stomach dropped. She hadn't calculated the animals' worth. "How much?"

Tony named a sum that raised a gasp from her rapt audience.

"Are you certain?" Moira's hands trembled.

"Maybe more. We're in army country now. The

rancher always liked army folks. Said they had deep pockets."

As she considered the tremendous sum of money, Moira hung her head. How could John Elder walk away from all that? Had he so little faith in their abilities that he wasn't even willing to try?

"I agree with Hazel." Sarah remained somber. "It feels like we're stealing. It's not right."

Moira felt a flush of heat creep up her neck. They didn't deserve that much if they only took the herd as far as Fort Preble. "What if we sell the herd and give the money to Mr. Elder? We'll only take fair wages." At a sudden loss, she faced Tony. "What is a fair wage?"

"I heard the boys talking plenty of times back on the ranch. Fifty silver pieces for a drive, start to finish."

The girls gasped and Darcy's eyes widened.

"That'd take forever to earn." Sarah spoke, her voice filled with wonder. "I worked in a hotel once. That was two bits a week."

Moira didn't know whether to laugh or cry. "This is more. A lot more." With fifty silver dollars she could hire a Pinkerton detective. Or even two. They'd find Tommy for certain. "We're not stealing. We're helping him out. Like when we rode his horses back from the livery."

Sarah chewed her bottom lip. "I suppose if we give Mr. Elder the money from the cattle, it's all right. You know, if we only kept our fair wages."

"Well, we may not have started this," Moira said. "But we can finish. We'll take our share of the pay and give the rest to Mr. Elder. That way we're all in the clear. He can't fault us for that."

Tony jerked a thumb over one shoulder. "I don't think he wants our help.'"

John had saddled his horse. He mounted and kept his head low as he kicked his horse into a gentle canter.

"See? He's leaving."

Moira's heart shattered. Without his expertise and guidance, the future loomed before her, bleak and foreboding. She'd known he was a loner. She'd known he didn't want a bunch of orphans around beyond a certain reluctant obligation. Yet somewhere in her heart she'd hoped he was different. She'd hoped he'd stay.

"Mr. Elder isn't part of this anymore. It doesn't matter how many people quit on us as long as we don't quit on each other. Right?"

Something passed between Tony and Darcy. A look Moira didn't quite understand. Yet the odd exchange stirred the hairs on the back of her neck. The moment quickly passed and their expressions mirrored acknowledgment. Whatever bit of silent communication they'd shared seemed to have set them in accord.

She'd keep an eye on those two. There was an undercurrent there. Moira returned her attention to the other girls. If anyone dissented, the plan was lost. "Are we all in agreement? A show of hands."

Tony's hand shot up first, followed immediately by Darcy, then Sarah, then Hazel. Moira felt the heat of excitement flowing through her limbs. Her blood pumped, invigorated. It felt good. Having a goal. Having a purpose.

She glanced at the kick of dust John Elder had left in his wake and an unexpected ache settled in her heart, shadowing her excitement. She shook off the pall. There was no use wishing things had turned out any different. She refused to beg John Elder for help.

Moira cleared her throat. "Mr. Elder might not believe in us, but that doesn't matter. We believe in each other. We have each other. And that's enough for me."

She shook off the cowboy's rejection. They were doing something good. Something worthwhile. He could run as far as he wanted, but he couldn't run from himself. She'd learned that truth the hard way. Some lessons were like that. He'd find out for himself.

John rode a safe distance away before stopping. Once out of view of the campsite, he dismounted and sat on a squat boulder. Nothing but red soil and the occasional shrub tree met his gaze. He glanced at Champion. The animal circled and whined.

"Don't look at me. It's not my fault." John snorted. "Don't get that judgmental gleam in those brown eyes of yours. I suppose you'd have stayed, too."

Another high-pitched whine met his question.

"Well, of course you'd rather stay with the girls. They've done nothing but coddle you the whole time. And feed you."

Champion nuzzled his hand.

"Yeah. You've gone and let yourself go all right. But we can't save them. We'll follow from a safe distance. Then, when things go horribly wrong, and things are bound to go horribly wrong, we'll be there."

Another whine.

"What's that supposed to mean?" Champion tilted his head to one side. John scoffed. "You don't actually think they can do this, do you? What do a bunch of girls know about driving cattle? About riding the trail, about hardship…."

He kept thinking of Moira's haunted eyes. She wasn't a quitter that was for certain. She could be married with a family of her own instead of searching for a brother she hadn't seen in years.

The thought led him to his own brothers. After Robert had lost his wife, their brother Jack, a Texas Ranger at the time, had set out to find the killer. He'd searched for over a year, never giving up, never slowing. The killer's trail had led him right to a lovely widow and her newborn girl. Even when Jack had known the truth might break her heart, that the widow's late husband had been a killer, he hadn't quit. His perseverance had paid off. He and the widow were married and their family had grown with two more boys.

John hung his head. Moira had questioned his honor. He was trying to save their lives and someday they'd thank him for it. Maybe not soon. But someday.

Champion barked and padded in the direction of the herd, then glanced over one shoulder.

"No. We're not going yet. They have to see how hard this is. We can't help yet."

The dog lifted both ears.

"You won't convince me."

Another bark.

"You do what you want. I'm done with the lot of you."

John pushed himself upright. He glanced around and found Champion sitting in the same spot, staring in the direction of the herd.

"Dog!"

Nothing.

"Champion."

Nothing.

Of all the betrayals he'd felt that day, this one stung the worst.

Chapter Seven

Moira couldn't stop looking over her shoulder, searching the horizon for any sign of John Elder. She missed the way his hat rode low on his forehead. The way his left hand curled on his thigh when he rode. She couldn't help wishing he'd stayed.

It was a foolish wish, and she was foolish for caring. Too bad her traitorous heart wouldn't listen.

The girls had saddled the horses and scouted the river for the lowest crossing. Pops had taken Hazel and crossed the water in the chuck wagon, scouting the next leg of the trail. When they'd discovered the point where the water stayed below the wheels, they marked the spot with a pile of stones.

After gathering the group at camp, Tony sketched out their path in the dirt. Moira stood guard for any sign of dissent or rebellion. To her immense relief, once the girls had declared their allegiance, the planning had fallen into place. Only one piece left her uneasy. While Tony had the most experience, the girls looked toward Moira for the ultimate guidance.

Which left her as the only adult in the group. The person in charge.

Moira ducked her head and tied a scarf around her neck as modest protection against the sun. "It's past noon, we should have left hours ago. We'll have to make the best progress we can today."

Tony stuck out her chin. "The hardest part is crossing the river. Once we're over, the rest will be easy."

Moira linked her hands behind her back and braced her feet apart. She'd gone over everything with Tony and Pops earlier. The instructions were simple, the execution deceptively straightforward. "Let's go over this one more time. Pops has taken the wagon on ahead with Hazel. Tony will be the point man. I'll take the right flank and watch the swing."

She paused and studied their reactions, breathing a sigh of relief when no one questioned her orders. "Once we drive the herd out of the gulley, we'll turn them east toward the creek. Sarah will watch the left flank. That leaves Darcy as the drag man. It's a small herd, and while we'll lose sight of Pops and Hazel, we won't lose sight of each other. Since we might not hear each other over the noise, don't forget the signal. Pops gave us each a red bandanna. If you get into trouble, wave your bandanna. We'll halt and regroup. Does anyone have any questions?"

The girls remained silent, solemn. After a moment, Sarah spoke, "I feel like we should have a name."

"What kind of name?"

"I dunno. For us. Something that says who we are."

Moira laughed. "How about the Calico Cowboys?"

The girls exchanged slow grins.

Sarah adjusted her bonnet. "We're the Calico Cowboys."

"The Calico Cowboys," Darcy repeated. "I like that, too."

Sarah closed her eyes and took a deep breath. "I think we should offer up a prayer."

The girls nodded.

They clasped hands and formed a circle. With Darcy on her right and Tony on her left, Sarah began, "Dear Lord. Please keep us safe on our travels. Guide our feet and guide our thoughts toward the path of righteousness. Give us peace on our journey. Amen."

"Amen," the girls spoke in unison.

They took their places and scrambled onto their mounts without assistance. Moira led her mount near a large boulder and clambered astride. She'd been getting tips from Tony and she'd chosen the easiest mount, the one John had assigned her last evening. If she mostly let the horse have its way, it seemed to know what to do.

Adjusting her skirts in the saddle, Moira recalled the previous night, how John had clasped her waist, his hands strong and sure. She quickly brushed the memory aside. He was gone now. They were on their own. For everything. Even something as simple as mounting a horse.

With a last glance toward the group, Tony kicked her horse into a gentle canter toward the point. Sarah and Darcy took their positions. Moira heaved a sigh. It was all well and good hearing how things must be done. Listening and doing were two separate things. They had to make this happen with no practice.

Moira swallowed around the lump in her throat. The cattle were enormous. They munched the grass, the horns occasionally clacking each other or a protruding rock.

She sat for a moment, nonplussed. Of all the things they'd planned for and discussed, she'd never once considered the mechanics of stirring the beasts into action.

"He yaw!" Moira shouted. "Go."

The enormous bull nearest her lifted his head for a moment before resuming his unhurried grazing. "Go on, you lazy beast. We've got five miles before sunset."

The animal snorted.

From the flank and the drag, Moira heard the faint echo of Sarah and Darcy joining her encouraging shouts. The cattle paid them no mind.

Moira chewed her lip. This particular dilemma had never even occurred to her. That they wouldn't even be able to start the herd. She hollered louder. Nothing happened. Well, one or two of the cattle wandered closer. If she didn't know any better, she'd think they were mocking her. One enormous bull shook its horns left and right, jiggling the muscles along its neck. Oh, yes. That animal was most definitely mocking her.

Sucking in a deep breath, she hollered again. And again. Exhausted, she shouted one last time. "Move, you stubborn bea—beasts!" her voice cracked.

Darcy reined her horse closer. "At least the drummer won't have any trouble finding us."

Moira brushed the hair from her forehead, wishing she had a hat. "We'll figure it out. Take the flank again."

As a last-ditch effort, she decided to rein closer. The horse jerked right instead. Moira whipped around and realized someone held the bridle.

John Elder met her astonished gaze. "I don't recommend going any closer. It's not safe."

"I suppose you've come to gloat at us." Moira kept her gaze averted. The humiliation stung. "As you can probably see, we can't even get them started."

The cowboy squinted into the distance. "Most tasks are more difficult than they appear."

"Is that what you came back to say? How encouraging. Thank you so much for the confidence. As you can tell, it's going swimmingly thus far."

He kept his focus on the horizon. "I see that."

Moira remained stubbornly silent. She wouldn't give him the satisfaction of seeing her frustration. "You want us to quit now and save you the trouble."

John placed his gloved hand over hers. "I'm keeping you safe."

She felt the warmth of his fingers. His touch was firm and weighty, comforting. Her body swayed toward his strength. She snatched away her hand. There was no use growing accustomed to something fleeting.

Swallowing hard against her potent feelings, she avoided his gaze. "Are you going to help us or not?"

"The first sign of trouble and I'm putting a stop to this crazy stunt. Is that a deal?"

Her lips parted in surprise. "I—"

"Cover your ears."

Moira was still staring in confusion when he let out an earsplitting whistle. The cattle picked up their heads. The biggest, a dappled red bull who'd been staring her down all morning took a resigned step forward. The old moocher tossed a baleful glare over one enormous shoulder. Moira stuck out her tongue.

Once their leader set off, the others soon followed. First, one ambled forward, then another and another. Soon, like a great rumbling train they formed a line, moving together three to five abreast. The flank swung toward Moira. John nudged his horse toward her and pointed.

"Move ahead. They're used to this. Don't get too close. Stay within ten or twenty feet. That's enough. Give the horse his head, he'll do all the work for you. It's his job. He's been trained by the best."

A wicked grin tipped up the corner of his mouth.

"Trained by the best, you say?" Moira noted his proud nod. "And who would that be? One of your older brothers?"

His expression shuttered and she instantly regretted her teasing. He'd helped them out and she'd rewarded his assistance with an insult. She hadn't meant…what did it matter? He'd taken her prodding the wrong way and she had only herself to blame.

He tipped his hat. "Keep this pace. I'll stick with you for a spell. Once you're started, I'll check on the others."

Moira let slack in the reins. The horse maintained a steady distance from the cattle. Their hooves kicked up dust, rumbling the ground beneath their feet.

"They're moving!" Moira shouted over the thunder of hoofbeats. "Can you see that? They're actually moving. We did that."

He appeared completely oblivious to their remarkable accomplishment.

She reached out and yanked on John's sleeve. "We're doing it, don't you see? We're actually making this happen!"

Their gazes clashed and her breath lodged in her throat. The space between them sparked with emotion. The air crystallized around her, full of promise and renewal. For a moment anything seemed possible. More than that, *everything* seemed possible.

He reached in his saddlebag and pulled out a pair of leather gloves. "Take these."

"Is that your only pair?"

"The only extra."

"Thank you."

Moira reached across the distance and accepted the gloves. John held the halter of her horse as she awkwardly tugged the enormous gloves over her fingers. She'd give them to Tony first thing. She'd have asked John to pass them on, but she had a feeling her request would put him in an awkward situation. He couldn't outfit them all and pointing out the shortfall only exposed their weaknesses.

They'd scrounged up the bandannas that morning and managed hats for everyone save Moira.

She set her chin in a stubborn line. They'd take care of themselves. "And thank you for coming back."

"You won't be thanking me for long. This isn't going to be easy."

"You think it's been easy for those girls up to this point?"

John tossed her a sharp glance. "I don't suppose it has."

"I'm betting they're tougher than they look."

"What about you, Miss Moira O'Mara? Are you up to the challenge?"

Moira thought of the endless hours of rolling cigars. The pungent scent of tobacco that permeated her clothes and hair and leached its way beneath her very fingernails. The pads of her fingers had been perpetually darkened, perpetually calloused. The work was easy. Monotonous. And it gave her too much time for thinking. Too much time for thinking how nice it would be without the infernal tick, tick, tick of Mr. Gifford's watch. He'd fill the presses with the completed cigars at each interval, and if a space remained empty, some punishment was meted out. Sometimes it was no break, sometimes no dinner.

Moira shook off the memories. "I know a thing or two about hard work."

Her answer must have mollified him because he lapsed into the silence. A familiar silence that once again gave her too much time for thinking.

When she'd gone to the Giffords', she'd thought she was stepping into a dream. At first she'd thought their fortunes had improved. But it had all been a distortion. The Giffords were just another false facade. Once the doors closed, the beautiful picture had blackened. They were all pretending, pretending to be something they weren't.

It was exhausting keeping up appearances.

Moira glanced around her. Out here everything was stripped away, elemental. There were no rocks, no trees to cower behind. There was just wind and brush and miles of nothing. She was dirtier than she'd ever been. Her hair needed a good washing and soon she was bound to attract as many flies as the cattle. The primitive conditions liberated her soul. No false fronts here. This was survival, pure and simple.

John's question hung in the air between them. *Are you up to the challenge?* Moira squinted into the distance. Tony waved and Moira sketched a hesitant wave in return. A sudden ache squeezed her heart. Developing a relationship with the girls wasn't wise. Who knew what the future held for any of them? After they sold the cattle, they'd be scattered like spring blossoms in the wind. The closer they grew, the more difficult the parting. She'd use her age as a barrier and hold herself apart.

John's expression turned grim as he watched the play of emotions on her face. "Surviving in the city is still different than making it in the country."

"At least out here you know the enemy."

"How do you mean?"

"It's easier to hide among people. Easier to put up a false front. Out here there's no hiding."

"There's nothing to hide behind, that's for certain." He swept his arm in a wide arc. "What about you? Are you hiding from something?"

"Disappointment, I suppose."

He was far too perceptive for his own good. Moira recalled an advertisement seen in the St. Louis train station. A tableau featuring a handsome, suited father holding open a book while his equally perfect family gathered around him. Those folks only existed in pencil drawings. Back in that old cow town, in the bottom of her leather bag, she kept the picture she'd sketched from the advertisement. She couldn't get the image out of her mind. She wanted that picture. She wanted those relaxed smiles. When she pictured Tommy, it was like picturing that perfect life. She'd have a dress that touched the floor and didn't show any ankle. A dress she'd pick out herself for once. A dress that no one else had ever worn. A pair of boots that fit right and didn't need papers stuck in the toe.

"Hey," the cowboy interrupted her thoughts. "Forget I said anything. We're all disappointed in something. This wasn't exactly what I was expecting either."

Moira forced an easy grin. "I'm sorry things didn't turn out for you."

She'd been shortsighted. Caught up in her own survival. She hadn't given his predicament much thought and he'd lost as much as the rest of them. More even. More because he had more to lose. Since he had a home, she'd convinced herself he wasn't suffering. A selfish oversight on her part. He deserved compassion and sympathy as much as any one of the girls.

The cowboy rested his wrist on his saddle horn. "Nothing ever turns out the way we picture. Sometimes it's better and sometimes it's worse. Right now I'm going to see it through."

"I guess that's fair."

He halted his horse and caught her mount by the bridle. "I don't regret the past twenty-four hours. No matter what happens, no matter what I said before. I'm glad it was me in that alley. It terrifies me when I think of all the ways that could have gone wrong."

Her head throbbed. She hadn't known it until that moment, but she'd needed to hear his confession. He might resent the situation, but he didn't resent them—the girls and Moira.

"You're good to say so."

"It's true."

He released the bridle and her horse shied away. "If I'd have known how things were going to turn out, I'd have taken a bath before I left yesterday. I'd give anything to feel clean again," she said.

"You're cleaner than Wendell, that's for certain."

Moira gave a ruthless laugh. "His hair was held to his head with dirt and grease. I bet if he gave it a good washing, it'd all fall out."

"He'd probably look better."

Moira jerked her chin toward Tony. "You should check on the others."

"Sure. Keep the flank in line. Remember what I said, let your mount do the work. Signal if you have trouble."

"I will."

"And don't get too close. The horns are lethal."

"I won't."

"And don't—"

"Enough," Moira cried. "We'll be in Canada before you finish this lecture."

Looking sheepish, John tipped his hat once more and kicked his horse into a canter. "I'll be back around."

"I'm sure you will."

She watched his progress, feeling the loss of his company. Sun sparked off the Snake River in the distance and Moira shivered. If she didn't screw up her courage for the next test, the whole drive was doomed.

She'd never found the right moment to admit that crossing the river terrified her.

"Well, Mr. Elder," Tony said, lifting the brim of her leather hat. "Looks like we've reached our first test."

The ground sloped beneath his horse's hooves, driving them inexorably downward toward the riverbed. "That sure didn't take long."

John had circled around the herd, checking on each girl in turn. Despite his worst fears, they handled themselves well. All the while, he kept thinking of Moira's obvious joy when they'd started the herd moving that morning. He'd never seen such elation from such a simple task. They hadn't saved the world. They hadn't done anything really. He'd whistled and the cattle had done what they'd been doing for the past several weeks. Champion nipped at their heels, spurring them into action, just as the animal had been trained. Nothing very special. The cattle responded by habit, following each other nose to tail.

Yet the simple task had lit Moira's face as though he'd given her a new pony on Christmas morning.

She remained at the center of his attention, the enchanting freckles scattered like buckshot over her cheeks and nose.

Near as he could tell, he'd gotten outwitted because he let her. At least that's what he was telling himself. Sparring with Moira left him invigorated, rejuvenated.

He fisted his left hand and braced his knuckles against his thigh. Over the past few weeks he'd forgotten how much he loved riding the trail, how much he relished the freedom and the untamed spaces. Not that he didn't enjoy modern conveniences. He liked staying in town just as much as the next fellow. He was looking forward to having his own house. To building his own ranch.

Once he had his own cowhands, he'd see things were done his way.

Tony snapped her fingers. "Are you listening?"

John started. "What were you saying?"

She indicated a spot along the riverbank. "That's the pile of rocks we left to mark the shallowest passage."

He shook his head, clearing his thoughts. He'd get them all killed if he didn't stay focused. "You already scouted the crossing?"

"Of course."

"I'll take the lead across with you. After the first half of the herd makes it, I'll circle back around and check the flanks. If one of the cattle gets into trouble, don't go near it. They'll thrash about and you risk getting killed."

"Okay."

"Keep an eye out for strays. Even with the rain we had yesterday, the river is shallow. The cattle are accustomed to the routine by now, but one or two of them still might balk. Let me know if you run into trouble. Don't push them, though. Let Champion and me handle that."

"Mr. Elder," Tony said, her cheeks flush with excitement. "If you don't quit talking, we'll still be here come next spring."

John sheepishly tugged on his ear. "I'll lead the way."

"This'll be easier than roping a penned calf."

A half grin lifted the corner of his mouth. He'd expected a lot of things. He'd expected uncertainty and caution. He hadn't expected the overwhelming excitement and enthusiasm. Their eager anticipation of the adventure reminded him of his first cattle drive. How long ago had that been? Seemed like forever since he'd been young.

Tony kicked off beside him and together they splashed into the river. John's horse slipped for the first few steps, then caught its footing. As the chill water gushed into his boots, he hissed in a breath. The nights were cooler up north, and the river's chill temperature brought the tale. He hadn't much time before the first frost.

A splash sounded behind him and he followed the rumbling progress of his finest bull. A great beast of an animal with a mean temper and an insatiable appetite. If John made it as far as Cimarron Springs, this bull was his best asset. As the animal pushed ahead, unhampered by the rushing water, he tamped down his fears.

Behind the bull, the first line of cattle followed without a hitch and John blew out a sigh of relief. Tony had positioned herself opposite him in the river, keeping the funnel of cattle narrow and contained. He pointed to an outcropping of brush trees in the distance. "Head toward that point. Sarah can take up your position. I'll catch up with you once we've gotten the whole herd across."

Tony grinned. "Have we passed your test yet?"

"Not hardly."

"I take that as a challenge."

"I was afraid of that."

He rounded back and took note of Sarah's position on the left flank. She'd reined her horse into the river where the water met the animal's belly. A moment of pride flashed in his chest. She'd positioned herself perfectly, and without any direction from him. She'd done it on intuition.

The right flank had bulged with the cattle wandering out of line. One particularly lazy beast had paused in the middle of river and lapped at the water.

John and his mount fought their way against the tide and urged the beast into motion. Once corrected, the others followed. He kept watch on their progress for a few moments more, then searched for Moira.

She remained on the bank. Champion danced around the legs of her horse, tracking the cattle, nipping at their heels and skirting away from their horns. For the next few minutes he marveled at how well everything was proceeding. The girls were green, but they had good instincts. Tony kept the lead cattle moving northeast and Sarah kept the water crossing manageable.

With only a few dozen cattle on the opposite bank. Darcy, the drag man, appeared near the shore.

John flagged her. "Move ahead and keep the right flank steady."

She offered a distracted nod in return.

He caught Moira's attention. "You and Darcy will be the last ones across. You want me to stay?"

"No. We're fine. You keep up with Tony."

A slight hitch in her voice caught his attention. "Are you certain?"

"We're plenty capable, Mr. Elder. It's not like I'm afraid of a little water."

Chapter Eight

Terrified was more like it.

Moira glanced down and her whole body trembled. Her horse, sensing her unease, remained stock-still. Champion barked and nipped at the heels of the last remaining cattle on the shore.

Moira pressed a hand against her roiling stomach. The cattle were crossing. Tony was a dot in the distance. Sarah and Mr. Elder moved up the line of cattle, letting their numbers increase to four and five abreast once they reached the top of the riverbank.

Darcy lifted her head. "My feet are freezing from this water. It's your turn. I'll meet you on shore."

Without waiting for an answer, Darcy and her mount splashed through the water, emerging from the icy river on the far side.

Her heart pounding, Moira kneed her mount deeper. The animal waded in until the water seeped through the seams of her boots. Moira sucked in a breath at the icy chill. No wonder Darcy had wanted dry land.

Though the reins remained slack in her hands, her mount drove through the current. Moira kept her eyes plastered on the horizon. Rushing water pulled at her boots, sucking her skirts around the horse's belly.

White-hot terror shot through her veins. Her limbs paralyzed and she remained frozen. The horse paused. Moira squeezed her knees and dug her heels into its flanks. "Keep moving."

Her mount moved a few lengths forward and stopped once more.

Moira groaned and glanced around her. John Elder had trained his horses well. Too well. The animal wasn't budging until the last bull climbed out of the water. Unless she wanted to swim the distance, she was stuck.

Champion nipped the final two heads of cattle into the water and splashed in beside them. Keeping its head above water, the dog surged past her toward the opposite shore.

Even as the glacial chill invaded her limbs, Moira broke out in a cold sweat. It felt as though the river was pulling at her, desperately trying to tug her under.

Her horse took a step forward and every muscle in her body tightened. Moira gripped the saddle horn with both hands and hunched her back. The water surged along her thighs. Fear pumped through her veins, blinding her vision.

For a moment she worried she'd lose control, scream or cry or burst into a thousand pieces. She dug her heels into the horse's flanks once more. If John Elder saw her now, he'd know her weakness, her fear. If he realized her terror, he'd have a weapon against her. A reason to call a halt to the cattle drive.

She caught sight of Darcy waiting on the shore. She hadn't much farther. As the water rose around her, a tangle of mane hair swirled around her fingers. As she came abreast of Darcy, the girl leaned over and adjusted her foot in her stirrup. Her hat tumbled from her head, landing in the shallow water near the shore.

The cows rumbled past, stirring the water. Darcy reached out. A wave lapped at the brim, carrying the hat beneath the belly of an enormous bull.

Darcy cried out. "Grab my hat. It's going right past you!"

Moira peeled her fingers from around the saddle horn. The brim bobbed along the water just out of reach. She leaned forward.

Darcy huffed. "Reach for it! I haven't got a spare."

Moira stretched out her hand and touched the brim. Her mount slipped in the muddy embankment. She shrieked and groped for the saddle horn. Her fingers, stiff with cold, missed their purchase. The rushing water reached her shoulders and drew her beneath the dark surface.

Moira surged upward, gasping and sputtering. Her right leg slipped over the saddle while her left foot remained caught in the stirrup. Her stomach churned with terror and frustration. Reaching for her ankle, suffocating waves lapped over her head.

Panic scattered her thoughts. She flailed her arms and arched her back. For a brief moment her face breached the surface. She caught Darcy's horrified expression, the space between them separated by a dozen cattle, their lethal horns clicking together as they slipped up the embankment, falling to their knees and rising again in a powerful heave of muscles.

There was no way for Darcy to reach her. Not before the water pulled her under once more.

Moira kicked out and caught her horse's right flank.

The animal started into motion, dragging her toward the shore.

Her boot slipped off and her foot sprang free. She thrashed her arms and felt for the bottom. The current snatched at her, dragging her into deeper water. She sucked in a mouthful of water. Gagging and coughing as her head bobbed.

The water closed around her, blurring her vision. Her heart thumped erratically as though clinging to the last vestiges of life.

She realized with a sudden clarity that she was going to die. She was going to drown before they even crossed the Snake River.

John had already started back when he heard the panicked shouts. Blood hammering in his ears, he kicked his horse into a gallop and found Darcy frantically pointing toward Moira's riderless horse.

"She's over there!" Darcy shouted. "She went under."

He urged his horse toward the water's edge and searched beneath the murky surface.

A tangle of brilliant red hair floated on the water. He slid from his mount and struggled toward the beacon. Reaching beneath the surface, he caught hold of Moira's limp body, then locked his arms around her waist and hauled her toward the embankment. She was heavier than when he'd held her before. The skirts of her water-logged dress had nearly doubled her weight.

He clumsily made his way over the muddy shore and laid her on dry ground. She whimpered and spread her arms akimbo like a carelessly tossed rag doll. Her eyes remained half-open, dull and unresponsive. Icy fear twisted around his heart.

She coughed and gasped and her body spasmed. John sagged at the glorious sound. Crouching beside her, he slipped his hands behind her neck and turned her head aside, letting her expel the water she'd swallowed. When the retching calmed, he eased her head on his bent knee. Her mass of snarled red hair soaked his trousers.

He brushed the sodden strands from her forehead and rested the back of his hand against her cool skin. Her face remained ashen. She moaned, her body trembling.

Darcy hovered over them, her hand over her mouth.

John searched the horizon. "Ride ahead and tell Tony what's happened, then fetch the wagon. We'll need a fire and warm blankets."

Darcy looked as though she might say something, then appeared to change her mind. She whirled and grasped the reins of her mount.

Moira's head lolled to one side and she puffed a weak breath. He lifted her into his embrace and she shivered violently.

Her eyes fluttered open and she coughed. "I'm all right now."

"Then you can walk back?"

She struggled partly upright and he pressed a gentle hand against her shoulder. "I was only teasing."

A bloom of color appeared on her cheeks. "I can't swim."

"I gathered as much."

She tugged limply on the buttons of her borrowed coat, the material plastered against her body, swollen with moisture and uncooperative against her fingers, nearly blue with cold.

He brushed her hands aside. "Let me help."

Together they worked her arms from the sodden

sleeves. She sat upright and wrapped her arms around her legs, resting her chin on her bent knees, her teeth chattering. He shrugged out of his slickers and draped the heavy material around her shoulders.

She pulled one of the edges tighter together and trembled. "You were right, you know."

"About what?"

"I didn't even it make it twenty yards."

The woeful note in her voice tugged at something in his chest. "Actually, you managed about twenty-two yards."

She offered a weak chuckle.

Searching for kindling, he scratched in the dirt beneath the scrub trees lining the bank. "You're not the first person to fall in the river during a trail drive. My brother Matt once got his pant leg caught in some brush. Had to cut him out of his britches. Let me tell you, with six brothers, you never want to be caught in your drawers."

Moira rubbed her cheek against her bent knee. "I bet you never let him live that down."

"No. We did not."

He discovered the charred end of a log as big around as his leg. Considering this was the shallowest part of the river, it didn't surprise him that others had crossed here before. Other folks had obviously rested and warmed themselves here before pushing onward.

After gathering an armful of twigs and tinder, he removed a tin of matches from his breast pocket and struck a flame against the base. Some of the grass was partially green, sending up more smoke than flames. He got down on his hands and knees and blew at the spot till the embers glowed.

Shivering, Moira scooted nearer the fire. Without asking he kneeled beside her and gathered her against his chest. At that moment warmth was more important than manners and propriety. He held her stiffly, shielding her from a bitter wind that had kicked up as the day progressed. She relaxed into his embrace and he savored the feel of her in his arms. Tipping her head against his shoulder, her breath whispered in a sigh. His heartbeat pitched.

He chafed her upper arms and his fingers caught in a tangle of drenched hair. He wound the strands around his palm and wrung the moisture. With painstaking care he repeated the process on the rest of the soaking mass. Her eyes fluttered closed, her eyelashes casting soft shadows against her cheeks.

His perusal drifted toward her lips. This close, he could count each uneven freckle dusting her face. He noted how they were darker on the delightfully rounded tip of her nose and lighter as they flared over the pink apples of her cheeks.

He'd never been a man easily turned by a pretty face. He admired a beautiful woman as much as the next man, but he'd never felt the need to wax on like he'd heard other fellows. Studying Moira, he wished he had more words. More of the flowery descriptors he'd scoffed at in school.

He knew if he tried to put his thoughts to paper with pen and ink, he'd never do her justice.

A splash sounded, jerking him back to the present. Their horses had wandered nearer the river, snuffling along the bank and drinking the crisp water.

John cleared his throat and leaned back, putting some space between them, breaking whatever hold she had on his wayward thoughts. He pushed off from his knee and stood, then reached out a hand. She grasped his fingers, her own icy cold. He clasped them tighter, offering what bit of comfort he could.

"What happened to your gloves?"

She tugged on her hand, but he held firm.

"I lent them to Tony." Her voice was husky from her ordeal. "She's the only one of us who knows how to rope. She needed them more."

He flipped her palm over in his hand and rubbed his thumb along the raised marks, the skin abraded from working the reins. She curled her fingers into a fist.

All of the doubts he harbored about the cattle drive and his unlikely crew came rushing back. "Your hands are too delicate."

"They're not. They're rough and chapped. Not a lady's hands at all."

They both turned toward the sound of hoofbeats. Sarah reined her horse before them. "Is everything all right? Darcy said there'd been an accident."

Moira moved away from him, her steps halting. "I took a tumble into the water. It was my own fault."

John touched her elbow lightly, ensuring she was steady on her feet before putting some distance between them.

Sarah wasn't the best rider of the bunch. Not the worst, either. She appeared more comfortable in the saddle already. "Did you find the wagon?" Moira asked.

"We've caught up with them. We're having some trouble with the cattle, though. They scattered after crossing the river and we can't get 'em all back together. They've separated into two groups."

Moira plucked at her limp skirts. "You ride on and

help, Mr. Elder. I'll stay here for a spell. See if I can dry out some more."

"I can't. You know that. I can't risk your safety. What if something happens?"

"It's only for a half an hour or so."

"In a half an hour you fell off your horse and nearly drowned in the river."

She tossed her head and gave an irritable tug at her damp hair. "It's not like I'm going to run afoul of anyone. We're in the middle of nowhere."

Leaving her all alone didn't sit right with him. "You'll get lost catching up."

"Really?" Moira gestured in a sweeping motion with one arm. "I can see halfway to Fort Preble. Don't know how I'd get lost."

"I don't like it."

"Then leave Champion. He'll keep watch."

"What if you don't put out the fire properly and you start a brushfire."

Moira lifted an eyebrow. "What? And ruin all this beautiful scenery?"

John scowled.

"It rained yesterday. It's not like we're in a drought."

She shivered and he realized she wasn't moving until he agreed. "I will build up the fire and leave you for precisely—" He fished out his pocket watch. "One hour. If you're not caught up, I'm sending someone back."

Moira's gaze remained transfixed on the pocket watch. She swallowed convulsively and jerked her head in a curt nod. He tucked his watch away and she appeared to relax.

The exchange was odd, leaving him uncertain. While he gathered more brush and stoked the flames, Moira removed her boot and stretched her stocking feet toward the heat. She wiggled her toes and leaned back on her elbows.

"You sure you're all right?"

"I'm certain."

He glanced at her askance, relieved her earlier wariness hadn't returned. "One hour."

"Yes, you mentioned that. One hour and you're sending a search party."

She closed her eyes, effectively dismissing him. He gazed into the distance, content there wasn't anything in sight except a few stray cattle and a couple of wild gobblers in the distance. He didn't see how anyone, even Miss Moira O'Mara, could possibly stir up trouble in this desolate environment.

Moira scrunched her hem beneath her fingers, feeling only a slight dampness. They'd set the fire well away from the cattle, though she didn't figure anything would spook those beasts. She heard the occasional whoops and hollers as the rest of the group rounded up the strays.

Her stockings were suspended by a stick she'd rigged near the fire. They weren't quite dry, but it appeared as though the rest of the team needed help gathering the herd once more. Champion's perpetual barking drifted over the wind. The dog returned occasionally, as though assuring itself of her safety, then darted off again.

The few cattle lingering near the river's edge wore perpetual expressions of boredom, with only the occasional grunt of discontent.

Darcy urged her horse into a trot and approached the fire, her expression glum. "I asked you to fetch my hat, not get yourself drowned."

"You're welcome," Moira replied with a wry grin. "Glad you appreciate the effort."

Darcy tossed her hair over her shoulder. "Are you dry yet? I'm tired of the drag. And there's still a couple of strays by the river."

Moira had been huddled before the warming fire for a mere twenty minutes. Despite the cowboy's gentle wringing, her hair dripped down her back and she had only one boot. She'd lost the other in the river.

She glanced at Darcy's sulky expression and back at the cheery flames. "I'm ready. I'll take over."

"Good. I'm tired of taking your turn." Darcy appeared almost triumphant as she galloped toward the line of cattle in the distance.

"Seems like your head is big enough to keep your hat on tight," Moira grumbled.

She doused the fire with three canteens full of water and kicked additional dirt over the embers, then doused them again. Heaven forbid a brushfire ignite the fresh grass. The cowboy would never let her live that down. She grappled onto her horse and glanced behind her.

A calf munched grass on the edge of the river. The animal was mottled a deep russet and red, with the darker color more pronounced around the head and shoulders haunches. Moira spurred her mount closer. Champion appeared once more and barked and bounced around the animal's legs. After a disgruntled snort, the calf lumbered up the embankment.

The calf labored and slipped, falling onto its forelegs with a bawl of distress.

Moira squinted into the distance. By the time she asked for the help, the poor animal would only dig itself deeper.

Champion splashed through the water, barking and nipping at the calf's hind legs.

The calf's eyes grew large, the whites showing stark against the red fur around its face. The animal brayed and snorted.

As the dog nipped at its hooves, the calf grew more agitated, thrashing from side to side. "Shoo," Moira ordered. "Give her some space, Champion."

She slipped off her horse and stumbled down the embankment. Moira pressed her palm against the animal's haunches and pushed. Though the calf was young, it still weighed several hundred pounds. Her feeble efforts were useless. "Easy there, big fellow. It's going to be all right."

Another animal appeared on the horizon. An enormous cow towered on the bank, flipping its head up and down and shaking the folds along its neck. The animal bawled, a lonesome sound that sent a shiver down Moira's spine.

"Go on, get up there," Moira urged the calf.

The cow at the top of the embankment lowered its head and snuffed. One sharp hoof pawed at the loose red soil.

A shot of fear skittered down Moira's spine. "You must be Mama. Well, Mama, tell your baby not to worry. We're going to get him out of here."

The mother threw back her head and bellowed.

Moira slid farther down the muddy embankment. She fought through the muck and braced her hands against the calf's backside.

"Keep moving before your mama decides to come down and fetch you herself. Then you'll both be stuck."

The animal thrashed, kicking up mud and spattering Moira's already-damp dress. She brushed a smear of mud from her forehead with the back of her hand. "Thatta boy, keep it up."

Two things happened almost simultaneously. The calf pitched forward and Moira slipped on the slimy embankment. Her boot caught beneath the calf's leg. The animal dug its sharpened hoof into her ankle and surged forward.

Moira yelped.

The mama cow on the embankment brayed.

Champion barked.

The calf caught its footing and skittered up the hill. Moira pushed herself into a standing position and attempted to follow. Her boot stuck in the mud. She yanked and her stocking foot slipped out of her boot.

Moira groaned.

She reached elbow-deep in the slimy mud and felt around. Nothing. She grimaced. Her boot had disappeared beneath a layer of mud. She took one step toward the stream and winced. Her tender ankle screamed in protest. Crouching, she rubbed the sore spot.

The mama cow and her baby remained perched on the embankment, balefully watching her troubles.

"Go on now!" Moira shouted.

She limped up the hill and stumbled right into John Elder's arms. He took one look at her mud-splattered dress and his brows drew downward into a frown. "Why didn't you fetch help?"

"I didn't need help."

His gaze encompassed her disheveled appearance and exasperation coasted across his face. "Yep. Doesn't look like you need any help at all."

He extended his hand and Moira grasped his fingers. He stretched out one leg and braced his foot against the embankment, then easily pulled her up the remaining distance. "You know," he said. "Stubbornness is not a virtue. It wouldn't kill you to ask for help once in a while."

Moira glanced down at the torn hem of her dress where the calf's hoof had shredded the material, and nearly wept. She didn't exactly have a warm bath and a change of clothing waiting for her back at camp.

She lifted her skirts and discovered the hole in her dress revealed her leg clear up past the knee. She dropped the material. "I didn't need help. I got the calf free all by myself."

The cowboy seemed singularly unimpressed by her accomplishment.

He grasped the reins of his mount and turned away. "And nearly got trampled in the process. You die, I gotta dig a hole for you."

His implacable expression was unnerving and her lips parted in shock.

"All right, maybe I'm taking this too far." The cowboy rolled his shoulders. "I'm used to giving this speech to men and the rules are different. Men respond to death and dismemberment and all that. I can see I'll have to take another approach."

Moira wrapped her arms around her body. "Dismemberment?"

"Forget that," John continued. "How about this? If you don't care about your own neck, think of those girls. They look up to you. They're counting on you. If you go and get yourself killed, I'll have a bunch of bawling girls back at camp."

Moira flushed but remained silent.

His mouth worked and he fisted his hand on his thigh.

"Okay, I guess that wasn't much better either. Don't get yourself killed on my watch, all right? I'll feel bad."

"All right."

"Good. Then we're in agreement. Now finish drying off and take up the drag. We've still got a whole day ahead of us and this was your idea in the first place."

He dismounted and approached her horse. Moira made a face at his stiff back. There was no need to over-act. *Dig a hole for her.* Indeed. He whipped around and she quickly resumed an implacable expression.

He led her horse nearer and she grasped the reins. Leaning down, he cupped his hands for her to step in. "Where is your boot?"

"In the river."

He glanced at her stocking feet. "Where is your other boot?"

"In the mud."

"Why doesn't that surprise me?"

He boosted her onto her mount and wiped his muddy hands against his pants. Moira adjusted her skirts and avoided his glower.

Together they set off for the herd in uneasy silence. Her leg throbbed and despite his dry slicker, she felt the cold seeping into bones. After his stern lecture on *death* and *dismemberment,* she wasn't giving him the satisfaction of showing her discomfort.

The herd appeared before them, the cattle back in line, the stream of bodies snaking over the horizon. Tony's hat bobbed along near the lead.

John slowed his horse. "Look, I shouldn't have yelled at you. When I came back to check and didn't see you, I guess I got a little scared. Might have pushed my temper."

"Thank you for the apology."

His head tilted upright. "It wasn't an apology. It was an explanation. And next time, ask for help."

Moira gaped at his retreating back. That infernal man had her all tied up in knots. One minute he was drying her hair and cradling her in his arms, the next minute he was shouting and carrying on.

John Elder sure made it difficult to like him sometimes. Which was probably a good thing. For a minute there, she'd been liking him a little too much.

The cowboy was a distraction she didn't need. Not now. Not ever.

Chapter Nine

John pushed the girls relentlessly. Better they realize the difficulties of the trail before they strayed too far from Fool's End. They'd realize soon enough the task they'd undertaken was easier said than done, and then he'd be finished with this crazy cattle drive. Keeping eight hundred head of cattle moving in one direction against the elements and the girls' inexperience wasn't a task for the weak at heart.

He cast a surreptitious glance at Moira. Of all the girls, she'd suffered the most that day. She'd been doused and muddied. She hadn't worn the gloves he'd lent her and her palms had already blistered. He'd resolved to treat them like men, and then he'd cradled her in his arms. Not the way he treated his men at all.

John impatiently drew his drifting thoughts away from Miss O'Mara and her troubles. The sooner he ended this debacle the better. His young crew was green and untried. As long as everything went well, they were fine. They weren't prepared for a disaster.

A form in the distance caught his attention and relief flooded his veins. They'd caught up with the chuck wagon and it appeared Pops already had a cook fire blazing. John's stomach rumbled in anticipation.

The girls had been on their horses for six hours and counting. By now they should be sore, hungry and ready to call it quits on the cattle drive. For good.

He dismounted and followed Moira as she limped before him. Not the weary gait of someone who'd spent too long in the saddle, she walked as though favoring one leg.

He jogged until he caught up with her and grasped her arm. "You okay? What happened to your leg?"

"It's nothing. It's been a long day, that's all."

With a tip of his head, he motioned toward the chuck wagon. "Why don't you sit? I'll take care of your horse."

She threw back her shoulders. "I carry my weight."

His steps slowed. "Suit yourself."

Sarah slid off her mount and her knees buckled briefly before she righted herself. She arched her back and rubbed her backside. "How can sitting all day hurt so much?"

"Because you're not sitting," Tony stated proudly. "You're riding."

"Well, I just discovered some muscles I never knew I had," Sarah said. "And those muscles are hurting."

"Don't get too comfortable. We've got to divvy up the watch."

Darcy hobbled into the campsite clutching the reins of her horse. "I don't know who's got the first watch, but it ain't me. I'm hungry, I'm tired, my back aches, the balls of my feet are sore, I'm sick of flies, and I'm sick of smelling cows."

"Well, ain't you just a ray of sunshine after a long,

hard day." Tony chucked her on the shoulder. "A little hard work never killed anyone."

"If you don't shut your yapper I'm going to shut it for you."

Tony raised her arms. "Somebody got off on the wrong side of the horse today."

John stifled a grin. "We'll take two hour shifts. First shift will start right after dinner. Everyone else will stay behind and help set up camp. Any volunteers?"

"Not me," Darcy reaffirmed.

The others glanced around. Everyone was too tired or too nervous to speak up.

Tony snorted. "It's all right, I got this. Schoolhouse rules. Everyone put in a shoe and we'll figure this out fair and square."

As though on cue, the girls crowded around her, the tips of their boots touching. Tony motioned for Moira. "You too."

Moira touched her chest. Tony nodded. She hobbled toward the group and glanced around, and added her bootless foot to the press of pointed toes.

"First one out is the last one on watch and we go in order from there." Tony knelt and placed her fingers on the toe of her own boot. "One, two, the cow said moo."

She spoke in a singsong voice, and with each word in the rhyme, she touched the next shoe in the circle. "Three, four, the lions roar. Five, six, the monkey does a trick. Seven, eight, he's swinging on a gate. Nine, ten, big fat hen."

The word "hen" landed her on Sarah's foot.

Tony flapped her wrist. "Sarah's out. She takes the last watch." Tony rested her hand on the next one in line, Moira's stocking foot. "Apples, peaches, pears and plums. Tell me when your birthday comes."

The last word landed on Moira's toe once more.

"June," she replied.

"*J-U-N-E* spells June and you are not it. Darcy is out."

Darcy heaved a sigh of relief and flopped on the ground. She tipped up her chin and let the setting sun warm her face.

"One potato, two potato, three potato, four. Five potato, six potato, seven potato more. I'm out." Tony sat back on her heels. "That means you take the first watch, Moira."

John waded through the seated girls. "Dinner first. Then watch."

Moira's shoulders slumped. "Food sounds wonderful."

"Hey," Darcy dug her heels in the dirt. "When is his watch?" She jerked her thumb in John's direction. "Ain't he the trail boss and all?"

"I'm the boss, all right, and I'll have you mind your tone." The sooner Darcy accepted his authority, the better. There might come a time when he needed a quick response from her, and he didn't want her constantly questioning his every move. "Pops and I will take midnight to two and two to four. We're used to the schedule and we'll stay awake."

Tony stuck out her chin. "We'll do our part. Same as the men."

"I know you will." He hooked his thumbs into his belt loops. "I've made my decision and I give the orders. My word is first, last and most binding."

"All right, boss. That puts Moira from six to eight, me from eight to ten, Darcy from ten to twelve. You and

Pops have midnight to four which leaves Sarah from four to six."

Darcy grunted. "I should have taken the first watch. Six to eight sounds better than ten to twelve. I'm bushed."

"Yeah," Tony said. "You should have. But you didn't. Now let's eat."

As she walked past, John stuck out an elbow and lightly tapped her upper arm. "Good work doling out the watch assignments."

"That's how we decided who 'it' is in hide-and-seek. I figured it would work for this, too."

"Fair and unbiased. I like your style."

Her eyes lit up. "Thanks, boss. You're not so bad yourself."

She'd puffed beneath his meager praise and he made a mental note to offer more words of encouragement throughout the day. His men usually preferred good-natured insults and the occasional ribbing. Dealing with girls required a whole new set of skills.

John halted. He didn't need any new skills. This was the end of the line. No use planning for a future that was never coming around.

As he moved toward the wagon and dinner, an enticing aroma wafted through the air, a scent he didn't usually associate with a trail ride.

Pops appeared with a tin plate in his hand.

John peered over his shoulder. "What's that?" He caught sight of two-tone chunks of meat stirred through the beans. "Is that bacon in the beans?"

"Sure is. Sarah came up with the idea. Since the girls don't eat as much as the boys do in the morning, we figured we could spruce up the beans a bit with the bacon.

Added some mustard and brown sugar. Mighty tasty, if I don't say so myself."

"Brown sugar? Mustard? This isn't some fancy hotel. This is a cattle drive." John's voice had taken on alarmingly high pitch. "How can we convince them to quit if you're serving them gourmet grub?"

"It ain't me serving them, it's Sarah." Pops scooped a forkful of doctored beans into his mouth and grinned. He chomped and swallowed, appearing as though he'd dug into a porterhouse steak and not a can of tinned beans with some flecks of fatted bacon. "I'm here to eat. Iff'in you want them to quit, that's your problem."

John's left eye ticked. The backboard of the chuck wagon had been flipped out into a makeshift buffet. A white handkerchief with embroidered pink roses and greenery at the corner had been folded into a triangle. A tin cup overflowing with wildflowers anchored the napkin in place.

John grunted. First bacon then black-eyed Susans. What was next?

He scooped the mouthwatering beans onto his plate and reached for a biscuit. His fingers sank into the soft bread.

"What's this?" He sniffed the unusually pleasant aroma and bit into the golden brown, flaky crust. A delicate tang infused the moist-textured grub. "If that's buttermilk I taste, I'm firing you on the spot. What happened to the hardtack? Where are the weevils?"

Sarah took a hesitant step forward. "Don't you like them? Pops had some buttermilk left from his supply trip into Fool's End."

Her crestfallen expression tugged at something in his chest.

He swallowed the delightful concoction. For a moment he feared his eyes would roll back in his head at the blissful flavor. "It's fine. Not bad at all. Just not what I'm used to."

Sarah beamed.

John stomped toward the fire. She needn't act as though he'd doled out some hefty praise. It was just a little buttermilk and some fatback.

He lifted his boot and hopped back. The girls had laid out a blanket and reclined on the surface.

He skirted the covering and plopped onto the prickly grass.

Pops held the handle of his Dutch oven and lifted the heavy cookware aloft. "Save room for peach cobbler."

"Are you pulling my leg?" John held his plate away from his body. "Peach cobbler? This is a cattle drive. No one serves peach cobbler on a cattle drive."

"Then I guess you won't be having any."

The cook meandered past and lifted the lid. A plume of steam drifted toward John. He held his breath and averted his gaze. Pops circled back around. The old coot wasn't playing fair. John exhaled his breath in noisy frustration and caught a hint of the succulent aroma. His mouth watered.

Sarah watched his reaction and plucked at the blanket. "Hazel helped make that special."

John suppressed the low growl in the back of his throat. He'd look surly if he didn't partake. "Well, um, if Hazel took all the time… I wouldn't want to be rude."

"I'm sure you wouldn't." Pops rolled his eyes. "Quite the thoughtful fellow all of a sudden, ain't ya?"

John lifted his fork and Hazel cleared her throat.

He paused.

She glanced pointedly at his hands. "Did you wash?"

"Did I wash what?"

"Your hands."

"Uh." Heat crept up cheeks beneath her watchful stare. "I forgot."

Hazel tsked. "There's water in the wreck pan."

He dutifully stood, crossed to the wagon, and rinsed his hands in the wreck pan of sudsy water. Upon sitting down, Hazel cleared her throat once more.

John tilted his head. "What did I do now?"

"You haven't said grace."

He mentally added another item to the list of things girls did differently than boys on a cattle drive. He supposed some of the changes weren't that bad.

After dropping his plate on the grass at his left, John folded his hands and bent his head. "Dear Lord, thank You for our safe crossing of the Snake River, thank You for this bountiful feast. Please continue to watch over us. Protect us from harm. And if there's any chance there's a stagecoach full of cattle hands just over the rise, tell 'em I can switch out with a bunch of girls."

Tony elbowed him in the gut.

John grinned.

As he reached for his discarded plate, a grasshopper leapt into his beans. He grimaced and flicked the insect off with his thumb.

Sarah raised an eyebrow. "The grasshoppers are as thick as cold porridge around here. That's why we're sitting on the blanket."

She smoothed her hand over the insect-free surface.

He gulped down another forkful of beans. "A little grasshopper never hurt anything."

Life on the trail was tough. Cattle drives weren't

about cherry or peach cobbler and bacon baked beans. They were hard work and adversity. Throwing down a blanket and adding a little buttermilk to the biscuits didn't change the facts.

Keeping his head low, he stood and crossed back over to the chuck wagon. Pops had set out the peach cobbler and an additional set of tin plates. John filled his cup of coffee before scooping a dollop, then resumed his seat on the prickly scrub grass.

Each bite melted onto his tongue with the flavors melding in perfect harmony. Engrossed in the tasty dessert, he barely registered Moira rising and placing her dishes in the wreck pan.

He glanced up as she walked past, noting that same hitch in her gait.

She wore a pair of battered boots and he realized Tony was in her stocking feet.

"You sure you're all right?" he asked. "Looks like you're limping."

Her spine straightened. "I'm fine. Tony's feet are smaller than mine. There's nothing wrong."

John scraped his plate with tine edge of his fork. "You let me know. Pops has a kit for cuts and scrapes. You have to be careful out here. A wound can go septic real fast if it's not tended."

Tony perked up. "It's true. Back when I lived on the ranch, one of the cattle hands only had one leg. Said he lost it in the war. He got gangrene in his big toe and they cut off his leg below the knee."

Sarah's pale skin grew even whiter. "Because of his *toe?*"

"I know, right? I mean, can you imagine if it had been in his ankle. They probably would have sawed off his leg at the thigh." She chopped the edge of her hand against a spot high on her leg. "That bone is huge. I wouldn't want anybody sawing through that."

Sarah abandoned her plate of cobbler on the blanket. "Could we talk about something else?"

"Yes, let's talk about something else." John stood and dusted his pant legs. "Nobody is getting anything chopped, hacked or severed on my watch."

Sarah pressed her fingers against her mouth and heaved.

He threw up his arms. That was yet another problem with having women in the camp. A man had to watch what he said all the time.

Moira limped toward the remuda. Safely away from camp, she lifted her skirts and tugged down the flap of her borrowed boot, revealing a purpling bruise and an ugly red scrape on her ankle. The calf's sharp hoof had bitten into her flesh.

The injury was far too shallow to go septic.

A little scrape was the least of her worries. The sun was setting and it was her turn for watch. Weariness enveloped her and her whole body ached. While she'd never considered herself a sedentary person, the day had proved far more exhausting than she'd anticipated. Though she was accustomed to working late at night— her job as a maid at the hotel had been mostly after regular hours when the patrons were asleep and wouldn't be bothered by the presence of the staff—she'd been keeping a more regular schedule for the past week.

Her eyes burned drily from sleeplessness as she approached the remuda. The saddles were stacked on their pommels in a neat line as John had instructed when they'd made camp. Moira scooped her arm beneath the cumbersome saddle and staggered backward.

Tony appeared and grasped the other side. "You really should ask for help. These saddles are too big for one person."

"You already helped me this morning when you saddled my horse. It isn't fair to make someone else do my work all the time." Moira groaned. "I have to learn to do this by myself."

Tony pressed her lips together. "The way I see it, we're sharing the work. You help me, I help you."

Moira was saved from an answer as they heaved the saddle over the horse's back. She fished beneath the animal's belly and grasped the girth strap. Tugging her lower lip between her teeth, she clumsily threaded the leather belt through the D ring.

Tony sighed and brushed her hands away. "Not like that. This here is the latigo."

She pulled the leather through the D ring of the girth strap, back up through the D ring on the saddle and repeated the process. "Now you've got a double loop. See? The next thing we're going to do is tie the knot."

She ran her fingers beneath the leather. "Don't tighten it too much. Just push the tail end back through the D ring, pull it down and across, then up through the D ring again. See how you've made a loop? Now push the tail end of the leather through the loop and you've made a knot."

Exhaustion enveloped Moira as she tried to concentrate on the rapid-fire instructions.

Tony grinned and untied the knot. "Okay. Now your turn."

Watching the motions and actually performing the

task were two entirely different things. Beneath Tony's watchful eyes, Moira repeated the instructions. Her back ached between her shoulder blades and her fingers worked, clumsy and uncoordinated.

Tony grasped the leather and ceased her fumbling efforts. "Not like that. You take the strap *under* the D ring."

Moira corrected her direction and looped the leather, then slid the end through, forming a knot.

Rubbing her chin, the younger girl nodded. "That'll do. Now you've got to tighten the strap, otherwise you'll end up beneath the horse's belly."

Tony grasped the outside layer of the long double loop they'd made with the leather strap and tugged, creating more slack. Then tightened the knot once more. At one point she reached beneath the horse and heaved on the strap.

Reaching up, she pulled on the saddle horn. "That'll hold firm." She glanced toward the horse's head. "Course, you're never gonna get anywhere unless you have a bridle."

She grasped what appeared to be a tangle of leather and expertly looped the halter over the horse's head, slid her thumb into the side of the animal's mouth and positioned the bit. "We'll save the bridle lesson for tomorrow. Mostly because I think you could use some instruction on horsemanship. You haven't ridden much, have you?"

"Once or twice, when I was very young."

When her parents were still together and they enjoyed a few good times. The memories seemed far away, almost as though they belonged to someone else.

Tony tromped toward a second horse. "Let me saddle this one. I'll show you some stuff from the ground and then we'll mount up and I'll give you a few more lessons."

"That's really not necessary." Moira turned her attention toward the setting sun. "I need to start my watch."

"You fell off in the river today. If you fall off on the ground, it's gonna hurt a lot worse. Not to mention if you lose control of your mount and get yourself killed, that means we're a man down and it's more work for the rest of us."

Moira gaped. "You sound just like Mr. Elder."

"Good. He's an excellent trail boss. And have you seen the way he handles his horses? I barely see him move, but they follow his commands. I saw an Indian once in a show at the fairgrounds. That fellow rode bareback with only a single rawhide strap half hitched under the horse's jaw for guidance. I never saw anything like it. I bet John Elder is that good."

"He mentioned he trained all the horses himself."

"That's saying something. These are some of the best horses I've ever ridden."

A grudging admiration for the cowboy filtered through Moira's numbed thoughts. John Elder handled himself well. He was patient and kind and other than a few spots of annoyance, he kept his temper.

Mindful of her debt, Moira assisted Tony with lifting her saddle. The younger girl made quick work of the rigging before leading her horse near Moira.

"Always approach a horse from the left side."

"How come?"

"I dunno. That's just what you do. You're going to have to mount for real this time. There won't always be a rock or a fence around every time we stop. Anyway, approach on the left and grasp the reins and the saddle horn in your left hand, facing the horse's rump. Then place your left foot in the stirrup. This is where it gets a little tricky. You have to kind of lift yourself up until you're standing on that left foot, then throw your right leg over the horse's back."

She demonstrated the "tricky" move with remarkable ease.

Moira attempted the motion three times before successfully swinging her leg over the saddle. Safely perched upon her mount, she caught her breath and patted the animal's neck. "That wasn't so bad now, was it?"

Tony sidled her horse nearer. "Now for the lessons. We'll practice and keep watch at the same time."

For the next forty-five minutes, the two circled the herd while Tony barked out instructions and corrections. About a half an hour into the session, Moira sensed herself steadily improving. The animal responded better, turning with her movements. The progress was minor, but the control eased her anxiety.

Tony touched the brim of her hat. "I think you know enough to keep you in the saddle tonight. We can do the same thing tomorrow."

"Thank you. For everything."

"No problem. We're a team."

The cattle munched grass and dozed, mostly ignoring her quiet direction. Her horse had good instincts and the cattle appeared to recognize its authority. As the evening progressed, her exhaustion leveled out.

At the prescribed time, Tony rode up to relieve her. The younger girl appeared refreshed and almost cheerful to be riding again.

They dismounted and Moira switched out her boots. When she mounted again, it only took her two tries.

On Moira's way back to camp, John appeared in the glow of the three-quarter moon. He glanced at her seat, her back straight and tall in the saddle, and a look of approval coasted across his face. "You're a fast study."

"Tony helped me out."

"Well, you did a good job following instruction. Now get some sleep. It's another long day in the morning."

They hadn't made it far, only a few miles from their starting point, but the small gain felt like a victory. A victory dampened by the doubt she sensed in John's considering gaze.

"I know we didn't make it very far today, but we've made progress."

"You girls did well, but it doesn't change the facts. We're in Indian Territory. We're vulnerable. More so than most. I can't take the risk."

"I'm not asking you to make a decision. I only want you to consider all that we've accomplished today."

"No decisions until morning."

Moira hesitated in the purple glow of twilight. She felt as though she should say something, or do something. Offer some sort of gesture for all the trouble he'd gone to on their behalf.

Before she could gather her thoughts, John tipped his hat and rode away. Moira sighed. She'd try again tomorrow.

She appreciated his dilemma. The girls' safety remained at the forefront of her thoughts. Despite all the reasons they shouldn't go forward, she felt compelled. The empty space in her heart didn't bother her quite as much out here. The loneliness didn't have such a fervent pull.

She needed the money, they all needed the money.

Lately she'd had doubts about her search. She'd pinned all of her hopes on a reunion. The more time passed, the more she worried her hopes were misplaced. All this time she'd thought if she could explain what had happened all those years ago, Tommy would understand. Hearing the sheriff talk had brought on new fears. Her brother hadn't just run away, he'd moved on with his life in ways she hadn't even considered. Would there be a place for her in his life? They'd always had each other. What if, when she finally found him, he didn't feel the same way anymore? She couldn't bear to lose him again. She was so tired of being alone.

Moira hung her head and prayed for guidance.

Chapter Ten

Moira woke with a start. She glanced around the tent and counted sleeping bodies. Hazel, Darcy and Tony were there but no Sarah. Panic snaked down her spine before she recalled that Sarah had taken the last watch. Moira took a few deep breaths, willing her heart to resume its normal beating once more.

Despite accounting for the girls' whereabouts, a sense of unease remained. She sat upright and kicked off the blankets, then straightened her rumpled clothing as best she could. Her dousing in the river the previous day hadn't done much for her by way of a bath, and she cautiously sniffed her sleeve. She didn't smell like a bed of roses, but she didn't smell quite as bad as a cow yet either. And that was saying something.

If there was one thing she missed from civilization, it was hot water. Her hair was a tangled mess, and she brushed through the gnarled strands with her fingers. When she'd braided the length into some semblance of restraint, she emerged into the brilliant morning sunlight. Sounds of the early dawn surrounded her. The call of birds, the low of the cattle and the clatter of the Dutch oven as Pops prepared the morning meal.

The sizzling scent of frying bacon filled the air. Moira inhaled a deep breath and froze. Sheer, black fright swept through her, paralyzing her limbs.

Perched on the hillside overlooking the camp were five Indians. Their stance was still and emotionless, chilling her fear into a cold knot in her chest. She couldn't make out much from the distance, but from their dress it appeared there were three females and two males in the group.

Moira backed away, keeping her eyes pinned on the distant group. She cautiously approached the tent John and Pops shared and scratched on the flap. For a moment she lost control of the spasmodic trembling in her hands. Pressing her fingers against her head, she tried to stop her brain from imagining what might happen to them, but the horrifying image crowded her thoughts.

"What is it?" a mumbled voice called.

"Trouble," Moira replied, her voice husky.

A moment later John stumbled from the tent, his hair mussed and the dark shadow of a beard covering his jaw. Her heart beat a rat-a-tat-tat at the sight. For a moment, she forgot the danger. Every time she thought she'd grown accustomed to his looks, he turned her tongue-tied and addled.

He frowned. "What's the trouble?"

Moira startled and pointed toward the hillside.

His throat worked. "Stay here."

Moira grasped his arm. "What are you doing?"

"I'm seeing what they want."

"Is that safe?"

"They've got their womenfolk with them. It's not a

war party." He lifted the corner of his mouth in a half grin. "If it was a war party, we'd already be dead."

"That's hardly comforting."

Despite his assurances Moira sensed the fear pulsating through his body. Only yesterday he'd cautioned her against their vulnerabilities. Today his worst terrors were realized.

He set off up the hill and Moira trailed behind him. He turned once and she raised an eyebrow. "You said it was safe."

He appeared to consider her answer before nodding. "Chances are, they've already scouted us. It's not like I can hide the fact that I'm traveling with a bunch of women and children." He held out one arm. "Still, it's best if you stay behind me."

Moira chafed at the order before realizing the absurdity of any objection she might make. They were alone and helpless. Mr. Elder had a gun and Pops had his rifle. While the Indians didn't appear to be carrying weapons, there was no telling what was beyond the gently sloping hills or how many more of them waited in the distance.

Once they reached the top of the rise, she stumbled back a step. As Moira had observed before, there were three women and two men in the group. On the ride from St. Louis, she'd thought about Indians and wondered what they looked like, how they acted—if they were as savage as the newspapers and books had led her to believe.

The picture in her head didn't match up with reality. The elaborate headdresses and clothing she'd seen in drawings back home were absent. The men were dressed in simple buckskin pants with fringed sides, their chests bare. The women wore leather tunics decorated with intricate beadwork.

The three women and the younger man appeared to be from the same family, or at least the same tribe. Their faces were broad, their noses flat, their cheeks rounded. The oldest, a man with grayed hair at the temples, had a broader forehead and a slimmer hawklike nose. Instead of shoulder-length hair like the first man, he wore his in two long braids that dusted the tops of his knees.

Upon closer study, Moira noted the hair bound in the braids was two-tone, leading her to believe he'd wound horsehair or something similar into the braids to make them appear longer. He caught her staring and she flushed and looked away.

John Elder said a few words in language she didn't understand.

Moira whipped around. "You speak their language?"

"Some Apache. Let's hope they know Apache, too."

The oldest man spoke, his gaze fixed on Moira. John answered then turned toward her. "He likes your hair."

She grasped her braid and backed away.

The Indian chuckled and he and John exchanged more words.

John glanced at her from the corner of his eye. "He says not to be afraid. He's not going to scalp you. He said red hair is considered bad luck."

"That's comforting."

"Well." John scratched his head. "Come to think of it, he might have said good luck. My Apache is a bit rusty."

Moira pursed her lips. "Did you ask them why they're here?"

John gave a quick shake of his head. "That's not how this works. First we'll invite them to share our meal.

Keep things friendly. Why don't you go down and let Pops know we're expecting company." He kept his face impassive. "And warn the girls. I don't want an uproar when they wake up and find Indians around the fire."

Hesitant, Moira nodded. She set off for the tent and caught sight of Sarah riding in from her watch. The girl's face was pale and she stared at the group gathered on the hillside. Moira waved her over and stood before the tent.

"It's all right. Mr. Elder is talking with them now. He's inviting them for breakfast. I'll let the others know."

"Who is going to take the next watch?"

"I think we'll skip the next watch. We should stick together. In case there's more."

"You think it's a trap?" Sarah wrapped her arms around her body. "What do they want from us? Are we going to die?"

Moira tamped down her own fears. "We can't think like that. We'll continue about our day as though everything is normal. There are still chores to be done."

"I'll feed and water the horse and join you." Sarah visibly calmed at having a task.

Moira rested her hand on her shoulder. "Stay sharp. If something happens, never mind the rest of us. If there's trouble, take whatever opening you can find and run. Don't look back."

"I will."

Moira ducked inside the tent and shook the girls awake. "We've got some special company in camp."

Tony blinked and yawned. "How special?"

"Indians."

Hazel squealed and Moira quickly shushed her. "Mr. Elder is talking with them now. Get ready and come out for breakfast. Try not to stare. Sarah is feeding and watering the horses. As far as we're concerned, this is just another day."

"Another day when we might all end up with arrows through our hides," Tony grumbled.

Moira shushed her. "Not now."

"Well I heard stories on the ranch. They'll cut you down and gut you without even a by-your-leave."

Hazel began to sob quietly and Moira hugged her against her side. "That's enough. Not one more word. If you can't keep a civil tongue in your mouth, Antonella, you should remain in this tent. We've trouble enough."

Moira stepped into the sunlight and stuttered to a halt. Seeing the Indians on the hill was one thing, having them clustered around the fire was quite another. She swallowed hard and forced her steps closer.

From the corner of her eye she watched as Pops added more bacon to the pan balanced over the cook fire. His hands wobbled.

The five Indians and John gathered in a neat half circle around the fire. They all sat cross-legged, their elbows resting on their bent knees. Even the cowboy. Moira brushed her skirts behind her knees and took the place beside him.

He tilted his head. "They think you're my wife. Let's keep it that way."

Moira glanced at the eldest Indian. He stared at her hair, his black eyes curious, his gaze intense, as though trying to peer into her soul. She turned away.

While John and the Indians spoke, Pops arrived with plates of bacon and rounds of cornbread fried in the left-over grease. The Indians accepted the food and ate with gusto, using their fingers. Pops must have realized they'd eat that way, since he hadn't offered up any utensils.

The girls emerged from the tent, Tony first, her face blank, clutching Hazel's hand. Darcy trailed behind them, her lips clenched in a thin white line. Sarah returned from caring for the horses and hovered uncertainly on the edge of the campsite. Moira motioned them over.

The two groups of people observed each other with wary curiosity. One of the women spoke, a mixture of English and Apache that Moira had difficulty following. John had a better time pulling out the words. He replied and turned toward the group.

"Most of the elderly and the children in their group died last spring. An influenza outbreak. Brought by the settlers, no doubt. Near as I can tell, they were relocated by the army from a place farther south. I'm guessing with the settlers moving in and the buffalo hunters spread over the plains, resources are thin."

A portion of Moira's fear dissipated. On closer inspection she realized the Indians' cheeks were hollow, their ribs showing, their legs painfully slim. With a sudden, awful clarity she realized that she hadn't seen them as people up until this point. In her head she'd referred to them as savages, in her mind's eye she'd seen them as less than human. The stories she'd heard, the brutality, had created a myth.

The truth was much less savage. And much more tragic.

The woman who'd been doing the bulk of the talking clicked her tongue and nodded her head. "Safe passage," she said. "Safe passage."

John spoke a few words and she replied. He shook his head. The woman repeated something and the cowboy frowned. "I can't quite make out what she's saying, but I think they're on their way to Fort Preble for medicine."

The woman gestured and talked with her curious mixture of Apache and English.

John frowned in concentration. "Her only remaining child is ill. She believes it's a white man's illness and she's hoping the white man's medicine will cure the child."

The eldest Indian, the one with the long braids and the hawkish nose, shook his head and scowled. Clearly the plan had not met with his whole approval. The woman met his scowl, her gaze defiant.

John spoke and gestured. At one point the Indians stood and walked a distance away.

Moira leaned over and whispered in his ear. "What's going on?"

"A trade. I hope. I'm offering them the choice of several head of cattle in exchange for safe passage to Fort Preble."

Moira watched their guests. Hawk Nose made a great show of considering the plan. The younger man in the group replied sharply. The two Indians remained locked on each other, caught in a fierce battle of wills. Moira shivered. After a moment Hawk Nose spoke quietly and the younger Indian jerked his head in a nod.

Hawk Nose gestured toward her hair. "Mine." He spoke.

Her scalp tingled. "Oh dear. He wants to scalp me."

"No, no. He wants a lock of your hair is all."

She automatically reached for her braid. "What should I do?"

"It's up to you."

Tony leaned closer. "We're outnumbered and outgunned. I say we give 'em what they want before they take it by force."

"It's only hair." Darcy shrugged.

Sarah glanced between the two groups of people. "I don't see that there's any harm."

Moira chewed her lower lip and considered the Indians. After a long moment, she carefully unraveled her braid. Hawk Nose didn't show any sign one way or another whether or not he was pleased with her choice.

She faced the cowboy. "Can you help?"

John reached into his pocket and pulled out a knife. He unfolded the blade and grasped a handful of her hair. The strands were impossibly soft and springy beneath his fingers, as though her curls had a life of their own.

He stared into her eyes. Her pupils were dilated and her breath came in short, hollow gasps. She was terrified of the Indians and putting on a brave face.

Outnumbered and outgunned.

Tony had a way of sizing up the situation in her succinct, blunt fashion. Right now they were balancing on a fine line of good humor and dumb luck. Near as John could tell, the Indians saw them as some sort of novelty. They'd seen plenty of settlers, buffalo hunters and horse traders cross their land. He didn't suppose they'd ever seen eight hundred head of cattle led by five females, four of them children.

While he made a show of leisurely piercing through Moira's hair, he considered the outcome of the meeting. If the Indians rustled their cattle and tore off for the low country, they risked bringing down the army scouts. A decade past it might have been a fair fight. Now, the meeting was anything but unbiased. The Indians were short of able-bodied men, victims of disease and famine brought on by the dwindling land and buffalo.

As long as he mollified this bunch and sent them home with a nice steer, there was a good chance he and the girls had bought their safe passage.

Moira blinked. Her brilliant eyes were shadowed, yet trusting. Her fear kindled a fierce protectiveness in him.

He wrapped a hunk of hair around one finger and slid his knife blade near the base. "You sure?"

She licked her lips and his gaze dipped.

"If it'll keep old Hawk Nose from taking my whole scalp, I don't figure I have much choice."

Tony cleared her throat. "Maybe we shouldn't talk about them when they're sitting right in front of us."

"They don't understand," Darcy protested.

Tony's gaze slid across the group of Indians. "It's not something I want to bet my life on."

John's blade slid through the strands as easily as slicing through warm butter. He set down his knife and yanked a length of fringe from his buckskin chaps and wound the length around the base.

Hawk Nose reached across the distance and accepted the offering. He rubbed the hair between his thumb and forefinger, then lifted the strands toward the sunlight and tilted his head. John's stomach tightened. It hadn't seemed much of a sacrifice before, yet he didn't like the Indian having a part of Moira. Even something as simple as a lock of hair. The gesture felt personal, intimate.

The three women erupted into chatter and reached for the lock. They took turns studying the hair, holding it near their heads and speaking amongst themselves. Hawk Nose snatched the hair and stuffed the curiosity in the pouch at his hip, ending the commotion.

The Indian glanced between John, Moira and the girls. "Not your children," he said in his clipped Apache.

John shook his head and said, "Family." Or what he hoped meant family.

He must have gotten a close enough word because the Indian woman who spoke some broken English nodded her approval.

Hawk Nose blinked his approval. "Many fine sons to come."

John assumed he was referring to his and Moira's future as a "married couple." He swallowed. "Yes."

The situation was too complicated for his broken Apache. There'd be no explaining how he'd wound up with four orphans and a fiery redhead. Certainly not an explanation to satisfy his unexpected guests.

Moira tugged on his sleeve. "What did he say?"

"He said thank you for the meal." John didn't quite meet her eyes.

He needn't tell her the rest. He stood and motioned for the leader. Together they approached the herd and the younger Indian followed. The tall man wove through the cattle, unmindful of the clacking horns and the lethal hooves. Without asking he returned and grasped a coiled rope from the pile of gear near the chuck wagon. Once again he disappeared into the herd.

The girls stood and huddled behind John. For the first time since he'd met the girls, they remained unnaturally silent. The Indian returned, leading an enormous bull. John took a step back and bumped into Moira.

Hazel gasped. "He can't take Ironsides."

"Who?"

"Ironsides. That's the bull he's taking."

John rubbed his forehead. "Please tell me you did not name all eight hundred head of cattle."

"Only about twenty. And that's Ironsides."

"Well, your bull has a new home."

"They're gonna eat him." Tears welled in her dark eyes.

Tony scoffed. "What did you think was going to happen? They're all gonna get eaten sooner or later. That's why you don't go naming farm animals. Leastways you end up naming your dinner."

Hazel burst into tears and dove into the tent.

John pressed his fingertips into his eyelids until he saw stars.

"I'll see to her." Sarah patted his arm.

The Indian ignored the drama and led the bull away from the herd.

Pops moved to stand beside John. "I seen a lot of things in my life. I ain't never seen an Indian lead a bull like a trained dog."

John winced at the muffled sobs emanating from the tent. "He took my best rope."

"Probably the luckiest thing that will happen this day."

As the group of Indians faded into the distance, the tension in John's shoulders eased. If he'd ever been more terrified in his life, he couldn't recall the time. Pops wandered off and Moira moved toward the fire.

John touched her arm. "Should I talk with her? Hazel?"

"No. She's old enough to learn the truth. I think we all need a moment alone."

Moira trudged into the distance, disappearing behind a small copse of brush trees. Unsettled by the look in her eyes, he jogged the distance and found her sitting with her hands wrapped around her knees, her head bent and her shoulders trembling.

John knelt beside her and placed a hand on her shoulder. "What is it? What's wrong?"

She rocked forward. "I have never been so scared in my entire life."

"I was just thinking the same thing." He caught her around the shoulder, catching a bit of her loose hair in his grip.

Her head lifted. "Do you think they'll be back?"

"I doubt it. At their heart, they're an honorable people. They won't break their word."

"But what about all the raids? The massacres?"

"I don't like murder of any kind, that's for certain." John gathered his thoughts. "The settlers changed their way of life and they fought back. It's not much different than the War Between the States. Right or wrong, people will fight for their survival." He turned his head and his chin grazed the top of her hair. "One side wins and one side loses. That's how most things end."

"And so much death in between."

She turned her head and stared up at him. He lowered his head, brushing his lips against her forehead. Her eyes fluttered closed. He pressed a kiss against her temple, feeling the rapid pulse beneath her skin. Her pale ivory skin was creamy and smooth. Her cheeks matched the blush of a peach's skin. She tipped back her head and their lips met. He'd only meant to offer her a modicum of comfort, but her gentle sigh wreaked havoc on his resolve. He pulled away and cupped her face, searching her eyes. The sweet, misty look on her face drew him forward.

His lips moved tentatively over hers. She swayed against him. He continued his leisurely exploration, giving her every chance to pull away. Her trembling hands wound around his neck and pulled him closer.

A shrill scream split the air.

Moira's forehead bumped his nose. "The Indians. They've come back."

John's stomach dropped. He leapt to his feet and glanced around. "It's not the Indians."

He'd expected more trouble. Just not this soon.

Chapter Eleven

Moira reached the commotion mere paces after John. "What's wrong? What's happened?"

The girls had gathered around an outcropping of rock on the edge of a shallow dip in the grassland. A narrow overhang of ragged weeds indicated the presence of a tiny cave, an opening fit only for an animal. The mouth of the hole opened beneath a ledge at the base of a flat rock. About the size of a barrel, the darkened mouth stretched into the embankment. Out of the opening came Champion's steady barking.

Hazel clasped her hands together. "It all happened too fast. I was standing here when Champion started barking. Then it brushed past my leg."

Tony tilted her head. "When what came past?"

"An animal."

"A possum?"

"No. It was soft with a fluffy tail. I think it's a cat. Champion chased it in there." She cast an accusing glare at John. "Now it won't come out."

"Well, uh." John adjusted his hat. "I suppose we best

leave whatever it is alone. Once we're all gone, it'll come out soon enough."

"I think it's hurt."

John hesitated. "Even more reason to leave it alone. A frightened animal is dangerous."

"It's a cat."

"It's not a cat. We're too far from town for strays."

Hazel set her jaw. "I'm sure it's a cat."

"Trust me. It's not a cat. I've been walking this trail for twenty years and I can guarantee you that."

Moira studied the determined set of Hazel's shoulders. She had a bad feeling if he didn't check out the animal, Hazel would go in after he turned his back.

John caught her gaze and an unspoken communication passed between them. He must have come to the same conclusion.

"If I prove it's not a cat, will you leave it alone?"

"I promise. But it's a cat. I'm certain."

Smothering a sigh, John knelt.

Moira edged closer. The hollowed-out area stretched deep into the ground, narrowing until the dog disappeared into the darkness. Stale dust and the rank scent of a wild animal sent her nose wrinkling.

Muffled barks echoed through the recesses of the tiny cave.

She didn't know much about nature, but this didn't seem like a good idea. "John is right, Hazel. If we all leave it alone, the animal will come out on its own."

Sarah patted the younger girl's back. "They're right. We shouldn't go messing with wild animals. For all we know it's a bunch of shoats."

Hazel remained stubbornly silent.

John gave a slight shrug. "It can't be very big. I'm

guessing it's a prairie dog Champion chased out of its den. I'll take a quick look." He doffed his hat. "This won't take long."

Moira accepted the hat and clutched it to her chest. A tingle of apprehension danced along her spine. "I still don't think it's such a good idea."

The cowboy angled his head and glanced up at her. "I'll be quick. We don't have much time. Looks like there's a storm coming."

Moira followed his gaze.

She'd been so engrossed in the excitement over the Indians and then distracted by John's kiss, she hadn't noticed the growing wall of white, fluffy clouds in the distance. "They don't look so bad."

Her cheeks warmed beneath his glance and she unconsciously touched her lips. Somehow, in that moment, everything had changed. Of course she'd thought he was handsome, what girl wouldn't? She'd known he was kind, considerate. Now she was thinking about him in a whole new way.

Had anything changed for him? She couldn't read his inscrutable expression.

"Those clouds will get worse, trust me," he said. "They'll get bigger and taller and darker. Then we'll have a storm on our hands. At least we're out of harm's way from the river. It's late in the season, but we're still risking a flash flood. The more we talk, the more time we waste."

Moira huffed at his quiet rebuke. Her earlier sterling thoughts of him tarnished a bit. "I'm only trying to save you from a bite. Or worse."

John reclined onto his left hip. He leaned in, positioning his body until he held most of his weight on this left elbow and shoulder. With the heel of his boot he pushed off, scooting into the darkness. His head and shoulders disappeared.

Moira held her breath.

"Oh no."

His boots kicked a furious tarantella in the dust.

The cowboy rolled out of the cave as though he'd been shot out of a cannon. A flurry of fur and squealing followed close behind. As John scrambled to his feet, the ball of fur flattened him back against the ground.

A screech sounded, immediately followed by an ear-splitting yelp. Champion leapt onto the pile.

"I told you it was a cat!" Hazel shouted.

"Stay back," John shouted. "It's a bobcat."

Champion and the angered cat rolled in the dust. The dog soon realized he was outmatched with a painful yowl. Champion released his clenched jaw from the animal's neck and sprang backward.

Dazed, the bobcat shook its head a few times before streaking into the distance. Moira caught sight of the cowboy sprawled on the ground, an angry slash across his cheek with two drips of blood sliding beneath his chin. He swiped at the blood with the back of his hand and made to push himself off the dirt.

His hand landed smack on the back of a startled skunk.

Moira clapped her hands over her mouth and stumbled away.

Champion had chased the bobcat into a den with a previous occupant. A burst of noxious odor hit Moira like a wall. John lunged. He clutched his face and staggered upright. The girls shrieked and scattered like shrapnel. Champion whimpered, tail tucked between its legs, slinking away, muzzle down.

Hazel pinched her nose. "That's not a cat."

Her eyes watering, Moira clutched John's arm. "Skunk."

"Skunk," he repeated, his voice hoarse. "I didn't think of that."

Pops appeared on the hill, then halted, waving his hand before his face. "Who got skunked?"

"That would be me." John coughed and sputtered.

"Well, don't just stand there," Pops shouted. "There's a watering hole about fifty paces ahead. Go rinse off."

John held his hands before him like a blind man. "My eyes are swelling shut. I can't see a thing."

Moira buried her nose in the crook of her elbow. "I'll lead you."

The odor was alive, slithering down her throat and coating her mouth. Moira coughed.

John groped along his puffy cheeks. "What's happening to my face?"

Her own eyes watered profusely, tears running down her face. She pried them open and got a good look at the cowboy. His cheeks were swollen, the sockets around his eyes puffy and misshapen, even his lips were bloated. His face was rapidly becoming unrecognizable.

"Take my hand." Moira linked her left hand with his and wrapped her right arm around his waist.

Sightless, he extended his right hand, feeling his way. Together they stumbled toward the creek.

Tony jogged toward them, stopping a safe distance and pinching her nose. "You need help?"

Moira glanced over her shoulder. "Get some rags.

Have Darcy catch up with Pops and Hazel. He's gonna need a change of clothes and some soap."

"Soap isn't going to help with that stench."

Moira swiped at her runny nose. "Well, it sure can't hurt."

She spotted the depression and followed it down to a stagnant puddle left by the wet fall weather. John tripped through the muddy hoofprints and waded in to his waist. Moira followed close behind, worried at his lack of sight. He pressed his face into the shallow water and threw back his head, showering Moira with water droplets.

"Hey!"

"Sorry," he mumbled.

Moira wiped the moisture from her cheeks. "You're not sorry at all."

"Nope."

She laughed and skimmed the heel of her hand along the water, kicking up a splash.

He waded deeper and Moira splashed after him, catching his elbow. "Not too far."

Halting, he turned and grazed her shoulder with his elbow. "Sorry." He reached for her and stumbled, threw out his arms, and sank deeper into the water.

Moira struggled, pulling them toward the bank until the water grazed her waist. She snatched his hat and filled the crown with water, then dumped the contents over his head.

The cowboy gasped and sputtered. "You might give me a warning next time."

Moira laughed. "Where's the fun in all that?"

John reached beneath the water. After a moment his hand emerged clutching his familiar, faded blue bandanna.

He mopped at his face "Another."

Moira obliged, dumping a hatful of water over his head. After ten or twelve dousing, the odor abated somewhat and Moira stepped back. The swelling in his face had gone down, though his eyes remained blistered and closed.

Keeping her arms above her waist she circled until she was upwind of the cowboy. He turned in her direction, running his hands down his face.

His reaction had her worried. "Have you ever been sprayed by a skunk?" she asked.

"I'm happy to say I've never had the pleasure."

"I think you had a reaction. I've never seen a swelling like that before. Mrs. Gifford only had a bit of red after she was sprayed."

"Who is Mrs. Gifford?"

"My foster mother. I worked for Mr. and Mrs. Gifford for years."

"Wait, I don't understand. You worked for them? I thought you said they were your foster family."

Moira smirked. Since he couldn't see her face, she didn't have to hide her reactions. "Orphans are little more than indentured servants, serving out our time until we come of age."

"Surely it's not like that for everyone."

"Too many. It's a hard life out west. It makes people hard. I could spread out blame, but what's the point. Folks shouldn't have children if they're not going to care for them."

His whole body stilled. "Your parents couldn't help dying, Moira. You must see that."

"My parents weren't dead, Mr. Elder. Not right away. My pa ran off. He figured his money went further supporting one man instead of a family. My mother was sick. Tuberculosis. She couldn't care for us."

"I'm sorry, I didn't mean—"

"It's all right. They're both gone now. My brother left the Giffords first." A sharp pain gripped her heart. "I stayed. I thought he'd come back for me. He never did. When I came of age, I set off on my own, too. I got a job cleaning rooms after hours at a hotel not far from the Giffords and waited. If Tommy came looking…well, I didn't want to be far."

Except he'd never come. And the longer she'd waited, the less hope she had. The more she worried he couldn't forgive her, the more she realized she had to find him and set things right.

"Moira, I'm sorry for bringing up the past. Of reminding you of the pain. Truly I am."

He stepped closer, blindly reaching out his hand. Moira flinched away. She didn't want his pity. There were truths in life, that was all.

"I've been looking for Tommy ever since. Once we're together, we'll be a family again, things will be different."

He'd make her whole again. She wouldn't be a burden or a charity. She'd be family. He'd forgive her for what had happened.

"That's an awful lot of responsibility to put on a person. An awful lot of hope to pin on someone."

"It's not worth talking about. You wouldn't understand."

He *couldn't* understand. He was a loner, but Moira needed family. She needed love and belonging. She needed something to fill the empty parts of her soul.

There was no use explaining loneliness to someone who'd never been lonely.

John sank deeper, tipping back his head. "I thought you were afraid of the water." His shirt plastered to his body, outlining the muscles of his shoulders, the corded strength of his arms.

Moira shivered.

"I'm afraid of running water."

"You're afraid of indoor plumbing?"

"No!" She chuckled. "Ponds and lakes don't bother me so much. It's the rivers and streams. I'm afraid I'll be swept away."

"We're not getting very far today. Why don't we call it quits and let everyone rest. We'll pull out the washtub and give everything at camp a good scouring."

Moira blushed. She'd gone forty-eight long, hard hours in the same clothing. She'd been soaked twice, but that was different. She needed soap and water and a good scrubbing. A thorough washing sounded wonderful.

"How do I look?" John asked suddenly.

"Horrible!" She replied quickly, grateful for the change of subject. In the two days since she'd let go of civilization, she hadn't yet adjusted. "You look like you've gone three rounds at the fights. And lost."

"What else do you see?"

"That's an odd question."

"It's strange, not being able to see." He turned a lazy circle, sending ripples toward her. "I can't see you, but I'm picturing you. It makes a fellow think about things. Reminds me of playing blindman's buff as a kid. When I think of you, you're very serious. You're always looking at where you're going, never what's around you."

"I don't want to trip."

"We're not walking now. Humor me. Tell me what you see?"

"No Man's Land."

"And what does No Man's Land look like?"

"Red."

"You're terrible at this, you know?" John raked his hands through his damp hair. "Haven't you ever played I Spy? I spy with my little eye, something green. You'd be surprised at how much people never notice. Look at us right now. My eyes are closed and even I see more than you do. I see black clouds."

"They're gray."

The cowboy shot her a look of pure disgruntlement. "You lost your turn. Don't interrupt."

"Fine."

"The sun is reflecting off the water, shimmering, there's catfish."

"This pond is too small for catfish. Besides, how can you see a catfish if you're blinded?"

"I didn't see it, it bit my toe."

A twitch of a smile flickered around the edges of her mouth. Grateful he couldn't see her reaction, she clamped shut her lips. "I hope it hurt."

His face distorted in a way that told her clearly he was attempting not to smile. "Of course you don't."

The fool man didn't even have the sense to be embarrassed. Moira chewed her lip and glanced over her shoulder. Where on earth were the others with the supplies? The soap and the change of clothes.

"The water is cold," John said. "So it must be spring fed. Which means there are trees around. The trees are spindly, already losing their leaves. A storm is coming, but the clouds aren't dark enough yet. They're building in the sky like mountains."

"Your mouth has been leaded, not gilded."

"I hear the cattle. They're gathering, too. Trampling down the hill looking for water. Pretty soon that old bull will wade right in up to his waist. I never once saw a bull who liked water as much as that old lazybones."

He was right, already the cattle dotted the area around the watering hole. They were keeping a wary eye on John and Moira, waiting for their turn.

Instead of admitting that, she said, "It's a good thing you're a cowboy. You'd make a terrible poet."

"Keep your voice down, you're disrupting my artistic genius. And they're not cows," he said with exaggerated patience. "They're long-horned Texas steer, and they'll gore you for mocking them. If you're going to be a trail boss, you should talk like a trail boss."

Her cheeks warmed despite the chill water. It suddenly occurred to her what a ridiculous turn her life had taken. A simple twist of fate had stranded her in Indian Territory on a cattle drive with a reluctant cowboy.

"My brother Tommy and I had a game, too. We'd imagine where we'd be if we could be anywhere in the world at any time in history. What about you? If you could be anywhere, where else would you be?"

"I'd pick a week from now. In Cimarron Springs," he announced immediately. "Warming my feet before my own fire with my boots set firmly on my own stool."

"But what about your family? Wouldn't you rather be with them?"

John guffawed. "Only once a year at Christmas. When it's too cold for hunting and the women are around making sure we're all on our best behavior."

Her smile faded. "Don't you miss them?"

"Of course I do. But that's the way of things. People grow. They move on. Jack and Robert have their own families now."

"But you could still be a part of their lives."

"Of course. But things change. We can't go on like we're still kids."

"Things don't have to change," she said.

"You know what would happen to this pond if the spring dried up? If the water didn't keep pumping out? It would go stagnant. Moss would grow on the surface and all the tadpoles would die. The whole place would turn rank. Life is like that. Things have to change to stay alive."

Is that what she'd done? Had she grown stagnant? No. That wasn't it at all. She was preserving her family. That was an honorable goal.

He had everything. He had a home. And he didn't want it. He didn't understand and he never could. He was carefree and unencumbered, waxing on about shimmering streams and imaginary catfish. He'd lived his safe life near the ground, never understanding what it was like to live up high, inching along a thin wire without a net. Never knowing where your next meal would come from or where you'd sleep that night.

Even with his face swollen and the faint stench of skunk drifting over the rushing stream, he was handsome. It wasn't just his looks, there was something compelling about him, a pull that kept her waist-deep in a freezing pond when she could be curled up before a warm fire instead.

He had effortless charm and an easy way. Perhaps that was the problem. He was right about her. She always kept her head down. She was drawn to his sense of adventure.

He ran his hand down his face and for a moment she sensed a rare vulnerability. In that instant his shoulders appeared less broad, his expression worried, though muddled by the swelling, distracted. She'd come to think of him as invincible, certainly indefatigable. His patience never lagged, his temper rarely flared.

He'd taken a rotten situation and put a humorous spin on the events, and not for his own benefit.

John took a step forward and stumbled. Moira reached out and steadied him. His shirt was soaked through, plastered against his torso. The heat of his shoulder radiated through the chill water, warming her hand.

Her breath grew shallow and uneven.

She took the bandanna from his free hand and dipped it into the water, wringing out the excess. Her touch cautious, she laid the cool cloth against his creased eyes. He winced and Moira pulled back.

His hand covered hers, pressing the cloth into place. "It's all right."

Moira shivered against the husky timbre of his voice.

"You're freezing." He wrapped his arm around her shoulder. "Lead me toward the bank. If we don't get you out of this water, you'll catch your death."

Together they struggled through the thick mud toward the bank, then collapsed on the dry, prickly grass.

Moira glanced up. "It looks like the cavalry is coming."

Pops appeared on the horizon, his bulky form moving faster than Moira had thought possible. Sarah and Hazel jogged beside him.

John touched her hand. "You haven't told me where you'd rather be."

"I'd go back in time and right a wrong."

His head jerked around. "What wrong?"

"It's nothing. Never mind."

"Has anyone ever told you that you're stubborn as all get-out?"

"They tell me all the time. I just never listen."

"That's because you're stubborn," he replied gruffly.

John accepted the blanket Pops draped around his shoulders. "Someday I'll get my answer, Miss O'Mara."

She tightened the blanket Sarah had given her and glanced at the sky. True to John's prediction, the clouds had grown and darkened. They hadn't made any progress yet that day and they were going to be halted by a thunderstorm.

Pops swung his arm in an arc. "Get yourselves back to camp. I've got a surprise waiting."

John sighed. "Please tell me it's not another skunk. This day can't get any worse."

A clap of thunder met John's muttered question.

"Yep," Pops replied. "Looks like this day just might get a touch worse at that."

Moira trailed behind the group. When she was with John, he consumed her thoughts, her focus. She hadn't thought about Tommy in hours. She hadn't considered what she'd do next. She hadn't even thought about the sheriff's promise or what she might find at the telegraph office in Cimarron Springs. Moira scoffed. She hadn't thought of anything beyond the present. The oversight felt like a betrayal.

When she'd lived with the Giffords, she'd felt trapped. At least the choice of searching for Tommy had been taken from her. Not anymore. She had no excuses for faltering in her goal. Glancing in John's direction, she shook her head. She'd vowed not to be distracted and it was time to keep that vow.

No more kisses. No more banter. This was business. They were driving a herd of cattle. Once they reached Cimarron Springs, they'd never see each other again.

John groaned. He still couldn't see well. Despite a good dose of Pops's magic cure-all, a syrupy concoction with a foul aftertaste, his eyes remained swollen and his vision blurred. "You didn't tell me the surprise."

"The drummer caught up with us." Pops muttered something unintelligible. "Now where is my ladle?" John heard the distinctive clink of tin cups and cutlery as Pops searched his chuck wagon. "That's funny. I don't remember putting it there. Anyway, he's unhitched his horses. Looks like he plans on sticking around a while."

"The girls must be chomping at the bit."

"Not like you'd think. You gotta remember, they've got no money. They're not getting their hopes up. Don't know how they'll get outfitted. I think they're afraid to ask. They've got their pride you know."

John absorbed the quiet rebuke. Of all the roadblocks he'd considered, pride hadn't been on the list. "Two days ago I had a crew of men. I didn't have to worry about this stuff."

"That was two days ago. This is now. You've got other problems."

"Point taken." John pressed his bandanna against his swollen eyes. "Make up some nonsense about a gear allowance. Buy him out of gloves and anything else they need."

Pops clicked his tongue. "We've only got another day or two before Fort Preble. That's a lot of money spent without much chance of return."

John thought of Moira's hands, the blisters already forming on her palms. "I guess I owe them something. They've gotten us this far. I can always sell off a bull or two, or wire the bank for money."

"Robert will wonder why you're wiring for money."

"Let him wonder. It's none of his business."

The jingling of bells signaled the arrival of the peddler and John tensed. "I still don't like the idea of a stranger in camp. I don't need word getting out. We're too far from Fort Preble."

"Don't worry. I've crossed paths with Swede before. He's harmless."

John pulled the bandanna from his face and squinted. "Is there anyone you don't know?"

"I've been walking this trail for thirty years. You're bound to run into the same faces. Don't worry about Swede. We go way back. He'll keep your secrets. He won't be spreading rumors about our crew. And he's promised me a deal on a new frying pan for bringing in the business."

"I knew it. You have an addiction to frying pans."

"And taken a liking to good food."

"At least we agree on one thing."

By the time the drummer lumbered into camp, John could open his left eye and make out hazy images. He couldn't recall a time when he'd felt more helpless, more inadequate. While the girls set up camp and made use of the washtub, he'd bathed and changed his clothes at the nearby watering hole. He'd worn the bar of soap to a whittling, but he still felt the skunk's odor glazing the back of his throat and saturating his hair.

The others steered clear, giving him a wide berth. Someone had pressed a steaming hot cup of coffee into his hands and quickly retreated. Someone else had slapped a tray of food before him. Tony, judging by the forceful presentation.

Having a stranger in camp while he wasn't at his best force left him feeling exposed. Since he'd discovered that rubbing his eyes only made them worse, he'd forced his hands back to his sides. No matter how much they itched and annoyed him, he remained stoic.

With his eyesight impaired, the rest of his senses heightened. The air had turned heavy and he feared an oncoming storm. Voices swirled around him and he felt disconnected and out of sorts.

He pushed off from one knee and stood. The girls remained huddled around the campfire.

"I need you outfitted," John declared. "All my men have full kits. You'll need hats, coats, gloves, a change of clothes and sundries. It's part of crew pay."

Tony sat up. "No fooling."

"No fooling. A crew can't function without gear. You're my crew. Every one of you should have a canteen and a pocketknife as well as a box of matches. You'll carry them with you in your saddle bags at all times. Jerky as well. If we get separated, those items are the difference in survival."

Tony sidled nearer the wagon, keeping a wary eye out. Her hesitation confounded him. A look passed between Darcy and Tony, raising his hackles. Darcy had performed well on the ride, but a certain rebellion in her demeanor kept him wary. While he didn't know the source of his unease, he trusted his instincts.

Sarah held Hazel's hand and they both kept their heads bent. He searched the surrounding area and realized Moira had taken her turn caring for the horses.

A man rounded the corner of the wagon. He sported a dark, scruffy beard that covered his face and stretched well down his neck. His black hair was parted down the middle and hung slightly over his collar. He wore mud-brown trousers held in place by a pair of suspenders, and his red union suit showed beneath the rolled-up sleeves of his chambray shirt.

Hazel buried her head in Sarah's shoulder.

The movement caught the newcomer's attention. His gaze narrowed. Darcy scooted away.

The newcomer stalked toward the girls.

John blocked the man's progress and caught him by the collar.

The newcomer spun around. "Are you John Elder?"

"I am."

"I'm Swede. Sheriff Taylor sent me."

"I figured as much." John kept his grip on the man's collar. "You want to explain what you're all fired up about?"

Swede jabbed a finger at the cowering girls. "I ain't letting them near my wagon. That one stole an apple off me cart not two days ago."

Hazel cowered into Sarah's arms.

John's suspicions crystallized. Even before the sheriff's arrival, he'd suspected they were thieves working together. Without proof either way, he'd let the issue remain unresolved. The arrival of the drummer had forced his hand.

John released his hold on the man's collar. "Surely you can forgive a slight transgression."

"The apple is what I know'd about. Who knows what else they took when I wasn't looking."

"They're children." John recalled his thoughts from that first day. "Starving children forced into desperate measures."

Swede wiped his nose on the back of his sleeve. "That ain't my problem."

John glanced to the hinged door on the wagon, already propped open, revealing a colorful array of wares. "You've come a long way to leave empty-handed."

The drummer tore his gaze from Hazel. "I ain't letting them girls pilfer my stock either."

John considered his options. As he mulled his choices, Moira appeared.

His breath hitched. Her hair remained damp, the curls darker and lanky at her shoulders. Her cheeks were flushed from her time spent in the sun and her eyes sparkled with curiosity. She wore the same dress she'd been wearing since the moment she'd dropped from the sky. The blue was faded from washing, the fabric worn thin. And she was the most captivating sight he'd ever laid eyes on. She glanced between the two men and a wrinkle appeared between her cinnamon-colored brows.

Swede's attention flicked in her direction and he appeared to quickly dismiss her. John didn't realize he'd been holding his breath until he released the pent-up air in his lungs.

"I'll vouch for them," John announced.

Darcy's eyes widened. Hazel raised her head. Sarah and Tony turned in his direction.

John shrugged. "I'll vouch for them. They're my crew. They're my responsibility. They'll do right by you."

Tony fisted her hands on her hips. "You'd do that? You'd trust us. Even after what he said?"

John mulled over the question, the implications of his answer. "I want an honest day's work for an honest day's wage. You've done that. You've never given me any reason to believe I can't trust you."

He considered the earlier reticence from the girls. They weren't afraid Swede would recognize them, they were afraid John's assistance came with a cost. They'd been conditioned throughout their lives, trained that their worth came with a price. Even among the four of them there were uneasy allegiances. Snatches of remembered conversation filtered through his memory.

They didn't entirely trust one another. They certainly didn't trust him.

What about Moira?

The deeper he dug, the more he realized he didn't know much about their pasts. They were young enough he figured he didn't need to dig far. He couldn't unravel the events that had led them to this point. One thought hadn't escaped him: Fool's End was an odd place for a bunch of orphans.

While he couldn't change what had brought them to this point, he could offer them his trust.

Moira remained motionless near the tent, sensing the undercurrents, no doubt.

Swede tugged on his suspenders. "You'll vouch for them girls with your wallet. If I find anything missing, I'll hunt you down for payment."

"I consider that fair."

The drummer puffed up.

"You needn't act like you've done anything special." Sarah flipped the hair from her eyes. "Mr. Elder has given us leave to purchase whatever we need. Why would any of us steal from you?"

The drummer squinted one eye. "Because you're thieves, that's why. It's all you know. Once a body gets a taste for thieven' he don't wanna work no more. You're like a bunch of magpies, you are, always looking for something shiny."

Moira gasped. "What is the meaning of this? Who are you and what gives you the right to say such horrid things?"

John tossed her a sharp glance. "We all need each other. The girls need new gear and Swede has stock. The sooner we get the girls outfitted the better. We can all be on our way again."

"I got my eye on ya'." Swede pointed at his face and then at Hazel. "You most of all."

Pops lumbered around the wagon carrying the Dutch oven by a hooked metal pole attached to the lid, his gait hitched against the heavy load. He glanced at the newcomer. "Taking over the business from your father, are you, Swede?"

The drummer blanched. "I didn't know you was part of all this."

"Swede, you've got your dad's beard and your mother's coloring," Pops spoke to the drummer. "I thought you were working out of Silver Springs."

"We moved up to Fool's End. More business."

"You'll not be getting any business by insulting your patrons. That's for certain. Why don't you keep an eye on this stew instead?" Pops wrinkled his nose and glanced at John. "Wouldn't hurt to buy yourself a new slicker. You're still sending off a powerful stench."

John lifted his elbow and caught a nauseating whiff of his sleeve. "Will do."

He'd placed his trust in the girls. He sure hoped his faith wasn't misguided.

Chapter Twelve

Moira glared at the drummer. He ate his stew with gusto, filling his bowl twice more while the girls rummaged through his wagonful of supplies. She snatched a pair of denim trousers and held them at her waist. The hem stretched well beyond her feet. She'd need four rolls in the cuffs, but at least she'd be able to ride more freely. Satisfied with the fit, she added another pair to her pile.

Hazel's clothing proved the most difficult. The drummer had brought a selection of clothing suitable for an adolescent boy.

The smallest of the group held up a pair of trousers over her head and the cuffs reached the dirt at her feet. "Everything is too big."

"Don't worry," Tony said. "We'll find you something."

Moira caught sight of a beautiful leather case. She flipped open the hinged lid and discovered a sewing kit nestled in the velvet-lined interior. The kit contained a pair of silver scissors with ornate detailing on the handles, a delicate thimble and wheels of cardboard with the spokes wrapped in a colorful array of thread. There was even a lidded cylinder for needles.

Tempted for a moment, she glanced over her shoulder. Would John balk at the expense? The men remained in deep conversation around the campfire.

Darcy caught her gaze. "Don't do it."

Moira started. "I beg your pardon?"

"You're thinking of stealing that. I can see it in your eyes. You can't. It's too big."

Moira slammed the lid over on the kit and set it aside. "Don't be absurd."

A hint of skunk caught her attention. She turned and found the cowboy leaning over her shoulder. He glanced at the kit then at Hazel.

She'd tugged a chambray shirt over her head and the hem reached well below her knees. John reached for the kit. "Looks as though we're going to need this."

He rested the leather case atop Moira's pile of clothing before setting off toward the cattle in the distance.

Darcy's expression turned speculative. "I think he likes you."

"Don't be silly."

"It's not a bad thing. Having someone like that take a shine to you. Could be real useful. For all of us."

Moira tensed. "What are you implying?"

The girl raised one shoulder in a slight shrug. "Well, he's not bad-looking and he seems nice enough. A girl doesn't have much choice out here. You could do worse."

"I'm doing fine on my own. I don't like the direction of your thoughts."

"You're not doing any better than the rest of us. You're just faking it better. You might have fooled Mr. Elder, but you haven't fooled me. I know your kind."

"You don't know me." Moira shoved the sewing kit off her pile of clothing and stacked her new boots on top instead. "You don't know anything about me."

She grasped her bundle against her chest and walked a few paces away from the wagon. Her heartbeat raced and her hands tingled. She thought of Mr. Gifford, how he'd once sidled up to her in the hallway and pressed her against the wainscoting, his hot breath on her cheek.

John wasn't like that. Their relationship was different. Her thoughts scattered. What was she thinking? They didn't have a relationship.

Moira glanced over one shoulder at Darcy. "Find yourself something to wear. We have a job to do."

Keeping his eyes open was exhausting. John rested his head against the wheel of the chuck wagon. A heavy weight landed near his bent knee.

He groped and discovered the pitted leather of a well-used valise with the word O'Mara stamped on a brass plate. "Give it to the redhead."

"My orders were to give it to you. That's what I'm doing."

John inclined his head. "Hope it wasn't hard finding us."

The man cackled. "I'd sooner track a slug. I left shortly after Sheriff Taylor found me. After that I took the road out of town. I cut off the path and circled back. Still beat you to the watering hole."

John felt his ears heat. "My crew did well considering they'd never seen a longhorn before two days ago."

"At least you're going in a straight line. That's something."

"Yep. That's something."

Swede tugged on his suspenders. "The sheriff filled me in on your situation, and I added a few extras to the stock. Things that appeal to the girls."

"Put it on my tab."

In for a penny, in for a pound.

The girls' chatter ebbed and flowed around him. After a moment, he sensed someone else approaching.

He knew it was Moira before she spoke. There was something about her. Her footfalls, the way she smelled like peony blossoms. He didn't quite understand the connection, but since that first moment, something sparked between them when she was near.

"Is there anything I can get you?" she asked.

"Nah. I'm fine. You get everything you need?"

"You've set the girls free in a candy store. I don't think any of them have had anything new in ages."

"Send his wagon back empty. Everyone should have something new once in a while."

She touched his forehead, her fingertips featherlight. He sucked in a breath.

"The swelling has gone down," she said. "Can you see?"

"It's better. How's the smell?"

"Better."

"You're not much of a liar, Miss Moira O'Mara."

She laughed and he recalled what Swede had brought. "There's something special for you."

He hooked his hand through the handle and hoisted the valise over his lap.

Moira gasped. She immediately knelt on the ground and rummaged through the bag, emerging with a dog-eared sketchbook. She flipped through the pages then hugged the book to her chest.

Curious, he glanced over her shoulder. "What have you got there?"

"My sketchbook."

She proudly displayed a page featuring a young boy. The details were flawless, delicately formed and perfectly displayed. He forced his sore eyes further open. "You're very talented. That's truly wonderful."

Moira blushed. "I practiced a lot."

He took the book from her hands and flipped through the pages. Every inch of every page was covered in sketches. Her subjects were disparate: people, animals, flowers, anything and everything. She had a great eye for particulars and an excellent sense of perspective. John angled the paper and realized the sketches covered both sides.

Moira tugged the book from his hands. "I don't like to waste space."

"You're good. Real good. You're running out of pages, though."

"I still have some space in the back."

John cast a surreptitious glance at her bag. She didn't have much.

She clutched the handles to her chest. "How did you talk the sheriff into sending this along?"

"I asked."

"I can't believe he agreed."

"He's not such a bad guy."

Moira snorted. "Did you have to pay him?"

"Nope. He wanted information."

"About what?"

"Land. He was looking to buy some land suitable for raising horses. Wondered if I had any leads where I was heading. I put him onto a parcel down the creek in Cimarron Springs."

Moira laughed. "Wouldn't that be the way? You'll be neighbors with the man who kicked you out of Fool's End."

"He saved those girls' lives."

"He did no such thing! We could have gone back into town but for him."

John had considered the events of that first evening over the past few days, and he had a bad feeling the girls hadn't acted alone. "Those girls weren't safe there and you know it. Not after, well, you know."

"I don't think we should paint Sheriff Taylor as the hero of this story."

"Heroes don't always look like we expect them to."

"I never expected you to defend the man. Especially after he ran you out of town."

"I had a lot of time to think today. It occurs to me that maybe I was wrong about some things."

Moira stood. "Well, I'll leave you to your thinking. It's my turn for watch and I can't be late or Darcy will pitch a fit."

He found himself longing for her return. When another moment passed, he let his thoughts drift. John enjoyed the silence for five whole minutes before Pops appeared.

The older man sipped on his ever-present tin cup of coffee. "We've gotten the girls outfitted. They've set up the tents and worked out a watch list. It's going to storm tonight. Looks like it's gonna be a real humdinger. We've got extra stakes on the tents in case there's wind."

"All right."

"Look, John. I'm sorry about setting this whole thing

into motion. I know you're sore. And maybe you're right. After this morning, well, we got real lucky. I can't help but think if it had been the old crew and us, things might not have gone so well. As it stands, we're lucky we made it out with our scalps. Maybe it's too dangerous for these girls out here. But I didn't see any way of stopping them. And I sure didn't want them out here alone."

"I get it."

"You sure you're all right?"

"I lost my men, my herd and my horses. One of my orphan crew nearly drowned. I got sprayed by a skunk and can't see out of my left eye. I assaulted a deputy sheriff and got kicked out of Fool's End. No mean feat considering it's a town with as many outlaws as law-abiding citizens. It's about to rain and I've got a leaky tent full of females. Oh, and my slicker is in the fire because it smells like skunk. Other than that, I'm doing all right."

"It doesn't sound all right when you say it like that." Pops rummaged through the drawers lining the sides of the chuck wagon. "You're starting to sound like Jack before he settled down and relaxed a bit."

John bolted upright. "What's that supposed to mean?"

"Easy there. It don't mean nothing except you sounded like Jack just then, you know, back before he met Elizabeth. There's something about a woman that changes a man. Jack was all full of right and wrong. He was all black and white. Always trying to force things his way. Not the sort of fellow who'd marry the widow of an outlaw."

"He must have changed all right, because that's just what he did," John said.

When Jack had set out after their sister-in-law's killer, he never expected the man would already be dead, or that he'd left a widow and child behind. Jack had fallen in love with the widow and child and brought them back to Paris, Texas. He was definitely a changed man, that was certain.

He and Jack hadn't gotten along well, before Jack married Elizabeth. They'd grown closer of late. While Jack hadn't encouraged him to leave after the fight with Robert, he hadn't questioned his decision to leave either. It was as though Jack understood his need to put some space between him and Robert.

No matter what Jack was like now, John didn't appreciate the comparison to the "old" Jack. The stubborn, hardheaded Jack.

Pops shook his head and continued his work.

John pressed the backs of his knuckles against his swollen eyes, thankful they weren't nearly as sore as an hour before. At the low rumble of thunder in the distance, he turned up his collar. They wouldn't make any progress today. Not with the rain and his green crew. He'd send out the boys in this weather, but he didn't dare risk the younger girls.

While he enjoyed the rare respite from his duties, a drizzle misted the air. Instead of wind and lightning, the drops were barely more than a haze. The girls disappeared into their tent and John sidled into the narrow space in the center of the chuck wagon, his knees bent against the sideboard. He laced his hands behind his head and stared at the overhang. Pops's words kept ringing in his ears. He was behaving like Jack. He was forcing the situation into a preordained shape. He was stubbornly jamming the pieces together when he knew good and well the puzzle had changed.

Just because his new crew was different from his old

crew didn't make them better or worse. They were simply *different*. As the trail boss, it was his job to bring out the best in his men, even if they were women.

It was high time he did his job.

After the drummer's exit and after everyone had washed and changed into a fresh set of clothes, they'd made the decision to set out on the trail once more. The clouds had moved north and the rain had let up. The time had gone past one in the afternoon, but Moira figured some progress was better than no progress. Even Hazel could tell John was chafing at the bit. Despite the Indians and the skunk, he'd made the decision to press onward.

The rest of the day passed beneath the monotonous drone of flies and the plodding of hoofbeats. The terrain remained even and unchanged, the horizon a faint line in the distance. Once she'd jerked upright, realizing she'd fallen into a slight slumber.

Tony circled around. "Look sharp. No sleeping on the job."

Moira yawned. "I always thought falling asleep in the saddle was a tall tale. I think different now.

Clouds covered the sun and kept the air cool. Moira's horse mostly took the lead. Better trained than her, the horse seemed to realize when one of the cattle was about to stray out of line. After what seemed like hours, John lifted his fisted hand and called them to a halt.

Moira slumped. "How far was that?"

"About six miles."

"Six? Is that all? Seems like we've gone fifty."

"We lost half the day. That's half the distance."

Since they'd had an easy day, she wasn't near as sore as she'd been the first. Already her muscles were accommodating the change in activity. That evening they gathered around the campfire. They'd rotated the watch backward from the night before, which meant Sarah had the first watch and Moira the last.

The air had a chill and Pops added extra logs to the fire, building the flames higher than normal. The sun sank in the distance, leaving behind the darkened haze of twilight.

Tony splayed out, her feet stretched toward the warmth, her head propped on a saddle. "You know what this night needs? Some good scary stories."

"I don't think it's a good idea," Moira said. "You girls won't sleep a wink after a round of scary stories."

"Nah." Tony had perked right up with the idea. "We'll be fine."

"I love scary stories," Darcy added.

Hazel plopped down. "Me too."

"Good." Tony grinned. "I'll get started. Everyone gather around."

The girls giggled and pulled their rough wool blankets around their shoulders against the cold.

"Go on," Hazel urged. "Tell us the story."

"I heard tell why all the soil in the Indian Territory is red," Tony whispered.

Even Darcy leaned in closer. "How come?"

Tony spread her arms. "A thousand years ago, a great monster roamed the plains."

"What did it look like?" Hazel gasped.

"It was big as a two-story building." Tony gauged her rapt audience. "As big as a four-story building. It was black as night, with enormous claws like a bear and horns that stretched as wide as main street. It had razor-sharp fangs as tall as a grown man, that stuck out of its jaws. The beast roamed the plains in the dark of night, searching for prey. The monster ate buffalo like they were no bigger than spring peas. And everywhere the beast hunted, the blood of its victims spilled on the earth and left the whole territory red."

"Oooh." Hazel wrinkled her nose. "What happened to the beast?"

"Don't know. Maybe it's still around."

"That's dumb." Darcy scoffed. "That's not even a scary story."

"You got a better one?"

"I heard a whole family in Mississippi was murdered with an ax—"

"That's a tale for another time," John broke in. "Moira's right. You won't sleep a wink with that kind of talk."

A coyote howled in the distance. The girls shivered and huddled closer. "Are we in danger?"

"Nah," the cowboy continued. "It's probably just the Ivory Coyote."

"What's that?" Hazel sat up straighter.

"The Indians say every five hundred years an Ivory Coyote is born. Its fur is as white as an elephant's tusk and its eyes are as red as a garnet. See, the coyotes never howled until the most recent Ivory Coyote was born, must be going on two or three hundred years ago."

"They live that long?"

"They live for five hundred years."

A stump popped in the fire, collapsing in a shower of embers. The air around the flames shimmered in a mirage, turning everything outside their vision hazy and muddled.

Moira rubbed her upper arms.

Tony kicked back on her saddle pillow. "What started them howling, then?"

"Well, a bunch of settler children found the Ivory Coyote and her litter of pups. They'd never seen the like before. It was too tempting. When the Ivory Coyote went out hunting that night, they stole the pups away."

"They stole her pups?" Hazel exclaimed. "That's so sad."

"Is that why she's howling then?" Darcy asked. "For her lost pups?"

"Those coyotes will howl for another two-hundred years, until the next Ivory Coyote comes to take its place."

"That still ain't scary." Darcy huffed. "Who cares if some old coyote is howling for her lost pups?"

"Because she's also looking for revenge."

Moira turned. "What kind of revenge?"

"She snatches the settler's children."

The cowboy goosed Hazel in the arm. The little girl shrieked and giggled. The girls yelped and laughed.

"I knew you were only fooling." Darcy grumbled.

Drawn toward the commotion, Champion trotted into the firelight. The animal wove its way among the girls, sniffing each one in turn, as though assuring their safety. Once satisfied with the inspection, Champion lay near Moira, pressing its entire body against the length of her thigh.

She stiffened and held her hands out of reach. Champion rested his snout on her knee and stared at her with velvety-brown eyes. She cautiously brought down one hand, gently stroking the top of the dog's head.

Hazel crawled closer and scratched behind the animal's ear. "He likes it when you do this."

Moira repeated the gesture on the opposite ear. If

she didn't know better, she'd think the dog was grinning at her.

"See," Hazel said. "He's smiling."

Moira studied the girls. They'd worked hard over the past two days, stretched beyond their skills.

Hazel tired of petting the dog and joined Tony. They played a game, clapping their hands together and repeating a singsong rhyme.

"My mother told me to open the door,
But I didn't want to.
I opened the door, he fell through the floor,
That silly old man from China.
My mother told me to take off his coat,
But I didn't want to.
I took off his coat, and out jumped a goat.
That silly old man from China."

Moira shivered. John leaned over, extending his hand, the handle of a tin cup full of Pop's ubiquitous coffee clutched between his fingers.

"You cold?"

"No." Moira wrapped her fingers around the cup for warmth. "It's the rhyme. I never did like the words."

"My mother told me to take off his hat,
But I didn't want to.
I took off his hat, and out jumped a cat.
That silly old man from China."

John shrugged. "Seems simple enough to me."

Darcy joined the group, and Hazel and Tony rearranged to accommodate her.

The three resumed their clapping with another song.

"Three sailors went to sea, sea, sea
To see what they could see, see, see,
But all that they could see, see, see,
Was the bottom of the deep blue sea, sea, sea."

John caught her gaze. "How are you holding up?"

"I've never been more miserable," she answered truthfully. "Or more satisfied. I'm exhausted, sore, and my hands are raw. I've got an itchy sunburn on the tip of my nose and the back of my neck. I'm more tired than I ever recall being in my life, yet I'm not ready for sleeping. I want to be right here, under the stars, listening to the girls play and laugh."

Something inside her was shifting. Her beliefs about herself, about the world. She'd set out with a goal: find her brother, reunite their family. The steps in her life had been simple and straight. She wasn't the sort of woman who drove cattle or told scary stories around a fire.

"I think I understand what you're saying. A hard day's work can make a man feel useful. Needed."

"Not always." Moira sipped her coffee and recalled her life with the Giffords. "Did you know it takes three different kinds of leaves to make a proper cigar?"

"Nope. I did not know that. You don't seem the type of woman to imbibe."

"It's how the Giffords earned their money."

"The foster family that took you in?"

Moira nodded. "Mr. Gifford never had much of a job. He was always looking for a way to get rich quick. They had a maid and a cook because everyone who was anyone in St. Louis had a maid and a cook. They took in

Tommy and me because they didn't have their own children, and children made a man look respectable. That's what Mr. Gifford said, anyway. Success and fame were always just around the corner for Mr. Gifford. In a way I suppose I admired his optimism. No matter how many times his schemes failed, he was always ready for another. Always staying one step ahead of the debtors."

"That's not optimism. That's idiocy."

"The cigars were his one, steady source of income. The tobacco farms paid us piecemeal."

She pictured his gold watch, the links of the chain stretched between his brocade-vest pockets. The steady tick, tick, tick. The monotony that gave her too much time for thinking. Too much time for dreaming.

Tick, tick, tick.

"That's how your foster family earned a living then, rolling cigars?"

"No." Moira stood and dusted her pant legs. "Mrs. Gifford didn't like how the tobacco left her fingers yellowed. Mr. Gifford felt he lacked the dexterity for such delicate work. Which meant the work fell to Tommy and me."

She laughed, the sound hollow even to her own ears. "I suppose it seems perfectly normal to you. Growing up on a ranch, you must have worked hard. Even as a child."

"I suppose," John began. "But what you're speaking of sounds more like child labor than chores. Is that what you were talking about earlier? When you said you'd like to right a wrong."

"Something like that."

She couldn't admit what she'd done. The more she knew about the cowboy, the less she wanted him to know about her life. She wanted him to like her, to respect her.

He might regret kissing her, he certainly hadn't brought up the subject, but she didn't want him to regret knowing her. She'd gotten him all wrong from the beginning.

He might be separated from his family, but at least he hadn't betrayed them.

Chapter Thirteen

Two nights later, following supper, the girls lounged around the fire once more. In a few short days they'd fallen into a regular routine. They went about their chores without fuss. Most of the animosity from the first few days had withered away beneath the weight of exhaustion. John was even growing accustomed to the improvement in the food.

Hazel sat cross-legged, her elbows propped on her knees, her chin cradled in her hands. "Why aren't you married yet?"

"Well, uh. I'm just not," John replied.

Tony whittled at a stick. "She means, what's wrong with you?"

"Nothing is wrong with me. Why would you think something is wrong with me?"

"You're a good-looking fellow. Got yourself a nice herd of cattle. You're plenty old enough. Why ain't you got a wife and kids by now?"

He caught Moira watching him and a flash of heat crept up his neck. "I guess I haven't found the right lady yet."

"Or you're not looking."

"I think he's doing something wrong." Tony eyeballed the sharpened end of her stick. "Maybe you're not approaching things the right way."

"What things?" John glanced around. "I'm not approaching anything. I just haven't gotten around to courting anyone yet."

"You better get around to it soon," Tony replied. "You're not getting any younger. And where you're going, there's not too many available women."

"How do you know?"

"Well, it stands to figure. The farther west you go, the fewer women. My pa used to say, there's a woman behind every tree in Kansas. Both of 'em."

"Well, I don't see the need to force anything." John didn't like the direction of this conversation. Lately he'd been thinking more and more about settling down, having a family of his own. He didn't need the girls goading him. "If the right woman comes along, well, we'll see."

Pops appeared in the firelight, a tin of raw bread dough in his hands. "What about that girl you was dating back in Texas?"

John fidgeted. "Ruth Ann?"

"Yeah, that's the one. Whatever happened with her?"

"You remember well enough." Moira had finally ceased looking at him as though he was about to disappoint her at any moment. He didn't need Pops dredging up the past and casting him in a bad light. "She married Alex Stillwell. They've got a pecan farm and five children."

"I didn't ask *who* she married. I asked *why* she didn't marry you."

"That's personal." Best to end this conversation here

and now. He didn't need Moira wondering what was wrong with him. "What have you got there?"

"A bit of bread for cooking over the fire. Sarah got it started this morning." Pops handed him the pan.

"What am I supposed to do with this?"

"Give me a minute."

Pops set off for the chuck wagon and returned a moment later with several slender twigs about two feet long apiece. He handed each of the girls a stick. "These are for cooking. Let me show you what to do."

He sat next to John and pinched off a fistful of the bread dough, then rolled it into a rope between his palms. Keeping hold of the bread with one hand, he grasped the stick with the other, then wound the dough around one end. "Be sure to pinch the ends together so it stays put."

He held the stick over the fire. "Just keep twirling it till the dough gets nice and golden brown."

The girls crowded around John, reaching for the dough. In short order, only a marble-sized ball of dough remained. With much giggling, the dough was formed into long snakes. More than one piece hit the dirt and had to be discarded. The activity kept the girls distracted, but not for long.

After Moira left for her watch, Hazel nudged him. "Why didn't you marry Ruth Ann?"

"Well, it's not so much why didn't I marry her, but why didn't she marry me."

"So?" Tony lifted her eyebrows. "Why wouldn't she?"

With Moira gone, he wasn't as self-conscious about opening up. "We were too young. Or at least I was too young. She didn't think I could care for her properly."

"Did you draw her a picture?" Hazel asked.

"Um. No. Can't say that I did."

"I'd like it if someone drew me a picture. I think Moira would like it, too. She likes to draw a lot."

"A picture," Pops said. "Never would have thought of that. But it's not a bad idea."

"I'll keep that under consideration." John twirled his piece of dough over the fire. "Although I don't see how drawing pictures can make someone like you."

"Sure can't hurt," Tony said. "Doesn't seem like what you're doing so far is working out all that well."

"I can always count on you to put things into perspective."

While the girls laughed and talked, John considered his future. The girls had obviously decided he and Moira belonged together. Considering their odd circumstances, the assumption fit. They were relatively close in age, they were both single. Other than Pops, they were the two adults in camp that the girls relied on.

He tried on the notion for size, letting the idea roll around in his head. He'd never felt for anyone what he felt for Moira. Not even Ruth Ann. His childhood sweetheart had been a friend. In retrospect, he realized their parting had been inevitable. Neither of them had felt deeply enough for the other to fight for their relationship.

Maybe in a year or two, when his ranch was up and running and he had a steady source of income—when he proved he could care for Moira—maybe he'd see if she was interested in the idea as well.

He wasn't making the same mistake twice. He wasn't courting a woman until he knew well and sure he could care for her.

The breakfast bell clanged the following morning. Tony stuck her face in the tent. "Mr. Elder says we're pulling out in twenty minutes. With or without you sleepyheads."

Moira glanced around. "You certain? I just went to bed."

The nights were cooling yet Moira kicked off the covers and wiped at the fine sheen of sweat on her forehead.

"It's morning, all right. You can tell by the sun."

Moira tossed a shoe in her direction, but the girl ducked out of the tent and avoided the blow.

Moira slipped into her denim trousers and tugged her blue chambray shirt over her head, knotting the long tail ends at her waist. Even those simple tasks left her winded and she sat back on her heels. After closing her eyes and counting to ten, she reached for her boots and pulled them on, wincing as the new, stiff leather brushed against her right ankle.

The scratch on her ankle had healed well at first, then yesterday she'd scraped it and reopened the wound. The previous day she'd sweated despite the cooler weather. She'd hardly slept the previous evening for the throbbing.

She rested for another few moments and stood, then stepped toward the tent flap. The world spun and she paused, pressing two fingers against her temple. After sucking in a few more breaths, she emerged into the morning sunlight.

Four faces stood in a half circle around the tent opening.

Sarah crossed her arms over her chest. "If you don't ask for help, that wound is going to go septic and then we'll have to cut off your leg at the thigh."

Moira's eyes widened. "Don't be silly. It's only a scratch. I'm fine." She steadied herself with a hand against the tent.

"Well, we're not going anywhere until you let us have a look."

"We're wasting time." Moira spoke in her most commanding voice. "Mr. Elder will be none too pleased."

"Mr. Elder is the one who called this meeting," a masculine voice spoke.

Moira groaned. "If it's that big of a deal, you can take a look."

The group disbanded, appearing disappointed at her easy capitulation.

Sarah brushed past. "It's not a crime to ask for help, you know."

"I don't need any help."

"Whatever."

John cleared his throat. "Have a seat over here. Let's look at that ankle."

She dutifully took her place on the edge of the chuck wagon and stuck out her leg.

John crouched before her and tugged off her boot. "You should have showed this to someone sooner. This appears infected."

"Do what you need to do. There's no call for a lecture."

He rested his forearm on his bent knee. "Actually, there's every need for a lecture. You're part of my crew. If I tell you to have a scrape checked out, you check it out. Our success is dependent on the health of the crew."

Moira bit her lip and looked away. "I am sufficiently chastised."

He held her ankle and turned her leg from side to side and his hands dwarfed her foot. She'd never considered herself particularly dainty. Next to John she felt positively tiny.

The cowboy took a bottle of liniment from a kit at his elbow and unstopped the cork. He poured a measure onto his bandanna and pressed it against the scrape.

Moira hissed.

"It'll only burn for a minute."

True to his word, after the initial sting, the pain slowly faded. He pulled away the bandanna and examined the wound once again.

"I'm going to wrap this. Keep the dirt out."

"Make it quick. We've a whole day ahead of us."

He grasped a roll of binding and carefully wound the bandage around her ankle. "I'll change this tonight and check for infection."

Moira stared at the top of his hat. "Thank you."

She couldn't recall the last time someone had looked out for her this well.

The brim lifted, revealing his dark eyes. "You're welcome. Say, I wanted to ask you something. Would you like it if someone drew a picture for you?"

"What kind of a picture?"

"Maybe a tree or something."

"I, ah, I suppose. Why do you ask?"

"I just wondered."

Her heart skittered a beat. Covering her unease, she reached for her boot and tugged the leather back over her ankle.

The cowboy held out his hand. Moira tentatively reached out her fingertips. He clasped them, helping her balance as she stood. She put some weight on her foot, testing the bandage.

"It's better."

He threaded their fingers together and stared at their clasped hands. "You don't have to be strong for everyone. You don't even have to be strong for yourself all the time. We're a crew together, we help each other. Support each other."

"And what happens when we reach Fort Preble?"

"What do you mean?"

"What happens when I become dependent on you and then you're not there anymore?"

"Well, it'll be different, that's for sure. Town life is quite a bit different from trail life."

"It's not only that." She'd promised herself she'd remain aloof from the girls. The more time they spent together, the more difficult keeping her promise became. "Once we're back in town, everyone will go their separate ways."

"You can write letters."

"That'll never happen. Out of sight is out of mind for people. Once this is over, we'll never even think of each other again."

"Do you really think that?"

"Don't you?" She avoided his dark gaze. Lately she worried that she'd miss the cowboy most of all.

She didn't understand her feelings for him, but she recognized they were strong. And they frightened her.

"I think it's important to enjoy the time we have together. Here. Now. If you're worrying about the future, or living in the past, you can't properly enjoy the present."

"Strange words coming from a man who's running from his own family."

Hurt flickered across his face, quickly masked by his easy grin. "Don't forget. Check with me tonight. We'll change the dressing."

He turned and strode away. An unexpected burst of

anger flared through her chest. She'd expected him to fight back. Defend himself. Defend his actions. Instead, he'd closed the subject and left her feeling like a first-rate heel.

He was kind to the girls, good to the animals. He was fair and open-minded. And he didn't care a whit about moving hundreds of miles from his family. How did all those contradictory things exist in one man? Last night the girls had teased him. He'd had a sweetheart, Ruth Ann. The admission had shocked her.

Almost as much as realizing she was jealous.

John's crew had finally picked up speed. The next two days took on a rhythm and they made good time, fifteen miles each day. There was little need for instruction.

He'd pulled a watch in the middle of the night during a brief squall, letting the rain sluice off his hat and dribble into his boots. Despite the discomfort, he slept better than he had in weeks. The following morning the smell of frying bacon teased his nostrils and pulled him from a restful slumber. Circling around the wagon, he stretched and yawned. A quick look in the mirror attached to the wagon post showed his face had returned to normal. He opened and closed his eyes a few times. They were still a mite bloodshot, but he no longer looked like he could scare a rattler out of its skin.

It had taken seven days to make the trip. Fort Preble sat in the distance, tall chimneys puffing smoke from cook fires. He hadn't expected they'd make it this far. Suddenly the idea of going the distance didn't seem so far-fetched. They were a few days from the Kansas boarder and a few more from Cimarron Springs.

He shook off the idea. The closer his destination

came, the farther it seemed. He'd closed his mind against the dangers of the trip. With each day, he realized the chances of a disaster grew.

The more he got to know the girls, the more he worried that something would happen. This morning his unlikely crew had crouched before the cook fire. They were filthy and exhausted, and, quite possibly, the best crew he'd ever had. The idea of putting together another crew at Fort Preble to make the rest of the distance soured his stomach.

Moira rode into view, her new hat low on her head. She slid off her mount and approached him. "We've got riders. Two of them. They're coming toward camp. Fast."

John reached for his gun. "Let me handle this."

At the rebellious gleam in Moira's eyes, he set his jaw. "Let me handle this," he repeated.

Keeping his fingers on the stock, he watched as the two riders approached. They could be anyone with their enveloping slickers and their hats pulled low against the rain. John widened his stance.

"What business do you have here?"

The first rider lifted his head and glanced around. "That's not the crew you left with."

John's jaw dropped. Of all the people he'd expected to see, he wasn't prepared for his brother Jack.

John reached out, clasped his hand in a quick shake. "You're a long way from home. Did you run out of fugitives in Texas or did Elizabeth send you to check up on me?"

"Both. Elizabeth is beside herself with worry. She'd probably faint dead away if she saw you now."

John shielded his eyes from the sun and met his brother's steady gaze. "I sure am glad you're here."

Relief coursed through him. His thoughts came into focus. He'd come all this way to prove his point, when the answer was already in sight. He'd inherited his share of the ranch from their father before he was ready, before he'd broken free of childish jealousies and developed the confidence and conviction that came with maturity.

Looking back on the past few days, he realized he'd sacrifice his pride if it meant the girls' safety. Nothing else mattered.

All this time he'd fought hardest with Robert, and the truth was humbling. Robert had lost his wife, he lived with guilt, and he struggled beneath the weight of responsibility that came with raising two children alone. Robert hadn't saved his wife, so he was driven to save the rest of them. He just went about it the wrong way sometimes.

A good man knew his strengths, but it took a bigger man to admit his weaknesses.

John had lectured Moira because her stubborn pride prevented her from asking for help, when he had been guilty of the same offense.

He'd set out on this journey filled with pride, and he'd discovered humility in the process.

"I sure am glad you're here," John repeated. "I could use the help."

Chapter Fourteen

Moira glanced between the two men. "Do you two know each other?"

"You could say that," John said. "Meet my brother, Jack Elder. Jack, this is Miss Moira O'Mara."

The resemblance was unmistakable. John was an inch taller than his brother was and wider in the shoulders, though they both shared the same rugged good looks. Jack was clearly the older of the two. Gray hair showed at his temples and deep lines tracked across his forehead.

"Pleased to meet you, Miss O'Mara." Jack faced his brother. "You and I need to talk about your crew. Alone."

Moira held up her hands. "No. Absolutely not. Those girls are my responsibility. Anything you have to say to John you can say to me."

The cowboy jerked his head in a nod. "This concerns her, too."

"Your call," Jack replied.

Moira glanced uneasily at the second rider. Jack followed her gaze. "That's Sergeant Baker from Fort Preble."

The second man braced his hands against his saddle

horn. "I'm just along for the ride. This is Sheriff Elder's show."

Pops rounded the corner of the chuck wagon and his eyes widened. "What brings you this far from Texas, Jack? You missed the cows?"

The senior Elder brother dismounted and the two men clasped shoulders in a quick, perfunctory embrace that clearly demonstrated their affection.

"You old coon dog," Jack Elder teased. "Aren't you too old to be trailing across the country?"

"I'm not that much older than you, and don't you forget it."

"Well, I *am* too old." Sheriff Elder rubbed his hip. "I think I'm getting a bit of the rheumatism."

"I've got some of my cure-all."

"How about some coffee instead?"

"There's always coffee over the fire when I'm in charge."

Moira watched the three men from a distance. They shared a history and their easy affection kept her isolated, staring in from the outside like a child pressing her nose against an ice cream shop window. With their easy relationship, the distance separating them might have been miles instead of a few feet.

Pops poured steaming hot brew into a tin cup. "How is Elizabeth? What about your young'uns?"

"Elizabeth is fit and healthy. We're expecting another child before Christmas."

John slapped his brother on the shoulder with a grin. "You never said."

"We were waiting to be sure. It's been five years since our last was born."

"You're awful cheerful for a man who's about to give up sleep for the next year."

"I wouldn't have it any other way." Sheriff Elder's expression sobered. "Which is why I can't stay long. I don't know what you did, but you've made a stubborn enemy. Some deputy sheriff wants your head on a platter."

Moira groaned. "Wendell."

"He sounds like a real weasel. He's claiming one of your crew stole from him. Says he's got plenty of other people willing to say the same."

John braced one shoulder against the metal ribs of the chuck wagon. "I was afraid something like this might happen. Still doesn't explain how you got roped into all this."

"I had some business up in Cimarron Springs. Elizabeth and I were worried when you didn't show. I figure you're a grown man who can ask for help when he needs it, but once Elizabeth is worried, there's no going back."

John snorted softly. "I remember."

"Anyway, it was pretty easy to backtrack. I figured you'd be stopping at the fort for supplies. They'd heard of you all right. They'd been warned about your arrival. Wendell wants you all arrested and sent back to Fool's End." Jack waved his coffee cup through the air. "I expected a more dangerous-looking crew after the deputy's dustup. And boys."

Moira made a sound of frustration. "This isn't fair. We cleared everything with the sheriff."

"Evidently, the sheriff was only temporary. He's been transferred to another town. I pulled some strings with the boys at the fort," Jack continued. "I did what I could. Since it's a state official making the case, I had the jurisdiction transferred to the U.S. Marshals. That means we can take the girls across the Kansas border. Marshal Garrett Cain has agreed to take over the case for me."

"Couldn't you handle this?" John asked. "Throw out the whole nonsense?"

"The deputy knows you came up through Indian Territory with longhorns. He'd have kicked up a fit if I sent them back to Texas."

"I still don't like it," Moira said. "What do we know about the marshal? Can we trust him?"

"Don't worry. I've met Marshal Cain. He's a good man. If there's anything that can be done, he'll figure it out."

Moira paced before the brothers. "They're children. Who cares about a few apples they've taken for survival? Where is the forgiveness?"

"Wait." Jack held out his hands. "Let's go back a step. How did y'all end up together anyway?"

John sketched out the story. He kept to the facts, downplaying his own role. Moira glanced between the two men. Jack Elder remained respectfully quiet during the explanation, yet she sensed he had more questions.

"If you weren't my own flesh and blood," Sheriff Elder said, "I'd say you were lying."

John grinned. "I gave them the idea. I told them about Gramps in forty-nine."

"Not sure how much of that story I believe."

"I believe more of it now."

"You did good, John."

The cowboy didn't reply, yet Moira sensed his pride.

The two brothers exchanged a glance. John studied his boots. "Moira, I can't shake the belief that Wendell is after you for some reason. Something personal."

"Me?"

Her thoughts flew back over their encounter in Fool's End. This had gone beyond a bit of revenge for whatever disturbance her brother had caused.

Sheriff Elder rubbed his chin. "Can you think of any reason the deputy would want you back in Fool's End. What brought you there in the first place?"

"I was searching for my brother. He sent a telegraph from there. Part of the message was missing, but I made out *Fool's End* and the name *Grey*. It was the first I'd heard from my brother in almost four years. I came as soon as I could. Mr. Grey said he'd never met Tommy. Something didn't sit right."

"It doesn't make any sense." John tugged on his ear. "Why wouldn't he admit that he knew your brother? If he's exacting some sort of revenge, what for? And we're certain your brother wasn't in Fool's End the whole time?"

Moira's stomach plummeted. "I don't know. I didn't check. Mr. Grey said he was gone... I took him at his word."

"Let's not panic until we think about this." John touched her cheek. The gesture was comforting. "The sheriff had heard of your brother. He said he'd moved on. There's no reason to believe Tommy was still there at the same time."

Her breathing came in quick, shallow gasps. "What do we know about Sheriff Taylor? What if he was working with Mr. Grey? He said there had been a dustup over Mr. Grey's daughter. What if he was lying?"

"No. I don't think so. The sheriff let us leave without much of a fuss. Wendell was the one who wanted your return. If Sheriff Taylor was involved, he wouldn't have let you leave that easily."

Moira shifted and Jack turned in her direction.

"And the telegram didn't say anything else?"

"Not much. I brought it along. Would you like me to fetch it?"

"Wouldn't hurt."

Moira retrieved the telegram and returned in short order.

Jack held the singed pieces between his thumb and forefinger. "What do you make of that word?"

The cowboy leaned closer. "Looks like it starts with a *w*."

Jack tucked the papers back into the envelope and handed it back. "I can do some digging on my way back to Texas."

"I don't know if that's such a good idea," Moira said. "I don't trust Wendell. If you start asking questions, who knows what he'll do."

"Don't worry about me, miss. I've been dealing with men like the deputy my whole career. I'll be careful."

An awkward silence descended and Moira realized the brothers were looking in her direction. She stood and dusted her pants. "I'll leave you two gentlemen."

Jack clasped her hand in both of his. "Pleasure to meet you."

Moira returned his easy grin. She wouldn't have thought it possible, what with all the trouble the girls had caused for his brother, yet he seemed genuinely at ease with her presence.

"Pleased to meet you as well."

And she was pleased. Watching the two men together filled her with warmth.

She left more confused than she had been all week. If the brothers got along so well, why was John traveling four hundred miles to get away from them?

When Moira moved out of earshot, Jack's expression sobered. "You're lucky you made it this far without a catastrophe. There are rivers and Indians and who knows what else. Not to mention those cattle are deadly if spooked."

"Bobcats and skunks."

"Huh?"

"That's what else is out here. Moira nearly drowned in the Snake River, Champion was almost mauled by a bobcat. And I got skunked."

"Who is Champion?"

"The dog."

"I thought the dog's name was Dog."

"Not anymore."

"I'll bet you didn't come up with that name. You've never been real imaginative when it came to naming things."

"No," John conceded. "Actually the girls came up with that name. And now he won't answer to anything else."

"Well, it's better than Dog. That's for certain."

"Which reminds me, we also ran into a group of Indians," John said.

"You ran into Indians." Jack shook his head. "It's fortunate Elizabeth didn't know what was happening. She'd have pitched a fit."

"I thought I'd planned for everything," John said. "I sure hadn't planned for any of this."

Of all his brothers, he'd known Jack the least growing

up. His brother's job as a Texas Ranger had taken him to all corners of the state. He hadn't been around much. When he'd married and taken over the role of sheriff in Paris, Texas, they'd grown closer.

Jack glanced at the cattle. "You realize things might be hostile at the border."

"I know." John blew out a hard breath. "Any chance of lenience?"

"None. The ranchers and farmers will meet you at the border with rifles. They're taming the West one farm at a time. They don't want cattle chewing through their crops and bringing disease."

"What do you think about Texas fever? When I left, I figure the stories were exaggerated. You know, because the farmers and ranchers didn't want the cattle trampling through their fences and grazing on their land. After our stop in Fool's End, I'm not so certain. I heard a few things that had me worried."

"It's real, all right, and getting worse. I think in the beginning there might have been a question. Not anymore. Texas cattle carry something that's killing off the Midwestern stock."

"But our stock is immune?"

"Looks that way."

John pressed two fingers against his temple "I'll see if I can sell the herd in Fort Preble. Winter is coming. I'm hoping they'll need the stock."

"I'm sorry," Jack continued. "I know the boys give you a hard time. None of us wanted this."

"I took a shot. It didn't work out."

"You know you can always turn around and go home. There are able-bodied men for driving cattle out here."

"No. Robert has enough to worry about. I couldn't see that before."

Jack dropped his head and stared at the reins clasped in his hands. "It changed him, losing Doreen. It changed all of us. You were probably too young to remember, but he wasn't always like he is now."

"I'm only four years younger. I was old enough to remember, and too young to understand."

"He's hard on you. I've seen that. That's why I didn't stop this cattle drive. I figured both of you could use the distance."

John didn't mind losing face to his brothers, but starting over took time. What if Moira wasn't willing to wait? Anything might happen between now and then.

And he hadn't even gotten the courage to ask her if she'd even consider courting sometime down the road. "Selling the herd is the best choice. I don't see how kicking and screaming is going to change anything."

"You're unencumbered. You can travel. You'll have a bit of money from the sale of the herd. Go to Europe. See the continent like them fancy fellows back east. Worse comes to worst, I'll put the homestead on the market. I can't seem to shake that property. It's gone through two owners and it always comes back into Elizabeth's name."

John rubbed his face. "Don't sell the property. I'll still take over the deed."

"Suit yourself."

"I won't need much."

Jack slapped his gloves against his leg and stared into the distance. "What are going to do with the horses?"

John blinked. "The remuda?"

"Yeah. You're selling the herd. What about the horses?"

"Hadn't thought about it yet."

"Let me know. I have buyers. And they *will* pay top dollar."

"I might take you up on that offer."

"It's none of my business, but you were always more of a horseman than a cattleman." Jack patted his horse's neck.

"There's more money in cattle than there is in horses."

"A man doesn't need much."

"I need security if I want to build a future. If I want a family." The words escaped before John could call them back.

Jack faced his mount and adjusted the saddle. "Taking care of someone is more than putting a roof over their heads. That's probably the easiest part. The hard part of taking care of someone is building their trust."

John kicked at the dirt. The girls had trusted him. How would they feel once they realized he was quitting? Probably they'd be happy. They'd have their pay, they were out of Fool's End. There was help for them in Cimarron Springs.

Jack faced him once more. "You're doing the right thing by those girls. They're young, they're defenseless. You've gotten lucky this far. Maybe someone higher up is watching out for you. I don't know. But anything can happen. It's best they're not riding the trail anymore."

"Believe me, I've thought of that."

"Marshal Cain is a good man. You can leave the girls in his hands. You've done more than most men already."

Hadn't John said the same thing to himself a week before? "I have to see this through. Some of those girls have families. If I can reunite them, *then* I'll have done a good thing."

"Even Miss Moira O'Mara?"

"Especially Moira."

John didn't want his brother reading anything into the relationship. He might have had a chance before he lost the herd. A chance of building a future for them. Now he was starting over. Moira deserved better. No matter what Jack said, she deserved someone who could provide for her. Until he knew whether or not a horse ranch was viable, he couldn't make her any promises.

He'd help her find her brother. That much he could do. Once they were reunited she wouldn't have much use for a failed rancher anyway.

John stuck his hands in his back pockets. "Can you make arrangements for us in town?"

"They've got barracks set aside for visitors." Jack led his horse toward the remuda. "You'll hardly recognize the place. It's doubled in size since we drove that herd up to Wichita in seventy-one." His brother halted. "Do you trust them?"

"How do you mean?"

"They're pickpockets. And how long have you known Miss O'Mara? Maybe the deputy isn't lying after all. You think she knows more than she's saying."

"She's not lying."

"I trust your instincts."

John grinned. "I've been waiting my whole life for one of you to say that."

"If Dad had lived longer, he'd have taught us better. We tried to fill in for him. We did the best we could, but we were too young ourselves."

"I know that."

Jack strapped a feed bag onto his horse. "What's the

story on Miss O'Mara? You think she'll settle in Cimarron Springs?"

John sensed a deeper meaning behind the question. By the time he built up the homestead, she'd probably be married and starting a family of her own. There was no reason to believe she'd wait for him. No reason to believe the idea had ever even crossed her mind.

"I doubt she'll stay around long," John replied. "I'm guessing she'll make sure the girls are settled, then she'll be gone again. She won't quit until she finds her brother."

"Loyalty is an admirable trait in a person."

"Yep."

"And you don't think she was working with the girls? That's the one part of Wendell's story that rang true. Those girls were organized. Feels to me like there was an adult involved. Someone older. More savvy."

"Those girls were definitely working together, but Moira wasn't a part of it. I've had my doubts about Darcy. Something's not right there. But Moira's problems begin and end with Grey. He wants revenge for something. And I have to wonder how bad does he want it? How far is he willing to go?"

"I'll check it out. You know, we're all assuming this goes back to Mr. Grey on account of the telegram. Maybe we should be taking a look at Wendell."

"He doesn't seem smart enough to start something on his own."

"I still think it's worth checking up on." Jack glanced at the chuck wagon. "That does not smell like Pops's usual mash."

"The food is different when you bring girls on the trip." John patted his stomach. "I've never gained weight on a cattle drive before."

"Are those flowers?" His brother squinted at the posy of black-eyed Susans on the back of the chuck wagon.

"Wildflowers. Wherever we go, they always seem to find wildflowers. I can't figure it out."

"That's because you're not looking."

"I'm a man."

"Tell you what. I'll send Sergeant Baker on ahead and stick around for lunch. You've been on the trail for six, almost seven days? We'll take the girls into town. Let them get cleaned up and sleep with a roof over their heads. We can all eat dinner in town."

"They'd like that."

"You said some of the girls have family. I can start digging up information at the fort."

"I haven't thought that far ahead." John scratched his forehead. "I know Tony has an uncle. Sarah has family, but I'm not certain she's welcome with them. There's no one for Hazel."

"What about the dark-haired girl?"

"Darcy. That's the one I told you about before."

"Cimarron Springs is a nice town. Good people. You might find your solution up there."

"I tried to take a shortcut, Jack. I should have taken the long way."

"You were in that alley for a reason." His brother looped the reins around his fist. "Sometimes you have to sit back and trust in God's plan. Stop pushing and step back a pace. He'll lead you where you need to be."

John kept his silence. He might be the most easygoing of the Elders, but he'd never been one to sit back and wait for anything once an idea got hold of him.

Sarah approached them, a plate in each hand. "Would

you like a scoop of peach cobbler? We didn't have any fresh so I used some tinned."

"Peach cobbler?" Jack's face lightened.

"I'm telling you, this isn't your normal cattle drive," John said.

Jack accepted the plate with a grin. "I could get used to this."

Wishing he felt as optimistic, John glanced at the place where the girls had gathered around the chuck wagon. They'd known all along that the end of the line was Fort Preble. He'd pay them fair and square, but there was no way he was leaving them on their own. He had a bad feeling his new plan wasn't going to go over well.

Chapter Fifteen

"**H**is brother is going to change everything," Darcy declared. "You mark my words. They're up to something, the Elders, I can tell."

Moira had the uneasy feeling that Darcy was correct. "I have an idea, but I'm not entirely certain."

She searched for the cowboy. Somewhere along the way she'd begun to think of them as a team. With the arrival of his brother, the balance had shifted. He wasn't consulting her any longer. Once again she felt an unaccustomed prick of jealousy. Outside of the cattle drive, he had a whole other life. A life that didn't include her.

John strode toward them, his shoulders squared, his dark hat low on his forehead. The muscles rippling beneath his chambray shirt quickened her pulse.

Moira looked away. "The girls would like to know what's next."

John Elder stood beside her, as though they were still a team. "We're driving the cattle into town this afternoon. I'm fixing to sell."

"No!"

"You can't."

"But we've come this far!"

"What will you do?"

"Wait." John raised his voice, silencing the protests. "I know I considered hiring a short crew and pushing onto Cimarron Springs. This is the right thing. I can't guarantee my herd isn't carrying disease. If I sell them here, at the fort, I won't be risking an outbreak. We talked about the risk before. Jack has been up north. Texas fever is real."

Tony stuck out her chin. "We're on our own after that, right?"

"No," John said. "You're underage. The deputy from Fool's End is stirring up trouble. The fort is too small, but the train goes through here. We'll regroup in Cimarron Springs together. I won't leave until everyone is settled."

John sketched out his plan. While Moira didn't like leaving the cattle any more than the rest of the girls did, she admired his principles. How had one week altered the course of her life? When she'd set out on her journey, she'd known exactly what she wanted, exactly what she was seeking.

Not anymore.

Oh, she still wanted to find Tommy. She'd never give up on that. Except she wondered if there was room for something more. Had she closed herself off too much?

After John completed his speech, Tony remained defiant. "There's no chance you would let us set out on our own? I ain't ending up on that orphan train again."

"Just because I'm selling the herd doesn't mean I'm giving up on you guys. We're a team. You're my Calico Cowboys."

Hazel tugged on his sleeve. "How did you know that was our name?"

"Because I listen. Because it fits. We'll break down the camp this afternoon and drive the herd into town. Jack is going on ahead and he'll let the boys at the stockyards know we're coming."

"Then what?" Sarah asked.

"There's a train to Cimarron Springs tomorrow. That'll give everyone a chance to clean up and get a good night's rest."

Hazel raised her hand. "What about Moira?"

"That's up to her. She's of age and she's free to do as she pleases. The rest of you are still minors and under the care of Marshal Garrett Cain until other arrangements can be made."

Moira straightened. "I'm coming with you. We're in this together. We'll search for Tony's uncle."

"What about the rest of us?" Sarah asked.

"I don't know." John didn't like the unpredictability any better than the girls did. None of their futures were certain. "But I meant what I said. I'm fixing to make Cimarron Springs my home. I'll be there to make sure everyone is settled."

John clasped Moira's hand. His fingers were rough and strong and gave her a sense of protection. "You're sure this is what you want?"

"I'll keep looking for Tommy while we settle the girls in Cimarron Springs. Maybe Sheriff Taylor will think of something. Anyway, it doesn't matter. We're talking about the Calico Cowboys, right?"

John jerked his head in a nod. "That's settled. I don't think anybody at Fort Preble has seen an all-girl crew before. I want you sitting high and proud in the saddle.

You've done something amazing. Let's give those army boys a show they won't forget."

Moira felt the tug on her heart once more. She clutched this precious time together, knowing it would be over all too soon.

With practiced efficiency the girls finished lunch, broke down the campsite, saddled their horses and took their places with the herd. They worked quickly, with few words. A sense of mourning permeated their routine. For a short time they'd been a part of something bigger. They'd strapped together their meager skills and accomplished something that was larger than any of them alone.

The accomplishment had stretched Moira's endurance to the breaking. She'd been tested again, only this time she'd proven worthy of the test. For the first time in a long time her life had possibilities. She wasn't trapped by circumstances.

Once the horses were saddled and ready and the tents and equipment stowed, the girls mounted and gathered. Hazel resumed her position next to Pops on the chuck wagon.

John gave the signal and sent up a whistle. Champion barked and nipped at the cattle's heels. Their hooves rumbled into motion while Pops kept the wagon to the side and watched them pass, a great river of cattle.

Moira whooped and hollered, pushing the cattle into action. She paused and drank in the scene. She catalogued everything in her memory: the sights, the sounds, the smells. Even the ever-present buzz of the flies. She didn't know the future, but she didn't figure she'd ever see the like again. After seven monotonous days on the trail, her life had blazed into motion once more.

As they neared the town, Tony circled back from the point. "I think you should lead the herd when we go through town."

Moira adjusted her hat. "You're more experienced. It should be you."

"We voted already and we all decided. None of us would have made it this far if it weren't for you."

"I didn't do anything."

"Are you fooling? You did everything. You came up with the plan to get us out of the brothel. You were the one who decided we should drive the cattle."

Emotion burned behind Moira's eyes. "What about Mr. Elder—John?"

"He's agreed. He's taking the drag." Tony lifted the corner of her mouth in a smile. "It would mean a lot to us."

Moira fisted her hands on the reins. "Then I'd be honored."

Her heart pounded as they approached the town. The cattle kept up their steady pace, nose to tail, unaware of the monumental occasion. Moira straightened her collar and adjusted her hat. She tugged her new gloves over her wrists and sat tall in the saddle.

Enormous timber walls rose before her; the great doors of the fort were propped open. The enclosure had no windows, only narrow slits for rifles. They'd contained the settlement inside the walls, safe from Indian attacks. A dirt road bisected the two sides. The only way to the stockyards on the far side of the fort was straight through town.

Moira lifted her face toward the sky and offered a brief prayer of thanks for their safe arrival. They had done something amazing.

The area inside the fort teemed with activity. Uniformed men and bustled women walked the narrow boardwalks. Smaller buildings dotted the parade grounds. An armory, no doubt, and what appeared to be a blacksmith's shop.

A young boy jogged toward them. "It's true! You're girls, ain't ya?"

Moira grinned. "Yep."

"I gotta go tell my pop it's true."

He dashed off and Moira waved to Sarah across the herd. As they moved down the dusty street, she noticed a small knot of folks standing before the blacksmith shop. They pointed and elbowed each other. Moira felt her cheeks burn. With each building they passed, more folks emerged onto the boardwalk.

A man waved his hand and shouted. "Look over here!"

Moira turned and a sudden burst of light blinded her. As her eyes slowly adjusted once more, she realized the man had taken a photograph.

The cattle, seasoned by weeks on the trail, barely twitched an ear at the commotion.

Moira figured by the time Hazel and Pops brought up the drag with John, the whole town would be watching them pass.

The stockyards appeared and Tony kicked her horse into a canter and joined her at the point. The young boy who'd spotted them on the edge of town sprinted toward the gate. He quickly released the chain and hopped on the lowest rung as the gate glided open.

The first steer rumbled into the enclosure.

The boy balancing on the fence gaped at her. "I never seen a girl riding point before."

"You have now."

"My dad thought it was a joke."

"Girls are just as capable as boys."

"Never would have thought it if I hadn't seen it with my own eyes."

"Don't you forget it."

The cattle filed in and eventually Darcy and Sarah joined Tony at the gate. The gentleman with the camera rushed toward them, his progress burdened by his cumbersome photographic equipment.

He quickly plopped his three-legged box onto the dirt packed street and held up his arms. "Don't move. This picture is going to make me famous." He leaned around the black draping. "It'll make all of you famous."

"I don't want to be famous, mister," Tony declared. "I could go with a hot meal, though."

Four hours later, Moira sat in the dining area off the barracks in her faded blue poplin. The other girls had purchased new dresses with their earnings that afternoon. They'd all taken long, hot baths and were upstairs trying on their new finery. Since she already had a perfectly good dress, Moira had saved her money for her uncertain future. Slipping into her worn outfit wasn't exactly difficult, and she'd arrived for dinner ahead of the others.

An elegant lady sashayed past in a bustled acid green poplin and Moira cupped the worn patches at her elbows. Sheriff Jack Elder appeared, his broad shoulders filling the doorway. He doffed his hat and ducked beneath the transom.

He searched the room and Moira stood, tugging her skirts over her ankles. This dress wasn't as short as the other was, but the difference brought a flush of heat into her cheeks.

He raked his hands through his hair. "Miss O'Mara. John should be along any moment."

"The girls are running late as well." She motioned toward the bustling restaurant area. "Shall we wait for them at a table?"

Once seated, the tension in her neck muscles eased. At least with her legs tucked beneath the table her skirts touched the floor. Seated, the sheriff wasn't quite as intimidating either.

Jack folded his hands on the table. "Must be nice to be back in civilization again."

"Yes and no," Moira answered honestly. "It's difficult to explain."

"Try me."

"I once took a riverboat ride up the Mississippi. It was windy and the boat swayed through the whole trip. Even after I was back on shore, I felt like I was still moving. I suppose that's what it's like. Like I'm still in motion."

"I know what you mean. Back before the trains crisscrossed the country, I rode for days on end. Same kind of thing. You get used to the motion and you can't hardly sit still anymore."

Moira smoothed her collar and tucked a stray curl behind one ear. Jack Elder wasn't the man she'd expected. His relationship with his brother wasn't what she'd expected either. There was an unspoken respect between the two men.

He smoothed the dark hair from his forehead. "My wife, Elizabeth, is never going to believe me when I tell her what happened. How you and John found each other in Fool's End."

She felt her cheeks heat. "I promise you I never stole anything from Mr. Grey."

"I believe you. A man has to trust his instincts in this job."

While his announcement was hardly a stellar endorsement, at least he believed her. "Thank you."

"I'll stop through Fool's End and see what I can dig up. Chances are someone knows why Wendell is fired up about you and the girls."

Moira recalled the sheriff's pregnant wife. "You mustn't go to all that trouble. I'm sure you want to be home."

Something shifted in his expression. A look she didn't quite understand. "I'm anxious for home, that's for certain. A few inquiries won't take long."

"What's it like? Your ranch?"

"Elizabeth and I don't live on the ranch. We live in town."

Moira started. "Oh, I just assumed…"

"I left early. I knew even as a boy I couldn't stay. I've never been a cattleman. Besides, men have a way of fighting for their territory. There were seven of us boys on that ranch. And if a man doesn't like fighting, he'd best make his own way. It's hard though, setting out on your own."

"Like John?"

"He never had much of a chance winning with our brothers. He was the baby. Sometimes in a family people get set on roles. That's what happened with John. Ma always told us to look out for him. I guess after she died we took the job too serious. If we let him grow up, it was like we lost a part of her."

Moira folded her hands in her lap. She'd been wrong

about him the whole time. She'd framed his actions based on her own experiences, and she'd been misguided. He'd cared for them all, his unlikely crew, watched out for them, risked his reputation and his life for them.

Jack cleared his throat. "I don't mean to frighten you away from our family. We're a noisy bunch, but we look out for each other."

And she had absolutely nothing to offer him in return. She was an orphan with fifty-six dollars to her name. Moira snorted softly. Fifty of the dollars she now possessed had come from John for their work on the cattle drive.

A sound caught her attention and she turned. Three of the four girls crowded the archway of the restaurant. Jack rose from his seat.

They were like a posy of wildflowers. Sarah wore a simple two-piece outfit in delicate pink calico. She had a lace collar and new kid boots peeked out from beneath her hem. Hazel had chosen a yellow party dress with several flounces. The ensemble was a touch too formal for the occasion, but Moira didn't suppose anyone cared. Tony appeared uncomfortable in her simple shirtwaist and dark navy skirt. She ran her finger around her collar and tugged.

Tears sprang into Moira's eyes. Sarah hovered on the edge of womanhood, not quite an adult, yet not quite a child either. Tony and Hazel wore the bright-eyed enthusiasm of youth.

Moira checked the stairwell. "Where's Darcy?"

"She didn't feel well." Sarah swept her pink skirts aside and approached the table. "She said she wanted to rest."

Moira half rose from her chair. "Maybe I should check on her."

"She's fine." Tony flapped her hand dismissively. "She's been acting strange since we left the mercantile."

"I suppose." Moira resumed her seat. Darcy had been quiet after their shopping trip. And goodness knew the past few days had been exhausting for all of them. "I'll check on her after dinner."

Content that Darcy was old enough to seek them out if she needed assistance, Moira once again studied the three remaining girls. With each new pair of shoes, with each new piece of clothing, the experience which had brought them together was slipping further into the past, further out of reach. They were all beautiful, all filled with the promise of a new beginning. Who knew what would happen after today?

Everything had changed and Moira's heart ached for the loss. Despite the hardships, the past several days had been wondrous.

Hazel rushed over. She paused before the table and twirled, her new yellow skirts fluttering. "Isn't my dress beautiful?"

Moira pinched one of her braids. "It's lovely. You're lovely."

Tony flopped onto a chair and planted her elbow on the table, rattling the cups and saucers perched at each setting. "I miss my other clothes."

Sarah sniffed. "I never thought I'd say this, but me too."

Moira thought of her trail outfit carefully tucked in the bottom of her valise beneath a stack of newspaper. She'd captured the wild smell, the moment and the feelings the scent recalled.

Hazel took her seat and shrugged. "I don't know which I like better. I think I like them both equal."

"Me too," Moira replied softly.

"I'll be the envy of Fort Preble," a familiar voice spoke.

Moira glanced up and gasped. John stood behind her, one hand braced on her chair, one hand on Hazel's chair. He'd shaved and his dark hair was neatly trimmed over his ears. He wore a dark gray coat with fabric-covered buttons and matching waistcoat, black trousers and a white turnover shirt collar with a black string tie.

She'd thought him handsome in his work clothes. In his formal attire, he snatched the breath from her lungs. Glancing down, she discreetly covered the careful mending on her sleeve where she'd torn the thin fabric.

They might have been a family. A big, noisy, loving family. He inquired about Darcy before taking the empty chair on Moira's right, across from his brother. For the next several minutes, their banter circled the table. Succulent dishes came and went, tea and coffee were served. The girls, decked out in their finery, displayed their best manners.

As the conversation ebbed and flowed around her, Moira's thoughts drifted further away.

"I can't believe you're passing on chocolate cake," John spoke beside her.

She pushed the plate toward him. "I couldn't eat another bite."

He accepted the offering with a boyish grin that sent her heart fluttering.

Sheriff Elder pushed back his chair and crossed his arms over his chest. He had a naturally commanding presence. The girls quieted and their expressions grew somber.

"I'll miss you girls after tomorrow," he said, his voice gruff.

John rested his fork on his plate. "The next stop is Cimarron Springs. It's a chance for a new beginning. A fresh start for everyone. I've got business in Fort Preble. Looks like I'll be able to sell the cattle for a fair price. I'm looking at using the money to purchase a few more horses. I'll be a week or two behind the rest of you."

Sarah gripped her hands together on the table. "No matter what happens, we're not going back on the orphan train."

The two brothers exchanged a look. "We're all in agreement on that. There's a boardinghouse in town and the landlady is willing to keep you for the next few weeks in exchange for some help around the place. She needs help with canning and yard work."

Sarah's face brightened. "I've never canned before, but I like to cook."

Tony stuck out her chin. "I don't know. Sounds like a trick."

"It's the best we can do right now," John said. "I'll finish my business in Fort Preble and we'll take another look at the situation. Give it a chance. It's better than sleeping on the street and stealing your dinner."

Tony's cheek bloomed pink at the reminder. "And you'll help me find my uncle?"

"I promise. You have my word. I have the information I need on your uncle. I'll do everything I can to find them. What I can't do is make promises about the results. All I can do is try."

Sarah glanced away.

Tony brushed at her eyes. "I trust you."

"What's going to happen to Champion?" Hazel spoke. "Can we take him with us?"

"I need him for a little while longer," John replied. "Don't worry. I'll take good care of him. You'll see him again."

Hazel's lower lip trembled. "I'll miss him."

"He's going to miss you, too. Don't worry. We'll be back before you know it."

After dinner the two brothers set off to complete the business Jack had mentioned earlier and the other girls retired to their rooms, chattering amongst themselves. Moira hovered in the restaurant after the others, feeling lost. Everything was settled. Everything but her future.

Recalling Darcy's absence, she took the steps two at a time and paused outside her room. She rapped three times.

"Go away," Darcy called.

Moira leaned her shoulder against the doorjamb. "No. I'm not leaving until I know you're all right."

"I'm fine. Don't worry. Just a touch of the collywobbles is all."

"Can I bring you something to drink? You must be thirsty."

"Maybe later."

The hairs on the back of Moira's neck stirred. There was something off about Darcy's voice. A certain hesitation in the other girl's answers. Looking left and right, she took a step closer and leaned her ear against the door.

A thump sounded from inside the room. Alarmed, Moira twisted the knob.

A male voice spoke, "Get a move on."

Moira shoved open the door and found a blond-haired

cowboy sprawled on the chair in Darcy's room, his hands linked behind his head, his feet crossed at the ankles.

"What is the meaning of this?" she demanded.

Darcy leaped to her feet. "It's not what you think."

Glancing between the two, Moira tightened her lips. "Actually, I don't know what to think. Who are you, sir?"

The man smirked. "Who are you, sir," he mocked in falsetto voice. "Why don't you mind your own business?"

"This girl is my business. She's in my charge."

"Well, she and I are getting married." He smacked his lips. "It ain't your business anymore, is it?"

Hazel appeared in the doorway. "Is everything all right?"

"See if you can find Mr. Elder and his brother," Moira ordered.

Hazel scooted away and the man guffawed. "They ain't gonna help you none."

"What is this all about?" Moira faced Darcy. "I need an explanation. Something…"

Darcy wrung her hands together. "He's my fiancé. We met in Texas before travelling to Fool's End."

"But you're only fifteen."

"I lied. I'm eighteen this month." Her gaze skittered away. "You've got no hold on me."

Staggering back a step, Moira pressed her hand against the wall for support. She didn't know much, but she could make a few assumptions. "You were the one who recruited those girls, weren't you?"

Darcy stuffed a hairbrush into a bag at her feet and shut the top. "It's none of your business what I done."

The answer cemented Moira's suspicions. "You recruited Hazel, Sarah and Tony," Moira repeated. She glared at the cowboy who was picking beneath his fingernails with the pointed tip of his knife.

He smirked. "She couldn't even get that right, could you, Darcy?"

Moira touched her throbbing temple. Bits of conversation flitted through her head. She recalled the glances exchanged between Darcy and Tony. The animosity, the feeling that something else had been going on the whole time. "The whole thing was planned. You gave the girls shelter and food for stealing for you. Then, when people grew suspicious, you made certain they were caught. That way you could slip away and no one would be looking for you. Except it didn't work out that way, did it?"

The man grunted. "Darcy got herself caught. I lost seven days, I did. Been waiting in this two-bit fort full of stiff collars. I overheard the sheriff talking about your crazy plan. Never thought I'd see girls leading a bunch of cows." He chuckled. "That's the funniest thing I ever heard."

Darcy glared. "It wasn't stupid. We did it. We drove that herd."

"Took you long enough. And it's not like it's that far." He nudged her hip with the toe of his boot. "Them cows could have walked on their own and gotten here faster."

Moira blocked the door. "You don't have to go with him. You're with us now."

"It's over, Moira. I'm not like the rest of you." Darcy lifted her bag. "I love Preston. I belong with him."

The man stood. "Yeah. She belongs with me."

He was young, not much older than Moira, exuding a certain shifty charm with his blond hair and lanky frame. While a girl might be taken by his glib manner, she doubted he'd fool anyone for long. She'd thought

Darcy smarter than someone like Preston, but everyone had a blind spot.

They pushed past her toward the door. As though unwilling to look her in the eye, Darcy rushed ahead, skirting the banister and rushing down the stairs. Moira made to follow her, but the cowboy grasped her shoulder.

"Get your hands off of me," Moira spoke, her teeth clenched.

"Don't you get uppity with me, you little troublemaker." He leaned closer, his breath whispering against her cheek. "Unless you want to come along."

Moira strained away. "Never."

The man laughed and shoved her. Moira stumbled and cracked her head against the doorjamb. Stars exploded in her head before the whole world went black.

Chapter Sixteen

His blood boiling, John took the stairs two at time; Jack pounded close behind. Moira lay on the floor of Darcy's room, her eyes closed and her face unnaturally pale. He knelt and cradled her head with his hands. His brother crouched on the opposite side.

Moira groaned and her eyes fluttered open. "What happened?"

He felt along her head and discovered a raised knot. "I was hoping you could tell me. Hazel said there was a man in Darcy's room."

Moira limply raised one arm. "She says he's her fiancé. She went with him willingly."

"Then how'd you end up on the floor?"

"He pushed me and I tripped. It's not as bad as it looks."

John cursed his inattention. He'd known something was suspicious about Darcy the whole time. She'd seemed older, more mature than the other girls. More worldly. He should have realized there was a man involved.

John met his brother's concerned gaze. "Find them."

With a communication born of family connections, Jack tightened his jaw and stood.

John slid his hand beneath Moira's knees and hoisted her into his arms. After what he'd heard from Hazel, he didn't want to leave her alone in the room. Sarah reached the top of the stairs and gasped.

"Which room belongs to Moira?"

Sarah led the way and opened the door to the sparsely furnished room. John carefully rested her on the bed.

Tony hovered near. "They're sending for a doctor."

"I'll be all right," Moira said. "I feel more foolish than anything."

She struggled upright and he gathered pillows behind her back. "Did you get his name?"

"Preston," Tony answered from the door. "His name is Preston. We never did know much else about him."

Moira pressed her hand against her head. "How long were you working for him?"

"I never figured he'd follow us," Sarah said. "I always thought… Well, I always thought Darcy sorta liked him more than he liked her. I figured once we were caught and he didn't come for us, well, you know. I figured Darcy would forget about him. That's why Darcy was reluctant about the escape."

"At first, anyway," Tony said. "Once she figured out he saved his own hide, she took her chances the same as the rest of us."

"Then she didn't know Preston was at the fort?" John watched the girls for any sign of deception.

"No. I don't think she knew until she saw him today. That's when she started acting strange."

Moira touched the back of her head and winced. "I sure am tired of feeling unsafe all the time."

John tucked two fingers beneath her chin. "If the doc checks you out and says you're okay, and if you rest a while, I'll show you a couple of tricks for defending yourself."

Seeing Moira hurt had ignited a rage in him he'd never felt before. He fought against the guilt and anger; he might have had his suspicions, but he hadn't seen this coming.

He tucked a curl behind her ear. "Promise you'll never scare me like that again. It took ten years off my life, finding you like that."

Moira offered a shy smile. "You must be getting tired of rescuing me."

"Never."

His chest swelled. He may not be a hero, but she sure made him feel like one.

After receiving a clean bill of health from the doctor and a good night's rest, Moira and the girls met John back in the barracks' restaurant.

Tony had donned her trail drive clothing and was itching for the instruction on self-defense that John had promised earlier. "It isn't fair that we're not safe. That other people can take advantage of us just because we're smaller. No one tells the boys they can't go out alone at night."

"The question isn't whether it's fair or not," John replied. "The point is keeping you girls safe."

"I wish I had been packing a gun. I'd have shot him," Tony declared.

"We're going to use the resources we have," John said. "And those resources are brains and common sense. We'll need some space to work."

Moira helped Sarah push the chairs against the wall. While she didn't have much confidence in learning skills to outmuscle a grown man, she was willing to listen. Once they'd cleared the room, the girls took their seats on the line of chairs while Moira stood a distance away.

John Elder paced before them, his arms crossed over his chest. "I grew up with six older brothers and I learned a few things. First off, don't make yourself a victim. A bully isn't looking for a fair fight, he's looking for an easy win. Look how Miss O'Mara is standing."

Moira started at her name.

"She's got her arms crossed over her chest, her chin is tucked. She's making herself smaller. She doesn't want to be noticed. You know what a bully sees? He sees a victim. Stand up straighter."

Moira glared and planted her hands on her hips. "Like this."

"That's much better. Her head is up and she's taking up more space. Showing confidence. She's less of a target."

Tony fisted her hands. "Are you saying it's our fault?"

"No. No." John waved his hands. "I'm offering you tools. The most important thing to remember is that fighting is your last option. When you're fighting a larger opponent, chances are, you're not going to win. You have two other choices before fighting back." He held up his thumb. "You can run." He stuck out his index finger. "Or you can hide. When you're in a vulnerable place, stay alert. That means being aware of your surroundings. Know your escapes, know your hiding places. If your head is up, you're aware."

Sarah folded her hands. "What if you don't feel very confident?"

"Fake it. People believe what they see. If you have to fight, get your attacker on your level. Use what you have. An elbow in the stomach doubles your attacker over and you've got a clean shot at a face. Don't forget to scream. Make noise. It's not time for being ladylike."

"I'm not sure if I could do that." Sarah glanced around.

"Of course you can. This is your life. It's not Sunday tea in the parlor. Use everything you have."

"Wendell caught me off guard," Tony spoke. "Otherwise I would have socked him." She swung her arm in a wide arc.

"And chances are, he'd have socked you back. Men are bigger and stronger than you are. Your best defense is a good offense. Watch his hands. You can duck out of the way if you see him cock back his elbow."

Tony swung her arm again.

"No," John admonished. "Not like that."

He searched the group and his gaze lit on Moira. "Watch me, I'll show you." He carefully pulled her around beside him. "Stay on the balls of your feet, that way you're ready to run at the first sign of trouble. Keep your hands up and protect your face."

Moira lifted her arms and John shook his head.

"I feel ridiculous."

"Not like that." He circled around behind her and wrapped his arms around her waist, not touching, but she could feel the heat of his body through her clothing. "Keep your elbows tight to your body and hands up."

Moira swallowed around the lump in her throat. "Like this?"

"That's it." He stepped to her right. "You're looking

for an opening, a chance for escape. Go for the vulnerable spots. Eyes, ears, nose, throat."

Moira tightened her fist.

"The best way to win a fight is to avoid it altogether," the cowboy continued. "I can't repeat this enough—trust your instincts. If someone is making you uncomfortable, put as much distance as you can between you and that person. If you have to be out at night, make certain you're not alone. All of you were picked up when you were alone."

"I walked right into him," Moira mumbled.

"What was that?"

"The deputy. I walked right into him. I was distracted, I had my head down. I bumped into him. Then he looked at me and he just kept looking. Like he was studying me or something. I could have run or hollered. I knew there was something strange about the way he kept staring at me. But I didn't do anything. I just stood there."

"That's what I'm talking about." John clapped. "Moira brings up a great example of why it's so important to be aware of your surroundings. It's also a good case of why you should trust your instincts. I never trust a man who's mean to dogs or children. Anybody who picks on somebody more vulnerable isn't trustworthy."

"But what if that person seems nice at first?" Sarah asked, her voice low.

"Most folks can't hide their true natures for very long. Even when they're charming, you can see bits and pieces of the real person showing through the cracks. Never settle for a man who drinks too much or treats you bad. You're better than that."

"But what if you're not?" Sarah asked. "What if you're not better than that?"

The cowboy grew serious. "We're all God's creatures. You're all worthy of love and acceptance, and anybody who tells you any different is wrong. Just wrong."

"Even if you've done something bad? Even if you messed up?"

"What would the world be without forgiveness?"

Tony stepped forward. "This is a lesson on defense. Y'all want to hash up the past, that's fine. But I don't feel bad. I did what I had to do. We all did. There wasn't much other choice."

Moira dropped her arms. "Is this about Preston?"

Hazel sat in one of the abandoned chairs pressed against the wall. "It was Darcy's boyfriend that got us into trouble."

Moira had already pieced together the circumstances, but she wanted to hear it from the girls. "How?"

Sarah squirmed in her seat. "I guess we were drawn to each other from the beginning. Darcy had been on her own the longest. She was confident. She knew things."

"She had nice clothes. She knew stuff." Tony hung her head. "At first we were just taking food. Then she convinced us we should take more."

Sarah heaved a sigh. "You can convince yourself of anything, I suppose, if you try hard enough. The stealing was getting out of hand, but I didn't know how to back out. I tried once, but Darcy said she'd turn me in."

"Preston was the worst," Hazel said and the group turned in her direction. "Darcy wanted him to like her."

Moira pressed a hand against her throbbing forehead. "You're probably right."

Having seen Darcy's boyfriend, Moira didn't doubt the draw he had over her.

Sarah stared at her hands. "What do we do now?"

"What do you mean?"

"What about Darcy?"

"I don't think there's much we can do," John said. "Jack searched. He didn't find a trace of either of them. They're of age. You can't save someone who doesn't want to be saved."

Moira glared at him. "We should at least try."

"If we drag her back here, she'll only run away again."

"But we'll be abandoning her."

Tony snorted. "She abandoned us first."

Moira gaped. "Matthew says, 'If a man have an hundred sheep, and one of them be gone astray, doth he not leave the ninety and nine, and goeth into the mountains, and seeketh that which is gone astray?'"

They stared at her, their looks pitying.

John spoke first. "We don't even know where to look. And she doesn't want to be found. We only know their first names. They're adults according to the law. They may have gone in any number of directions."

"It's not right. It's like we're leaving her behind. Abandoning her. I shouldn't have started this. If we'd never gone on the cattle drive…"

"Then what?" Tony shook her head. "She would have caught up with Preston earlier."

Sarah toyed with the embroidered cuff of her sleeve. "She knows where we're going. She knows we'll be in Cimarron Springs. The town can't be that big. If she wants help, she knows where to find us."

"Someone should care." Moira choked off a sob. "We should care."

"We do care." Sarah touched her arm. "But she doesn't want our help. She never did."

Not for the first time Moira recognized the gulf separating them. Never once had they mentioned Preston or his involvement. The girls had known why they were being held, yet they hadn't trusted her with the truth. Even John had suspected the real story long before she had. He'd been trying to tell her all along, only she hadn't listened.

She'd mistaken his easy nature for apathy. She'd been wrong. He was more watchful, more attuned to the needs of everyone around him. Even *her* needs.

Tony perched near Hazel. "Darcy always kept a wall between us. I knew she wasn't going to stick around long. She was with us, but not. We all knew she was going to leave sooner or later. You must have realized that?"

Somewhere Moira *had* realized that. She'd pushed the truth aside, because she knew if she accepted that Darcy didn't belong, she'd have to admit that she didn't belong either.

John pulled a chair out and straddled the seat. "We've all done bad things at one time or another. Doesn't mean we're bad people."

"Do you think God forgives us?"

"Of course He does. The hard part is forgiving yourself. Tomorrow you're getting on a train for Cimarron Springs. It's a new start. For everyone."

Moira's throat tightened. She'd started over more than once in her life. Always before she'd seen a new beginning as a challenge. Not anymore. She didn't want anything to change. Because once they reached Cimarron Springs they'd no longer be the Calico Cowboys. John Elder didn't need them anymore.

She wanted him to need *her*.

Chapter Seventeen

Moira spent the first week in Cimarron Springs sketching. She splurged on a new sketchpad and pencils. The pictures poured from her fingers in a frenzy. Normally sketching was her hobby. As the leaves fell and the brisk fall air tinted her cheeks pink, the drawings became her obsession.

A full month had passed since they'd arrived in Cimarron Springs. September had turned into October, and the weather was temperate. She hadn't seen much of John Elder in that time. He was traveling more often than not, though he did check up on the girls when he was in town.

She captured the memories as quickly as her fingers allowed, whittling her pencils down to the nub. The work kept her from thinking. About the past, about the future, about anything. She didn't have to think about how she didn't belong. While the other girls had flourished, Moira puttered around without a clear direction.

Sarah backed her way through the door from the kitchen and spun around, a mason jar in each of her hands. "Look! We've finished canning the peaches."

Moira flashed an indulgent grin. "Is there any room next to the tomatoes and the apple butter?"

"I can't help it. This is the most fun I've had in ages. You should come and join us."

"That's all right. I'm sketching."

Sarah whistled her way back into the kitchen. She and the boardinghouse owner, Agnes, had been inseparable almost from the day the girls arrived. The two shared a love of cooking and baking, and, most recently, canning. They'd spent the past week in the kitchen whipping up dish after dish.

A knock sounded. Realizing Agnes was up to her elbow in peaches, Moira answered the door and discovered Deputy McCoy. The young man was tall with jet-black hair and brilliant green eyes. From what Moira had gathered, all of the McCoys shared the distinctive coloring. From the few snatches of gossip she'd heard, David had recently married his sweetheart, a pretty blonde with blue eyes and a smile that must have broken more than one heart before she fell in love with David.

He gripped his hat brim. "The marshal has some news. For Tony."

The younger girl appeared in the doorway. "About my uncle?"

"He didn't say. I can walk you over."

Tony glanced at Moira. "Will you come along?"

"Of course."

Moira quickly donned her bonnet and the three of them walked the short distance to the marshal's offices. A few people tipped their hats along the way, smiling greetings. She returned their good wishes with a hesitant wave, always feeling like a bit of a fraud. The girls were a novelty around here.

Upon arriving at the offices, the marshal motioned them toward the two sturdy wooden chairs before his desk.

They exchanged greetings and Moira took the chance to study the marshal. He was older than his deputy was and more world-weary. As though sensing a kindred spirit, she knew instinctively he'd seen more in his life than his young deputy.

He brushed the mahogany hair from his coffee-colored eyes, took his own seat behind the desk. She caught the scent of fresh paint and wood shavings.

The marshal noted her curiosity. "We had a fire not long ago. Had to take the place down to the studs and start over."

"Oh dear. Was anybody hurt?"

"Nope. It all worked out. Rather well, if I do say so myself."

He grinned and Moira shook her head. "You seem awfully pleased," she commented.

"Well, got myself a wife out of the deal."

"JoBeth, from the telegraph office?"

"That's the one."

Moira recalled seeing her once or twice when she visited Agnes. "Your Cora is quite precious."

The girl often accompanied JoBeth on her visits.

"That's my niece. Although we'll have a baby around the house next spring." Flaming color infused his cheeks. "Uh, shouldn't have let that slip. We haven't told anyone yet."

Moira hid a grin at his mixture of pride and embarrassment. "Your secret is safe with me."

Tony shifted impatiently. "Enough with the chitchat. How come you called us in?"

Marshal Cain smiled indulgently. "Of course. You should be aware that while I have some good news, I have some bad news as well. I think we've found your uncle. My wife sent out a few inquiries since she works at the telegraph office. Anyway, we found him in El Paso. He's out of work right now and doesn't feel he can properly care for you."

Tony blinked rapidly. "Well. It's not like I need much. I can work, too."

"As to that," a voice spoke from the doorway. "I might have a solution."

Moira bolted upright. John Elder stood in the doorway. His welcoming grin sent her heart beating erratically and her palms dampened. "Mr. Elder. I didn't realize you'd returned," Moira said.

"Only got in this morning."

"You're chitchatting again." Tony crossed her arms over her chest. "What's your idea, cowboy?"

"Marshal Cain told me about your problem this morning. I need some extra hands at the ranch. I'm building up a stock of horses. You'll have to live in Cimarron Springs. But if your uncle agrees, you'll be together."

Tony launched herself from the chair and threw her arms around the cowboy. He staggered backward and patted her back.

The girl sprang away. "I have to tell Hazel and Sarah." She dashed toward the door and paused. "You coming?" she asked Moira.

"In a minute," Moira replied. "I won't be far behind."

Tony slammed out the door in a flurry of petticoats. Moira smiled at the cowboy. "Thank you. That was a very kind thing for you to do."

He propped one shoulder against the doorjamb. "Not really. Works out for both of us."

"How many horses have you acquired so far?"

She was falling in love with him.

She'd been skirting the truth for ages. For a time she'd wondered if her feelings would fade, if she was confusing her blossoming love for him with the adventure they'd shared. She'd convinced herself that she'd kept her feelings in check. She couldn't have been more wrong.

He was always polite and deferential toward her, and sometimes she wondered if he liked her as well. Yet he hadn't tried to kiss her again. And they hadn't been alone since the cattle drive.

There were things she needed to settle. With Tommy. With the Giffords. She had nothing to offer John Elder. She was a twenty-two-year-old woman who could roll cigars and drive a herd of cattle. Two skills John had little need of. And even if she did declare her feelings, was there a chance he might return them? The risk terrified her into silence.

"I've acquired thirty-four more horses," John said. "I've got a line on another twenty up north. Mustangs. Good stock."

The marshal cleared his throat and Moira started. She'd forgotten he was even there. When John was in the room, he captured her attention. A sheen of sweat covered her forehead. She'd nearly blurted out her feelings before a near stranger.

She grasped a newspaper from the marshal's desk and fanned herself. "That sounds like quite a herd. You've got a lot of work ahead of you."

"I do. It'll take a while. Building up the ranch." The tips of his ears turned red. "It'll be worth the wait."

What was he saying? *It'll be worth the wait.* Was he trying to tell her something?

The marshal's chair creaked and Moira jerked upright. She'd forgotten about him again. He didn't appear annoyed at the oversight.

"What about Sarah?" Moira changed the subject. "Have you found her sister yet?"

"Well, that's the thing." The marshal straightened the cup of coffee resting on the corner of his desk. "I don't think Sarah wants her sister found. All the information she's given me has been vague. I discovered a gentleman I thought might be her brother-in-law, but he didn't seem real interested in answering my queries. I'm just not certain how much more I should look."

Moira fanned herself more vigorously. "Her sister's husband didn't want her before. I suppose she's worried that's still the case."

"It's a good assumption." The marshal sipped his coffee.

The sight sent a sudden rush of melancholy through her. She missed Pops drinking coffee over the cook fire. She saw him once in a while, around Cimarron Springs. He'd stayed in town. He'd said he needed the rest, but Moira had the feeling he couldn't leave until they were all sorted out. Until everyone had a place. But the relationship was different now, more formal. Just as she knew it would be when they'd parted ways at Fort Preble.

The marshal lifted one shoulder in a careless shrug. "I don't see why Sarah can't stick around Cimarron Springs. She sure has taken a shine to Agnes. The feeling appears to be mutual."

John pushed off from the doorway. "Would you be

willing to speak with Agnes before we set something into motion? I don't want Sarah disappointed again."

"I'll have my wife take care of it. She and Agnes go way back. Wouldn't be surprised if she brings up the subject first."

Moira didn't have any doubt of the outcome. The solution was ideal—for both of them. Despite her confidence, she was grateful for John's careful handling of the situation. He was correct, the girls had suffered enough disappointments. They didn't need any more.

John crossed his arms over his chest. "That leaves Hazel."

"And Darcy," Moira added quickly.

The cowboy frowned. "We've talked about this. She's an adult. She's getting married. There's nothing we can do unless she wants our help. Near as I can tell, she doesn't."

"He's right." The marshal kicked back in his chair. "I've gotten some reports out of Illinois. Could be a coincidence, but there's a couple that matches the description of your friend and her fiancé. Appears Preston likes to cheat at poker. He's going to meet a bad end if he's not careful."

"Keep us informed," Moira pleaded. "I know Darcy is a touch prickly, but she was a good worker. She pulled her weight along with the rest of us. I don't like the hold that man has on her. She was different when she wasn't around him."

"I'll let you know if I find out anything else. I wouldn't get your hopes up, Miss O'Mara. Love has a way of making people do strange things."

Afraid she might reveal something in her expression,

Moira kept her gaze firmly affixed on her lap. Any moment she'd blurt out the words and shock them both.

I'm falling in love with you.

Then what would she say? *Would you like to go for ice cream?* She'd gone and lost her wits like Sarah's Great-Aunt Sylvia.

"That leaves us with Hazel," John said.

The marshal braced his hands against his desk. "My wife and I could take her in. She's not much older than our little one."

"No." Moira half rose from her seat, caught the startled gazes of the two gentlemen and plopped back down again. "That is to say, I don't think we should disrupt her life just yet."

"The offer stands. There's always room for her with us."

"Thank you. That's very kind."

The obvious question hung in the air. What was she going to do? For the past month she hadn't let herself think about much of anything concerning the future. The more time passed, the more she worried she'd never find her brother, Tommy.

I love you. How do you feel about a wife who betrayed her own brother?

"I should go." Before she blurted out something revealing and embarrassed all of them. "If you discover anything else of importance…"

"Don't leave just yet." The marshal lifted a hand. "I haven't showed you the best part. You're famous. Check that paper you're fanning yourself with."

She loosened her death grip on the paper enough to read the headline. The Calico Cowboys of Cimarron Springs. Her jaw dropped. "Where did you get this?"

"A reporter from the *St. Louis Chronicle* was at Fort Preble when you came through. They even sketched your picture."

Moira recognized the four girls on their horses before the stockyard gates. "He never said he was a reporter."

"Either way, the *Omaha Bee* picked up the story as well." The marshal slid a second newspaper across his desk. "You and the girls are quite a sensation."

John tugged the newspaper from her limp fingers and read, "'Led by a feisty redhead, the girls arrived at Fort Preble under the watchful eye of their stoic trail boss, John Elder.' Huh. You're feisty and I'm stoic?"

"That's enough." Moira touched her warm cheeks. "I'd rather absorb this news in private." Never in her wildest imagination had she thought about the story appearing publicly. "It's quite odd, discovering that one has become a sensation."

Was that why people were tipping their hats and waving on the boardwalk? Because some overzealous reporter had fashioned them into a sideshow?

The marshal took one look at her face and flipped over the newspaper. "It'll blow over soon enough. I'd warn the girls to keep up their guard. I've seen things like this happen before, and we're bound to have a few reporters showing up."

Moira groaned. "Reporters? You really think so?"

"Don't worry. My deputy will keep a watch out. As long as we don't add any fuel, this will blow over soon enough."

"I suppose that's not the worst thing. If there's nothing more…" She wanted nothing more than to escape and gather her thoughts in private.

The marshal's expression grew somber. "There is one more thing."

The cowboy straightened. "You need a moment alone?"

"No. You better stay. This concerns you, too."

Moira rested her forehead on the edge of the desk. "I don't think I can handle any more surprises."

John didn't like the tone of the marshal's voice. "Well, spit it out. What's so serious?"

"It's Hazel. She's been stealing from the mercantile."

"That's outrageous." Moira snatched John's hand. "Are you certain?"

He glanced at their intertwined fingers. Had she taken his hint? Did she understand that he was building up his ranch before he courted her? He wasn't certain. He'd dropped enough clues to his feelings. When he'd spoken earlier, she'd had an odd expression on her face. Was that a good sign or a bad sign?

"I'm certain," the marshal continued. "Mr. Stuart complained. Then Agnes found a stash of candy and baubles when she was cleaning out the girl's room."

He lifted a sack from the floor and dumped the contents on the table. Contraband scattered across the surface. Beads and ribbons and penny candies.

Moira lifted a peppermint drop. "Why steal something if she's not even going to eat it?"

"I don't know. But it's got to stop. I've given her some leeway considering what she's been through. I don't think we're doing her any favors by not addressing the problem."

John squeezed Moira's trembling hand. "We'll handle this."

Together they crossed the distance to the boarding-house. The girls and Agnes had gathered in the parlor, laughing and chattering about the discovery of Tony's uncle.

Agnes lifted her head when they entered. "This calls for a celebration, wouldn't you say?"

"I think we should make a cake." Sarah stood and dusted her hands. "Chocolate."

Tony nodded. "That's my favorite."

The girls bustled into the kitchen and Moira placed a hand on Hazel's shoulder. "Why don't you stay behind?"

The young girl paled. "This is about Mr. Stuart's store, isn't it?"

Moira nodded.

Hazel sat on the divan and Moira and John flanked her. Moira spread the contents of the bag on the table. "These things were discovered in your room."

A single fat tear rolled down the little girl's cheek. "Are you going to send me away?"

"Absolutely not," Moira declared.

John admired the fierce note of protectiveness in her tone.

Hazel's face brightened, then fell once more. "Sarah and Tony have a family. I don't have anything."

"That doesn't give you the right to take things."

"Am I a bad person?"

Moira sighed. "No. Remember what Mr. Elder said at the fort? Well, he was right. We have to forgive ourselves before we can move on. I have my own confession to make. I stole something too once."

Hazel gasped.

John gaped. His memory flitted over something she'd

said the day he'd gotten skunked on the trail. If she could go back to any time in history, *she'd right a wrong*.

"What did you steal?" Hazel asked.

"I stole a watch." Moira snapped open her reticule and fished out a brass watch. "When I was your age I lived with a family that wasn't very nice to me."

"Like Mrs. Vicky?"

"Very much like Mrs. Vicky. This watch belonged to Mr. Gifford. My brother and I rolled cigars and Mr. Gifford timed us. I hated the sound of the ticking. One day, I couldn't stand it anymore. When he left it on the table, I took it. I don't even know why. It happened so quickly. I hid it in the pantry behind a tin of crackers."

"What happened then?"

"Mrs. Gifford and I went to the store that morning. When I came back, my brother was gone." Moira's voice grew thick with emotion. "You see, Mr. Gifford thought Tommy had stolen the watch. They fought and…" Her voice broke. "They fought and Tommy ran away. I figured Tommy would come back and I could explain things, admit what I'd done. Only he never came back."

John's throat tightened. Her obsession over her brother crystallized in his mind. No wonder she wouldn't be at peace until she found him.

Hazel blinked. "Did you ever find him?"

"No. I'm still looking. I kept this watch because I didn't know what else to do. After so much time had passed, I was afraid of admitting the truth. Of confessing what I'd done. It's time I returned the watch. It isn't right, keeping it after all this time."

"What if he's mad?"

"I have to take responsibility for my own actions."

Hazel stared at the table. "I guess I should return these things."

"Mr. Elder and I will accompany you. But I think it's important we set things straight before we move on. For both of our sakes."

"Can I help make the cake?" Hazel said.

"Of course," Moira said.

She left the room, and Moira kept her face averted.

John ached to reach across the distance, but he was afraid she'd pull away. "That was a very brave thing you just did."

"I should have done it a long time ago. I was holding on to the past, I guess."

"I think you still are."

She tucked her chin to her chest. "What else would you like me to do?"

"Forgive yourself."

"I can't. You must see that. Tommy has to forgive me."

"What happened with Tommy wasn't your fault." John touched her chin and turned her face toward him. "Listen to me. You weren't there when Tommy and Mr. Gifford fought. You don't know what happened between them."

"I know I set the whole event in motion." Tears welled in her eyes. "And Tommy must blame me. I haven't heard from him since that day."

"You mustn't give up hope."

"If it wasn't the watch, then it was just me."

"No, it wasn't you."

John had been relentlessly searching for her brother since before they'd left Fort Preble. Two days ago they'd received a telegram from a man who'd seen their story in the paper. A man who claimed to be her brother. The marshal thought it was legitimate, but no one wanted to see Moira disappointed.

Her words added fuel to his hunt. He thought of his brothers, of Jack and Robert, their children and their wives. Anything could happen. There were no guarantees in life. He wasn't waiting until he had a successful ranch before he'd court Moira, he was only waiting until she squared things with her brother. He didn't know what the future held for the siblings, and he didn't want Moira torn between the love of her brother and his love. If they needed time together, he'd wait. Only he loved her and he didn't want to wait. He wanted to start their lives together right then. He'd trust in God's plan. If the timing was right, he'd know.

If he found her brother, if he proved to her she could forgive herself…after that, he'd campaign in earnest. Maybe she'd have him, maybe she wouldn't, but he wasn't giving up without a fight.

"I almost forgot," he said. "I have something for you."

Moira sat with hands folded in her lap, her knuckles white. What did he have for her? She couldn't tell from his expression if the delivery was a good thing or a bad thing.

John returned a short while later with two enormous fabric-wrapped boxes.

He set the colorful packages on the low table before her and stepped back.

Moira tilted her head. "What are they?"

"You have to open them to find out."

She hesitantly lifted the lid from the first box and

gasped. A beautiful porcelain doll rested in the satin lining.

John cleared his throat. "It took me a while to find one with red hair."

Of all the things she'd been expecting, this had never crossed her mind. The exquisite doll wore an emerald green velvet coat with tiny brass buttons.

He gestured toward the other box. "There's more stuff in there. Clothes and things."

He rubbed the back of his neck.

She reverently lifted the doll free, enchanted by the details of her painted face and elaborate clothing. Keeping the doll firmly tucked at her side, she lifted the lid from the second box and revealed a trove of tiny clothing in satins and velvets, as well as several tiny pairs of shoes.

Her throat dry, she blinked several times. "I don't understand. Is this a mistake? Shouldn't this be for one of the girls?"

He reached for the box. "It was a dumb idea," he spoke gruffly. "I'll take it back."

Moira leaned away. "No you won't."

"Then you like the doll?"

If she didn't know better, she'd think he was embarrassed.

"I love her. She's beautiful. How did you find something so perfect?"

"I saw how much you liked Hazel's doll. I thought you'd like one of your own."

Moira opened her mouth to speak, but emotion caught her words.

He gestured again. "I bought one for Hazel, too.

Didn't want her to be jealous. And I got Tony a rifle and Sarah a fancy comb and brush."

"You didn't have to get us anything."

"I wanted to thank you."

"For what?"

"For reminding me of what's important. I don't regret coming out here. I'm where I need to be. But I'm a whole lot more thankful for the things I have. I'm not taking things for granted anymore."

She'd been wrong about her feelings. She wasn't *falling* in love with him. She was *in* love with him.

He paced before the fireplace. "Uh, well, looks like the girls will start school next week."

"Tony's not real pleased."

"She doesn't like being cooped up inside for too long."

Moira stared at the doll's lovely face, the eyes a shade of green she was used to seeing in the mirror. If she didn't know better, she'd think the doll had been specially made in her likeness. "I only went to school until I was twelve."

After the admission, she kept her eyes averted.

"That's better than me," John said. "I went to school until I was sixteen, but I stopped paying attention around eleven." He offered a lopsided grin. "You know that whatever happens, there will always be a place for you here."

Her chest tightened. She was foolish to read anything special into his words. She was simply another responsibility. Sheriff Taylor had called him an honorable cowboy. Of course he was looking out for her. He was looking out for her the same as he'd looked out for the other girls.

She cleared her throat. "How are things for you?"

"Good. Real good. The house needs work. The pastures are good, though. I need more hands. It'll be a proper working ranch soon."

"I guess things turned out okay."

"They did." He paused. "They'll work out for you, too. You'll see."

He knelt before her and cupped her face with both hands. "I'm fixing to kiss you, if you don't mind."

Too startled for thinking clear, Moira nodded.

The pull between them sparked into a flame as his lips found hers and his hands slipped around her waist. A fierce yearning took hold and she wrapped her arms around his neck, pulling him closer as she tried to pour her feelings into the kiss. The moment stretched out and new wondrous feelings surged through her heart.

He stood, stepped back a pace and planted his hands on his hips.

She gaped at his sudden withdrawal. "Did I do something wrong?"

Had her enthusiasm embarrassed him?

"Of course not, but I can't think while we're kissing and I have something I need to say." He crossed his arms over his chest. "I love you and I want to marry you. It'll be hard. I'm just starting out. I don't know what the years will bring, but I'll always take care of you. I don't want you to answer yet. Think on it for a couple of days." He heaved a breath. "This is harder than I thought it would be."

Her thoughts tumbled in confusion. He loved her, but he didn't want an answer. Why was he waiting? "Are you certain?"

"Of course I'm certain. I mean it though, I don't want

your answer until next week. I need to know you're with me all the way.

"All...all right." She wasn't sure what else to say.

He huffed out a breath as though he'd just run a mile. "Well, that's settled then."

After his hasty retreat, Moira sat in stunned silence.

He loved her, he wanted to marry her, yet he didn't want an answer yet. Was he uncertain of her feelings, or his?

Chapter Eighteen

A week following John's startling marriage proposal, Moira plucked weeds from the garden behind the boardinghouse. She had to make her decision today. Confusion had her thoughts jumbled. She kept waiting for a sign to give her some indication of why John had wanted her to wait before giving her answer. She was no closer to figuring out her next move and she'd decided to avoid people altogether. Part of her wanted to march right over to John's ranch and give him a piece of her mind. Why had he put her off? Was he having doubts? She'd snatched her bonnet from the peg three times this morning, and three times her courage had faltered before she reached the door.

When the gate squeaked open, she kept her head bent, hoping the person would note her lack of interest and move on. Footsteps padded through the rows of vegetables—late tomatoes and squash. She should have told John that if he didn't want an answer right then, he shouldn't have asked the question. She should have let the Cains take custody of Hazel. Should, should, should. Despite all the things she should be doing, here she was, crouching between the rows of pea vines, plucking weeds while wearing the gloves she'd kept from the cattle drive like a sentimental fool.

"Moira?"

At the familiar voice, her breath caught and her vision blurred. Certain she was mistaken, she kept her head bent and yanked another weed from the soft-tilled earth.

"Moira," her brother whispered. "Aren't you going to turn around?"

She lifted her hand above her head and swiped the moisture from her face on her shoulder. "I can't."

Tommy stepped closer and extended his hand. "Sure you can."

Moira grasped his fingers and he pulled her to her feet. She stared at him, searching his face, cataloging the changes the years had wrought. He wasn't the image of a gangly teen she'd locked away in her memory. He was inches taller and his face had changed. His cheeks were thinner and his shoulders broader than when she'd seen him last.

Her heartbeat raced and her stomach clenched. She'd waited four years for this moment and couldn't think of a single thing to say.

The corner of his mouth turned up in a hesitant grin. "Aren't you happy to see me?"

Collapsing into his arms, Moira sobbed. "I can't believe you're here."

He tightened his hold and murmured soothing words against the top her head.

Gathering herself, she stepped back and pinched off her gloves, then brushed at her dress. "I wish I'd have known you were coming. I would have worn something different. You should come inside. We'll have a cup of tea."

They stepped back through the kitchen. After hasty introductions and more tears, Agnes hustled them into the parlor with promises of tea and cakes.

They sat across from each other on the chintz-covered chairs flanking the fire. After all the anticipation, Moira found herself uncertain. "I'm sorry," she blurted.

Tommy rested his ankle on his bent knee. "For what?"

"It's my fault you ran away. And then you never came back."

"That wasn't your fault." He tipped forward and gripped the arms of her chair.

"But I stole Mr. Gifford's watch. Then he accused you."

Her brother collapsed back into his seat. "That wasn't the reason. Not the whole of it, anyway. I just figured the old fool lost his own watch. Never even occurred to me you might have taken it. We were going to have it out sooner or later. That part was inevitable. I was so full of anger. It wouldn't have mattered what he accused me of that day. I was leaving one way or another."

Nausea rose in the back of her throat. She was relieved and hurt at the same time. Questions filled her head. "Then you didn't stay away because you blamed me?"

"I stayed away because I knew I would only make things worse for you. Those first few months were rough. I found what work I could. Most times I was sleeping out in the fields."

"Why didn't you ever come for me?"

"I did. Must have been a year and a half ago. But you'd already left the Giffords."

For a moment she didn't believe him. Searching his face, she realized the truth. "Then you *did* try and find me?"

"I wrote every few months that first year. When I never received a reply, I stopped writing."

"They never gave me your letters."

"I should have guessed as much." He clasped his hands together and lifted his thumbs. "But I was struggling for my own survival."

"How did you finally find me?"

"This." He held up a copy of the *Omaha Bee*. "I read the story. I knew from the description and the name it had to be you. How in the world did you wind up on a cattle drive?"

"Looking for you, of course. One of the maids at the Gifford house found part of your telegram in the fireplace. I made out the name Mr. Grey and Fool's End."

"I only wish that maid had had the guts to bring you my letters sooner."

Moira waved his complaints aside. "You have to tell me. Why were you in Fool's End?"

Another knock sounded at the door. She made to rise and Tommy waved her down. "That's the reason now. She was waiting. Giving us a few moments alone."

Who was waiting?

Moira brushed at her skirts and straightened her collar. The door opened revealing a young woman with honey-colored hair pulled into a simple knot at the back of her head. She wore a smart gingham dress in shades of yellow with puffed sleeves and a high waist. With her hovering in the open door, the wind whipped at her skirts, plastering them against her belly and revealing the slight bulge of her stomach.

Moira's eyes widened. "Is this your…"

"Wife. Yes. This is Ava Grey. Well." He grinned. "Used to be Grey. Now it's Ava O'Mara."

The woman smiled shyly and rubbed her belly.

Moira rose unsteadily to her feet. "It's, uh, it's a pleasure to meet you, Mrs. O'Mara."

"Call me Ava. We're sisters now."

"Uhhh…well…uhhh…where are you staying?"

Tommy wrapped his arm possessively around his wife's waist. "Over at the hotel. Can you believe it? We're living up in Wichita. That's not too far. We can see each other as often as we want. Say, you should come by the hotel for dinner."

"Dinner?"

"Yes. And bring that fellow, what was his name?"

"John Elder," Ava replied in her breathy voice.

Moira's tongue felt thick and uncooperative. "How do you know Mr. Elder?"

"I wired looking for you." Tommy appeared sheepish. "I hadn't planned on coming out, but he sent the money. Sent enough for both of us. I told him I'd pay him back, but he wouldn't hear about it. Told me that he owed you and you didn't like asking for help."

Don't answer just yet, John had said. He was waiting. Not because he was uncertain of his feelings for her, but because he wasn't certain of her feelings for *him*.

Ava pressed a hand into the small of her back. "My father didn't approve of our marriage. That's why we left Fool's End."

"And that other fellow." Tommy's expression darkened. "This fellow Wendell had a crush on her. Kept stirring up trouble."

All the pieces of the puzzle fit together. Mr. Grey's feigned ignorance. Wendell's anger.

Her head reeled and her attention scattered as they chatted for a few more minutes, catching up on the lost years. When Ava's eyelids drooped with fatigue, Tommy quickly wrapped up the pleasantries.

He caught Moira in a quick shoulder embrace without releasing his wife. "I'll see you tonight. Can't wait to catch up."

Ava tucked herself against her husband's side. "I'm sorry about everything that happened. I knew my dad was angry. I never expected him to act so outrageously."

"Don't apologize," Moira said. "You can do me a favor, though."

"What's that?"

"Make your peace with him. Your father."

"But after what he did—"

Moira held up a hand. "He was frightened. He was scared he'd never see you again. Sometimes people do crazy things when they're scared."

"I don't know." Ava hesitated. "He was awfully mad when we left. He disowned me."

"At least let him know where you are. That there's a baby on the way."

The two exchanged a look.

"She's right," John said. "Moira is right."

"If you think so." Ava gazed adoringly at her husband.

The pair stared at each other with such devotion, Moira felt her own cheeks heat.

A few moments later, Moira stepped onto the porch and followed their progress. What had she been expecting? Tommy had moved on with his life. She'd been hanging on to her guilt for years. Using it like a wall to keep her from living. From truly experiencing life. She'd been afraid.

The watch had been returned and she didn't expect a reply.

She hadn't needed Tommy's forgiveness, he had never blamed her. She had needed to forgive herself. She'd needed to understand that she'd been a child unfairly tasked with an adult promise. Her brother had moved on with his life. They weren't kids anymore. Their relationship had changed. They would spend time together, visit, talk, but she couldn't expect things to go back to the way they were.

That's what John had been trying to tell her all along. She had wanted to go back and relive the years, take up where they'd left off, when she should have realized their lives would never be the same.

Tommy had a new family. It didn't mean they weren't a family as well, just that it had expanded. He was living his life. It was time for her to do the same. And she knew just where to start.

An hour later, standing before the door of the Elder ranch, Moira's courage faltered. She heard sounds from behind the house and circled around toward the corral. John stood in the center, his sleeves rolled over his forearms. He held a horse tethered by a long rope. The horse trotted around him while John flipped the extra length of cord in a wide arc.

He caught sight of her and did a double take. He clicked and the horse halted. Gathering the rope, he unhooked the lead before strolling over.

Moira's throat went dry. "I need your help."

"Miss Moira O'Mara. Asking for help. I never thought I'd see the day. You know, I was asking God for a sign, and I think He just might have sent it."

"I want to court someone."

He quirked an eyebrow. "And do I know the gentleman?"

"I believe you're intimately acquainted with him."

"I see. And what sort of help do you need?"

"First off, I don't know where to begin."

John planted his elbow on the top rail of the fence separating them. "You should tell him how handsome he is."

"He's quite the handsomest man I've ever seen."

"And you should compliment his intelligence. Men like to know a woman appreciates them for more than their good looks."

"He's quite the smartest man I've ever met."

John hitched his other elbow on the fence and rested his chin on his fisted hands. "And humble, too, no doubt."

"He's extremely modest."

"I'm starting to like this fellow."

"I've fallen in love with him."

John reached over the fence and cupped her cheeks with his work-roughened hands. "I suppose you ought to start there. With your feelings."

"I love you."

"I love you, too."

"I know, you already told me."

"I should have asked you to marry me properly, on one knee and everything. With a ring and some flowers or something. I was too nervous. You want me to try again?"

"Nope. It was perfect the first time." She smiled. "Thank you for letting me sort out things with Tommy."

"If you need time with him, I'll wait."

"No. I've been lingering around the edges of life, not wanting to get hurt. Not wanting to lose people. Now that we're together proper, I don't want to waste a single minute."

He slid his hand into her hair and angled his head.

Their lips met in a sweet kiss and Moira sighed. "I should warn you. I have some conditions."

"Tell me."

"We're having dinner with my brother tonight."

"I can meet that demand."

Moira kissed him again. "And I want Hazel to live with us."

"Agreed."

He pressed his forehead against hers. "And I have one condition of my own."

"What's that?"

"I want a short courtship."

Moira clambered over the tall fence and launched herself into his arms. "Agreed."

Epilogue

One year later

Moira leaned against the stall door and sighed. John joined her and wrapped his arm around her waist, then rested his hand on the slight bump of her expanding stomach.

Five puppies whimpered and snuffed beside their mother in a nest of hay. They were squirming, fluffy bundles of brown-and-white fur, a mix of their sheepdog mother and collie father.

He shook his head. "Hazel, you're going to name every one of them, aren't you?"

"I've already decided on names," Hazel declared. "That's Violet, Rose, Daisy, Marigold and Lily."

"I should have guessed," John said.

Champion sniffed around the edges and lay down with a whimper. The mother belonged to their neighbors, the McCoys, but the sheepdog had taken up residence at the homestead shortly after Champion had arrived. The two families had tried to discourage the relationship, but love had won out.

John pointed at Champion. "Don't look so proud of yourself."

Moira elbowed him in the side. "You're one to talk. I believe a certain father-to-be recently bought the general store out of cigars."

The tips of his ears reddened. "Point taken."

Moira pecked him on the cheek. "I love you."

"Mmm-hmm."

"Is that all you're going to say?"

"Kiss me proper and I'll try again."

Moira tilted back her head.

"Ah, no," Tony spoke from the large double doors leading outside. "Are you two kissing again? Give it a rest. We've got a visitor."

John groaned and glanced over his shoulder. "Who is it?"

"You better come see for yourself."

Moira exchanged a glance with John and shrugged. "I guess we better see for ourselves. Hazel, will you keep an eye on the puppies for us?"

Hazel nodded without looking up. Since the puppies had been born two weeks ago, she'd barely strayed from the barn.

John kept a protective arm around Moira's shoulder as they emerged into the sunlight.

Her eyes widened. "Darcy?"

"Yep." Tony smirked. "It's her all right."

"Tony," Moira pitched her voice in a warning. "Be nice."

"Yeah. I miss you, too," Darcy grumbled.

She appeared years older than when Moira had last seen her, though only twelve months had passed. Her hair was caught in a loose knot at the base of her neck, with several loose strands falling over her shoulders. Her faded blue calico dress was rumpled and bags showed beneath her eyes.

"Preston is dead," Darcy said, her expression bleak.

Moira pulled away from John and embraced Darcy. "I'm so sorry."

She hadn't thought much of Preston, yet she mourned his passing for Darcy's sake.

"He got in a fight outside Chicago. Never recovered."

"Why don't you come inside?" Moira motioned toward the house. "You can sit for a while and have some lemonade."

A sound caught her attention, and for the first time she noticed a basket sitting at Darcy's feet.

Darcy knelt and lifted a bundle into her arms. "This is Preston Jr."

Tony made a strangled sound in her throat. "You had a baby with that moro—"

"Tony!" Moira shushed her. "Let's carry the rest of Darcy's things inside. I believe we all have some catching up to do."

Moira struggled against her shock and dismay. Darcy appeared too exhausted to answer the myriad questions flitting through her head.

Tony gathered the basket and a satchel and hooked her arm. "Follow me." She paused and stared at the face peeking from beneath the folds of the blanket. "He's pretty cute. I guess."

"Here." Moira reached out her arms. "Why don't you let me carry little Preston."

Darcy instantly relinquished the bundle. "I'm so tired. I don't think I've slept in the three months since he was born."

She yawned and pressed a fist against her mouth.

"Let's not stand here yapping then," Tony said, though her voice had softened considerably since she'd spotted the baby. "Come on inside."

Moira stood in the fading sunlight and stared at the tiny, perfect infant in her arms. He was impossibly small and light, his eyes closed. He yawned, and his fingers splayed, then fisted once more.

In a few more months, she'd have one of her own. Sometimes she felt so much love for the new life growing inside her, her heart ached from it.

"Oh, my," Moira crooned. "Isn't he precious?"

John leaned in. "I should have seen this coming, but I didn't."

Her stomach plummeted. "You're not angry, are you?"

"Of course not. But you know what this means, don't you? Darcy still has a lot of growing up to do. If we take her in, chances are, we'll end up raising this baby just as much as her."

"Would you mind that very much?"

"It's you I'm worried about." He rested his hand on her rounded belly.

Moira blinked back tears. She never tired of looking at him. She'd memorized the tiny flecks of gold around his irises. The small creases that appeared at the corners of his mouth when he smiled. Beneath the warmth of his love, she'd learned to love herself. And that realization had opened her heart to a pure joy like she'd never experienced before.

She sighed. "You once said heroes don't always appear the way we expect."

"You know I can't deny you anything when you look at me that way. As though I'm your hero."

"You are."

A blush crept up his neck at her compliment. "We shouldn't make any hasty decisions."

"Darcy has no place else to go," Moira said simply. "And we've got enough love, it seems a shame not to share it."

"If you're certain."

"All babies are a blessing."

John adjusted his hat to the back of his head. "It's going to be crowded when your brother and his family come to visit next week."

"I know."

"And Robert will be here the following month to purchase a few horses for his ranch."

"We'll make do."

"You know you can't save everyone." He pressed his forehead against hers, the dozing baby between them, the brim of his hat shading them from the last rays of the evening sun. "But I love you for trying."

"I do have one question."

"What's that?"

"Are you going to tell Hazel that some of the puppies are boys?"

John chuckled. "Just as long as she doesn't name the new baby."

"But she's already made a list."

"Now I'm terrified."

"She thinks Lancelot is a good name."

"No."

"Chester."

"Definitely not."

"Aphrodite."

"*Absolutely* not."

Moira trailed him back to the house, calling out increasingly ridiculous names along the way. When he paused on the porch, she smiled. "Thank you for knowing me better than anyone, and for loving me anyway."

He wasn't perfect, he had his faults, but then again, so did she. Together they made a good match.

"I love you, too, my fiery redheaded wife." He scratched his chin. "And I'm kind of warming up to the name Lancelot."

"No!" Moira shrieked.

They stepped into the house, still laughing, while behind them the setting sun cast golden shadows over the prairie.

* * * * *

Winnie Griggs is the multipublished, award-winning author of historical (and occasionally contemporary) romances that focus on small towns, big hearts and amazing grace. She is also a list maker and a lover of dragonflies, and holds an advanced degree in the art of procrastination. Winnie loves to hear from readers—you can connect with her on Facebook at Facebook.com/winniegriggs.author or email her at winnie@winniegriggs.com.

Books by Winnie Griggs

Love Inspired Historical

Texas Grooms

Visit the Author Profile page
at Harlequin.com for more titles.

SECOND CHANCE HERO

Winnie Griggs

For God has not given us a spirit of timidity;
but of power, and of love, and of a sound mind.
—*2 Timothy* 1:7

With sincere thanks to my generous friends who are always ready to brainstorm with me— Connie, Amy, Christopher, Dustin, Renee, Beth and Lenora. And to my fabulous editor Melissa Endlich, whose suggestions are always aimed at making my work tighter and stronger.

Chapter One

Turnabout, Texas
April 1897

Verity Leggett took firmer hold of her daughter's hand as they approached the street crossing. There wasn't much in the way of carriage or horse traffic this time of morning, but she always preferred to err on the side of caution, especially where Joy was concerned.

Suddenly Joy stopped in her tracks and pointed to her right. "Look, Mama, a dog."

Verity stared suspiciously at the hound slinking out of an alley two blocks away. She was glad they weren't headed in that direction. Joy loved animals with all the indiscriminate abandon her five-year-old heart could summon. She definitely hadn't learned the value of caution yet.

"I see him." Verity hitched the handle of the hatbox she carried a little closer to her elbow. "But Miss Hazel's dress shop is this way. And don't forget, you can play with Buttons when we get there."

Distracted by thoughts of the cat who resided in the

dress shop, Joy faced forward again, cradling her doll, Lulu, in the crook of her arm, and gave a little hop-skip. "I brought a piece of yarn for Buttons to play with."

"I'm sure Buttons will be quite pleased." Verity knew her droll tone was lost on her daughter, but that was okay. It was just so good to see how well Joy was thriving since they'd moved to Turnabout a year ago.

As Verity guided her daughter onto Second Street, her gaze slid past the closed doors of the apothecary and the saddle shop to focus on the last building on the block. Good—the dress shop was already open. She gave the hatbox a little swing and grinned in anticipation of Hazel's reaction to her latest millinery creation. It was just the sort of flamboyant frippery her friend liked.

The new sign Hazel had recently hung over her shop door was an example of just how far her friend would take her love of the dramatic. It was elaborate in shape, brick red in color, and was emblazoned in fancy gold lettering that proclaimed the establishment to be Hazel's Fashion Emporium. Her friend was quite put out that folks in town still referred to her business as simply "the dress shop."

Then, almost as if drawn to it, her gaze moved to the closed door of the shop next to Hazel's. The window bore the name Cooper's Saddle, Tack & Supply in crisp white letters. Mr. Cooper, the owner, had moved to Turnabout just a couple of weeks ago and had opened his shop on Monday. She hadn't officially met him yet—only seen him from a distance in church and around town. Not that she was in any hurry to get to know him better. After all, she was twenty-four years old and a widow. Hardly someone who would be looking to form attachments of that sort.

And even if she had been looking for such a thing, Mr. Cooper was not at *all* the type of man she'd be attracted to. There was a guarded air about him that, even from a distance, made her think he wasn't all he seemed, that he held something tightly leashed inside himself. Perhaps it was just her imagination, but it was enough to put her guard up. Some women might be attracted to men who seemed just a little bit dangerous or adventurous, but she preferred someone who was dependable and reliable, someone like her late husband, Arthur.

Still, something about the man tugged at her imagination…

The door to the saddle shop opened as if on cue, and her pulse kicked up a notch. But to her surprise, instead of Mr. Cooper, a small brown dog padded out. The animal looked around, then sat on its haunches next to the doorway, for all the world as if it were guarding the place.

Surely that animal didn't belong to Mr. Cooper? She would have pictured him with a large hunting dog— not this small, cuddly-looking pet that reminded her of a child's stuffed bear.

Joy, who was chattering to her doll, Lulu, about Buttons, hadn't noticed the animal yet. Verity braced herself for the gleeful clamor that would come whenever her daughter *did* notice.

A heartbeat later Mr. Cooper himself stepped out, broom in hand, and Verity paused the merest fraction between one step and the next. There was no denying that there was a presence about the man, much more impactful up close than from a distance. It wasn't his size—he couldn't be more than a couple of inches taller than she was, maybe five foot nine. Nor did he seem to be actively trying to command attention. In fact just the opposite. But there was a hardness about him, an air of stoicism and confidence—or was it a kind of self-containment?—that was hard to ignore.

Then he bent to scratch the dog behind the ears, and her impression of him shifted. His closed expression softened to something resembling exasperated affection, and the dog responded with tail-wagging exuberance. His brown hair, worn a bit longer than normally seen around here, was nearly as dark as his dog's coat and it had the slightest of waves to it.

Mr. Cooper straightened, obviously ready to sweep the walk in front of his shop, and only then noticed the two of them approaching. His expression closed again and he paused to let them pass.

It seemed she was going to meet the newcomer now, whether she wanted to or not—at least enough to exchange greetings. His gaze might be impassive, but still Verity's nerves jangled at being the focus of it. She tamped that feeling down, but before she could offer a greeting, Joy spotted the dog.

"Oh, look at the little doggie, Mama. Isn't he cute?"

Verity nodded, studiously *not* looking Mr. Cooper's way. "Yes, he is."

Joy, however, seemed to have no qualms about meeting Mr. Cooper's eyes. "Is he your doggie, Mister?" she asked brightly.

The man's expression eased into a slight smile. "He is. His name is Beans."

Verity blinked. What an odd name to give a dog. Even odder still that such a fanciful name had come from such a decidedly *un*fanciful-seeming man.

"Can I pet him?" Joy asked.

Verity, worried about allowing her daughter to approach a strange animal, stepped in before Mr. Cooper could respond. "Stop pestering Mr. Cooper—it's not polite. We need—"

"It's no bother." His voice had a husky, gravelly quality to it. But it wasn't unpleasant. In fact she rather liked the sound of it.

"Beans won't hurt the child," he said. Then he turned back to Joy and gave her another smile. "If your mother allows it, Beans and I don't mind."

Joy looked up at Verity. "Can I, Mama, please?"

"*May* I," Verity corrected. She glanced at the dog. The animal appeared friendly enough, so she gave a reluctant nod. "Very well, but just a quick, gentle pat. We need to get along to Miss Hazel's shop."

Smiling brightly, Joy rushed over to the dog and knelt down to stroke its head and talk nonsense to it for a minute. The dog accepted the attention with a happy wag of its tail. A moment later it had its two front paws planted on Joy's knees and was trying to bathe her face with his tongue.

Verity made a small involuntary move to intervene, and then the sound of Joy's giggles stopped her. She supposed there was no real harm in letting her daughter have fun with the animal for a few minutes.

Instead, she forced herself to look away from Joy and face the dog's owner. Up close, Mr. Cooper was even more interesting. There was an ever-so-slight dimple in his chin, but it in no way took away from his firm jawline or the chiseled planes of his face. It was those piercing blue-gray eyes, however, that drew her in, made her want to learn more about him. Combine that with his guarded air, and he had a definite presence about him. He wasn't exactly what you'd call handsome—his features were too irregular for that. No, not handsome, but arresting.

Yes, most definitely arresting.

Then she realized he was waiting for her to say something. "I hope you don't mind," she said with what she hoped was a neighborly smile. "Joy has such a love for animals, it's impossible for her to pass one by without stopping to pet it."

"Beans seems to be enjoying the attention," he said noncommittally. Then he glanced toward Joy. "My sister was the same way."

She noticed something momentarily cloud his expression, but it was gone by the time he turned back to her. Then she realized he'd used the word *was*. She'd passed away then. Was his loss recent?

Verity decided to change the subject. "It's nice to see someone making use of the old boot shop."

He nodded. "It's working out well for what I need."

Definitely not much of a conversationalist. She tried again. "How are you liking Turnabout so far?"

"The folks here are neighborly and it seems like a good place to set down roots."

Is that what he wanted to do—set down roots? Stability and responsibility were certainly fine traits to aspire to. But did that mean he'd been a drifter before he came here?

"I'm pleased to hear it." Then, remembering that poignant mention of his sister, her smile warmed. "And if you're looking to leave your past behind you," she said softly, "and find a new place to belong, then you've come to the right place."

At the flash of surprise in his eyes, she realized just

how presumptuous that must have sounded. Embarrassed, she quickly turned to Joy and held her hand out. "Come along, pumpkin. Time to tell the dog goodbye. Thank Mr. Cooper and let's be on our way."

Joy obediently turned to Beans's owner. "Thank you, Mr. Cooper. Beans is a nice doggie." She held out her doll. "And Lulu likes him, too."

Risking a glance his way, Verity saw that he was giving her daughter a broad smile, apparently choosing to ignore her own ill-conceived remarks of a moment ago.

"You're welcome," he said, executing a half bow. "Both of you. Anytime."

Verity decided he should smile more often—it transformed his face, making him appear much more approachable. But perhaps he reserved his smiles for puppies and children.

As if to punctuate that thought, he turned back to her, his expression once more merely polite. Then he nodded and took firmer hold of his broom.

Intrigued by these contradictory glimpses of the man, and still embarrassed by her earlier words, Verity put a hand on Joy's shoulder and gently nudged her toward Hazel's shop.

And tried not to think too hard about the fact that she'd like to see one of those warmer smiles directed her way.

Nate Cooper swept the sidewalk in front of his shop, his thoughts focused on the mother and daughter who'd just walked away.

He glanced down and noticed Beans watching them, as well. The animal's tail was still wagging, but much slower now. "You like that little girl, don't you, boy?"

Beans looked up as if he understood the question, and
Nate paused long enough to give him a quick scratch behind the ears. "Well, don't worry," he said as he straightened. "I'm pretty sure she likes you, as well."

The little girl—Joy, her mother had called her—had
certainly been taken with his four-legged companion.
Her giggles had been sweet proof of that.

For just a heartbeat, she'd reminded him of Susanna.
Joy's physical resemblance to his younger sister was only
superficial—honey-colored hair and a button nose—but
it was the way the child had responded to Beans that
had tugged at him. Susanna had loved animals with that
same wholeheartedness, especially dogs.

It was surprising how, after all these years, little re-
minders like that could hit him in the gut with such
force.

As he pushed the broom, his thoughts shifted from
the child to her mother. There were definitely no bittersweet memories to ambush him when thinking of her.
Quite the opposite.

This wasn't the first time he'd noticed her since his
move to Turnabout. She was a member of the small choir
at the local church. Both times he'd attended the service there, he'd taken notice of her. Not at first, though.
The drab widow's weeds she wore and her dark hair
had made her a shadow that the eye easily skipped past.

But all that changed the moment she began to sing.
Her face took on such a luminously serene yet passionate glow, as if she truly felt every word, every note she
sang. And even from where he sat he could see a fire
in her large green eyes that drew him. He hadn't been
able to take his gaze off of her until the preacher began
his sermon.

There'd been none of that fire in her today, though. In fact, the way she'd reacted when her daughter approached his little bit of a dog, she'd seemed nervous and something of a handwringer. Did that enchanting spark come through only when she sang?

Still, knowing it was there, he was intrigued enough to want to unearth it. And just now he'd found he liked her speaking voice too, a difficult-to-describe mix of genteel lady and country girl. There was something else he'd noticed as well, something that hadn't been apparent until he'd seen her up close just now. Right below the left corner of her mouth was the faintest of small scars. It didn't detract from her appearance. In fact, if anything it added an element of interest to her otherwise merely pleasant features. It also made him want to find out how she'd gotten it.

But it was when she'd relaxed enough to show him a genuine smile just now that she'd really caught his attention. The words that had accompanied her smile, however, had startled him. It was almost as if she'd understood his private yearnings.

Had she really meant what she said, or was it just some sort of polite bit of verbiage she would have said to any newcomer? And if she knew what sort of past he was trying to leave behind him, would she still have uttered those words?

She'd obviously known his name, but he had no idea what hers was. And since she hadn't offered, he hadn't felt it appropriate to ask.

But now he wondered—should he have asked? There'd been a time when he would have known how to carry on a polite conversation, but his social skills had grown rusty with disuse.

If he was ever going to fit in here, though, he'd need to relearn.

"I think the sidewalk is clean enough."

Nate looked up to see Adam Barr standing there, an amused half smile on his face. Adam was the closest thing Nate had to a friend these days, and was the person to whom he owed his current toehold on stability.

Nate returned the smile. "Just enjoying the morning sunshine."

Adam nodded and Nate knew without any exchange of words that his friend understood his meaning.

Nate leaned against the broom. "And what is the town's esteemed banker doing on this side of the street? Checking up on me?" He was only half joking. The bank, where Adam had his office, was a block and a half in the other direction.

"Not at all." Adam nodded toward the apothecary. "Reggie asked me to stop by Flaherty's for her."

Nate frowned. Reggie, Adam's wife, was expecting their third child. "She's not taken ill I hope."

Adam shook his head. "No, nothing like that. It's for Patricia. She's developed a rash and Reggie asked me to pick up some ointment for it." Beans had joined them now and was sniffing at Adam's boots. The man stooped down to absently scratch the animal behind the ears. "So how *is* business?"

Nate shrugged. "Slow. I sold a bridle Monday and yesterday Ed Strickland brought in a harness for me to mend." He tightened his hold on the broom handle. "But it's only my third day so I didn't expect a rush of business just yet." But it would need to pick up soon if he was going to pay his bills.

Adam nodded toward the display window. "I imagine that's getting you some interest."

Nate glanced at the item Adam was referring to and felt a small tug of pride. It was a saddle—one of the few possessions he'd brought with him to Turnabout. He'd made it himself and spent a lot of time and effort on it. The display piece was a visible testament to his skill as a saddler. "I've had a few inquiries, but nothing serious yet."

"I predict it will catch just the right eye soon." Then Adam glanced ahead. "Looks like Mr. Flaherty is opening his doors, so I'll let you get back to your sweeping." And with a nod, Adam headed for the apothecary.

Nate brushed the broom over the sidewalk one last time, his thoughts still with his friend. When Adam had invited him to move here to Turnabout, he'd described the town as a good place for fresh starts, something he'd known Nate was seeking. Nate had now seen firsthand just how well things had worked out for Adam. His friend, who hailed from Philadelphia, had truly made a life for himself in this town. He'd married a local woman and now had two children with a third on the way. He also had a position as manager of the local bank and had become an accepted, even prominent, member of this community. All that in spite of having spent six years in prison. Of course, not everyone here knew that part of his past.

Nate, whose own past was similar to Adam's, both in where he'd come from and where he'd been, passionately wanted that kind of future for himself. At least the being accepted and belonging part.

It wasn't that he didn't want the family part too—he

absolutely did. It was just that he knew it was better—for everyone—if he didn't pursue that dream.

For one thing, he had no luck whatsoever in relationships. More often than not, he ended up hurting the very people he cared most about.

For another, he could never pursue a serious relationship with a woman without letting her know what he'd done. And what woman would want to marry a man with a past like his? Especially not a certain widow whose face popped into his head at the thought. No, it was best all the way around if he just settled for a comfortable, neighborly relationship with the folks around here.

After all, what more could a man who'd robbed a bank and then spent nine years in prison paying for it expect?

Chapter Two

"I can't wait to see the latest of your fabulous creations."

Verity firmly pushed aside thoughts of the very interesting Mr. Cooper as she smiled at her friend Hazel's extravagant compliment. "I'm not sure about fabulous, but I do hope you like it." She glanced toward Joy, who sat on the floor playing with Buttons. Maybe someday, when they had a house of their own, she could get Joy the pet she so passionately wanted. In the meantime, perhaps Aunt Betty and Uncle Grover wouldn't mind a caged pet, like a sweet little songbird…

"Oh, my…"

Her friend's delighted exclamation pulled Verity's thoughts back to the present.

Hazel lifted Verity's current millinery creation out of the hatbox and studied it, her eyes gratifyingly alight with admiration. "I do believe this is your best one yet. It's absolutely exquisite." Then she shook her head in mock confusion. "Who would guess that your restrained demeanor hides a woman with such a stylish flair?"

Verity drew up at that. "I'm a widow, remember. My

restrained demeanor, as you call it, is not only appropriate but expected."

Hazel seemed unimpressed by her reasoning. "You've been widowed over a year now, so it's okay to put off wearing such dreary colors all the time. And we both know that before you were even married you dressed much more conservatively than the rest of us."

Verity knew her friend meant well, but the words still stung. As if her mourning for Arthur would automatically end based on a date on a calendar. Besides, she had already added some color to her wardrobe. True, she still wore black skirts, but her shirtwaists contained gray or lavender or even some dark green. In fact, her Sunday best was the only solid-black dress she still wore, and she'd even added a bit of gray to the collar and cuffs of that one. It was only proper that, as a widow, she didn't try to wear bright colors or frills.

As for the rest, with that scar on her face, she'd never been one of the "pretty girls," and she'd long since come to terms with that.

Verity gave her friend an exasperated look. "Not all of us are as comfortable with flamboyant airs and drama as you are."

This shop was proof of that. Color and furbelows were everywhere. Besides the dress forms that displayed examples of her work, there were bolts of fabrics in every shade imaginable, from pastels to deep jewel tones, both solids and prints, spools of lace and cord and ribbons, trimmings such as feathers and beads and medallions, fashion plates displayed artfully around the store—and all arranged in a manner to catch the eye and entice one to come close to admire and touch and perhaps purchase.

Verity loved it here, loved how it made her feel, as

if she was inside a fantastical daydream where nothing harsh could intrude.

But she was just a visitor here—it wasn't *her* world.

"Which is a shame."

For a startled moment Verity thought her friend had read her thoughts. Then she realized Hazel was merely responding to her last statement.

Hazel's grin had an I-know-best twist to it. "I think a little flamboyancy and drama in your life is just what you need."

Verity relaxed and returned her grin. "That's what I have you in my life for. And why I create these hats." One of the things she'd missed most about Turnabout when she'd married Arthur and moved so far away was her friendship with Hazel. They'd kept in touch with the occasional letter, but being able to spend time together was so much better.

When Verity had moved back to Turnabout after Arthur's death last year, she and Hazel had picked up where they'd left off.

Joy's giggles drew her attention and she glanced in that direction. The girl was jiggling her bit of yarn in front of Buttons. Hazel's cat was trying to bat at it with one of her front paws, much to Joy's delight.

Verity turned back to see Hazel rotating the hat this way and that, trying to view it from all angles. Wetting her lips and affecting a casual expression, Verity gave in to the urge to do a little probing. "Have you met your new neighbor yet?"

"You mean Mr. Cooper?" Hazel glanced out the door, as if she could see around the corner to his shop. "Just casually. He seems rather mysterious, don't you think, just showing up here out of the blue?" Her eyes sparkled with saucy speculation. "I know he's a friend of Adam Barr's, but still, one can't help but wonder what his story is. Especially when he looks right at you with those striking eyes."

Verity popped her hand on her hip in mock outrage. "Hazel Theresa Andrews, I thought you were sweet on the sheriff. Has another man finally caught your fancy?"

Hazel tossed her head. "I'm getting tired of waiting for Ward Gleason to take notice of me. It certainly won't hurt anything to let him know I have options." Then she narrowed her eyes. "Why do you ask? Do you have *your* eye on Mr. Cooper?"

Seeing the speculation in her friend's expression, Verity tilted her chin up defensively. "Don't be silly. I don't even know the man."

"He didn't happen to be outside his store when you walked by just now, did he?"

Hazel was too perceptive by half. "He was. And yes, we chatted for a moment. But only because Joy wanted to pet his dog. You know she can't pass by an animal without wanting to play with it."

"So you *did* meet him."

"Not exactly." She waved a hand. "I mean, no introductions were exchanged. But saying hello was the neighborly thing to do." Verity mentally cringed when she heard the defensive note creep into her voice.

And of course Hazel pounced right on it. "Well, now, isn't this an interesting turn of events. Our meek-as-a-lamb, practical-as-prunes Verity is interested in the very rugged and far-from-meek-looking Mr. Cooper."

"Don't be silly," she said, drawing herself up even straighter. "I have no interest in the man beyond a natural curiosity."

"Of course you don't." But from the knowing smile on Hazel's lips, Verity could tell her friend didn't believe her protests. It was time to steer this conversation in a different direction.

"Thanks for letting Joy play with Buttons," she said. "She looks forward to it whenever I tell her I'm headed over here."

To Verity's relief, Hazel accepted the change of subject as she carried the hat to the nearby cheval glass. "Buttons enjoys it, too," her friend said absently as she placed the hat on her head at a sassy angle. Then she preened, turning and tilting her head different ways to admire the effect. "Oh, I love it, especially the flirty way the brim is folded. If it wasn't yellow I'd consider keeping it for myself." She glanced over her shoulder at Verity. "Yellow never was my color."

Verity disagreed. With Hazel's vivacious red-gold hair and sparkling green eyes, there was very little that didn't look good on her. But she kept her opinion to herself.

Hazel removed the hat and turned back around. "Now, you on the other hand, with that gorgeous mahogany-colored hair and your fair complexion, would look stunning in this."

"Not particularly suitable mourning attire," Verity said drily.

Hazel sighed dramatically. "I've already said my piece on *that* subject. But I can tell your mind is made up." Then she shrugged. "Ah, well, it'll look nice in the window next to that lavender dress with the scrumptious lace."

Verity fidgeted with her sleeve. "I do wish you'd let

me pay you something for displaying my hats in your shop."

"Well, I won't, so let's hear no more about it." Hazel patted a few stray hairs back in place before moving away from the mirror. "And don't think it's because I'm feeling altruistic. I'm getting something out of it, too. My sales have definitely gone up since your hats went on display next to my dresses."

Verity had been thinking lately that she'd like to open a millinery shop of her own one day, and Hazel's words gave her an added nudge in that direction. Despite Uncle Grover's and Aunt Betty's assertions that they liked having her and Joy stay with them, she couldn't— wouldn't—live on their charity forever. It had been fifteen months since that awful day Arthur was killed. It was time for her to move on with her life, to decide what kind of future she wanted for herself and Joy.

If she could start her own business and make a go of it, she might just be able to afford to have a home of her own again. But there was so much risk involved in such an undertaking, risks she wasn't sure she could afford to take. It definitely wasn't a step to take lightly. For one thing she'd have to save up more money before she could even get started. And what if she failed? Besides, the one time she'd mentioned it to Uncle Grover, he'd counseled her about all the pitfalls she could face and she'd gotten the impression he didn't think it was something she should even attempt.

Still, every time she allowed herself to dream about the future she wanted for herself and Joy, the yearning to take more control of her life grew.

"Have you heard about the plans for the Founders' Day celebration?"

Verity pushed away her daydreams and focused on Hazel's question. "You mean there's going to be more to it than the town picnic this year?"

"A *lot* more. Ever since Mayor Sanders realized this is the seventy-fifth anniversary of Turnabout's founding, he's wanted to do something special, which to him means something bigger and flashier."

That was Mayor Sanders, all right. Some things about this town never changed.

"He's talking about a grand festival," Hazel continued, "sort of like a county fair, with games, contests, food, performances. He's even talking about bringing in a traveling circus or an acting troupe."

Verity listened with only half an ear as Hazel recounted the discussion from yesterday's town council meeting. Instead, her thoughts drifted back to Mr. Cooper.

Hazel was wrong. She wasn't taken with the man. Well, not exactly. She was merely curious about him. When she looked into his intense eyes, she still got the sense of something controlled but dangerous. Yet seeing him with that little lapdog had contradicted that impression. Showing kindness to a small animal and speaking of putting down roots seemed to indicate a man who was compassionate and responsible.

Which was the real man? Or was it possible he could be a combination of both?

The sound of a dog barking outside made her think again of the small dog itself. Beans—what a whimsical name for the animal.

Perhaps someday—there was that nebulous *someday* again—if she could find a similar lapdog, one that she knew was well behaved, she could get it for Joy.

Verity glanced over her shoulder to check on her daughter again, but neither the five-year-old nor the cat was in the same spot any longer. She turned fully around. "Joy?" Where had the girl gotten off to?

Hazel paused midsentence and glanced quickly around the shop. "She probably followed Buttons to one of his hiding places. Check behind the counter."

"Joy!" Verity said the name louder this time, using her no-nonsense, answer-me-now voice. She knew it was probably an overreaction, but she couldn't help herself. Her late husband's violent death had given her a terrible lesson on how tragedy could strike in the blink of an eye. And she'd found herself wanting to hold tighter and tighter to her daughter ever since.

When there was still no response, Verity's focus sharpened. If Joy was just behind the counter, why wasn't she answering? "Joy, this isn't a game. Come out this minute."

Still no answer. Could she have gone upstairs? Verity had half turned in that direction when Hazel spoke up, halting her in her tracks.

"She's out on the sidewalk."

Verity spun around and headed for the door. Why hadn't she kept a closer eye on Joy?

A warning shout sounded just as she stepped outside, closely followed by a gasp from Hazel.

She watched in horror as her daughter, intent on chasing Buttons, darted in front of an oncoming wagon. Verity raced forward screaming Joy's name. The child turned, then froze as she saw the horse bearing down on her.

Verity stumbled and realized with shattering clarity that she would never reach Joy in time.

Chapter Three

For an agonizing heartbeat, as the wagon bore down on her daughter, time froze. Verity felt every irregularity in the pebble that bit into her palm, could taste the tang of blood from where she'd bit the inside of her cheek when she fell to the ground, could see the dust motes hanging in the air before her.

Please, Jesus. Please, Jesus. Please, Jesus.

She wasn't sure whether she was uttering the frantic prayer aloud or if it was just shrieking through her thoughts.

From somewhere a woman screamed, but all sounds, save for the wagon's relentless rumbling progress, seemed to come from a great distance.

Verity spotted the moment the wagon driver spied Joy and tried to turn his horses.

And still Joy didn't move.

Then, from out of nowhere, Mr. Cooper shot past her, and time sped up with a whoosh. He dived toward Joy, reaching her a heart-stopping split second before the horse's hooves would have trampled the child, and pushing her out of the way.

Without remembering having moved, Verity was suddenly kneeling in the road with her weeping daughter clutched tightly against her. Her heart thudded painfully against her chest and her breath came in near gasps. She'd come so close to losing her precious baby. She could still feel the stab of keening desolation that pierced her the moment she'd realized she couldn't get to Joy in time. This time the prayer she sent up was one of thanksgiving.

"Mama, you're squeezing too tight." Joy's querulous complaint ended on a hiccup.

Verity had to fight down the hysterical bubble of laughter that wanted to leap from her throat. Instead she loosened her hold and pushed back just enough to examine her daughter, brushing aside a tendril of Joy's hair with fingers that trembled uncontrollably. "Don't you *ever* scare Mommy like that again."

Joy shook her head, then hiccupped again as her tears stopped.

Verity was vaguely aware that Hazel stood at her elbow and that a crowd had gathered, but her attention remained focused on reassuring herself that Joy really was okay.

Fortunately, her daughter appeared more scared and confused than hurt. The stains and smears on her pinafore were dirt, not blood.

"I'm so sorry."

Verity looked up into the pale, worried face of Nestor James, the wagon driver.

"Please tell me your little girl's okay," he continued as he crushed his hat in his hands. "I didn't see her 'til I was practically on top of her."

"It's not your fault, Mr. James." Though her voice

was still shaky, now that Verity knew Joy was okay she could be reasonable. "I should have kept closer watch over her. And it appears Joy isn't hurt—just shaken up. Thanks to Mr. Cooper."

She looked around for the man who'd saved her daughter.

And only then realized he hadn't fared as well as Joy.

He was sitting up, his movements slow and stiff. There was a darkening bruise on his forehead, he held his left arm stiffly and his sleeve was ripped and stained with blood and dirt.

Sheriff Gleason had bent down to lend him a hand up.

Verity immediately intervened. "Don't get up yet, Mr. Cooper. Not until I've had a look at you." There was no telling how badly he might be injured.

He gave her a startled look, which she ignored. Instead she turned to Sheriff Gleason. "Keep an eye on him, please." Then she turned back to Joy. "Do you hurt anywhere, pumpkin?"

Joy bent her right arm and lifted it for inspection. "I hurted my elbow. And Lulu got smushed."

Quickly noting that Joy's elbow was merely scraped, Verity bent down and gave it a kiss. "There, is that better?"

Joy nodded, swiping at the dirt and tears on her face with her other sleeve. Then she handed the doll up to her mother. Verity obediently gave the doll a kiss, as well. "There. You should both feel better once you've washed up a bit."

Then she gave her daughter a stern look. "Now, I want you to stay close to Miss Hazel while I check on Mr. Cooper."

"Yes, ma'am."

Hazel took Joy's hand and gave Verity a nod.

Inhaling a fortifying breath, Verity turned to check on the condition of the man to whom she owed so much.

Nate Cooper watched the woman's sudden transformation with fascination. A moment ago she'd been understandably shaky, emotional, on the verge of hysteria even, over what had nearly happened to her daughter.

He would have thought that the sight of his sorry state would have pushed her even further toward hysteria. Instead, she seemed composed and even decisive. Which was something of a relief. He'd rather deal with an oncoming wagon all over again than with an overly emotional woman.

But what had she meant by *have a look at you*? Did she fancy herself a doctor? He'd seen the kiss-it-and-make-it-better approach she'd used with her daughter and the doll—not exactly by-the-book medicine. Though, come to think on it, he wouldn't be particularly averse if she wanted to try that method with him...

He quickly pushed that entirely inappropriate thought aside as the woman in question knelt down beside him.

"Before I do anything else," she said softly, "I want to tell you how unbelievably brave what you just did was, and to let you know I'm so much more than grateful. You not only saved my daughter just now, but me, as well."

The woman's moss-green eyes glowed with a gratitude that verged on hero worship. That shook him much more than the accident with the wagon had. He hadn't been on the receiving end of such a look since he'd lost his sister nearly a decade ago, and he wasn't quite sure what to make of it. But hero worship was something he didn't want.

Or deserve.

He'd just been at the right place at the right time—nothing more. He'd seen Beans bark at the cat and send it running across the road. He'd then seen the child follow the feline. It had been pure instinct to go after her—nothing heroic about it.

"I'll be okay," he said brusquely, waving the woman away with his right hand. "You should see to your daughter."

The woman ignored his suggestion and began rolling up her sleeves. "Joy is fine, thanks to you. And that gash on your arm definitely needs some attention."

Without waiting for a response from him, she glanced up at the crowd milling around them. "Someone get me a pail of water to clean this up. And I'll need some clean rags, as well."

To his surprise, several individuals from the crowd nodded and rushed off to do her bidding. Then she turned to Sheriff Gleason. "Do you have a pocketknife I can borrow?"

The lawman never hesitated. He pulled out his knife, opened it for her and handed it over.

Nate raised a hand. "Now, hold on." These folks might trust the woman, but he wasn't ready to let her cut on him. "What do you intend to do with that thing?"

Her brow went up and there was an amused twist to her lips. "Don't worry, I'm not planning to operate on you. Yet." He was only partly reassured by her dry tone.

She took the knife and, with a quick movement, sliced his already ripped shirt all the way to the cuff.

He tried one more time to wrest control from the stubborn woman. "See, it's just a cut. I'll be okay. If it makes you feel better I'll go see the doctor." He tried to push himself up, but a sharp pain shot through his left ankle and he winced involuntarily.

"You are *not* okay." She put a firm hand on his right shoulder. "Don't move until I have a look at you." Her expression softened slightly. "Don't worry, I do have some medical training."

That would explain her air of authority. But was she serious? "You're a doctor?"

"Not exactly. But the town's doctor is my uncle and my late husband was a physician, as well. So you see, I've worked with doctors most of my life. I know what to do."

The "not exactly doctor" turned to the dressmaker, who still held the little girl's hand. "Would you mind taking Joy back to your shop until I've finished here?"

"Of course." Miss Andrews smiled down at the little girl. "Come on, sweetie, let's get you and Lulu cleaned up and then we'll see if we can find a cookie to snack on."

The woman's gaze lingered on her daughter as the two walked away. But a moment later a young man set the requested pail of water at her feet and she turned to smile up at him. "Thank you, Calvin. Now would you mind running over to the clinic and letting my uncle know he'll have a patient shortly?"

"Yes, ma'am." And with that the young man was off again.

Finally she turned back to him. "Since I'm about to tend to your injuries," she said with a caretaker's smile, "I should probably introduce myself. I'm Mrs. Verity Leggett."

Nate gave a short nod. "Mrs. Leggett. I'm Nate Cooper."

"Now that we've gotten the pleasantries out of the

way, let's get this arm cleaned up, shall we, so we can see what we're dealing with?"

He still wasn't comfortable with the idea of being examined by a female doctor, no matter how pretty or confident she was. It seemed vaguely ungentlemanly to put her through such unpleasantness. "There's no need to trouble yourself, Mrs. Leggett. I can get myself over to the doctor—"

She didn't let him finish. "I agree that my uncle should see you. And he will—just as soon as I make sure we have this cleaned up and the bleeding has stopped."

She dipped a cloth in the water and then gently dabbed at the gash, cleaning away the dirt and blood with her right hand while she supported his arm with her left. Her touch was gentle but sure, and not at all unpleasant.

As Mrs. Leggett bent over him, he could smell the faint scent of honeysuckle on her, could see the glint of sunlight tease out touches of auburn in her mahogany hair. The feel of her hand supporting his arm as she gently cleaned the cut was warm and strong in a uniquely feminine kind of way.

As she bent closer to study her progress, that stray image of her kissing her daughter's injury popped up in his mind again. Would she—

He abruptly pulled his thoughts back from that dangerous cliff. His reaction to her was a testament to how long it had been since he'd felt the gentle ministrations of a woman, nothing more. And he was certain she wouldn't welcome any indications that he felt anything other than gratitude.

When Mrs. Leggett had the cut cleaned to her satisfaction, she leaned back and studied it. "You're definitely going to need stitches, but I don't believe you've cut anything vital." She looked up then and met his gaze with a reassuring smile. "The bleeding has slowed, but I'm going to wrap it tight to make certain it doesn't start flowing again before we get you to the clinic."

When she had put action to words, she met his gaze again. "Now, your left leg seemed to be giving you problems when you tried to get up. Where does it hurt?"

So she'd picked up on that. "It's my ankle, but I'm sure it'll be fine in just a bit."

She scooted over and took his booted foot in her hands, again disregarding the niceties of social behavior. Her gentle probing had him gritting his teeth, but he did his best to not show any outward signs of pain.

She gently set the foot back down. "It's definitely swollen. I think we'll leave the boot on until Uncle Grover is ready to examine it. But you shouldn't be walking on it for now." Then she met his eyes. "Are you hurt anywhere else?"

His head pounded, his shoulder and ankle throbbed and he was starting to feel light-headed. Nothing a little rest wouldn't cure. "No."

Her raised eyebrow told him she wasn't convinced, but she didn't press. Instead she gave his good arm a light pat. "Don't worry, we're going to take very good care of you."

Despite his reservations, he had to admit he liked the sound of that.

Mrs. Leggett made as if to stand and the sheriff was at her elbow, lending her a hand.

She smiled up at the lawman. "Thank you, Sheriff. Would you find some men to help carry Mr. Cooper over to the clinic? I'll go on ahead to help my uncle get things ready."

The sheriff tipped his hat. "Yes, ma'am."

Carry him? "That won't be necessary. I just need a little help getting up."

She gave him a don't-be-ridiculous look. "You won't be doing any walking on that ankle, at least not until Uncle Grover takes a look at it."

The woman wasn't shy about giving orders. "Well, I certainly don't intend to let myself be carried through town like a sack of flour. I'd rather hobble. If I could borrow a shoulder to use as support—"

"Your hurt ankle is on the same side as your hurt arm so it would be inadvisable to put any strain on it."

She even *talked* like a doctor.

Before he could protest again, the man who'd been driving the wagon stepped forward. "I can take him to your uncle's clinic in the back of my wagon, if you like?"

Nate clamped down an uncharitable stab of annoyance that the man's words were directed at Mrs. Leggett rather than him.

But the doctor's niece nodded, as if she, too, thought it was her decision to make. "Thank you, Mr. James, that will work nicely. I'll leave this in your and Sheriff Gleason's very capable hands." And with another reassuring but rather condescending smile for him, Mrs. Leggett turned and walked into the dress shop. A moment later she stepped out again with her daughter held on her hip. With the little girl's head snuggled against her shoulder, she marched down the sidewalk.

His eyes followed her progress until she turned a corner and disappeared from view. He still couldn't quite get over her transformation into a coolheaded, would-be doctor. When she'd stopped in front of his store on her way to the dress shop, he'd gotten the impression that she was more diffident than decisive. But just now, she hadn't had the least bit of hesitation about taking charge and issuing orders. And she also hadn't been the least bit put off by either the blood, ugly gash or the fact that she'd had to kneel in the middle of the dusty street to minister to him.

Now that she'd tended to him, she'd changed back into the concerned mother again.

The movement of the wagon pulled his thoughts away from the puzzle Mrs. Leggett presented and onto more immediate matters. He watched as the men maneuvered the vehicle right up beside him, then braced himself to stand. His left side had taken the brunt of the blow. Both his shoulder and ribs felt as if they were on fire, and the gash she'd taken such pains to clean and wrap protested any time he attempted to move his arm. His ankle was the most problematic, though. She hadn't really needed to warn him not to place any weight on it—the offending joint was doing a thorough job of that all by itself.

But as long as nothing was broken, he should be able to deal with the discomfort, even if it meant using crutches to get around. After all, he didn't need the use of his legs to do his job. And he certainly couldn't afford for this to keep him out of commission for long. He was still in the process of getting his fledgling business established.

Not that he regretted his actions. Better *he* get hurt than something happen to that little girl.

Sheriff Gleason bent down. "I think it best you shove your pride aside for now and allow us to help you into that wagon. Mrs. Leggett isn't going to be happy if I let you put weight on that ankle of yours." He grinned.

"And right now I'm more worried about her druthers than I am yours."

Nate nodded. Being helped into a wagon might not be the most dignified way to board, but it was a good sight better than getting carried through town.

The sheriff nodded toward one of the other men. "Jeff, lend me a hand here." The two men positioned themselves on either side of Nate, then helped him up. The action shot a bolt of pain down his left side, and he had to clamp down hard not to let loose with a string of expletives. He'd spent too much time away from the company of God-fearing folk—he was having to learn how to act in polite company all over again.

The sheriff climbed in beside him, presumably to keep him from falling out, then called to Nestor to get moving.

Nate gritted his teeth throughout the jarring, interminable-seeming ride to the clinic. Perhaps he *would* take it easy today. The workday would probably be half over before the doctor was finished with him, anyway.

When they finally arrived at the clinic, Nate was guiltily relieved to see Mrs. Leggett and an older man who was presumably her uncle step outside with a stretcher—he would have had trouble taking more than a few steps on his own. Mrs. Leggett had changed into a clean dress and wore a crisp white apron over it.

"Mr. Cooper, this is my uncle, Dr. Grover Pratt," she said as soon as she was close enough to speak to him. "Uncle Grover, this is Mr. Cooper, the man who saved Joy's life."

Nate shifted. All this excessive gratitude was making him uncomfortable.

"Hello, young man. Let me add my thanks to that

of my niece. That was a very brave thing you did, saving our Joy."

"I'm just glad I was in a position to help her, sir."

Sheriff Gleason clamped him on his uninjured shoulder. "Don't let his modesty fool you, Doc. I saw the whole thing. Mr. Cooper here is a real hero."

Dr. Pratt nodded. "Let's start showing our appreciation by getting him inside, where he'll be more comfortable."

Sheriff Gleason and the wagon driver took the ends of the stretcher and Nate maneuvered himself onto it with a minimum of help. Mrs. Leggett stayed beside him as the men transported him into the clinic. Her hand rested lightly on his good arm, as if she wanted to make certain he didn't fall off. The feel of her hand on him was… comforting. Then she looked down and gave him a reassuring smile. Almost as if she truly cared about him.

Was this all part of her job as the doctor's assistant?

Stupid question—of course it was.

Once the men had deposited him on the padded table in the examining room, they took their leave. Nate sat on the edge of the narrow but sturdy table with his legs dangling over the side. By refusing to lie down, he felt marginally more in control of the situation.

To his surprise, Mrs. Leggett didn't follow the men out. Surely she didn't plan to assist in the actual examination?

"I have strict instructions to take extra special care of you." Dr. Pratt cast a smile his niece's way. "So let's get to it."

The doctor began to lay out some of his implements. "Verity, please help Mr. Cooper remove his shirt."

Apparently she *was* going to stay. And participate. He wasn't quite sure how he felt about that.

But she didn't seem the least bit disconcerted by her uncle's request. Her expression remained pleasant but detached and her movements were businesslike as she approached him. Still…

"That's okay, I can manage," he said as he quickly started working the buttons with his right hand.

"Don't be silly." From her tone, she could be speaking to a wayward child. "This is part of my job. Besides, your arm is hurt and it's best you don't move it more than necessary until the doctor can take a look at it."

By this time Nate had managed to free all of the buttons, but he let her help him ease the already-ruined shirt off his arms and shoulders. As he did so, he was very conscious of the old scars she would see on his torso. What would she think?

But it wasn't until she'd laid the garment aside and turned back to him that he noticed any sort of reaction. Unlike the recoil or emasculating pity he'd expected, however, it was a wince and flash of guilt that she quickly suppressed.

Glancing down, he saw the ugly bruise that had formed on his left side, no doubt from his contact with the wagon. Had she not noticed anything else?

Once more wearing that businesslike, doctor's-helper demeanor, she quickly moved around to remove the arm bandage she'd applied earlier. Her touch was every bit as sure and impersonal as before.

Once done, she stepped away and allowed her uncle to take her place.

"Well, Mr. Cooper, let's take a look, shall we?"

Nate nodded. "Please call me Nate. And your niece didn't seem to think it was too serious."

Dr. Pratt smiled. "Verity's got a good eye, but why don't you let me have a look, anyway?"

As Dr. Pratt performed his examination, he took his time and made a point of letting Nate know what he was doing and why. It was all very different from the treatment he'd grown accustomed to the past nine years.

Even though Mrs. Leggett did her best to remain unobtrusive, Nate found himself very aware of her presence. Her movements were deft and sure, and she seemed to anticipate her uncle's requests so that very few words were spoken between them.

Verity—that was a rather old-fashioned name, but somehow it suited her. And her daughter was named Joy. Both named for virtues. The jaded part of him wondered if they found the names a burden to live up to. Not the little girl, of course, at least not yet. But the mother?

After cleaning the wound and studying it, the doctor looked up to meet Nate's gaze. "You're going to need stitches, but I don't see any reason why this cut shouldn't heal completely with no lasting damage, other than a scar, as long as you take it easy the next few days."

That was a relief. He could deal with one more scar. It would be difficult, though, to do his work without full use of his arm.

The doctor moved on to examine Nate's shoulder and side. Nate did his best to bear the probing stoically and not show any signs of discomfort. Mainly because he didn't want to make Mrs. Leggett feel any guiltier than she obviously already did.

But a part of him admitted that he didn't want to display weakness in front of her, either.

Finally, Dr. Pratt straightened. "Well, your shoulder and ribs are bruised but not broken. That knot on your head is of some concern, but so far you aren't exhibiting any signs of a concussion. Now I'm going to take care of suturing your arm before we take a look at your ankle."

Nate nodded. "Whatever you say."

Dr. Pratt gave him a considering look. "I think this will go better if you lie down on the table."

Without a word, Nate swiveled and swung his legs up on the table, then lay back. The doctor offered him a strip of leather to bite down on, but Nate shook his head. This wasn't his first time to get stitched up, so he knew what to expect.

Mrs. Leggett, who had quietly laid out the necessary implements, stood beside her uncle as he applied the stitches, ready to assist as needed.

Nate kept his gaze fixed on the ceiling as the doctor went to work, refusing to utter so much as a whimper. But apparently he wasn't as impassive as he would have liked, because about halfway through the procedure, Mrs. Leggett moved next to him and applied a cool cloth to his brow. Surprised by the action, he left off staring at the ceiling long enough to meet her gaze. She gave him an approving, sympathetic smile that somehow eased the pain of the procedure. A moment later she had slipped back into her less personal, bedside demeanor and returned to her uncle's side.

When at last Dr. Pratt was done, he straightened. "You can sit up now if you like," he told Nate.

Nate had to admit, if only to himself, that it hadn't ended any too soon. It had taken all he had not to cry out a time or two. Only the fear that he would embarrass himself in front of Mrs. Leggett had kept him from doing so.

The doctor glanced toward his niece as he helped Nate sit up. "Verity, would you take care of wrapping his arm for me?"

"Of course." She reached into a cabinet and pulled out a roll of gauzy-looking cloth.

As she had out in the street earlier, she used her left hand to hold his arm with a gentle firmness while she wrapped the bandage around it with her right hand. She kept her eyes focused on her work so he was free to study her at will.

Trying not to think too much about the warmth of her hand on his, he found himself fascinated by the lone wispy curl of hair that had escaped her otherwise tightly controlled hairstyle. It swayed and danced with her every movement, an incongruously playful counterpoint to her businesslike demeanor.

His fingers actually itched with the desire to reach up and touch it, to let it curl around his finger and see if it felt as impossibly soft as it looked.

Startled once again by the direction his thoughts had taken, he forced himself to look away and found Dr. Pratt watching him thoughtfully. He suddenly felt like a schoolboy caught in some mischief.

A moment later, Mrs. Leggett was done and she stepped back and gave him a smile. "There. How's that? Not too tight I hope."

"It's fine, thank you." Not that he would have complained even if it hadn't been.

Dr. Pratt moved closer. "Now let's have a look at that ankle." The older man studied it a moment without touching him, then looked back up. "My recommendation is that we cut the boot off. Otherwise, you're going to find this much more than uncomfortable. And if your foot is broken it could cause even more damage." He spread his hands. "But the choice is yours."

Nate frowned. He didn't have the funds to spend on new footwear right now. And he was no stranger to pain. "Let's give removing it whole a try first."

"Very well. If you change your mind once I get started, though, you just have to say the word." He turned to his niece. "Verity, please stand behind Mr. Cooper so he has something to lean back against if he needs to."

With a nod, she did as her uncle asked, positioning herself at his back and gripping the edge of the table on either side of him.

And he was honest enough with himself to admit he liked the feel of having her all around him. But, knowing she wouldn't feel the same, he refused to take advantage of the situation.

He'd remain upright, no matter the cost.

With that in mind, this time he accepted the offer of a leather strap to bite down on.

Chapter Four

Verity could tell Mr. Cooper was doing his best to avoid leaning against her. She saw his knuckles whiten as his grip on the table edge tightened, saw his muscles tauten to unbelievable levels, saw the sweat bead on the back of his neck. This couldn't be good for that freshly stitched gash.

That reminder of his bandaged arm made her fingers tingle again. When she'd wrapped his arm earlier, she'd found it surprisingly difficult to maintain the polite detachment that usually came so easily to her. Instead she'd been keenly aware of the warmth of his skin, the sound of his breathing and the feel of his gaze on her.

That last had rattled her more than anything else. Why had he been staring at her with such intensity. What was he thinking? Did he believe it unladylike for a woman to do this sort of work? Or maybe he'd noticed her scar and was fascinated the way some folk were by such imperfections.

Uncle Grover asked him again if he'd prefer to have the boot cut off, but Mr. Cooper shook his head. Probably gritting his teeth too hard to speak, stubborn man.

A few excruciatingly long minutes later, he let out a single grunt of pain as her uncle managed to finally wrench the boot free. It was only then, as he reflexively sagged with relief, that he allowed himself to lean back against her.

She stood completely still, supporting his solid torso for the three heartbeats it took for realization to hit him. She knew the second it happened. He suddenly stiffened and then jerked upright again. Without turning, he tossed a mumbled apology over his shoulder. Was he embarrassed at what he might consider a show of weakness?

He removed the leather strip he'd been biting on and set it on the table beside him. Verity couldn't help but notice how deep an impression his teeth had made.

She moved around to assist her uncle and winced at how red and swollen his ankle was. As her uncle went about his examination, she kept an eye on the patient. Mr. Cooper bore it stoically, but she saw the muscles in his jaw tighten each time her uncle put the least bit of pressure on the injury.

At last her uncle straightened. "Well, the good news is you have a sprain, not a break."

"And the bad news?"

"You're going to need to stay off of it for a while."

Mr. Cooper frowned. That was obviously not what he'd wanted to hear. "How long?"

"If you want that ankle to heal properly I strongly suggest that you stay off of it for at least a week."

Mr. Cooper raked a hand through his hair. "But it's nothing that will keep me from my work?"

Uncle Grover gave him a severe look. "Only if you work sitting down."

"I do. And I suppose I can use a cane to get around."

"Crutches would be better. But with your bruised shoulder and the fresh stitches I've just applied to your arm, neither will be advisable for the next few days."

Verity saw the rebellion in Mr. Cooper's eyes. Then she realized that, like Hazel, he probably lived above his shop. Stairs would be very difficult, if not impossible, for him to navigate in his condition.

"What do you expect me to do in the meantime, just lie about?" His tone was short and clipped. "I have a business to run." Then, as if he realized he'd been abrupt, his expression lost some of its hard edge. "I'm sorry. None of this is your fault."

Verity disagreed. This was *all* her fault—he'd gotten injured because she hadn't kept a close watch on her daughter. "Perhaps I can assist you in some way," she offered. "I'm sure Uncle Grover can spare me for a few days."

Before her uncle could confirm what she'd said, Mr. Cooper spoke up. "I appreciate the offer, ma'am, but I don't think that will be necessary. I'll figure a way to work it out."

Was he just being polite? Or was it that he wasn't interested in having her around?

"You two can work that out later." Uncle Grover's stern look was aimed at them both. "For now, I would suggest Mr. Cooper stay here at the clinic, where we can keep him under observation."

"I don't think—"

Her uncle raised a hand. "If it's money you're worried about, don't." He met Mr. Cooper's gaze with an earnest, direct look. "You were injured helping my greatniece—there will be no charge for anything related to your injuries."

"That's very kind of you. But—"

How did he expect to go anywhere without help? "The only place you're going is to our infirmary." She could see another protest forming on his lips so she tried again. "You need to listen to my uncle. With that knot on your head, someone should keep an eye on you, at least for the next twenty-four hours, and since you live alone, this is the best place for you. Besides, I believe you live in an apartment above your shop, is that correct?"

"Yes, but—"

Uncle Grover joined the debate. "Even if you *could* make that climb to the second floor—" his tone made it clear that was doubtful "—it's not something you should be doing right now, not in your condition."

Verity saw Mr. Cooper's jaw tighten at the phrase "in your condition."

"If need be I can bunk downstairs in the shop for a few days."

"Young man, now you're just being stubborn."

"Besides," Verity added, "we have a nice comfortable bed right through there." She waved to a door in the far wall.

"It's just a sprained ankle. I'm not some sickly bed patient."

So his irritation stemmed from a bit of male pride. "Of course you're not. We just want to make certain we take good care of you. Besides, meals are provided, and I promise you Aunt Betty's cooking is something to look forward to. She has a pot of chicken and dumplings on the stove for lunch today."

Without giving their patient a chance to argue further, Uncle Grover turned to Verity and nodded to one of the cabinets. "Please fetch Mr. Cooper something more comfortable to wear while I prepare a draught for him. Then you'll need to step out so he can change."

"There's nothing wrong with the clothes I have on."

Was the man going to fight them every step of the way?

"I was being polite," Uncle Grover said. "Your shirt is now rags and the rest of your clothing is the worse for wear and, not to put too fine a point on it, filthy. For the sake of your health, and my niece's and wife's sensibilities, you need to change. There's a clean nightshirt we keep here just for such circumstances."

Verity hid a grin. Uncle Grover wasn't averse to using a bit of blackmail to get his way, especially when he felt it was for his patient's own good.

She placed a clean nightshirt on the table beside Mr. Cooper, then collected the soiled bandages and his discarded shirt and moved to the door. "I'll take care of these and let Aunt Betty know we'll have an occupant in the infirmary."

Uncle Grover nodded absently. "Thank you, my dear."

With a breezy smile for the still-glaring Mr. Cooper, she sailed out the door and closed it behind her.

She had to admit, she was pleased by the idea that Mr. Cooper would be under their roof a bit longer. It would give her an opportunity to get to know him better. Because she felt that the two of them were linked now in some intangible but very real way.

Partly because he'd saved her daughter's life.

And partly because she felt that little tug of attraction whenever she was around him.

Nate swallowed down the unpleasant-tasting draught Dr. Pratt handed him without a word, but refused the man's offer to help him change clothes. After the doctor made his exit, Nate frowned at the oversize nightshirt. This day had certainly taken an unexpected turn. It wasn't a very auspicious milestone on the road to his fresh start.

Then again, it hadn't been all bad. Getting to know Mrs. Leggett better certainly hadn't been an unpleasant experience. Of course, she seemed to think of him as either a patient or hero, neither of which sat well with him.

Best not to think on how he wanted her to think of him, though. With a huff of frustration, he snatched up the nightshirt.

Nate had barely finished changing when he heard a light tap on the door. Had the doctor forgotten something? But when he bade the person enter, it turned out to be Dr. Pratt's niece, rather than the doctor himself.

Verity entered the room and gave him an approving smile. Then she moved purposefully across the room. "Now let me get you settled into the clinic's guest room."

"Guest room, is it? I feel as if I was coerced rather than invited to stay there." He watched her, admiring her efficient movements.

"Oh, come now, it's not such a hardship to stay with us here, is it?"

How did he answer that? "I know you're doing what you think best." He offered her a half grin. "And *guest room* does sound friendlier than *infirmary*."

His answer seemed to satisfy her, but she dropped the subject. Instead she waved a hand toward a door across from the one through which she'd entered. "Our clinic *guest* room has comfortable beds for long-term patients. Fortunately, it's not in use right now so you'll have it all to yourself." She pulled a wheeled chair out from a corner of the room and pushed it over to him.

Ah, well, he supposed a conveyance that allowed him to sit up was preferable to that stretcher again.

She stood beside the examination table, obviously prepared to assist him.

"Where's your uncle?"

"He was called out to tend to another patient. Don't worry, I can get you situated." She moved closer to the examination table. "Just place a hand on my shoulder for support."

He didn't much relish the idea of treating her like a support post, but it didn't look as if he had much choice. "Thank you." He placed a hand on her shoulder, finding it both firm and soft at the same time. And then he caught the faint scent of honeysuckle again—it was all he could do not to inhale deeply.

Perhaps accepting her help wasn't such a bad thing after all.

He carefully slipped from the table, using her shoulder for balance more than support, then slid into the chair.

As soon as she saw that he was settled in, she moved behind the chair and set it in motion. "Don't worry, we'll see that you're made as comfortable as possible."

"I don't doubt that, but my shop—"

"Taken care of. I already asked Sheriff Gleason to have someone keep an eye on it so no one will be bothering it. If you'll let me know where you keep your key, I can go by a little later and lock it up for you."

The woman was nothing if not efficient. "But that doesn't take care of my dog."

"Oh, my." He heard the dismay in her voice. "I hadn't

thought of that." Then, as they crossed into the other room, "Of course we must see to your dog." There was a short pause where he could almost feel the wheels turning in her mind. "I suppose I'll just have to bring him here until you're well enough to go home."

From the way she said that, he could tell she wasn't particularly happy about it. Did she blame Beans for the accident? "Perhaps I should just go home after all."

"Nonsense. Joy has been after me for ages to get her a pet. You wouldn't want to deny her this taste of what it would be like, would you?"

Before he could respond, she moved on. "I don't imagine you could do much work for the next day or two, anyway. And for that I'm truly sorry. It's a poor reward for your valiant rescue."

He wished she'd quit bringing up terms like *rescue* and *hero*. She was right about his condition, though. He certainly didn't want to put out shoddy work by doing things one-handed. Nevertheless, it was frustrating to have to shut down his shop right now.

But he was suddenly feeling lethargic. Was it a delayed effect of his injuries? "Perhaps, just for today then. As to your question about the key, I keep it next to the till during the day."

Mrs. Leggett parked the chair next to one of two comfortable-looking beds. She turned down the coverlet, then straightened and faced him again. "Now let me help you into bed."

He nodded. While he was certain he could accomplish the task on his own, he found himself not quite so reluctant to accept her help this time.

She placed a hand around his waist as he stood, then helped him ease over to the bed. Once he'd swung his legs into the bed, she fussily arranged the light coverlet over him.

"There now." She stepped back. "That draught Uncle Grover gave you should help ease your pain and also help you to sleep, which is the best thing for you right now. We'll talk again when you wake up."

A sleeping draught? No wonder his lids were feeling heavy.

She pointed to a cord that hung in easy reach of the bed. "If you need anything, pull that cord. It'll ring a bell in the house and one of us will be right in to see what you need."

He tried to watch as she bustled about the room, but his eyelids were getting heavier. She pulled the curtains closed, cocooning the room in shadow. He lost sight of her for a moment, then suddenly she was there bending over him. "One last question. I'm afraid your trousers and shirt are in a sorry state. Would you like me to get you a fresh change of clothes when I fetch your dog?"

Were they really talking about his clothing now? "I suppose. They're in the wardrobe in my bedchamber."

She smoothed the covers over his chest one more time, and the gesture brought him back to a time when his family had been intact and his world had been pleasant and uncomplicated.

"Sleep now," she said softly. "We'll talk again when you wake up."

So he did.

Verity softly closed the door behind her. Mr. Cooper was a true hero in her book—literally a godsend to her and Joy. She was only sorry he'd paid such a steep price for his quick action and bravery. If only there was something she could do to make certain his business didn't suffer for his absence.

She headed for the kitchen, where she found Joy and Aunt Betty preparing lunch. Verity still felt the need to reassure herself that her baby was okay.

Aunt Betty looked up. "How's our patient doing?"

"He's settled in the infirmary." Verity moved to stand behind Joy's chair and placed a hand lightly on the girl's shoulder. "Hopefully he'll sleep for a few hours."

Her aunt nodded. "Poor man. Sleep's the best thing for him."

"Before he fell asleep, he reminded me that he has a dog." Joy's head went up at the mention of the animal. "I assured him I'd see to it while he's laid up." She gave her aunt a diffident look. "I can check on it several times during the day, of course. But I was wondering what you would think about my bringing the animal here instead. I know Uncle Grover doesn't like house pets, but it's a small dog, so it shouldn't be much trouble."

Her aunt hesitated for just a moment, then spoke. "Of course you should bring it here. I'm sure your uncle will agree, it's the least we can do for the man who saved our little Joy."

"Thank you." Relieved, Verity rushed to reassure her aunt. "And don't worry, I'll make sure the animal doesn't get in your or Uncle Grover's way."

Aunt Betty gave her a gently chiding look. "Verity dear, this is your and Joy's home now, too. You must learn to treat it as such."

Only it wasn't, not really. Verity felt that longing again to have a house of her very own. If only she could open a millinery shop with some assurance it wouldn't fail.

Joy, who was practically squirming in her seat, looked up. "Are you really going to get Beans?"

Verity smiled at the hopeful expression on her daughter's face. "I am. Would you like to come with me?"

Joy immediately slid from her chair. "Yes, ma'am."

As she and Joy headed out a few minutes later, Verity found herself moving with a bounce in her step. She tried to tell herself that it was just an eagerness to get this errand taken care of, but she knew better. Was it wrong of her to be so intrigued by the idea of getting a peek at Mr. Cooper's lodgings?

Then she pulled her shoulders back. Of course not. It was nothing more than a natural urge to learn more about the man who'd saved her daughter's life.

Or at least that's what she told herself.

Chapter Five

Obviously excited by the idea of seeing Beans again, Joy chattered all the way to Mr. Cooper's place. Fortunately, most of her comments were directed to her doll, Lulu, and didn't require a response from Verity. She kept firm hold of her daughter's hand the whole time, but her mind kept drifting to thoughts of what Mr. Cooper's place might look like and if it would provide new insights into the man himself.

When they arrived, Verity spotted Calvin Hendricks seated on the bench that sat between the apothecary and the saddle shop. Calvin was a local youth who was fast approaching adulthood. Apparently he'd been the one tapped by Sheriff Gleason to keep an eye on Mr. Cooper's shop.

"Hi there, Miz Leggett." Calvin stood, then turned to her daughter. "And hello, Joy. I sure am glad to see you walking around and looking good as new."

"Mr. Cooper saved me," Joy said, as if it was momentous news. Which, as far as Verity was concerned, it was.

"That he did. And it was right heroic of him, too." Calvin turned back to Verity. "How's he doing?"

"He's got some painful bruises, a gash on his arm and a sprained ankle, but thankfully nothing that won't heal. Uncle Grover stitched him up and he's resting at the clinic." She waved toward the saddle shop. "I'm here to fetch his dog and a change of clothes, and to get his key so we can lock the place up."

Calvin nodded. "Anything I can help with?"

"Thank you, but no. It shouldn't take me more than a few minutes."

"Well, if you change your mind, I'll be right out here." And the youth sat back down on the bench, as if to demonstrate he wasn't going anywhere.

Verity opened the shop door and stepped inside. She and Joy were immediately greeted by a yipping ball of excited dog. Joy stooped down to greet the animal and quickly had her face washed in doggie kisses.

Verity carefully closed the door behind them, unwilling to risk Beans running out and Joy following him in a repeat of the earlier mishap.

Deciding to tackle the matter of clothing first, she headed toward the stairs at the back of the shop. She slowly crossed the room, studying her surroundings with keen interest. The place had a definite masculine feel— all leather and wood and metal.

Harnesses and leather straps of various lengths and widths hung from pegs on the wall to her right. There was a worktable to her left. A selection of tools, most of which she didn't recognize, were displayed there. They were neatly arranged and organized, though his system wasn't immediately obvious. She imagined him working here, wearing the heavy canvas apron that hung on a peg behind the table, his head bent over his work, his strong, callused hands wielding those strange tools, his arresting blue eyes focused on his work.

The smell of leather hung heavy in the room, so strong she could almost taste it. Under that scent, she could also detect the aroma of oil and just a faint tang of metal.

Only when she reached the bottom of the stairs did Verity realize her daughter hadn't followed her. Appalled by her lack of attention so soon after Joy's accident, she spun around. "Come along," she said, holding out her hand. "We need to fetch something from Mr. Cooper's room upstairs."

Joy's lower lip pushed out in something suspiciously like a pout. "But I want to stay down here and play with Beans."

"Beans can come with us."

Her daughter's expression cleared. "Okay." She stood and waved to the dog. "Come on, Beans."

The dog obediently trotted at her heels, then bounded up the stairs with her.

The staircase led up to a landing that had an open sitting room straight ahead and a kitchen to the right. The rooms were stark, with only a bare minimum of furniture. Perhaps Mr. Cooper just hadn't had the time, or the funds, to do much more. But surely he would have brought some personal possessions with him, from his former home.

There was a door off to her left that she assumed led to his bedchamber. "Joy, you and Beans can play right over there. I won't be but a minute."

She marched to the door, then hesitated before opening it. It suddenly seemed invasive to enter his private space, even if she did have his permission. Which was silly. She was only going to fetch him a change of clothing and then leave. And she did have his permission to be here, after all.

Verity opened the door and stepped inside. A quick glance around showed a neatly made bed, a wooden chair and a small bedside table. On the opposite wall was a trunk and the wardrobe. Everything looked as if it had seen better days.

She noticed a picture on the bedside table, and her curiosity got the best of her. She went closer and discovered it was the image of a young woman. She was quite lovely, in a delicate, fragile sort of way. Her clothes were fine quality, her heart-shaped face very sweet and delicate. She had an ethereal quality to her and seemed to be everything Verity was not. Was this the kind of woman Mr. Cooper admired?

Who was she? She was obviously someone who meant a great deal to him as it was the only picture, the only personal item really, in the room. A family member? A sweetheart? And where was she now?

Verity straightened abruptly and turned away. What was she doing? She had no right to snoop into Mr. Cooper's personal life. He'd given her permission to take care of some necessities for him, not snoop into things that were none of her business. She marched to the wardrobe, grabbed a clean shirt and pair of trousers, then headed back out.

"Come along, Joy, time to go."

As she descended the stairs she thought how different his clothing smelled from what Arthur's had. Where her husband's had smelled of antiseptic, soap and cigars, Mr. Cooper's smelled of leather, of course, but also soap and something faintly woodsy.

She decided that she liked it.

* * *

Nate woke from his nap to see flowers floating in front of his eyes. What in the world—

Was he still dreaming?

"Do you like them?"

The flowers, which he now saw were in a glass jar, floated to the side and the little girl holding them finally came into view.

"Well, hello there, Joy. Does your mother know you're in here?"

"I just wanted to give you these," she said, not answering his question. She held the flowers out toward him a little more. "Do you like them?" she asked again.

"They're lovely."

Apparently this was the correct response, because her face split with a grin. "They're for you. From me and Lulu." She proudly held them out to him.

"Why, thank you. But who's Lulu?"

The child held out her doll. "My dolly."

He looked the doll in the "eyes." "Very nice to meet you, Lulu." Then he turned back to Joy. "The flowers are nice, but may I ask why you are giving me such a nice gift?"

"You rescued me and Lulu. You're a hero."

There was that word again. "It was my pleasure. But little girls really shouldn't play in the street."

"That's what Mama told me, too." Her tone wasn't particularly penitent. "But I wasn't really playing in the street. I was trying to catch Buttons."

"Buttons?"

"That's Miss Hazel's cat. He likes to have me chase him."

Nate let the girl's interpretation of the cat's motives stand. But he had a feeling Mrs. Leggett was going to have her hands full raising this one. "I see. But you still shouldn't have gone out in the street."

Joy pursed her lips in a stubborn line. Then she smiled. "I'll put your flowers right here on the table where you can see them whenever you want to." She put words to action, then came back to stand beside him. "Everyone is saying you're a hero. What's a hero?"

Now, how was he supposed to answer that? "First of all, I'm not a hero. I was just the first one to get to you. But to answer your question, a hero is a person who does something for other people who need help, without worrying about what it might cost him."

"Oh." She pondered that for a while then waved toward his bandaged arm. "Does it hurt a lot?"

He was touched by the worried look in her eyes. "I've had worse."

She hugged her doll to her chest. "It's my fault, isn't it?"

Another tricky question. He studied her woefully guilty expression, wondering how best to answer her. But before he could say anything, Joy spoke again.

"I'm sorry. And Lulu's sorry, too."

He smiled. "Apology accepted."

She brightened and changed the subject. "Beans is in the kitchen with Aunt Betty. We gave him some of the scraps from lunch. Me and Mama brought him here so he could be close to you. Do you want me to go get him for you?"

"Not right now—"

The door opened behind the little girl, and Mrs. Leggett came in carrying a tray. He sat up straighter, his stomach reacting to the delectable aromas with a rude rumble.

Mrs. Leggett, however, was staring at her daughter rather than him. "Joy, what are you doing in here?"

Her daughter looked at her as if that was a particularly silly question and waved toward the makeshift posy. "I brought Mr. Cooper some flowers, see? You said we should always thank people who do nice things for us."

He saw the woman struggle with whether or not to chastise the girl. "True," she said, finally. "But bothering Mr. Cooper is not a good way to thank him. I hope you didn't wake him from his nap."

"She wasn't bothering me," Nate said quickly. "I woke up on my own. But it was nice to have such a pretty face to wake up to."

And nicer still to have Mrs. Leggett's smiling presence here with him. Even if that smile was currently directed at her daughter.

Verity smiled as Joy preened at Mr. Cooper's compliment. He was a much more thoughtful man than she'd first assumed. She set down her tray and turned back to Joy. "We'll discuss this later. Why don't you go check on Beans?"

"Yes, ma'am." Before heading for the door, Joy turned back to the patient. "Thank you again for saving my life, Mr. Cooper. And I think you're wrong. You really *are* a hero." And with those words she skipped out of the room.

Once Joy disappeared out the door, Verity turned to her daughter's rescuer and shook her head. "I'm afraid Joy is much too impulsive. I hope she wasn't bothering you."

"Not at all." He sat up straighter and she hurried to his side, setting the tray down and plumping pillows behind him. All part of being a nurse.

He inhaled deeply. "Whatever you brought in with you smells wonderful."

"It's that bowl of my aunt Betty's chicken and dumplings I promised you. I thought you might be ready for something to eat."

He smiled and she liked the way it softened his entire face. "You thought correctly."

Verity lifted a napkin from the tray and handed it to him, then carefully set the tray on his lap. "How's this?"

"Fine, thank you."

Then, as she took the spoon, he frowned. "There's no need for you to wait on me."

"Are you sure?" She'd been rather looking forward to feeding him. "I know your arm and shoulder are injured."

"Just on my left side. My right arm is fine."

"Very well." She surrendered the spoon reluctantly. But for some reason she wasn't quite ready to leave. After all, she needed to keep an eye on him to gauge his condition.

"I locked up your shop when I fetched Beans," she said. Then she waved a hand to the small dresser across from his bed. "Your change of clothes is in the upper drawer and the key is on top."

"Thank you." He scooped up another spoonful of the chicken and dumplings, his gaze never leaving hers. "How long did I sleep?"

"About four hours. It's after one o'clock."

He grimaced and she hurried to reassure him.

"No, that's a good thing. You needed the rest. It helps you to heal faster." He didn't appear convinced, so she changed the subject. "How does your leg feel?"

"Better."

Not a very descriptive answer. "Uncle Grover should be in shortly to change the dressing on your arm and also have another look at your other injuries."

"Perhaps then he'll see that I can manage well enough to go home."

Why was he in such a hurry to leave them? There certainly wasn't anyone at his place to rush home to. Instead of responding to his comment, however, she crossed the room to open the curtains. "Let's let a little more light in here, shall we?"

When she returned to his side, she lifted the tray with the now empty bowl and smiled down at him. "Would you like some more?"

"Not now, thank you. But please relay my compliments to your aunt. That was very good, especially compared to my own cooking."

Was he dismissing her? Perhaps he wanted to rest some more. "Is there anything else I can get for you?"

He seemed to hesitate a moment, then raised a brow in question. "Something to read perhaps?"

That was unexpected. "Of course. What sort of books do you like?"

"What do you have on hand?"

"I'm afraid Uncle Grover's library consists mostly of medical tomes and journals. I believe Aunt Betty has some books of poetry and some devotionals. I have a volume of poetry, some Shakespeare, Dickens and a few of Mr. Twain's novels. And of course some children's stories for Joy. Oh, and I think I also still have a copy of yesterday's *Turnabout Gazette* if you haven't seen it." She waved a hand. "If none of that is of interest, I'd be glad to find you something at Abigail's library. Just let me know what sorts of books appeal to you."

"I've read Shakespeare and Dickens. Perhaps I'll try Twain. And I believe I will take a look at the *Gazette*."

Apparently he was well educated. Now that she thought on it, there was a certain refinement that crept into his speech from time to time. It embarrassed her that she'd made so many wrong assumptions about this man. She should know better than to jump to judgments.

"I'll fetch the book and newspaper for you as soon as I put away these dishes. Can I do anything else for you?"

After his *No, thank you* response, Verity made her exit and slowly headed toward the parlor, where most of the family's books were located. Her thoughts, though, were on Mr. Cooper rather than her errand.

There was still a faint air of something less than welcoming simmering below the surface in this man, a feeling of standoffishness. But for some reason it didn't scare her away—in fact it had just the opposite effect. She was beginning to see him as a brave, honorable, well-educated person who just needed someone to teach him to trust enough to open up.

If he had a wilder side to him, well, he seemed to have it well controlled. And that was a sign of maturity and responsibility, wasn't it?

The sound of a tap at the door pulled Nate from his reading. One thing he could say for this place, they respected a person's privacy. Which, after his time in prison, was another thing he'd never take for granted again.

He sat up straighter. "Come in."

Mrs. Leggett stuck her head in the doorway. "You have a visitor, but if you'd prefer to rest I can ask him to come back at another time."

There was only one person here in Turnabout who would be visiting him. "Not at all. Show him in."

She gave him an assessing look, as if gauging his condition, then nodded and withdrew.

Sure enough, Adam Barr strolled through the open door a few minutes later.

"Hope I'm not disturbing you," his friend said, "but Dr. Pratt said you're up for visitors."

Nate waved Adam to a chair near the bed. "Actually, other than being a bit banged up, I'm fine. I'd be back home if it was up to me, but Dr. Pratt practically strong-armed me into staying."

"He cares about his patients," Adam said. Then he grinned. "Are the ladies of the house smothering you with kindness?"

Smothering wasn't exactly the word he'd use, but he let it stand. "It's a definite change from what I've been used to."

"A little female attention is never a bad thing." Then Adam leaned back. "I hear you've become something of a town hero as of this morning."

Nate grimaced. "I just happened to be in the right place at the right time. You and I both know there's nothing heroic about me."

Adam frowned. "I know nothing of the sort. In fact, I have good reason to believe otherwise." He stroked the faded scar on his cheek, a reminder to both of them of how they'd met—in a prison fight.

When Adam had entered prison all those years ago, Nate had already been there six months. That first day, a couple of the more hardened inmates had cornered the new arrival as he exited the food line and Nate had weighed in to even the odds. The two had been friends ever since.

"That was just me looking for a fight—nothing more."

"That's not how I saw it." Adam crossed his arms and gave Nate a drawn-brow look. "Besides, I spent time in prison, too. Do you think that makes me less capable of acting heroically?"

Nate gave a sharp, dismissive wave. "You didn't belong there. I did."

That was one reason, besides his own selfish desire to be free of his past mistakes, that he couldn't reveal to the townsfolk that he'd spent time in prison. Because, since folks knew that he and Adam were already acquainted, any confession on his part might cause speculation about Adam's own past.

"You had your reasons for what you did." Adam shrugged. "But be that as it may, you served your time, so your debt is paid. And everyone deserves a second chance."

He *had* come to Turnabout looking for a fresh start, a place to begin again without the anchor of his past to weigh him down. Knowing that his friend believed in him allowed him to have faith that he might be able to pull it off.

He just wished he felt as if he deserved this second chance. He knew the Good Lord had forgiven him long ago, but he was still having trouble forgiving himself.

Then Adam changed the subject. "So how long do you plan to lie around here lollygagging?"

"Assuming Dr. Pratt doesn't tie me to my bed, I'm heading back to my place in the morning."

"Well, I wouldn't be in too big a hurry. I hear Mrs. Pratt is quite a cook."

"You've heard correctly. I've already sampled her chicken and dumplings and it has my own cooking beat by a mile." Then he turned serious. "Which reminds me, would you mind letting Mrs. Ortolon know I may not be able to help her at the boardinghouse for the next several days?" He touched the bandage on his arm. "I definitely won't be swinging an ax anytime soon." He'd been doing odd jobs at the boardinghouse in the evenings for meals and pocket change to help him get by until his business was better established.

"I'm sure she already knows, but I'll stop by when I leave here."

"Thanks." Nate brushed at a bit of lint on his coverlet. "Mrs. Leggett—she's a widow, I take it."

"She is. Her husband died a little over a year ago. She and Joy moved back here shortly after it happened."

Some time had passed, then. Of course, he knew from his own experience that one never totally "got over" the death of a loved one. "So she wasn't living here when he passed away." He hoped she'd had friends, people she could lean on, around her.

Adam shook his head then shifted in his seat. "There's something you should probably know if you're going to be around Mrs. Leggett much—her husband's passing wasn't peaceful. He died of a gunshot."

Nate froze for a moment as that sunk in. That must have been horrific for her. Had she witnessed it? Had Joy?

Then Adam cleared his throat and gave him a look that had a touch of sympathy in it. "It happened during a bank robbery."

Nate dropped back against his pillow as all the implications of that news thundered down around him like a rockslide.

Chapter Six

After Adam had gone, Nate retrieved his book, but he didn't open it immediately.

Adam's revelation changed everything. He couldn't stay here, couldn't trespass on this family's hospitality any longer than he already had, couldn't bear to have Mrs. Leggett look at him with that admiration and gratitude, not knowing what he now knew.

Injured ankle or no, he'd make it back to his place. He just wished he'd thought to ask Adam to bring a wagon around to transport him.

Deciding to test his mobility, Nate threw off the bedcovers and stood, putting all his weight on his good leg.

Before he could try taking a step, there was another tap at the door. He clenched his jaw and sat back down on the bed, but left both feet on the floor. It might not be Mrs. Leggett. It could be Dr. Pratt or even Adam, returning to say something he'd forgotten earlier. "Come in."

But, of course, it *was* Mrs. Leggett. She halted just inside the doorway and frowned at him. "What are you doing up?"

His frustration and guilt spilled out before he could

stop them. "For goodness' sake—I have a sprained ankle, not a bullet in my chest."

Her recoil brought him up short. None of this was her fault. "I'm sorry, I'm just tired of being treated like an invalid."

She recovered quickly. "Of course. But you *do* know that you have to take it easy if you want to heal properly, don't you?"

"I do. But I don't take well to mollycoddling. In fact, I can get absolutely churlish. Which is why I should head on back to my place now."

That set her back again. "Nonsense. We've already agreed that you should spend the night here. Nothing's changed."

Oh, but it had. In fact, *everything* had changed. "I know what I said earlier. But now that I've had my rest, I'm thinking clearer and I believe it's better if I go on home." He shifted, feeling at a distinct disadvantage dressed in this ridiculous nightshirt.

She crossed her arm like a schoolmarm confronting an unreasonable child. "Uncle Grover, as an experienced physician, would certainly know better than you how to deal with your injuries. And he has stated that it's important for someone to keep an eye on you for at least twenty-four hours."

He shrugged. "I'm sure I'll be fine." Then, before she could throw another argument at him, he added, "You may consider me foolhardy if you wish, but regardless of you or your uncle's warnings, I plan to head home as soon as you leave so I can get dressed."

He held her gaze, refusing to back down, hoping she'd give in to his determination. If she only knew the truth about him, she'd be showing him to the door rather than trying to convince him to stay.

Finally, the authoritative frown slipped from her expression and a furrow of uncertainty creased her brow in its place. "I see. You obviously feel quite strongly on the matter." She slid a stray tendril of hair behind her ear. "Have we done something to offend you? Made you feel unwelcome or uncomfortable in some way?"

"No, of course not."

"Then I don't understand. Why the sudden change of attitude and the rush to be gone from here?"

What could he say? That he was no longer comfortable here not because of anything they'd done but because of what *he'd* done, because of the kind of man he was? If he said that, he'd have to give her the whole sordid story, and this wasn't the time or place for that. If he was lucky, that time would never come. "I just don't want to be a bother," he said feebly. Then he waved a hand in near surrender. "If you're certain it won't put you or the doctor out..."

Her smile returned, as if he'd just given her a wonderful gift. "That's settled, then—we'll have no more talk of your leaving today." She became businesslike again. "Shall I help you get settled back in the bed?"

Nate shook his head, doing his best to not put her out more than he had to. "I'm tired of being a slugabed. I think I'll get dressed and sit up for a while."

He saw the objection form on her lips, but then she seemed to think better of it. "As long as you don't wear yourself out, I don't see any harm in that." She crossed the room to retrieve his change of clothing.

As she brought it over to him, she took a quick look around the room. "If you're going to be sitting up for a while, the most comfortable option may be to use the wheeled chair. I can put a pillow at your back to make it more comfortable."

"Whatever you think best." He might as well capitulate completely.

She wheeled the chair next to him, then retrieved a pillow from the spare bed and plumped it up against the back of the chair. Then she turned back to him with one fist planted on her hip. "I would tell you not to take advantage of the added mobility this chair gives you," she said, her tone dry, "but I know I'd probably be wasting my breath. So instead I'll tell you to be careful you don't put any strain on that left arm of yours."

Was that actually a hint of amusement in her eyes? Surely the straitlaced widow wasn't teasing him.

"Do you need help with anything else?" she asked.

"I think I can manage."

"Very well." She waved toward the bell pull. "Just remember to give that a tug if you find you do need something."

As he watched her leave, he decided that what he most needed was to get away from here as soon as possible.

Otherwise, his resolve to keep his distance from the intriguing—and now altogether off-limits—Mrs. Leggett was going to be very sorely tested.

As Verity closed the infirmary door, her smile faded. What was going on with Mr. Cooper? Why had he been so insistent that he needed to go home? It had almost seemed like he was fleeing from something.

Did he truly prefer to be alone? That was such a heartbreaking thought.

Well, someone needed to show him the joy that could

come with being an active part of a welcoming community. This town had certainly welcomed her back with open arms when Arthur had been killed. No, more than welcomed her, they had shown her love and compassion, praying for her and with her, letting her know she was not alone in her grief.

Of course she'd spent most of her growing-up years here in Uncle Grover's home, had been one of them, so to speak. But she had seen these folks offer that same warm welcome to strangers who needed a place to start afresh. Like Mr. Tucker and those ten orphan children who'd arrived here last year. He'd actually ended up married to the local widow Eileen Pierce and together they'd adopted all ten children.

Yes, sir, this town was a good place to make a new life for oneself, if one really wanted it.

Then again, perhaps that was the problem. Did he prefer to be left alone?

She shook her head. That was a foolish thought. Some people were forced by circumstances to cut themselves off from the world, but no one *preferred* to be alone. Even if a person thought that was what he wanted, he just needed to be shown the joys of having friends and neighbors who cared.

Well, if that's what Mr. Cooper needed, it was the least she could do for the man who had saved her daughter's life.

She smiled, her mind spinning with ideas of how she might accomplish that.

Sometime later that afternoon, Nate was roused from a light doze by a soft knock on the door. Sitting up straighter in the chair and hoping there were no traces of sleep remaining on his face, he bade the visitor enter.

It was Mrs. Leggett again. "How are you doing?" she asked. "Tired of sitting up yet?" No doubt it was part of her job here to check in on the patients occasionally.

He grimaced. "Actually, I'm much more tired of this forced inactivity. The book is good, but I'd prefer to be up and about."

"We can't have that, but would a change of scene help? While Uncle Grover doesn't want you to put any weight on that foot just yet, I could wheel you into the parlor or out on the porch if you'd like." A saucy note of challenge lit her eyes. "I could even sit down to a game of chess with you, if you play. But I have to warn you, I often beat Uncle Grover when we play."

Despite his intention to remain aloof, Nate found himself responding to this teasing side of her. "I haven't played chess in quite a while, but I've never been one to back down from a challenge."

Within a few minutes she had wheeled him into the parlor and up to a small table. Then she pulled the game board out from a cupboard and took a seat across from him.

Mrs. Leggett proved to be a thoughtful, strategic player. But she also liked to chat as she contemplated her moves. "Joy is enjoying having Beans here."

"I'm glad."

She moved one of her pawns, then leaned back to wait on his countermove. "If you don't mind my saying so, he seems like a rather odd choice of pet for a man such as yourself."

He shrugged. "Actually, Beans chose me."

"What do you mean?"

He made his move, then sat back. "I spent a few days in Kansas City on my way here. One day this ridiculously small mutt showed up outside the hotel where I was staying. It was obvious the animal had had a hard time of it." It had been raining and the dog was wet, dirty, scratched up and obviously starving.

"I stumbled on him at a weak moment and made the mistake of feeding him a few scraps." Nate shrugged. "He started following me around and I couldn't find anyone who'd lay claim to him. When he followed me to the train depot, I took him with me on impulse."

The truth was, the mutt reminded him of a dog his sister had adopted when she was a kid. And that's where the name had come from, as well. Because of her pet's dark brown coat, Susanna had named it Coffee Bean, but it had quickly been shortened to Beans.

Nate shook off that memory and focused on Mrs. Leggett again as she moved a pawn. "I guess you could say both Beans and I came here looking for a fresh start."

That drew a speculative look from her. Had he revealed too much?

He made a quick move on the chessboard, then changed the subject. "Joy is certainly an exuberant child."

Mrs. Leggett's expression took on a wry twist. "She is definitely a handful. Her lack of fear scares me sometimes."

There was that hint of timidity again. "Most children are born fearless. They have to be taught to fear. Surely you don't want your daughter to be fear*ful*."

Her posture turned defensive. "A little bit of caution wouldn't go amiss."

He didn't let that go unchallenged. "As long as it doesn't turn into excessive timidity."

She frowned at that, obviously disagreeing with his sentiment. But she didn't comment. Instead, she changed the subject. "Did you have a nice visit with Mr. Barr?"

Nice? That was much too soft and feminine a term to suit him. "Adam was just checking in on me."

"Do you mind if I ask how you and Mr. Barr know each other?"

Nate hesitated. How did he answer that question without revealing too much about his, and for that matter Adam's, secrets?

Verity saw the hesitation on his face. Was there some private matter there she'd inadvertently intruded on? How could she take the question back without making it worse?

Before Verity could figure that out, he spoke up.

"I've known Adam for a number of years." His gaze was focused on the chessboard rather than her. "We've maintained a correspondence since he's moved here. His letters made Turnabout sound so appealing that when I was ready to relocate I decided to try it here."

She realized he hadn't exactly answered her question. But she ignored that and moved on. "And where is home?"

"I was born and raised in Plattisburg, Pennsylvania."

"Do you still have family there?"

His jaw tightened. "No, they're all gone now. That's why I decided to try a change of scenery."

Verity's heart went out to him at that admission. She'd lost people in her life as well, but there'd always been other family members around to help her through the rough time. Mr. Cooper was definitely a man in need of a community.

But she'd pressed him enough for one sitting.

And apparently he thought so, too, because he changed the subject. He waved a hand toward the piano at the other end of the room. "That looks like a fine instrument. Do you play?"

She shook her head. "No, that belonged to my mother, who got it from her mother. I'm afraid I never learned to play. Joy's started to show some interest, though, so I'm hoping when she's a little older I can find someone to teach her."

"Actually, she's not too young to start now."

She looked at him with renewed interest. "It sounds like you know something on that subject yourself."

He gave her a little half smile that seemed to hide some other emotion. "I used to play, but it's been years."

She glanced back at the piano before meeting his gaze again. "I'm not sure if it's still in tune, but if you'd like to play while you're here, please feel free. It would actually be nice to hear it get some use again."

He lifted his left arm. "Aren't you worried about my using this arm too much?"

"Aren't there pieces written to be played with one hand only?"

He raised a brow. "Is that another challenge, Mrs. Leggett?"

She saw the amused twist of his lips, and something inside her nudged her toward a capricious response. Lifting her rook, she placed her fingertips to the area above her heart and schooled her features into a shocked expression. "Dear me, Mr. Cooper, I would never extend such a *taxing* physical challenge to an incapacitated patient." And with a sweet smile for him, she set her rook back down on the board. "Check."

He gave her a full-blown smile at that and inclined his head in acknowledgment. "Touché." Shifting in his chair, he focused back on the board.

The game went on for another twenty minutes, and the conversation turned to more impersonal topics as they continued their game. But her thoughts kept drifting back to his unexpected reaction to her question about Adam Barr. She knew both he and Mr. Barr were from Pennsylvania, but had no idea how they'd ended up here in Turnabout. Was Mr. Cooper hiding something to protect his friend?

Or himself?

Verity eventually lost the game, but she didn't mind. While she had enough of a competitive streak to enjoy winning, she also enjoyed just playing the game with a likable competitor. And Mr. Cooper was definitely likable. Even though he was undeniably guarded, the occasional peeks she caught of his self-deprecating attitude, his dry humor and his confident intelligence were quite an appealing combination.

She had just stood to put the game away when a bell sounded. She gave Mr. Cooper an apologetic smile. "That means we have a visitor at the clinic. I should check in to see if Uncle Grover needs me for anything. Would you like me to wheel you back to the infirmary or would you prefer to stay here?"

"I'll stay here, if you don't mind."

It was the answer she'd expected. "Of course. Make yourself at home." She crossed the room and grabbed a large wooden box.

"This is Aunt Betty's stereopticon," she said as she

set it on the table in front of him. "I'm sure she wouldn't mind if you took a look at it."

With that, she hurried away to check in with Uncle Grover.

Nate knew he was in trouble. Mrs. Leggett was becoming more than just an interesting woman to him. She was bright, kind, composed. And, when she let herself relax, had an unexpected sense of humor. Granted, he didn't have a lot of experience with women—he'd gone to prison at nineteen and before that, well, before that there had been other priorities in his life.

But he knew enough to know this woman was special.

And she was still very much off-limits to him.

Chapter Seven

Verity hurried up the walk. Uncle Grover had sent her to the apothecary shop to pick something up for him and she'd decided to stop by the library while she was out to pick up a book for Mr. Cooper. Her uncle was no doubt wondering what had taken her so long.

She delivered the packet to her uncle, chatted with him for a few minutes about how the Simmons boy was doing since his splint had been removed yesterday, then she glanced toward the far door.

"Has Mr. Cooper returned to the infirmary yet?"

Her uncle looked up distractedly. "I haven't seen him come through. As far as I know he's still in the parlor, where you left him."

Verity moved toward the door that connected the clinic to the house. "I suppose I should check on him then. He might be ready to get some rest."

Her uncle nodded and turned to the bookcase behind him, obviously searching for a particular tome.

As Verity stepped inside the house, she heard someone playing the piano. Had Mr. Cooper decided to try it one-handed after all?

She quietly moved to the open parlor door and paused on the threshold. Sure enough, Mr. Cooper sat in front of the piano, playing with his good hand. He wasn't using sheet music so he must be playing from memory.

He sat in profile to her, so she could see his expression as he played. There was a look of intense concentration tinged with frustration—no doubt because he was forced to play one-handed. Even so, he was doing a remarkable job.

When he was finished with the piece, he sat perfectly still, his hand still resting on the keys, his head down.

"That was lovely," she said softly.

His head jerked up and around to face her, and for a moment she saw an unexpected vulnerability there. Then he straightened and gave her a crooked smile. That vulnerability—if it had been there at all—was gone. "You must be tone deaf if you call that lovely," he said drily.

Relieved that he'd decided to take her intrusion without rancor, she smiled and stepped into the room. "Actually, my ear for music is said to be pretty good."

"Just because you sing in the choir…"

So he'd noticed that, had he? For some reason that cheered her. "Actually, I'm the choir director. So yes, I think that makes me somewhat qualified to judge." She remembered the book she carried and held it out to him. "Here, I picked this up at the library for you."

She saw a flicker of surprise in his eyes before he reached out to take it from her.

"Thank you." He studied the cover. "*Ranch Life and the Hunting-Trail* by Theodore Roosevelt."

She couldn't tell from his expression how he felt about it. "Have you already read it?"

"No."

"It's a new arrival to Abigail's library. I thought it looked intriguing."

"And so it does." He held it up. "Thanks again. I look forward to reading this."

Joy skipped into the room just then, Beans at her heels. As soon as the dog caught sight of Mr. Cooper, he bounded over to his side and put his paws up on the man's good leg.

Verity's gaze focused on the way Mr. Cooper absently reached down to scratch Beans's head. There was something to be said about a man who cared for his dog.

And a man whose dog cared so enthusiastically for him.

Joy turned to Verity. "Aunt Betty says to tell you that supper will be ready soon. And that she hopes Mr. Cooper is up to joining us at the table."

Joy turned to Mr. Cooper and stepped closer. "I hope you're feeling better."

"I am, Joy, thank you. And those pretty flowers you brought sure did brighten up my room."

Okay, there was another point in Mr. Cooper's favor—he was going out of his way to be nice to her daughter.

Joy smiled. "So I helped?"

"You most certainly did."

Joy stooped to pet Beans, but she kept her gaze on Mr. Cooper. "Was that you playing the piano a while ago?"

"It was."

Her expression turned wistful. "Mama says I can learn one day, too."

Her daughter's words drew Verity up short. Why hadn't she ever heard that longing note in Joy's voice when they discussed piano lessons before? Was that new? Or had Verity not been paying close enough attention?

She decided she'd talk to Zella, the church pianist, after the service on Sunday about giving Joy lessons.

Nate looked around the supper table with the sinking feeling that he was fighting a losing battle. As soon as he'd learned the circumstances of Mrs. Leggett's husband's death, he'd known he had to pull back and not try to forge anything more than a polite, neighborly relationship with this family.

Yet here he was, seated with them, eating their food, sharing their hospitality.

Once they'd settled in their seats at the table and Dr. Pratt had said the blessing, Mrs. Pratt reached for the bowl of peas that sat to her left. "Allow me to serve your plate, Mr. Cooper. You shouldn't be straining that arm of yours this soon."

"Thank you, ma'am." Everything about the doctor's wife seemed soft—her voice, her appearance, her temperament.

Dr. Pratt accepted the biscuit plate from his niece. "Well, young man, other than your accident this morning, I hope you're enjoying your move to Turnabout."

"Yes, sir. This seems to be every bit as fine a place as Adam assured me it would be."

"You mean Adam Barr?"

"Yes, sir. He wrote me several letters extolling the virtues of Turnabout."

"Adam is a fine young man. Despite being from back east, he's become an important and well-liked member of our community."

Nate wondered if the same would be able to be said of him someday.

Mrs. Leggett spoke up. "Turnabout is growing. When I returned last year after a seven-year absence, I was surprised by the changes."

She'd returned after a bank robber killed her husband, Nate reminded himself. Which meant she would be understandably unsympathetic to anyone who had ever robbed a bank.

He turned from her to Mrs. Pratt, hoping his guilty feelings didn't show. "This is a fine meal, ma'am. I appreciate your sharing it with me."

"You're quite welcome. It's always a pleasure to cook for someone who appreciates the effort." She reached for her glass. "I assume that was you I heard playing the piano earlier."

"Yes, ma'am. I hope you don't mind."

"Not at all. It was nice to have music in the house." She gave him a warm, motherly smile. "You're quite talented."

"Thank you." Yes, he was definitely getting in deep with these folks.

All through the rest of the meal the family made it a point to include him in the conversation and make him feel a welcome addition to the gathering.

When they pushed back from the table, Mrs. Pratt held a hand up to forestall her niece. "Let me take care of the dishes, dear. And Joy can help me. You should take care of our guest."

Nate tried to protest. "That's all right. I don't want to be—"

But the doctor's wife wouldn't let him finish. "Nonsense. You're a guest in our home and I pride myself on my hospitality."

Nate doubted she offered all residents of the infirmary this kind of treatment, but he couldn't continue protesting without running the risk of repaying her kindness by seeming churlish or ungrateful.

Mrs. Leggett moved behind him and took the handles of his wheelchair. "No point in arguing. Aunt Betty may look like a softie, but she normally gets her way." She steered him out of the dining room. "I know you've been cooped up indoors most of the day. If you like, I can wheel you out on the porch for a breath of fresh air."

He should refuse. "I'd like that."

In short order she had wheeled him out the front door. She parked his chair near the door then moved to stand by the rail, looking out over the front lawn.

Dusk had settled in and Nate saw the twinkle of a few fireflies in the distance.

He shifted in the chair. "Don't feel like you need to keep me company. I'm perfectly fine here on my own, and I promise not to tell your aunt if you want to slip away and take care of something else."

"I don't mind." She kept her back to him. "It's nice out here this time of day."

There was another long silence. Then she turned to face him. "So why leather working?"

"What do you mean?"

"You're obviously very well educated. You play the piano like someone who has practiced extensively. That doesn't sound like someone who would turn to making bridles and saddles for a living."

I do it because it was the work I was given while in

prison. But he didn't say that. "Are you saying someone who works with his hands can't be well educated?"

"No, of course not. It just seemed a curious combination."

"There is something satisfying about the work I do, something artistic and creative."

She nodded. "Sort of like the hats I make."

"You make hats? For sale?" Somehow that seemed out of character.

"Yes. That's why I was at the dress shop this morning."

"So you don't have your own shop?"

"Oh, no. Not yet, anyway. I just make them when the mood strikes me, and Hazel sells them in her shop for me."

What kind of headgear did she fashion? Sober bonnets like that black affair she wore most every day? Surely there wasn't that big a market for such dull headgear.

Then he had another thought. "You said *not yet, anyway.* What's stopping you?"

She seemed a little taken aback by his question, so he raised a brow in challenge. "I figure, since you quizzed me this afternoon, I would return the favor."

She relaxed and smiled. "I suppose fair is fair. But there's nothing particularly interesting about my answer. I said not yet because I'm not ready."

"I assume this is something you really want, not just an idle dream."

"Oh, yes. I want to be able to fend for myself and Joy, to not have to take advantage of the charity of Aunt Betty and Uncle Grover forever."

Had she given up on the idea of remarrying someday? "Well, then, what are you *really* waiting for?"

She gave him a puzzled frown. "You make it sound like it's something I could do at the snap of a finger. Starting up a business takes planning and forethought. Which you should know since you've just opened one yourself." She rubbed her hands along her upper arms. "But I'm sure it'll happen someday. And for now, I'm happy to muddle along doing three or four a month to sell at Hazel's shop."

He couldn't really picture her as a "muddle along" kind of person. But he'd let that slide.

Maybe he'd check out the dress shop window next time he passed by to see what sort of hats she created—it might tell him a little more about the kind of person she was. He suddenly had a stray thought of what she might look like in a different kind of dress, one that was a lively color with more flattering lines. One that didn't remind everyone who looked at her that she was a widow.

He stiffened as he realized what direction his thoughts had taken. "If you'll excuse me, I think I'll go back to my room now."

Her expression immediately shifted to one of concern. "Of course. You must be tired after the day you've had."

He grimaced. "It seems I've already done my fair share of resting today. But I wouldn't mind lying down and I'd like to dig into that book you brought me from the library." And the sooner he was away from Mrs. Leggett's company, the better.

For both of them.

Verity pulled the pins from her hair as she sat in front of her vanity. She lifted the silver-handled brush she'd inherited from her mother and pulled it through the thick tangle of her hair.

What a day today had been. She'd finally met the town's newest resident, Joy had come within a hair-breadth of getting seriously hurt, and Mr. Cooper had moved into the infirmary.

Such a good man. And modest, too. He seemed actually uncomfortable with accepting their gratitude for what he'd done.

Well, he had it whether he wanted it or not. And she'd make it her mission to see that everyone knew what a fine, brave man he was.

She paused and bowed her head.

Heavenly Father, thank You for seeing my daughter safely through her near miss today, and thank You for sending Mr. Cooper into our lives. I think perhaps You sent him to us for a reason and I hope that You will find a way to use me to help him in some way. Help me to always be open to whatever direction and work You have in store for me. Amen.

She turned down her lamp and crawled into bed, already looking forward to what tomorrow would bring.

Nate stretched, pleased to note that the twinge of pain in his right arm seemed less noticeable today than yesterday. He leaned back and studied the harness he'd been working on.

Not bad, considering he was moving slower than normal. Dr. Pratt had consented to allow him to return home this morning only after he'd promised to come back to the clinic tomorrow so his injuries could be checked. He wondered idly if Mrs. Leggett would be there.

Okay, maybe not so idly.

She hadn't seemed very happy that he was ready to return home. And he had to confess that he'd been more than a little pleased by that.

Nate glanced around his shop, trying to imagine how Mrs. Leggett had looked wandering through here yesterday, amid his very masculine wares and tools. Stranger yet, imagining her upstairs, moving through his quarters to find him a clean change of clothes.

What had she thought of his place, of how spare and impersonal it was? Had she been all business, quickly taking care of her task at hand and getting out? Or had she lingered, studying his things?

How would he have handled it if the situation had been reversed?

He glanced up as someone walked past his open door. It was Mrs. Leggett and her aunt. He watched as they passed by, tracking their progress across the large shop window. At the last minute, Mrs. Leggett glanced inside and gave him a warm smile when their glances met.

Was her primary emotion toward him gratitude? That wasn't what he wanted.

Nate leaned down and absently scratched Beans behind the ears. What *did* he want?

He'd thought he knew when he arrived here. But maybe it was changing.

An elderly gentleman stepped through the door just then, pulling Nate's thoughts back to the present.

"Now that we've finished with old business, let's move on to a discussion of the upcoming Founders' Day Festival." Regina—otherwise known as Reggie—Barr, head of the Ladies Auxiliary, looked around the room with an expectant smile.

Verity shifted in her seat. She was having trouble focusing on the discussions going on around her. The meeting was running longer than normal and she was anxious to get back home and check on Joy. It wasn't that she didn't trust Uncle Grover to watch her daughter, but she didn't want the girl to be a bother to him. Besides, she still hadn't quite gotten over the scare of Joy's near accident yesterday.

Verity let the discussion swirl around her, lending only half an ear to talk of prizes, games, competitions, music, parades, fireworks and goodness only knew what else.

The idea of the festival seemed a bit frivolous to her. But if these folks wanted to get excited about it, then she saw no real harm in it. Besides, it would be something Joy would have fun participating in.

Verity's mind turned to Mr. Cooper. He had spent the morning reassuring Uncle Grover that he was quite capable of taking care of himself. He'd seemed inordinately eager to leave them. Was it merely because he wanted to be back among his own things? Or was there another reason?

Realizing her thoughts had drifted into inappropriate territory, Verity sat up straighter and tried to pick up the thread of the discussion.

"Thank you, Daisy. Now for the next item on the list, Janell Whitman has volunteered to work with the schoolchildren to prepare a short play for our entertainment during the festival. She'd like to have a volunteer to help her."

Verity thought about volunteering, but Abigail Fulton, one of the younger members of the Ladies Auxiliary, immediately raised her hand.

Reggie pointed her pencil toward the young girl. "Thank you, Abigail."

Hazel raised a hand and spoke up without waiting to be recognized. "Let me know if you want costumes for the children—it'll be my contribution to the festival."

Janell gave her a broad smile. "That would be wonderful. I'll come by your shop tomorrow and we can discuss it."

Reggie looked down at her list. "All right, I think that was the final item on our agenda. Anyone have anything else we need to discuss?"

The meeting broke up shortly after that.

As they stood, Aunt Betty touched Verity's arm. "Don't wait on me, dear. I want to chat with Daisy about helping her with the refreshments for the festival."

Verity nodded and moved toward the door. Her thoughts turned almost at once from the Founders' Day Festival to Mr. Cooper. How was he faring now that he was back at his own place? Perhaps she should stop in and check on him.

As a concerned medical assistant, of course.

So lost in thought was she that she jumped slightly when Hazel came up and linked arms with her.

"Sorry if I spooked you," her friend said. "I just wanted to ask how Joy is doing today."

"She's doing fine, much better than Mr. Cooper."

"Ah, yes, the hero of yesterday's drama. I hear he spent the night at the clinic."

"Yes. Uncle Grover wanted to keep an eye on him for the first twenty-four hours."

"And was he a good patient?"

Verity ignored her friend's arch tone and answered the question as stated. "Other than not liking to be, as he put it, mollycoddled, he was fine." She brushed at a piece of lint on her skirt. "He moved back to his place this morning."

"Do I detect a note of disappointment?"

"Disapproval would be more accurate. He should have stayed under my uncle's care a little longer. But he does have a stubborn streak."

Hazel grinned, then changed the subject. "By the way, your hat sold already. Stop in and I'll pay you. And that means I'll be ready for your next creation whenever you can get it to me."

Verity nodded. "I already have a design in mind. I should have something ready for you in the next couple of days."

They chatted about fashion and the upcoming festival the rest of the way to the dress shop.

Verity exited the shop feeling the satisfactory weight of extra coins in her purse. Hopefully it would be enough for the first few piano lessons for Joy. Her steps slowed as she approached the saddle shop. Yes, she definitely should check in on Mr. Cooper to make certain he was doing okay.

Mind made up, she stepped forward purposefully. The little bell over his door jingled as she entered. Beans, who'd been soaking up the warmth in a puddle of sunshine, bounded to his feet and raced over to greet her. But it was Mr. Cooper she watched, even as she stooped to scratch the dog. Was he glad to see her?

He'd looked up at the sound of the bell, but his expression had closed off as soon as he saw her. Now he set down his work and leaned back. "Excuse me if I don't stand." His tone was self-deprecating as he motioned to the crutch behind him. "Is there something I can do for you?"

She gave Beans a final pat and straightened. "I've just come from Hazel's and thought I'd stop in and check on you." Was he not glad to see her? "How are you feeling?" she finished feebly.

"I'm managing."

"Is there anything I can do for you? I'd be glad to prepare some meals for you or take care of some of your housecleaning. After all, it's my fault you're in this fix."

"Mrs. Leggett, please stop trying to take the blame for my accident. It just happened—it was nobody's fault."

"There you go, being modest again. You really should learn how to take a compliment."

He didn't say anything to that—just continued to watch her in that uncomfortably unreadable way.

"You're staying off of that foot, I hope."

He spread his hands. "As you can see."

"And the stairs?"

"Only when absolutely necessary."

Before she could quiz him further, the shop door opened. She turned to see Cletus Keeter, a farmer from just east of town, entering with a harness in hand.

"Well, hi there, Mrs. Leggett. I heard about what happened to Joy yesterday. I hope she's okay."

"Hello, Mr. Keeter. Yes, Joy is just fine, thanks to Mr. Cooper here." She nodded to both men. "Well, I'll leave you two gentlemen to your business. Good day, Mr. Cooper, Mr. Keeter."

Mr. Cooper nodded, still not softening his politely businesslike demeanor.

As she stepped out on the sidewalk, Verity realized that, now that he was on his own again, it seemed it was going to be more difficult than she'd thought to break through Mr. Cooper's reserve. But she wasn't the least bit daunted. If there was a way to get past his guard, she was determined to find it.

Some things were just worth fighting for.

Chapter Eight

"Verity, do you have a moment?"

Verity, who'd arrived at the mercantile only a few minutes ago, paused in her shopping to find Janell Whitman approaching her. "Of course."

"As mentioned at the Ladies Auxiliary meeting yesterday, Abigail and I will be putting together a little program with the children as part of the Founders' Day celebration."

Verity nodded. "I'm looking forward to seeing them perform."

"I was thinking that perhaps we'd do a play based on the story of the founding of the town. Mr. Parker and Mr. Fulton have agreed to write the play for us."

"That will be fun."

"But the number of parts will naturally be limited and I'd like to make certain all of the children have a way to be involved."

Verity had always thought the town was blessed to have a teacher like Janell Whitman, one who really cared about the children. "I agree that we don't want anyone to feel left out. How can I help?"

"I thought one option would be to form a choir with the remaining children and have them put on a musical performance, as well."

Verity felt a little stirring of excitement as she began to see how the teacher was looking to involve her.

"The problem is," Janell continued, "both Abigail and I will be fully involved with the play. And of course neither of us have your talent when it comes to music. So we were wondering if you'd be willing to take that on."

"Of course." The chance to form a children's choir, even a temporary one, was something she would very much enjoy doing.

"Zella has already agreed to play the piano for you and lend a hand with directing the children as needed."

"She'll be a good help." Zella was the church pianist, and a more patient woman didn't exist. She'd be quite good with the children. "How many students would be involved?"

"I'm thinking seven from my group and Mr. Parker thinks about five from the older students in his group."

A dozen, then. But then she had another thought. "One more question. Would you object to having a few of the younger children join this little choir?"

Janell smiled. "Such as Joy, you mean? Of course not, as long as you're willing to work with them."

"What kind of program did you have in mind?"

"Nothing too elaborate. I was thinking two or three simple songs with an uplifting theme. But this will be your project and I'm sure whatever you decide to do will be fine."

Already Verity's mind was brimming with ideas. "All right. As soon as you get me the names of the children involved we'll schedule the first practice. In the meantime, I'll speak to the parents of some of the other younger children to see if any of them are interested in participating. And I'll speak to Zella after choir practice tomorrow about any ideas she might have."

Janell smiled. "Looks like you're definitely the right person for the job. I'll leave it all in your very capable hands." And with a wave, the schoolteacher moved on.

Verity finished her shopping while mentally making a list of things she could do while waiting for the names of the participating children. She could visit the parents of some of the children Joy's age to see if she could recruit a few more choir members. Eileen Tucker would be her first stop—Molly and Joey Tucker were Joy's best friends.

She could also talk to Hazel. The dressmaker had already volunteered to provide costumes for the children who were in the play. Perhaps she could also talk her friend into doing some short, simple, smock-like choir robes for the children's choir.

Yes, she'd go by Hazel's first. And since it coincidentally just happened to be right next to the saddle shop, perhaps she'd stop in and check on Mr. Cooper while she was at it.

Nate looked up from his workbench to see Adam striding into the shop. Truth to tell, he was glad of the interruption. Nice to have something to think about besides the way he'd been less than gracious with Mrs. Leggett.

He leaned back. "Here to get a harness repaired?"

"Just visiting."

Was Adam checking up on him? Was he worried about Nate's ability to repay his loan? Then Nate pushed that thought aside. He owed his friend more trust than that. He nodded toward a nearby chair. "Have a seat."

Adam looked around as he sat. "I don't see your crutch. Don't tell me your foot's healed already?"

"Not completely." Nate reached behind him and grabbed the walking stick he'd fashioned from a strong, straight branch and some scraps of leather. "I'm using this instead."

"How's the arm?"

"Much better." Nate rolled his shoulder to prove his point.

"Glad to hear it. Because I've come to ask you a favor."

Now, that was unexpected, but he welcomed the chance to repay, at least in part, the debt he owed his friend. "Name it."

"Zella Ford, our church pianist, has had a family emergency and has to go out of town to attend to it. She may be gone for a month or more."

Uh-oh, he didn't like the direction this was taking.

"If I remember correctly, you play the piano, don't you?"

Nate nodded.

"Good. Then I'd like you to consider taking her place during the interim."

Nate stared at his friend, trying to figure out what was behind this. Was this some misguided scheme to get him more involved in the community? "Why me? I mean, isn't there someone else here in town who plays piano and would be better suited?"

"Mrs. Peavy, our housekeeper, normally steps in on the rare occasions when Zella can't attend services."

"Well, then—"

"Mrs. Peavy is a generous woman and when Reverend Harper spoke to her about the situation, she agreed to step in. But she's been having flares of rheumatism in her hands lately and I'd like to spare her any extra use of them if I can. Besides, with Reggie expecting again, I'd like to selfishly keep her focus on our household."

"I see." Nate nodded, remembering what he owed Adam. "I suppose, when you put it like that, I can't say no."

"Good. The choir practices for an hour every Saturday at four o'clock."

"I understand Mrs. Leggett is the choir director."

"She doesn't care to be called that, but yes, the choir looks to her to lead their practices. And she usually works with Reverend Harper to make the hymn selections." He studied Nate. "That won't be a problem, will it?"

"No, of course not." It seemed the more he resolved to keep his distance from the widow, the more circumstances conspired to throw them together. But he'd already given his word. And there was no reason he couldn't handle this in a businesslike manner.

"Good. Because there is one other thing. Reverend Harper says Mrs. Leggett will also be working with some of the local children to put on a musical performance for the Founders' Day Festival. She'll need you to work with her on that, as well."

"Does she know that I'm taking Mrs. Ford's place?"

"I haven't said anything to her, or anyone else for that matter. I wanted to make sure you would agree first." He gave Nate that probing look again. "There's no reason *she* should object, is there?"

"None that I'm aware of." He grimaced. "In fact, she still considers me a hero."

Adam relaxed as the light of understanding dawned in his expression. "I see. Well, there's nothing wrong with that."

Nate answered with a scowl. Then changed the subject. "I assume there is sheet music. Back when I had access to a piano, the pieces I played were classical rather than from hymn books."

"I'm sure there is, but you'll have to ask Mrs. Leggett about that." Adam stood. "I'll let Reverend Harper and Mrs. Peavy know the good news."

"And Mrs. Leggett?"

"I'll leave that up to you. Remember, choir practice is tomorrow at four o'clock at the church."

As Adam left, Nate wondered if Mrs. Leggett would welcome the news or not. With his luck, she'd see this as one more aspect of him being a hero.

He groaned and decided it was time to take Beans for a walk.

Every Saturday, at three o'clock, Verity and four of her friends from the choir met at the Blue Bottle Sweet Shop and Tea Parlor for tea before they went to choir practice. It had become a ritual of sorts for the five of them.

Besides herself, there was Hazel, and Janell Whitman, Reverend Harper's daughter Constance, and Abigail Fulton, the young woman behind Abigail's Subscription Library.

Constance Harper was the last to arrive this Saturday, and she didn't immediately take her seat. Instead she stood facing them with barely suppressed excitement.

She was obviously bursting with news of some sort. "I have an announcement."

Verity smiled. "Whatever it is, it looks like good news."

Constance nodded. "Yes. Well, both good and bad. I'm afraid this is the last Saturday tea I will be attending with you ladies for quite some time." Then she grimaced. "That's obviously not the good-news part."

"Well, I should say not!" Abigail gave her friend a pouty frown. "The good news better be mighty good to make up for that bad news."

Constance coyly took her seat. "Oh, it is."

From the smile on the girl's face, Verity had no doubt that something wonderful had happened.

"Well," Abigail said impatiently, "don't keep us waiting."

"The reason I won't be here is that I'm going to pharmacy school in New York."

There was an immediate chorus of congratulations, followed by a stream of questions.

Finally Constance held up both hands, palms out. "Thanks, everyone. I will miss all of you, of course, but this is such a great opportunity. Mr. Flaherty has taught me a lot since I've been working for him at the apothecary shop, but he says there's more to be learned and he wants me to be ready to take over the business when he retires in a few years. So he's sending me to a pharmacy school. He's even offered to pay for my classes."

"Oh, Constance, that's wonderful."

"It sounds as if Mr. Flaherty sees something very promising in you. You should be proud."

"You must stop by the fashion emporium so we can chat about New York. I can let you know what to expect." Hazel had family in New York and spent a few weeks there every summer.

As their tea was delivered, Janell, who was seated next to Verity, turned to her. "How are your plans for the children's choir coming?"

"Very well. I've been in contact with the mothers of several younger children. In addition to Joy I have three other younger children recruited."

Janell smiled and shook her head. "You're a brave woman."

Verity returned her grin. "It'll be fun." Then she sobered. "I heard Zella is going to be unavailable to play the piano for us. I'll miss her, but Mrs. Peavy will do fine, I'm sure."

"Oh, haven't you heard?" Constance chimed in from Janell's other side. "Mrs. Peavy isn't taking Zella's place this time. Mr. Cooper is."

Surprised by that little tidbit of news, Verity sat up straighter. How interesting that they were going to be thrown together yet again. Did Mr. Cooper know about the children's choir yet? She hoped that wasn't going to be a problem for him.

"Well, now, isn't that an interesting development." Hazel's voice had a definite what-have-we-here edge to it. "Who would have imagined a man like him could play piano?"

Verity shot her friend an annoyed look. What did she mean *a man like him*? "He's actually quite talented."

"Is he, now?" Hazel was looking at her with a mix of amusement and speculation.

"He practiced on the piano in our parlor while he was staying at the clinic."

To Verity's relief, Eve, the proprietress, arrived with

a tray of sweets just then, and once they all had their refreshments, the conversation turned to other topics.

But Verity knew Hazel wasn't ready to let it drop entirely. Sure enough, when they left the Blue Bottle to head for the church, Hazel linked arms with her and nudged her with a shoulder. "So why didn't you tell me Mr. Cooper serenaded you with the piano while he was at the infirmary?"

"Because he didn't serenade me. He didn't even know I was listening until he finished playing the piece."

"Still, apparently he did more than lie in bed and re-cuperate while he was there. Tell me, is he as interesting as he seems? Did the two of you have some nice, long, get-to-know-you-better conversations?"

Verity drew her shoulders back in exasperation. "Hazel, really, he was a patient in the clinic, not a suitor."

"Not yet, anyway."

Verity gave her friend a stern look. "I know that look in your eye. Promise me you won't try to do any match-making."

Hazel sniffed and tilted her chin at a haughty angle. "You're just no fun at all sometimes."

"Promise me."

"Oh, very well." She good-naturedly changed the sub-ject to a discussion about the proposal for a big fireworks display to close out the festival this year.

As Verity entered the church a few minutes later, she felt her pulse quicken in anticipation. Would he already be here? Had he volunteered to take Zella's place or had he been pressed into service? How would he feel about taking direction from her?

She gave her head a mental shake. Her thoughts were

heading into territory it would be best to avoid. It was a good thing Hazel couldn't read her mind.

Mr. Cooper was already seated at the piano. He hadn't yet noticed her entrance, so she had time to study him.

He was thumbing through a hymnal, his expression unreadable. No one had approached him, but she wasn't surprised. It was that invisible wall he had erected around himself. Was he even aware he was doing it?

Well, making him feel a welcome part of the choir would be a good start. She marched down the aisle and went straight to the piano. "Mr. Cooper, thank you so much for agreeing to step in for Zella, especially on such short notice."

She turned to the gathered choir members. "Most of you have probably already heard about Zella having to go out of town to see to her brother for a while. We're very lucky to have Mr. Cooper to fill in for her. I've already had the pleasure of hearing him play the piano, and I can assure you he is quite talented."

Then she turned back to him. "Have you met everyone here?"

When he indicated he hadn't, she went around the group, introducing them one at a time. By the time the introductions were done, the last of the choir members had arrived and Verity was ready to begin the practice session.

Nate was impressed with Mrs. Leggett's leadership qualities. Just as when she took charge of his care right after the accident, she was firm but not bossy, and quick to lend a hand or lend praise where needed.

She had apparently spoken with Reverend Harper earlier about the scripture his sermon would be based on and chose songs that would complement his message. Some of the hymns were unfamiliar to him and he stumbled a bit the first time he played them. But she was as patient and gracious with him as she was with the rest of the choir.

By the time practice was over, he was confident he could play the hymns for the service tomorrow without any trouble.

The choir members began to slowly disperse, leaving in chatty groups of three or four. He saw the dressmaker, Miss Andrews, speak to Mrs. Leggett for a moment, but the widow waved her on and turned in his direction. Was she going to inquire after his health again?

"Thank you again for stepping in today. Your time and talent were greatly appreciated."

"I don't mind. I actually enjoy playing the piano."

"It shows in your playing." She hesitated a moment, then continued. "I don't know if anyone mentioned this to you or not, but I'm going to be working with a group of children to form a choir and present a program at the Founders' Day Festival. Zella was planning to help me, but now that she's unavailable—"

"You need another pianist. Yes, I'm aware, and I'm happy to step in."

Her relieved smile softened her features. "Oh, thank you. And I promise you won't regret it. Children are such a joy to work with."

Not ready to see her go yet, he asked the first question that popped into his head. "Do you know yet what kind of program you want to teach them?"

"I have some ideas, but I'm open to other suggestions if you have some to offer."

"Why don't you tell me what you're thinking first

and I'll see if it sparks any ideas." He slid over on the piano bench. "But first, have a seat. You're making me feel most ungentlemanly."

She complied, coming around the piano to perch on the opposite end of the bench from him.

He listened to her plans, asking questions and making suggestions. But all the time, a part of him was also aware of her nearness, her contagious enthusiasm.

If it was going to be like this whenever they were together, he was in trouble. He would just have to make certain that they were together only when the choir—either the adult or children's version—were with them. No more of these one-on-one sessions.

"I plan to have practice sessions every Tuesday and Thursday afternoon right after school between now and the festival," she said. "Will that be a problem for you?"

"I can work with that."

"This first Tuesday I will mainly be evaluating the children individually to see where they are musically, and to see how well they can understand and follow directions. I won't necessarily need the piano for that, so I suppose if you don't want to come—"

"You're going to have over a dozen kids to work with. You'll need some help. I'll be here."

"I was hoping you'd say that." She stood. "Well, I should be getting home so I can check on Joy. Aunt Betty loves her, but that little darling of mine can be a handful sometimes." She moved away from the bench. "I'll see you at the service tomorrow."

He stood, as well. "I'll walk you out." He reached for his cane. As they walked toward the door, she easily matched her steps to his without comment. But when they stepped outside, she paused and turned to him.

"Do you need any assistance with the steps?"

Did she think him such an invalid? "I can manage."

His tone had come out sharper than he'd intended and he saw her brow go up. "Sorry," he said, "I'm just used to taking care of myself."

She gave him an understanding smile. "Well, you're amongst friends now. There's no shame in asking for or accepting help."

Amongst friends—he liked the sound of that. But could he truly consider himself their friend so long as he kept his history from them?

Sunday morning, Verity took her place with the rest of the choir at the front of the church. Mr. Cooper was already in place at the piano. Was he nervous? If so, he didn't show it.

The church bell rang, signaling to the latecomers and dawdlers that it was time to come inside and find their seats. Taking his cue as smoothly as Zella ever had, Mr. Cooper began playing an instrumental piece. It wasn't a melody Verity was familiar with, and he seemed to be playing it from memory. There was no hesitation or stumbling. It was lovely.

Later, when the service was over, she approached Mr. Cooper with a smile. She had to wait her turn to speak to him, however, as several members of the congregation came up to compliment him on his playing and thank him for standing in for Zella. It did her heart good to see him receiving such warm acceptance from the folks here—perhaps now he wouldn't feel the need to keep himself so aloof.

When at last he was alone, she stepped up. "It seems

as if I'm not the only one who thinks your playing is exceptional."

He shrugged as he put away the sheet music. "I'm glad the folks in the congregation enjoyed it."

"Aunt Betty asked me to invite you for lunch."

He reached for his cane. "That is very kind of your aunt, but I've already made other plans." He glanced toward the Barrs, and Adam's wife, Reggie, gave him a small wave.

"Oh, I see." She'd been prepared to counter his I-don't-want-to-be-any-trouble arguments but hadn't even considered that he might have other plans. She also hadn't been prepared for the stab of disappointment. "Well, enjoy your meal."

She turned, but before she could move away, Joy skipped up to them.

"Hello, Mr. Cooper."

He gave her a smile. "Hello, Joy. How are you today?"

She noticed that his cool reserve seemed to melt away when speaking to her daughter.

"I'm fine, thank you," Joy responded. "I like your piano playing."

"Thank you."

"How is Beans doing?"

"He's doing just fine. Thank you for asking." Then he leaned in, as if to relay a confidence. "But I do think he misses seeing you."

Joy nodded solemnly. "I miss him, too." Then she gave Nate a this-just-occurred-to-me look. "Maybe I should visit him."

"Joy!" Verity chided. "It's not polite to invite yourself over to someone else's home."

Her daughter widened her eyes innocently. "But he

said Beans misses me. And I miss him, too." The child's tone implied that that was reason enough.

Mr. Cooper intervened. "I tell you what. I plan to take Beans for a walk over toward the schoolyard this afternoon. Would you like to come with us?"

"Can I, Mama?"

"May I," she corrected absently. Was he issuing the invitation more because he felt obligated or was it because he really wanted to? "Oh, pumpkin, I don't know—"

"You are invited, too, of course."

She looked from Mr. Cooper's impassive face to Joy's pleading one and nodded. "Very well." If nothing else, this would be a step along the path to getting Mr. Cooper out and about more.

Then she gave her daughter a no-nonsense look. "But only if you take your nap after lunch."

"I will, I promise."

Verity turned back to Mr. Cooper. "What time do you plan to take Beans for his walk?"

"Shall we plan to meet in the schoolyard around three o'clock?"

With a nod, Verity took Joy's hand and turned toward the door. She was happy they'd agreed to see each other later, but there was something about the way he'd issued the invitation, something in his tone and carefully schooled expression that made her wonder if he was regretting the invitation even as he was issuing it.

When they stepped outside, she informed Aunt Betty that they would not have a guest for lunch after all, then let Joy go with her and Uncle Grover while she turned to look for Hazel.

She spotted her friend across the churchyard speaking to Belva Ortolon. Belva was relatively new to Turnabout. She'd moved here about four months ago to help her aunt Eunice with the running of the boardinghouse.

When Verity approached, Belva gave her a smile of greeting. "Oh, hi, Verity. I was just telling Hazel how much I enjoyed the music this morning, and she tells me you picked out the hymns."

"I did." Verity liked the girl. There was an artlessness about her, an almost tomboyish quality that she found quite engaging.

Belva nodded approval. "'What a Friend We Have in Jesus' is a favorite of mine, so thank you for selecting it."

Before Verity could respond, Belva looked past her and straightened. "Oh, there's Mr. Cooper. I need to speak to him about something."

Surprised, Verity watched Belva approach Mr. Cooper and engage him in animated conversation. The girl seemed to know him rather well. Then Verity corrected herself—not girl, woman. She thought of Belva as a girl because of her youthful demeanor. But in truth she was a young woman of nineteen or twenty. By the time she herself had been that age she'd had a husband and daughter of her own.

Belva's aunt joined the pair just then and, together, the three of them made their way out of the churchyard. It occurred to Verity that Mr. Cooper hadn't actually *said* his lunch plans were with the Barrs. Could he be taking his meal at the boardinghouse with the Ortolon ladies instead?

Not that it was any of her business if he was.

"Mr. Cooper did a fine job playing the piano this morning."

Verity turned back around to see Hazel eyeing her with an amused glint in her eye.

"That he did." She fiddled absently with the tie on her bonnet. "He's starting to feel more comfortable with life here in Turnabout, don't you think?"

Hazel nodded. "How could he help *but* like it here?" She cut her eyes toward the man in question, then back to Verity. "And he apparently likes certain people here quite well." For a moment Verity thought she was referring to Belva. Then Hazel clarified, "I noticed how he watched you during the service this morning."

Verity waved a hand dismissively. "It's only because I'm choir director. He was taking his cues from me."

Hazel made a noncommittal sound, then changed the subject. "By the way, have you ever considered making hats to order?"

"I don't know." From the corner of her eye, she watched the trio make their way as far as Second Street, then they turned the corner and disappeared from view.

But Hazel was eyeing her with a knowing smirk so she quickly pulled her thoughts back to the conversation at hand. "Part of the fun for me in making hats is just going with whatever whimsy my imagination feeds me rather than trying to follow a set pattern or copy something from a picture. Why?"

"Eula Fay stopped by the shop yesterday to order a new dress to wear when she presides over the festival's opening ceremony. She asked if you'd consider making her a hat to match."

As Mayor Sanders's wife, Eula Fay always liked to look her best when she was attending some sort of official function. "I suppose, if the only parameter I had was that it should match a particular dress, I could do that."

Hazel nodded. "It would be a guaranteed sale for you. And it could generate some additional orders. You know how Eula Fay is—if she likes something she'll let everyone know."

"All right, you've convinced me." Verity hooked her arm through Hazel's and the two started down the sidewalk together. "I'll come by your shop tomorrow and take a look at the fabric and pattern you're using for the dress."

If she were to ever realize her dream of someday owning a millinery shop, she would definitely have to learn to create hats to order. Might as well start now.

But at the moment her thoughts were not entirely on hats. Part of her mind was focused on the fact that when she and Hazel turned on Second Street, neither Mr. Cooper nor the Ortolon ladies were in sight. Had they separated at Mr. Cooper's shop?

Or had they continued on to the boardinghouse together?

Chapter Nine

Nate turned onto Schoolhouse Road, Beans trotting at his heels. He wasn't sure why he'd invited Mrs. Leggett and her daughter to join him, especially after he'd promised himself to minimize his contact with her. He was already pushing matters by working with the choir and now with her children's program.

He could tell himself he'd only intended to invite Joy, but that would be a lie. He knew good and well inviting Joy would also mean he was inviting Joy's mother.

Beans's sudden yip brought him back to the present. The dog bounded away from him toward the schoolyard. Joy was already there, waiting on him. As was her mother.

Despite his resolve to remain merely polite, his pulse kicked up a notch. Okay, so he was attracted to her. But that didn't mean he had to do anything about it. If there was one thing the past nine years had taught him, it was to curb his impulsiveness. This was just a simple outing to give Joy an opportunity to play with Beans—nothing more.

Of course it was.

By the time he reached the schoolyard proper, Joy and Beans were already playing near the teeter-totter. Mrs. Leggett stood in front of the schoolhouse steps.

"Am I late?" he asked by way of greeting.

She shook her head. "I'm afraid Joy was getting impatient so we came out a bit early." She waved behind her toward the steps. "Shall we sit?"

He nodded and swept a hand, indicating she should precede him. She took her seat and fussily arranged her skirt, then looked up at him. "Aren't you going to sit, as well?"

Nate shook his head, thinking it best to maintain his distance. "I prefer to stand."

She frowned. "But your foot—"

"Is getting better every day. And don't worry, I'm not putting much weight on it." Ready to change the subject, he glanced toward the other members of their party. "It appears Joy and Beans are having a grand time."

She followed his gaze with her own. "Thank you so much for indulging Joy this way. I know you didn't have to include her in this outing."

He shrugged, uncomfortable as always with her gratitude. "It's just a walk I was planning to take, anyway."

"Still, it was a nice thing to do." She brushed at her skirt. "Did you enjoy your lunch with your friends?"

There was something odd about her tone, but he couldn't quite put his finger on what. Was she upset that he hadn't accepted her invitation? More to the point, how should he respond to her question? He hadn't lied to her earlier, but he'd done his best to mislead her so he could refuse her invitation without hurting her feelings. Truth was, he had eaten alone in his own apartment. He chose his words carefully. "It's always good to spend time with friends."

She looked at him as if she knew he hadn't really answered her question, but then nodded. "It is." Then she shifted and sat up straighter. "Perhaps now would be a good time to discuss the children's program in more detail."

Good, something neutral to discuss. "Of course. What size choir will you have?"

"I'm not certain yet—Janell, the schoolteacher, is going to cast her play tomorrow so she won't know for certain which children will participate in the choir until then. I'm meeting with her and the children at the end of the school day so I can meet them all. But Janell has already told me she anticipates there will be a dozen or so."

"That's a nice size. I assume they will be of various ages."

"Yes, including some children who are not yet school-age." She waved toward her daughter. "Joy for one. And at least two other children about her age—maybe three."

"Won't that be challenging?"

She grinned, not at all daunted. "Indeed it will." Then she raised her brow. "Does that make you want to back out?"

"Not at all." Truth be told, he was actually looking forward to it. "So how many songs will be on the program and how long do we have to put it all together?"

"I think three songs will make for a good program. And we have three weeks."

It seemed she wasn't afraid of a challenge. Of course, if anyone could pull this off, it was her. "So yesterday when we talked about this we decided the songs needed to be simple enough for four-and five-year-olds to learn, but interesting enough for the older children to not feel like it's beneath them. Did you come up with any songs that met those criteria?"

"I thought we'd start with something simple that most of them already know, 'Jesus Loves Me.' Do you know how to play that?"

"I haven't played it before, but I'm familiar with it. It shouldn't be a problem."

"Good." She cut a quick glance toward her daughter, then turned back to him. "Another song I thought of that might work with this group is 'Row, Row, Row Your Boat.' I know it's very simple, but if we have them perform it as a round, and add some hand motions with it, the older kids might find it challenging enough to be fun. What do you think?"

He nodded. "I think it will work. And since that one doesn't require a piano, I can help you with the rounds."

She nodded absently, her mind already seeming to move ahead. "I still need to figure out a third song. You don't have any suggestions by any chance?"

Nate hesitated. Then he decided that since she'd asked his opinion, that's what she'd get. "How about 'Down in the Valley to Pray'? It's easily divided into parts and simple enough for a children's choir. It can also be done a cappella."

A small frown line appeared between her eyes and he thought for a moment she was trying to find a polite way to tell him no. Then she lifted a hand, palm upward. "I'm afraid I don't know that one. Can you sing it for me?"

Sing it? On his own? That was definitely not something he was comfortable doing. "If you're not familiar with it, then perhaps we should go with something else."

"Oh, but you made it sound so intriguing. And I always love learning new songs." Then she tilted her head and gave him that challenging grin he found so irresistible. "You're not *afraid* to sing it, are you?"

"Afraid? No." He gave a self-deprecating smile. "I just know my own limitations and don't want to assault your ears with my braying."

She cast a watchful eye Joy's way again, then waved a hand dismissively. "Nonsense. I've heard you sing in church, remember? And I expect you to set a good example for the children. So you might as well get used to singing out with confidence."

He frowned and slid his fingers through his hair. Then, deciding he wasn't going to be able to get out of this, he gave in and sang the first verse and the chorus. When he was finished, he rubbed the back of his neck. He'd never done that before, sang solo for someone, not even Susanna. It made him feel more vulnerable, more exposed, than he liked.

But Mrs. Leggett was beaming at him approvingly. "What a lovely song!" She placed a hand on his arm. "Thank you so much for sharing it with me."

Everything inside him seemed to still for a heartbeat, as if wanting to soak in that unexpected touch. What was it about this woman that affected him so strongly? He fought to keep his expression in check and maintain an easy smile.

But either he failed or she felt something, too, because her expression shifted just the tiniest bit. Her eyes darkened and her breathing seemed to quicken. For a moment it felt as if something flowed between them at that point of contact. Then she abruptly withdrew her hand and the feeling was gone.

Averting her gaze, she called out to her daughter. "Joy, move away from the street."

"Yes, ma'am," the little girl responded with a wave. Mrs. Leggett kept her gaze on her daughter until the child had complied, which gave him time to collect himself.

When she turned back to him, her expression was once again serene. Had she felt what he felt?

"Where did you learn that song?" she asked.

In prison from a fellow inmate known only as Preacher. But he couldn't tell her that. "From an acquaintance. It was his favorite hymn." Hedging his answers like this felt as bad as lying.

"Well, I can certainly see why. You said it could be divided?"

He nodded. "You just repeat the whole thing four more times, replacing the word *father* in the chorus with *mother*, *brother*, *sister* and *sinner* respectively on each pass."

"The children are going to love it and so will their parents when they hear it. Thank you so much for singing it for me."

"Look." Joy's hail interrupted them. "I've taught Beans a trick."

Mrs. Leggett rose to go admire Joy and Beans's accomplishment and he slowly followed. Perhaps he should come clean, tell her the whole story of his past. It would solve the problem of her sending those admiring glances his way.

But could he bear to see her look at him with loathing?

Verity held firmly on to Joy's hand as they made their way to Hazel's dress shop the next morning. She had to admit, knowing she would be passing Mr. Cooper's shop to reach Hazel's added a certain zest to the trip.

Mr. Cooper wasn't out on the sidewalk this morning, but the door to his shop was already open. He looked up from his workbench as they passed, giving them a smile.

Joy tugged on her hand. "Can I go visit Beans?"

"Maybe after we get finished at Miss Hazel's. In the meantime, you can visit with Buttons."

That seemed to mollify the child and she continued on without further resistance.

"There you are," Hazel said by way of greeting.

Verity nodded as Joy immediately sought out the feline. "We had a patient at the clinic first thing this morning so I was a little late heading out." She closed the shop door behind her, unwilling to trust her daughter to remain inside.

"Nothing serious I hope."

"Turned out to be just a bad case of indigestion." Verity set her drawstring purse on the counter. "Now, let's see this material you have picked out for Mrs. Sanders's dress."

Hazel drew out a bolt of a deep orange fabric shot through with delicate stripes of yellow. As she fingered the soft material, Verity felt her mind playing with several possibilities. "You said this is for the festival's opening ceremonies?"

"It is."

Studying the fabric and thinking of the woman herself, Verity nodded. "I believe I can come up with something that will look fetching and that she'll like. Can you reserve about a half yard of this that I can use for trim?"

"Of course."

"And if you have some netting in this shade of yellow, I'll need some of it, as well."

"Just let me know what else you'll be needing and I'll get it gathered up. And of course I'll bill Eula Fay for it."

"I'll stop by her place and discuss some ideas with her before I get started, but I already have a few thoughts as to what I'd like to do."

Another customer walked in and Verity stepped back to let Hazel conduct business. But rather than taking her leave, she found herself studying some of the bolts of fabric on display. There was one in particular that caught her eye. It was a muted blue, a hazy-sky kind of color, just the shade she loved. She fingered the fabric and liked the suppleness of it, as well.

"That would look lovely on you."

Verity dropped the fabric guiltily. Then had second thoughts. "I've been thinking about what you said the other day, and my black dress *is* getting a bit worn. Perhaps a new Sunday dress wouldn't be amiss."

Hazel's smile widened. "Well, it's about time." Before Verity could stop her, she grabbed up the bolt and carried it to her worktable. "And I have the perfect pattern in mind."

"Whoa." Verity held up a hand. "I said *perhaps*—I haven't made up my mind yet. And this fabric is much too fancy for me. I would need to choose something a bit more conservative."

"Nonsense. If you've gotten far enough in your thinking to say it out loud, then you're definitely ready. And this fabric is perfect. Now, I insist you let me make this for you."

"Oh, no, you don't. I can take care of this. Besides, I have another project for you."

"What's that?"

"The children's choir I'm forming for the Founders' Day Festival, I don't want them or their parents to worry about finding new clothing. I was thinking that if I could provide some smocks for each of them, sort of like short, simple choir robes, that might sort of even things out for everyone."

"Of course. I can get a bolt of simple, inexpensive fabric and whip something like that up in no time."

"Actually, I thought we might get some of the members of the Ladies Auxiliary to help with the stitching if you can do the cutting and oversee their work. I know Aunt Betty was asking how she might help, and I'm sure there are other ladies who feel the same way."

Hazel grinned. "Even better."

"Good. I'll ask Aunt Betty to round up some volunteers and report to you." She retrieved her purse. "I'll find out which children will be involved this afternoon so I can give you a head count and rough sizes after that. And of course I'll pay for the fabric."

Hazel waved that offer aside. "Don't worry about that. I can cover it, especially since I won't be doing all the sewing." She put a finger to her chin. "Now, about this new dress of yours?"

"Let me think about it."

"Don't think about it too long. I'm going to set this fabric behind the counter for you so it will be there whenever you get ready."

Verity tried to tell her friend not to bother but finally gave up. Whenever Hazel got something in her head, it was difficult to dissuade her. "Come along, Joy. Time to go. Tell Buttons and Miss Hazel goodbye."

Joy popped up and said her goodbyes. Then she took hold of Verity's hand. "Can we go see Beans now?"

"Beans?" Hazel raised a brow in question.

"It's Mr. Cooper's dog," Joy volunteered. "I taught him a new trick when Mama and me visited them in the schoolyard yesterday."

"You did?" She turned to Verity. "And why didn't you tell me about this little expedition? I want details."

Verity shrugged. "There's nothing to tell—Mr. Cooper just allowed Joy to play with his dog yesterday. Now, if you'll excuse us, it's time for us to go."

Verity breezed out the door with head held high, perfectly aware that Hazel was not at all satisfied with that explanation.

But thoughts of her friend faded quickly, replaced by a mood-lifting touch of anticipation at the thought of seeing Mr. Cooper again. However, when she and Joy stepped through the doorway of his shop, she came to an abrupt stop. Standing there, talking to Mr. Cooper with a bright smile and sparkling eyes, was Belva Ortolon.

Chapter Ten

Joy immediately rushed forward to greet Beans, drawing Mr. Cooper's and Belva's attention. Verity pasted her smile back on and stepped forward. There was no reason for her to give in to that stab of jealousy. She and Mr. Cooper were merely friends, nothing more. If he and Belva were forming some sort of attachment, well, she was happy for them. Of course.

With that not-quite-true thought firmly in mind, she waved a hand. "Hello. Don't let me interrupt you. We just stopped in for a minute so Joy could say a quick hello to Beans."

Belva shook her head, her cheerful demeanor never faltering. "Oh, you weren't interrupting anything—I was ordering a saddle from Mr. Cooper, but we were done."

Ordering a saddle? As far as Verity knew, Belva didn't own a horse. But again, that was none of her business.

"Besides," Belva continued, "you're just the person I need to see."

Verity took a heartbeat to absorb this unexpected statement. "Is there something I can do for you?"

"I was just congratulating Mr. Cooper here on his

piano playing Sunday—wasn't it lovely?" She barely waited for Verity's bemused nod before continuing on. "Anyway, I mentioned that I had been thinking about joining the choir and he told me to stop thinking about it and just do it. So, since you're the choir director, I figure you would be the one to talk to."

Why the sudden interest in joining the choir? Belva had been in town for four months and this was the first time she'd mentioned it. Could it have anything to do with Mr. Cooper's involvement?

Not that that was either here or there. "Anyone with an interest is welcome to join," she answered with a smile she hoped was welcoming. "We practice every Saturday at four o'clock."

She hesitated a moment before issuing the second invitation, then chided herself for such churlishness. "And several us get together an hour earlier at the Blue Bottle for tea and conversation. You'd be most welcome to join us there as well, if you like. It's strictly optional." And since Constance had left this morning for her new adventure back east, there was an empty spot at the table.

"Oh, how lovely. Thank you."

"Hey," Mr. Cooper interjected. "How come no one invited me to this get-together? Aren't I a member of the choir now?"

Verity gave him a mock frown. "Technically you're the pianist, not a choir member."

Belva, who appeared confused by Verity's response, looked from her to Mr. Cooper and then back again. "But surely, if he truly wants to join you, I mean, I can sit out—"

Verity laughed, though it wasn't lost on her how quickly Belva came to Mr. Cooper's defense. "I was just teasing. Of course, if he was serious about wanting to join our little tea party on Saturdays, Mr. Cooper is welcome to join us. I meant it when I said everyone was welcome."

"Oh." Belva gave a sheepish grin. "I should have known you were just having a bit of fun." Then she turned to Mr. Cooper. "What about it? Are you going to join us?"

He rubbed his chin, as if giving it serious consideration. "It's tempting, but it sounds as if this is a ladies-only affair." Then he raised a brow. "Then again, I do like a good cup of tea."

Did the look he shot her have a glint of challenge in it? Verity lifted her chin. "Eve's teas are special—she adds syrups and spices to give them unique flavors. She has something new just about every time we go in. Most of the menfolk around here, though, consider it too frou-frou for their tastes."

He raised a brow at that. "I'm not most men and I'm not from around here." His lips twitched into a half smile before he schooled his expression again. "And I prefer to make up my mind for myself when it comes to what I like and don't like."

The look he gave her as he said that made her heart do a little flip-flop in her chest.

Then he turned to Belva. "How soon will you be needing that saddle?"

Was she dismissed? She stood there awkwardly fiddling with the collar of her dress, wondering if she should stay or go.

"Not for about three weeks," Belva answered. "Will that be a problem?"

"Not at all. It'll be ready when you need it."

"Well, if you'll excuse me, I have a few errands to run for Aunt Eunice." She turned to Verity. "It was nice running into you. And I'll see you on Saturday at the sweet shop."

When Belva had gone, Mr. Cooper leaned back and studied her curiously. "So, is there something I can do for you, or did you really come in so Joy could play with Beans?"

"It was mostly for Joy. But I did want to invite you to join me at the school this afternoon to meet the children who'll be part of our choir. If you'd like to, that is."

He seemed to ponder that for a moment. Then nodded. "Of course. What time should I be there?"

"I told Janell I'd be there at two-thirty."

"Then two-thirty it is."

"Well, then, I'll let you get back to your work." She turned toward her daughter, who was seated on the floor with Beans in her lap. "Time to go, pumpkin."

"But Mama, Beans and I aren't through playing."

"I'm sorry, but we need to go. I have a few more errands to run and I promised Aunt Betty I'd be back in time to help her hang out the laundry."

Mr. Cooper leaned forward. "It's all right, Joy. You're welcome to come back and visit anytime."

"You mean it?" Her precocious daughter's tone was quite solemn.

"Absolutely."

"Can I bring Mama, too?"

He glanced her way, his blue eyes seeming to darken slightly. "You may. In fact, I insist."

"Okay." Joy turned back to Beans. "Did you hear that? I can come back to play with you whenever I want."

Verity mentally sighed at her daughter's convenient misinterpretation of what had been said.

She foresaw a few battles between the two of them in the coming days.

Once Mrs. Leggett and her daughter had made their exit, Nate went back to work. He probably should have come up with an excuse to turn down her invitation. After all, she really didn't need him to go with her this afternoon. But for some reason, he hadn't been able to say no. His one consolation was that they would be in a room full of schoolchildren, not relatively alone in an empty schoolyard.

Nate forced his thoughts back to the order Belva had placed with him. A new saddle. It was his first major commission since he'd opened his shop and he was determined to do a good job.

Adam had loaned him the seed money he'd needed to set up and stock this place. And while he had no doubt his friend would extend the loan if he needed it, Nate was determined to make the payments on schedule. Because if he couldn't make a go of this place, then he might as well pack up and move on. He refused to be a drag on the man to whom he owed so much.

Then his thoughts circled back around to Mrs. Leggett. Was it wrong that he was so eagerly looking forward to seeing her again this afternoon?

When Nate stepped out of his shop just before two thirty that afternoon, he saw Mrs. Leggett approaching. Of course, she'd have to pass this way to get from her uncle's home to the schoolhouse. He shut the door behind him, then turned to wait for her.

As they exchanged greetings, they fell into step together.

"Where's Joy?" he asked. "Isn't she going to be part of this choir, too?"

"I left her with Aunt Betty. She'll get her introduction to the choir at the same time as the other young ones."

"How many?" he asked. Anything to keep the conversation light and impersonal.

"In addition to the children we meet at school today, there will be at least four others who are not yet school-age."

He sensed a quiet kind of anticipation about her, an eagerness, as if they were approaching a fun outing. She really *was* looking forward to this children's choir.

"So how well do you know the children who go to school here?"

"Most of them I at least know by sight. And I know some better than others, of course."

"So you're about to be assigned a group of children to teach that you have no idea whether they can carry a tune or not and how well they'll work together."

She tapped his arm lightly. "Don't be such a pessimist. They're children. And they're going to join the choir because they *want* to be in it."

"Or because they don't want to be in the play. There is a difference, you know."

"My, my, you *are* in a contrary mood today, aren't you?"

"I'd prefer to think I'm being realistic."

"Then you must think of this as a challenge. It will be up to us to make them love the choir, whether they are going into it for the right reasons or not. Do you think you are up to the job?"

He executed a half bow. "I will strive to follow your lead."

She laughed outright at that. It was a sound that brought a smile to his own lips.

They'd reached the schoolyard by then and he allowed her to precede him up the steps, suppressing thoughts of that simple but altogether electrifying touch yesterday.

When she reached the top, Mrs. Leggett opened the door herself rather than waiting for him, and stuck her head inside the building. "Are you ready for us?"

"Come on in" was the response from inside, and she opened the door wider and threw a smile over her shoulder as she entered.

When Nate followed her inside he saw Miss Whitman along with about a dozen students of various ages.

"Welcome, Verity." The schoolteacher waved them in. "And Mr. Cooper, it's an unexpected pleasure to have you join us, as well."

He set his hat on a nearby school desk. "I've volunteered to help Mrs. Leggett with the music, at least until your regular pianist returns."

"And we are all most grateful to have someone as talented as you fill in for Mrs. Ford."

He was grateful that she didn't wait for a response but instead she swept a hand toward the students. "These are the talented group you two will be working with on the musical performance. The rest of the students are in Mr. Parker's classroom reading over the play."

"And a fine-looking group it is," Mrs. Leggett said enthusiastically. "I already know many of you and I'm sure I'll get to know the rest of you quickly. But for Mr. Cooper's benefit, why don't you each step forward, one at a time, and give us your name and age?"

There was something about her tone and demeanor that made one want to please her. Did the children feel it, too?

One by one they stepped forward and introduced themselves, just as she'd asked. He hoped no one actually expected him to remember all these names. He did spot one familiar face in the group—Jack Barr, Adam's son. The boy gave him a toothy grin as he introduced himself, indicating he recognized him, as well.

Mrs. Leggett had a kind word for each of them. When the last child had given her information, Mrs. Leggett took the floor again. "Very good. Now, we're not going to have any sort of practice session today—I just wanted to get to meet you and let you meet me and Mr. Cooper. But we *are* going to discuss expectations."

One of the younger children raised her hand.

"Yes, Cora Ann?"

"What's expectations?"

"Expectations means I'm going to let you know what I expect you to do if you want to be part of this choir." Then she smiled. "I promise none of this is very difficult. First, practice sessions will be for one hour every Tuesday and Thursday right after school, over at the church. We expect you to attend every practice unless you are ill. Second, you must promise to do your very best."

Nate watched as she went down her list of far-from-onerous expectations. She had the children's full attention—they seemed to be listening closely and were nodding in the appropriate places. Would she be able to command their attention as easily when they got down to the practice sessions themselves?

When she was done, she turned to him. "Was there anything you wanted to add?"

He was caught off guard by the question, but rallied quickly. "Only that everyone be respectful of their fellow choir members. Remember, everyone learns things at a different pace."

She gave him an approving nod, then turned back to the children. "Do you all agree to try to meet these expectations?"

Almost as one they said, "Yes, ma'am."

"Very good." She beamed approvingly at the group. "And I hope you'll be pleased to know that there are four children who aren't quite school-age yet who will be joining us. They are Joey and Molly Tucker, Jeffery Unger and my little girl, Joy."

"But they're practically babies," one of the older boys protested. "Will they even be able to keep up with us?"

Nate frowned. "They will if we help them."

She shot him a surprised look that quickly changed to one of approval. Had she thought he had no opinion on such things?

Then she turned back to the children. "Mr. Cooper is right. The younger ones may require a little extra patience, but with some practice they should be fine, especially with the songs we've selected."

"What songs are we gonna be singing?"

"We've selected three songs for the program, but I think we'll wait until tomorrow, when the rest of our choir will join us, to announce what they are." She looked around the group. "Now, does anyone have any other questions for me or Mr. Cooper?"

When no one spoke up, Mrs. Leggett leaned back against the teacher's desk.

"Very well, then. I'm really looking forward to getting to know all of you better and to listen to the beautiful music we'll make together. Remember, our first practice is right after school tomorrow. Let your parents know and don't be late."

The schoolteacher stepped forward. "All right, children, you are dismissed for the day." As the children quickly filed out, Miss Whitman turned to the two of them. "Thank you both so much for taking this on. I know the children will do their best for you." She scooped up a stack of papers from her desk. "Now, if you'll excuse me, I saw Abigail arrive a few minutes ago so I need to go next door and help her get the children's play organized."

"Of course." Mrs. Leggett stepped aside to let the teacher pass and then, with a "shall we?" glance for him, headed toward the door.

Taking his cue, he followed her out. By the time they stepped out on the small porch, there were no children in sight.

"Well, what do you think of our choir members?" she asked.

"I think, as a whole, they're a much younger group than I'd expected." He hadn't seen more than two or three who looked like they'd hit their teen years yet. "Especially when you consider the four who weren't here today aren't yet old enough to be in school."

"The majority of them *do* seem to fall in the eight-to ten-year-old range." She didn't seem the least bit concerned by that. "It's a blessing for us, really."

"How so?"

"I find younger children much more teachable than the older ones."

He hadn't thought of it that way. Not that he was entirely convinced.

But she was moving on to another subject. "For our practice sessions, I was thinking it would be best to start with one song and practice it until they get it down right before moving on to the next. But do you think we should introduce them to all three songs when we get together tomorrow before we settle down to practice the first one? Or would that overwhelm them?"

How would he know? But she was waiting for his answer. "It seems to me that introducing them to all three songs first would give them something to look forward to. And if we sing each of them at the beginning of each session, it would get them used to that last song that they are probably not already familiar with."

"Good point. So you and I will sing them for the group first, and then we'll settle in to practice 'Jesus Loves Me.'"

"You're assuming these children actually can sing. Not everyone has an ear for music, you know."

"True. But if nothing else they can make a joyful noise. And, as you told Robbie, they'll manage okay if we help them." She met his gaze, her expression earnest. "I don't want any of these children to feel they are any less important to the choir than any of the other members."

He gave a short nod. "Of course. A joyful noise it is."

"I was wondering…" She paused, her fingers plucking at her collar.

"What is it?"

"Well, that song you sang for me yesterday—'Down to the Valley.'"

Had she changed her mind about using it? "If you prefer to substitute something else—"

"No, no, I love the song. It's just that, if I'm going to

teach the children, then someone really needs to teach it to me first."

Teach her? Watch her learn the words and melody, make them her own? It was very tempting.

But he wasn't sure he was much of a teacher.

Chapter Eleven

Verity saw his hesitation and wished she could take the question back. Had her request been out of line? Her cheeks warmed as she realized the spot she'd put him in. He had shut his shop to accompany her this afternoon, and now she'd asked for more of his time. He was undoubtedly trying to find a polite way to say no.

Before she could withdraw her request, however, he nodded.

"All right. Where would you like to do this? It's performed a cappella so we don't need a piano, but I'd prefer not to break into song right here on the sidewalk."

She appreciated his self-deprecating humor. And also his generosity. "Thank you, but I just realized you probably need to get back to your shop. Why don't we plan to meet a little early before practice starts tomorrow instead?"

But he shook his head. "Today is fine." By now they'd reached the corner of Schoolhouse Road and Second Street. He waved toward his shop. "As you can see, there's no line of customers waiting for me to open my doors. And the work I already have scheduled can wait a little longer without endangering any schedules."

Was his business slow, then? "I'm sure you'll get more customers as more people become aware of your work."

He merely nodded and changed the subject. "So, where shall we go?"

"We could go down by the church. It should be fairly quiet there today."

They turned their steps toward the church but hadn't gone far before they encountered Eunice Ortolon, Belva's aunt.

Verity intended to just exchange greetings and keep moving, but Eunice apparently wanted to have a conversation.

"Well, hello, Verity, Mr. Cooper. It's a fine afternoon for a walk, isn't it?"

Mr. Cooper nodded. "That it is, ma'am."

Verity could see the woman's mind working as she studied the two of them. Surely she didn't see this as anything other than what it was. But the woman was a notorious busybody—she loved speculating about anyone and anything she knew, or even thought she knew. And she didn't mind sharing those speculations with anyone who would listen.

Eunice gave Mr. Cooper an arch smile. "I hope your injuries are healing well. We've been missing you around the boardinghouse."

Mr. Cooper smiled politely. "I thank you for your concern, ma'am. And I certainly hope my absence hasn't caused you any inconvenience."

"We're getting by." She glanced at Verity and then back to him. "I understand you'll be helping Verity here with the children's choir. That's very kind of you. There's not many a gentleman who'd agree to step in for the church piano player, much less teach songs to a group of youngsters."

Verity's spine stiffened. Did Eunice think that such actions were beneath him?

"If that's true, then it's their loss," Mr. Cooper said easily. "I enjoyed playing for the church service. And I just met some of the children who'll be in the new choir and I'm certain I'll enjoy working with them, as well."

"It sounds like Verity here is lucky to have someone as enthusiastic as you are to help her." Eunice's tone still carried an edge of patronization

Verity lifted her chin, but kept her smile relaxed. "It's Turnabout that's lucky Mr. Cooper moved here, don't you think?"

Eunice's smile slipped momentarily, then came back in full force. "Of course. Well, I won't keep you from, well, from wherever you were headed."

Verity ignored Eunice's not-so-subtly buried question and moved on.

For a moment neither she nor Mr. Cooper said anything. What was he thinking? Had he been put off by Eunice's clumsy comments?

"It strikes me that Mrs. Ortolon is nothing like her niece."

Verity swung her gaze around to meet his. The words had been uttered in an idle tone, as if he'd been remarking on the weather, but there was a definite glint of amusement in his eyes.

She matched his impassive expression. "You mean she's shorter and has a brassier voice?"

"Exactly."

They shared a grin, and for a moment Verity felt an

unfamiliar emotion tugging at her, an emotion she decided not to examine too closely.

When they reached the churchyard, Verity swept a hand out. "Will this do?"

"It seems quiet enough."

By which she knew he meant there was no one around to hear him sing. This little touch of insecurity, and the vulnerability that it lent to such an otherwise strong man, actually seemed quite endearing.

"Would you like to sit on the steps?" he asked.

His question brought her thoughts back to the here and now. "Actually, this may sound strange, but what if we stroll through the cemetery?" She could see she'd startled him. "I promise I'm not being morbid. I've just always thought it was such a peaceful, beautiful place, especially on a bright spring day like today. But if it makes you uncomfortable—"

"Not at all. Lead the way."

Nate strolled beside her, wondering again at her unexpectedness, at how she could so enchant him without any obvious effort. The man who'd been her husband had been a lucky fellow.

She led him through the gate and then around the perimeter until they came to a large oak. There were two simple wooden benches, one on each side of the tree. She turned to him with a smile. "How's this?"

"It'll do." Actually, with her smiling at him like that, he would have agreed to sing in the middle of Main Street.

She took a seat on one of the benches, then looked up at him expectantly. "Well, then, teach me."

He cleared his throat and launched into the song, singing the first verse and chorus at a respectable volume. His reward when he was done was an absent, inwardly focused glance from his pupil.

"I think I have it," she said. "If you'll go over it again, I'll try to sing along."

With a nod he started again. She immediately added her voice to his. The sound of their voices together both startled and pleased him.

When they were done, she grimaced. "I mangled a few notes. Let's try it one more time."

He hadn't noticed her mangling anything, but he decided he could do this all day. He started again and this time when she joined in her voice was stronger, surer. And to his surprise, rather than copying him this time, she sang harmony, playing with some of the notes, making it up right there on the spot. And it sounded amazing. The beauty of their joined voices was something he could listen to forever.

When they were finished this time, she clapped her hands in pure joy. "Oh, that was fun. The kids are going to love this song."

Right now, it was his favorite, as well.

"I'll definitely need your help teaching it to the children, but at least now I feel like I can hold my own with it." She straightened. "Now, I'm sure you're eager to get back to your shop."

Not particularly, but he knew a dismissal when he heard one.

She led him out a different way than the one they'd taken earlier. Rather than following the perimeter, she silently led him on a winding path between the headstones.

Then she paused and placed her hands lightly on a pair of side-by-side headstones. "These are my parents," she said softly. "I like to stop by and say hello whenever I'm here."

He studied her bittersweet expression. "Have they been gone long?"

"They passed when I was five. Uncle Grover and Aunt Betty raised me."

"It was good that you had someone to take you in."

She removed her hands from the headstones and smiled up at him. "They were great substitute parents—I never doubted I was loved."

But she was still studying her parents' graves pensively.

"Do you remember them?" he asked.

She nodded. "Not a lot, of course, but images, emotions. I loved my mother, but I adored my father."

He could tell be the faraway look in her eyes that she was remembering another time and place.

"He was bigger than life, always full of energy, and he seemed to live to make me and Mother happy."

"Sounds like quite a man."

"He was. He had a way of making everything we did seem like fun. And he liked to take Mother on what he called adventuring—take hikes, camp out in the woods, canoe on water rapids, climb peaks—anything that seemed new or exciting. I have great memories of the two of them laughingly setting off on what looked, to my five-year-old self, like really fun excursions."

Her smile had a faraway quality to it. "They included me occasionally, in what I now know were the tamer of these outings." She touched the little scar near her lip. "I got this on one of the camping trips. Father said it was my badge of honor, the proof that I was an adventurer like him and mother."

"Did their death occur on one of these adventures?"

She nodded. "It was a hot air balloon."

Realizing what must have happened, Nate immediately held up his hand. "There's no need to tell me the details."

She seemed not to hear him. "I stood on the ground with a family friend and watched the balloon go up with them in the basket below. They both blew me kisses and then turned and kissed each other. They looked so happy and my only thought was that I wanted very badly to be with them." She paused a moment. "Then, when they were so far up that I could no longer distinguish them, the balloon caught fire in a big whoosh. It was over almost before the woman who was holding my hand fainted and hit the ground."

He quickly reached for her hand, wanting to offer her what comfort he could. "Verity, I'm so, so sorry that happened to you. That must have been horrific to see."

Her gaze slowly lost its unfocused quality and she smiled at him. "As you yourself said, Uncle Grover and Aunt Betty were really wonderful. Uncle Grover blamed my father's reckless, impulsive nature for getting my mother—his sister—killed, but he never held that against me. And anyway, I'm nothing like my father. I lack his thirst for adventure."

And then she seemed to suddenly realize he was holding her hand. Her cheeks pinkened and gaze dropped.

He gave her hand a quick squeeze and then released it. But he didn't apologize. Mainly because he wasn't sorry.

Did she also realize he'd called her by her first name? Because she certainly hadn't objected.

Then he struck an idle tone as he prepared to do a little more probing. "Is your former husband buried here, as well?"

She didn't seem put out by the question. She merely shook her head. "Arthur is buried in Kansas, beside his first wife."

So she had been the man's second wife. "Do you mind if I ask you what sort of man he was?"

She started walking again, and for a moment he thought she wasn't going to answer. He didn't blame her—it was something he had no right to ask.

Then she spoke up. "I don't mind. In fact, Arthur deserves to be remembered and spoken of from time to time."

There was a fondness in her voice, and some sense of reflection, as well.

"Arthur was a fine, decent man," she continued. "He was a good doctor, and a respected member of the community where we lived. And he absolutely adored Joy."

"Did he have an adventurous streak like your father?"

She smiled at that. "I'm afraid not. For one thing Arthur was somewhat older, nearly fifteen years my senior. And he had a more analytical approach to life, a trait that served him well in his work as a doctor."

But how had it served him in his role as a husband? Had he been dispassionate and analytical there, as well?

Nate didn't press her any further. But he did find it odd that she never once spoke of loving him.

Verity lay in bed that night staring at the ceiling, going over the events of the day. Singing a duet with him had been such an amazing, exhilarating experience. It had felt…exciting. And fun. And, oh, so right.

Almost as if their voices had been created specifically to complement each other.

Which was a totally ridiculous, fanciful thought.

Was that why she'd told him about her parents? A lot of people around here knew the story, of course, but she'd never spoken of it to anyone before.

The way he'd taken her hand, and looked at her with that sincere sympathy in his compelling blue eyes had been both comforting and affirming. His hands holding hers—strong, callused hands, hands that belonged to both a craftsman and a pianist—had made her feel both safe and empowered.

Which she supposed was why she had spoken so freely about Arthur today. Strange, but, except for the conversations she sometimes had with Joy, she'd spoken of her former husband more in that short discussion with Mr. Cooper than she had since she'd returned to Turnabout.

But even without Mr. Cooper's questions, she'd found herself ruminating on her marriage. Because telling him about her memories of her parents had had her making some comparisons with her own life.

Arthur had been a good husband to her and she'd been quite fond of him. She'd admired him, too. He'd been predictable, responsible and even-tempered. He was everything she'd told herself she wanted in a husband.

But thinking today of the all-encompassing, zestful love she'd witnessed between her own parents, she realized that she and Arthur had never shared anything like what her parents had. And she wondered now what it would be like to experience such a love.

She rolled over on her side and hugged her pillow. Arthur had never shared her love of music, either. Singing together with Mr. Cooper today, however, had been a surprisingly emotional experience. The way their voices had blended and intertwined, the look in his eyes as their gazes locked together—she'd never experienced that kind of connection before. It had been altogether addictively exhilarating.

Had Mr. Cooper felt the same thing?

And he'd called her by her first name. That had to mean something.

Didn't it?

Chapter Twelve

Verity nodded her thanks to Nate—that's how she thought of him now, even if she still used the more formal Mr. Cooper when she said his name aloud.

The two of them had just finished singing all three selected songs for the children. She had enjoyed singing with him today every bit as much as she had yesterday. Once Zella returned, would he consider joining the choir? It would be nice to sing alongside him every Sunday. Would the experience be the same as part of a larger group?

But right now it was time to focus on the gathered group of sixteen children. "So what do you all think? Doesn't that sound like a great program?"

Her question was met with mostly smiles and nods, but she also made note of the few who looked doubtful.

"Today we're going to focus on practicing 'Jesus Loves Me.'" That was the easiest and the one most familiar to the children. Hopefully it would help build the confidence of those who were feeling a bit overwhelmed.

"But we all already know that one, Mrs. Leggett," Derbin said.

"But do you know all four verses?"

"There's *four* verses?"

"There are." She looked around to include all the children in her remarks. "And I have an idea about how to perform this so that every one of you has an opportunity to really be heard."

The children leaned forward slightly. She noticed that even Nate raised a brow at that.

"Since there are sixteen of you, and the song has four verses, I'm going to divide you up into four groups of four singers each, and each group will be responsible for one of the verses."

"Do we get to pick which team we're on?"

Verity grinned at Jack's question. "No, Mr. Cooper and I will be figuring out the teams." She held up a finger. "But first, let's sing the first verse, the one all of you know, all together so I can get a feel for each of your voices."

She glanced toward Nate and without her saying a word he took his place at the piano. She turned back to the children. "Form a line here in front of me, oldest to youngest."

The kids scrambled to do as she asked. There was a little bit of giggling and rearranging as they figured out relative ages. Finally they were settled.

"Okay, now, stand up straight." She nodded to Nate. He played a short intro and then went right into the melody. She sang with them the first time, walking back and forth in front of them. When they got to the end, she nodded. "Sing it again, please."

This time she didn't sing along, but rather listened to each of the children in turn, assessing the strength of their voices and their ability to carry a tune.

When they were done for the second time, she smiled and nodded. "Well done. Let me discuss this with Mr. Cooper for a few minutes and then we'll form your groups." She moved to stand next to him at the piano bench.

"I want to put the four youngest together," she said. "They know the first verse really well and this will give them an opportunity to be heard rather than hidden behind the older ones. And I'm sure their parents will appreciate giving them a bit of the limelight, as well."

"That sounds like a good plan."

"As for the others, I think grouping them by voice range would be best, don't you?"

He nodded. "But you also want to be sure you don't group all the weakest singers together, regardless of range."

"Agreed." She made a few mental adjustments to her thoughts on the groupings, then signaled him to follow her as she turned back to the children.

"Okay, here we go. When I call your name, stand together with your group. Group one—Molly, Joey, Robbie and Joy. Group two—Mina, Jack, Peter and Alice. Group three—Harriet, Cora Ann, Susie and Derbin. And that leaves Becky, Mary Ellen, Fern and Kevin for group four."

She waited until all the children had arranged themselves into their groups, then spoke again. "As I said, each group will learn one of the verses to sing. But all of you will sing the chorus together. Now, I've written down the words for each verse." She began passing the pages around, one sheet per group. "I want each group to pick a corner of the church and go there to practice your part. In about thirty minutes we'll get back together and try to run through the whole thing."

Responding to her glance, Nate stepped forward. It was really nice to work with someone who seemed to be so in tune with her thoughts.

"If you'll work with group one—" she pointed to the youngest children "—I'll work with group two." She figured the older children could probably handle this one on their own. Fern Tucker was in group four and Derbin Greene was in group three. Both were good singers and good kids—they'd be able to lead the others.

She'd given Nate the youngest group to work with mainly because Joy was in it. She figured it would be better for everyone if she didn't work with her own daughter. And since the children were already familiar with the words and melody to this one, his biggest challenge would be making sure they all started and ended the song at the same time.

She forced her focus away from him and his group and onto her group. Since they were not as familiar with the second verse as they were with the first, they had to go through it a couple of times before the children were comfortable singing it through by memory. Once they had that down, she focused on their timing and harmonizing.

Finally, it was time to pull them all back together. "Okay, everyone, let's gather back in the front here. And this time when you line up, do it by groups. Group one stand here, then group two next to them and so forth. Mr. Cooper, if you'd return to the piano."

Once they were all in place, she gave them a big smile. "From what I heard coming from your groups, it sounds like everyone is ready. So, let's try it together.

Remember, each verse will be sung by only one group, but you will all sing the chorus together each time."

She waited for their nods before continuing. "One other thing before we start. I'm going to use a few hand signals to communicate with you during the performance. When I do this—" she held up a hand, palm out "—that means to stand up straight and focus on me. When Mr. Cooper plays the introduction, I will give you a countdown as so." She held up three fingers, one at a time. "And then when I do this—" she jabbed her index finger out in an aggressive pointing motion "—that means start singing. And when I do this—" she made a sweeping motion with her hand "—that means everyone join in. So keep your eye on me, okay?" She held up a hand and they all came to attention.

She nodded to Nate and he started the intro. She counted down with her fingers, then pointed to the youngest group. She had to smile as they sang. They weren't completely together, but what they lacked in technique, they made up for in enthusiasm. Even if they didn't improve before the actual performance, their parents would love watching them.

Though by no means perfect, they made it through the entire hymn without having to stop. They went through it a few more times, and once Verity thought they were comfortable with the song, she asked them to add some minor movement. As the time came for each verse, she had the group responsible step forward, then return to their places when they were done.

There were a few missteps, naturally, but all in all she was pleased with this first practice. When they came back together on Thursday they could polish this up and begin work on the next song.

Just as she was ready to dismiss the group, Hazel showed up with a measuring tape and notebook in hand. The dressmaker took quick measurements of each of the children for the smocks she planned to make.

When the final measurement had been taken and all of the children but Joy had gone, Hazel turned to Verity. "So how was the first practice?"

"I think it went quite well." Verity turned to Nate. "What did you think?"

"They're a good group of kids. Some of them already have excellent singing voices, some are going to need a little more work. But I think in the end we'll have a program the parents and friends will be able to appreciate."

Verity nodded. "I agree. And all of them seem willing to put in the work."

"Well, I have what I came for." Hazel gathered up her things. "If you two have additional work to do, I can take Joy back with me. You can stop in and get her on your way home."

Verity resisted the urge to roll her eyes at this not-so-subtle bit of matchmaking, but nodded, anyway. She knew Hazel would keep a close eye on her daughter, so she had no qualms on that account. "Well, there is something regarding our next practice I'd like to work out with Mr. Cooper." She turned to him. "If you don't mind staying a moment longer."

"Not at all."

Hazel held her hand out. "Come along, Joy. Buttons has a new bit of yarn he needs someone to dangle for him."

Joy went to her without hesitation. With one last grin over her shoulder toward Verity, Hazel led the little girl out the door.

A moment later, though, Joy raced back inside. What in the world was the matter?

"Joy, slow down before you fall and hurt yourself."

The girl immediately slowed her steps but continued forward. Verity saw Hazel step inside and pause.

She turned back to her daughter. "What's the matter? Did you change your mind about going with Miss Hazel?"

Joy shook her head. "I forgot Lulu." She reached into one of the pews near the front of the church and triumphantly picked up her doll. Squeezing her ever-present companion tightly, she turned back toward Hazel and made her exit for the second time.

Nate watched Joy leave, then turned to her mother. "That doll seems to be very dear to her." Susanna had had a special doll, also. Unlike Joy's wooden-headed cloth figure, though, Susanna's had been china and elegantly dressed in lace and silk. Still, it seemed both girls shared a similar love for their playthings.

Verity nodded. "It was given to her by her father." Her expression grew more solemn. "Just one week before he died."

Nate stilled at that reminder of her loss. And of the secret he was keeping from her.

But Verity didn't seem aware of him. Her gaze was unfocused, turned inward. "She was only four at the time and I think she's forgotten so much of him. He loved her very much—I'm glad she has that one thing of his she can cling to."

What about her? Was her memory of her deceased husband still fresh and raw? Or was he a beloved but fading memory that she thought fondly of from time to time?

And why did the answer to that very personal question matter so much to him?

"I'm sorry," she said, her cheeks pinkening. "I shouldn't have brought up such personal thoughts."

"No need to apologize. I'm honored that you would be comfortable sharing them with me."

Her smile immediately turned warmer.

Deciding his thoughts were now drifting toward dangerous territory again, he cleared his throat. "So what was this you needed to speak to me about?"

She took his cue and her expression took on a more businesslike cast. "I was thinking I'd like to change the second song to something else."

"And what brought this on?"

Her nose wrinkled slightly, as if she was trying to articulate a nebulous feeling. "It just doesn't seem to fit in with the other two."

He stilled at that. "And fitting in is important to you?"

Something in his tone must have caught her attention because she gave him a faintly puzzled look. "Well, of course. The program should be harmonious, don't you think?"

Fit in. Harmonious. Did she feel that way about the people she let into her life, as well?

Rather than answering her question, he asked one of his own. "What did you have in mind to replace it with?"

"That's just it, I can't make up my mind."

He moved around the piano. "Do you mind if we walk while we discuss this? I need to head back to my shop. Miss Ortolon asked to talk to me about her saddle design again and I told her to come at four-thirty."

"Oh. Of course." She fell in step beside him as they headed down the aisle. "I apologize for holding you up. We can continue this conversation another time, if you like."

He heard something different in her voice, but he couldn't quite put his finger on what. "Not at all. There's time to figure this out before Miss Ortolon arrives." He opened the church door and allowed her to precede him. "So back to your question, what attributes would a song need to have in order to *fit in* with the other two songs? Are you looking for another hymn?"

"Not necessarily, though a hymn would definitely work better than a child's rhyme." She paused, as if gathering her thoughts. "I guess I'm looking for something with an uplifting message."

She waved a hand with an apologetic air. "I'm sorry I didn't think this through earlier. I hate changing things up now that we've set the children's expectations." She grimaced self-consciously. "Uncle Grover always says being wishy-washy shows a lack of character."

He felt strangely protective of her and was insulted on her behalf. "Not at all. And you're not being wishy-washy. You're merely being flexible enough to make an adjustment when you spot a weakness."

He was rewarded with a warm smile. "I guess I'd never thought of it that way. That does sound nicer, doesn't it?"

He forced himself not to bask in her smile but to get back to business. "So, a new song. Given our time frame, it would need to be either something the children are already familiar with or something very simple."

"Agreed."

He rubbed his chin. "How do you feel about adding

a patriotic song? Something like 'America' or 'Columbia, the Gem of the Ocean'?"

"Why, that's a great idea." She smiled at him as if he'd said something brilliant. "I think 'America' will fit in perfectly. And you should be able to find the sheet music for it in the stack Zella left for you—she plays it every Independence Day. Which also means most of the children will at least have heard it before."

He nodded, a bit puffed up by her enthusiastic praise. "I'll come by tomorrow to look for it and maybe run through the song a couple of times just to make certain I can play it smoothly at Thursday's practice session."

"I'll be glad to help you with that if you like."

He definitely liked. But should he agree?

She spoke up again before he could decide. "It might be good for us to run through it together so we can decide whether to have the children sing it as a group or break it out by verses like we're doing the others."

How could he say no to that? "Of course." They'd reached his shop by then and he opened his door. "Would you like to continue our discussion inside?"

She started to say something then glanced down the sidewalk and her expression changed. "I think we're done for now. I'll let you get back to work."

He followed her gaze and saw Belva approaching. He turned back to her and nodded. "I'll see you at the church tomorrow then. Shall we say four o'clock?"

With a nod and a wave, she retraced her steps as far as the dress shop. He watched as she stepped inside, then he turned to greet Belva.

Verity didn't tarry long at Hazel's. Joy, naturally, didn't want to part from Buttons but reluctantly followed her mother out. Verity determinedly kept her gaze on her daughter as they walked past Nate's shop, though she was quite tempted to look. Were he and Belva laughing the way they'd been the last time she saw them together?

Nate had said Belva was stopping by to discuss her saddle design. What was there about saddle design that needed further discussion once the order had been placed?

Verity didn't like the idea that she was giving jealousy a toehold in her heart, but there was no denying she had. If she couldn't control her heart, she at least had to control where she let her thoughts take her.

With that in mind, she turned to her daughter. "So, Joy, what did you think of choir practice today?"

"It was fun."

"And what was your favorite part?"

"It was when Mr. Cooper practiced with our group. He has a nice voice."

It seemed Nate had managed to steal her daughter's heart, as well.

She let Joy's happy chatter, which required very little response, carry them the rest of the way home.

Nate listened to Belva's suggestions and took the appropriate notes. Back when he had been working part-time at the boardinghouse, Belva had gotten into the habit of chatting with him while he chopped wood or performed some of the other maintenance chores her aunt had lined up for him.

He wasn't sure why she'd taken to him the way she had—perhaps it was because she was fairly new to town herself and hadn't made any close friends yet. Or perhaps it was because, as she'd told him recently, he reminded her of a schoolteacher she'd had when she was younger, a man she admired and trusted very much. Whatever the case, it seemed he'd become a confidant of sorts for her. She'd confided secrets that she hadn't shared with anyone else. He hadn't reciprocated, of course, which made him feel even more of a fraud. But he hadn't asked to be put into that role, and there was nothing he could do about it now.

All that being said, normally he enjoyed her chatter—she almost felt like a younger sister—but today his mind was on Verity.

The doctor's niece was beginning to look at him with a certain softness, a certain interest that he couldn't mistake. The thing was, he wasn't sure if she liked him for who he truly was, or if she still had some kind of misguided sense of gratitude that she was mistaking for something deeper. And the answer to that mattered a great deal to him.

Whatever the case, he wasn't sure how much longer he could maintain a "just friends" attitude, especially when she looked at him with those lovely eyes of hers and that sweet smile on her lips. And even worse was this gnawing guilt that he was lying to her by omission.

The time was drawing near when he'd have to summon the courage to tell her his past.

And once he did, he wouldn't have the problem of having her look at him with such admiration at all.

"Mr. Cooper."

Belva's voice pulled him back to the present. "Yes."

She had a fist planted on her hip. "I don't think you've heard anything I've said for the past few minutes."

He didn't bother denying the accusation. "I'm sorry. What were you saying?"

She relaxed and waved a hand dismissively. "Oh, nothing much. Just nattering on like always. But it looks like this time, it's you who needs to talk. Anything I can help with?"

"Oh, it's nothing. I'm just distracted today." He tapped his notebook with his pencil. "I think I have your new specifications down and I don't see any problems incorporating them in the final product. Was there anything else?"

She shook her head. "That's all for now. I can't wait to see the finished saddle."

"Have you told your aunt about your horse yet?"

"I'm going to wait until the very last minute. I'm afraid something will happen to spoil my plans if I tell too many people." Then she gave him a little wave. "Thank you again. And remember, if you need someone to talk to, I'm available."

Someone to talk to—that would be very welcome. But the only person here he could safely confide in was Adam, and Adam was a big part of his dilemma.

Because his story wasn't his alone. If he ever reached the point where he was ready to talk about his time in prison and what he'd done to land him there, if the person he told was an intelligent person, she might begin to wonder just how he and Adam met. And Nate would *not* allow himself to be the cause of speculation about Adam's past.

No matter how uncomfortable keeping secrets from certain people made him.

Chapter Thirteen

The next few days passed in a pleasantly busy fashion for Verity. She met Nate at church Wednesday afternoon as they'd planned, and together they practiced the new song in what Verity thought of as perfect harmony. Singing with him had become a treasured experience for her. She loved the way their voices intertwined, the way his gaze held hers when they sang, the way they seemed to instinctively be able to anticipate one another. Perhaps, sometime soon, she could convince him to perform a duet with her during the Sunday service.

In the end they decided to go with the first three verses of "America" for the program and to let the children perform it as a group rather than assigning parts.

At Thursday's practice session, Verity had them start out by running through "Jesus Loves Me," the song they'd practiced during the prior session, a couple of times and then she introduced "America" as the replacement for "Row, Row, Row Your Boat." By the end of the hour-long session she was well pleased with their progress.

By the time Friday rolled around, Verity had Eula

Fay's hat completed. The mayor's wife seemed delighted with the result, lavishing effusive praise on Verity. It was enough to make her begin to think that perhaps she might just be ready to open her millinery business after all.

Despite his teasing comments earlier in the week, Nate didn't join them on Saturday for their weekly tea, but Verity hadn't really expected him to.

Belva, however, *did* join them. The other members of the group welcomed her and seemed genuinely delighted to learn she was joining the choir.

Despite the remaining pinprick of jealousy, Verity couldn't help but like the girl. She was perpetually optimistic, had a bit of coltish awkwardness about her and was always willing to pitch in and help where she could.

And later, at choir practice, she proved to have a tolerable enough voice to blend in with the rest of the group.

After choir practice, Hazel approached her. "Come with me and stop by the shop on your way home. There's something I want to show you."

Verity had hoped to walk with Nate but hid her disappointment. "Of course. Is it something to do with the choir smocks?"

"No questions—it's a surprise."

Verity rolled her eyes—Hazel and her love of the dramatic. But it was always easier to go along with her than try to argue.

"So, how are things going between you and Mr. Cooper?" her friend asked.

"He's been a big help to me with the children's choir. He has a way about him that they all respond to."

Hazel gave her a little nudge. "I didn't ask how he

was getting along with the children. I asked how he was getting along with *you*."

Verity waved a hand airily. "We've become good friends, and of course I have no complaints about his performance as a musician."

Hazel gave her a severe frown. "You, my dear, can be a most frustrating friend. I want details, not boring platitudes."

Verity placed a hand over her heart in feigned shock. "Boring?"

"Don't play the innocent with me, Verity Magdalena Leggett. You know exactly what I mean."

Verity laughed. "Let's just say we get along very well." By this time they'd reached Hazel's shop. "Now, what is this surprise you wanted to show me?"

"Patience, my dear." Hazel opened the door and led the way inside.

Verity's gaze went immediately to a dress form in the center of the shop. Draped on it was a lovely dress fashioned from that same shadow-blue fabric she had so admired last week.

She moved closer to examine it. Hazel had done an amazing job of keeping it simple but at the same time giving it a special feel. The slightly flared skirt was trimmed on the bottom with two rows of a darker blue ribbon, as was the waistband. The sleeves were puffed from the shoulder and then gathered at the elbow and snug on the forearm. Again there was dark trim on the bodice, but here it was done in a vertical pattern that Verity could tell would be quite flattering to the wearer.

"So, what do you think?"

Verity turned to her friend. "It's really lovely. I knew this fabric would drape beautifully, but I think you outdid yourself here. You should have no trouble selling this one."

"Oh, it's not for sale." Her friend had a very smug look on her face. "I made it for you."

Verity was taken aback. She couldn't accept such a gift. And yet…

"And before you say anything," Hazel continued, "you should know that I won't take no for an answer. In fact, I will be highly insulted if you don't accept my gift since I went to a lot of trouble to tailor it just for you."

Verity fingered the dress, enjoying the suppleness of it. It had been a long time since she'd had a new dress, at least one that wasn't made from pieces of other dresses and a new bit of ribbon or trim. "If I do accept it," she said carefully, "then you must at least let me pay for it." She'd find the money somehow.

"If you insist on repaying me, you can make one of your fabulous hats just for me and I will consider us even."

Verity knew it wasn't an even trade but she nodded agreement. She'd find other ways to repay her friend.

"Good." Hazel stepped forward to remove the dress from the form. "Let me just package this for you and you can take it home with you. And I expect to see you wearing it at church tomorrow."

A few minutes later Verity was headed toward home, a package in her arms and the humming melody of a song on her lips.

Yes, all in all, it had been a good week. And she had the glimmer of an idea how to make tomorrow even better.

Clothed in this new dress, she might just find the courage to translate her idea into action.

* * *

"There's something I'd like to talk to you about," Nate said as he followed Adam into the study.

Adam had invited him to join his family for supper Saturday evening and Nate had gladly taken him up on it. The meal was over now, and he and Adam had moved from the dining room to the study.

"Of course." Adam took a seat in one of a pair of large leather chairs that fronted the desk and signaled Nate to take the other.

Once seated, Nate rubbed the back of his neck, suddenly unsure how to start.

Adam steepled his fingers. "Would this, perchance, have anything to do with Mrs. Leggett?"

Nate noted the amused glint in his friend's eyes and nodded sheepishly. "Am I so obvious?"

"Let's just say I've noted the glances you've been giving each other." He propped his left leg on his right knee as he leaned back. "So, is it serious?"

Nate had no problem answering that question. "If you're asking if I'd like to pursue something more than a mere friendship with her, then the answer is yes."

"So why did you feel the need to speak to me about this rather than her? Do you want some information about her?"

"No, nothing like that. The thing is, I don't think I can take this any further without being honest with her about my past."

"I see."

He couldn't read anything one way or the other in Adam's demeanor. Did his friend understand what the implication was? "Of course I don't plan to mention anything about your connection to any of this. But Mrs.

Leggett is an intelligent woman." It was one of the things he admired about her. "She might very well put some of the pieces together."

"Nate, I know I've told you that my history is not well-known around here. But that wasn't meant to keep you from telling your own story if you felt the need." He leaned forward, his expression earnest. "The people who matter the most to me know all about my history. As for the rest of my friends and neighbors here—" he shrugged "—I hope I've proven myself to them in the three years that I've lived here. But, if some choose to believe the worst, then I'd like to think I can survive that."

He gave Nate a pointed look. "If Mrs. Leggett is important to you, and you feel led to tell her your story, then don't let any concerns about my feelings hold you back."

Nate felt humbled by his friend's trust. "Thanks. Mind you, I don't plan to tell her tomorrow, and it may not be next week, or next month, or even at all. I just needed to know that, if the time does come, I won't be betraying any spoken or implied confidence between us."

Later, as Nate walked home, he thought over what Adam had said. His family and close friends knew the truth and still accepted him. Of course, in Adam's case, he had been innocent of the crime he'd been imprisoned for. Not that his innocence had ever been officially established. Still, that had to have played into how those who knew his story viewed him.

Would that same kind of trust be afforded to him?

He supposed that depended on whom he told his story to. And how he told it.

This wasn't something he could figure out on his own. Bowing his head, he offered up a prayer, asking for guidance.

After church on Sunday, Verity approached Nate with a lunch invitation. "Aunt Betty has cooked a lovely pot roast and there is plenty to go around."

"Thank you, I'd be quite pleased to accept your invitation." He quirked an eyebrow. "Should I bring Beans? For Joy to play with, I mean?"

One of the things that endeared him to her was the bond that had formed between him and her daughter. "Of course. She'd like that."

Then, emboldened by the pretty new dress she wore, she gathered up her courage to take her invitation one step further. "Aunt Betty's been after me to gather some dewberries so she can make a cobbler. I thought, after lunch, I might take care of that for her. You're welcome to come along with me if you like."

He hesitated, and she thought for a moment he would decline. Had she been too forward after all? But he finally smiled and nodded. "It's a fine day for an outing and I'd be happy to repay your aunt with such a pleasant chore."

Verity exhaled the breath she hadn't been aware until now that she held. Issuing such an invitation to a single gentleman had called for a forwardness she hadn't been sure she had in her. It had felt both scary and exhilarating. Hazel would be proud.

She smoothed the skirt of her new dress. Perhaps she should have followed Hazel's advice and added some color to her life a long time ago.

Chapter Fourteen

"I see you've put away your walking stick. How's your arm and ankle doing?"

Nate turned to pass the breadbasket to Verity as he answered her uncle's question.

"They're healing nicely, sir. In fact, I'm thinking about resuming my work at the boardinghouse in another day or so."

He saw Verity's fingers tighten on the basket so he held on to it a moment longer until he was certain she had a proper hold.

"Do you think that's wise?" she asked. "I mean, given the kind of work she'll have you doing."

Her uncle spoke up before he could. "That depends." He turned to Nate. "Just be careful to start slow—I wouldn't be chopping any firewood or carrying heavy loads." He pointed his index finger at Nate in the manner of a judge pointing to an accused. "And mind you, if those injuries protest in any way, you stop what you're doing immediately."

"Yes, sir."

The conversation turned to inconsequential matters

after that. Nate enjoyed the meal, but even more, he enjoyed the company, the give-and-take that could only happen in a gathering of folk who were comfortable with each other. That was one of the things he'd missed most after he was thrown in prison.

He also couldn't help but notice the difference in Verity. He'd been pleasantly surprised by that new dress she was wearing today. Not only because the cut and color were flattering on her, but because of what it signified—she had put away her mourning clothes. Could it possibly be a signal of other, more subtle changes in her outlook?

And it wasn't just the dress. There was a new energy about her, a certain spark that hadn't been there before. It could just be her pleasure in wearing that new garment, but he didn't think so. Something internal seemed to have shifted and changed in her, as well.

Perhaps, when they went berry picking this afternoon, he'd be able to get some clues as to just what this all meant.

When at last the meal was over, Verity insisted on helping her aunt clean up before they went on their excursion.

As the women started clearing the table, Dr. Pratt turned to Nate. "What do you say we get out of the ladies' way? How do you feel about a game of chess? Verity tells me you're quite the strategic player."

So she talked about him to her uncle, did she? "It would be my pleasure, sir."

As he followed the older gentleman into the parlor, he couldn't help but remember what Verity had told him about how her uncle had such disdain for her father, but hadn't held her father's adventurous nature against her.

It had been a rather peculiar statement to make and he wasn't above doing some subtle probing.

Nate waited until they were seated and the game was set up. "I understand Mrs. Leggett grew up here with you and your wife." That was a nice neutral opening.

"That's right." Dr. Pratt glanced up from the chessboard. "She's like a daughter to us."

Had that been a warning of some sort? "She told me what happened to her parents."

The doctor moved a pawn, then leaned back. "Did she, now? I'll admit to being surprised. She doesn't ever talk about the accident. Or about her parents at all."

"Not even with you?"

The older gentleman tugged on the corners of his vest. "When she was younger I used to tell her tales of her mother as a little girl. But it's been some years now since we spoke of it."

Nate made his opening move. "And her father?"

Dr. Pratt's face hardened. "We don't speak of her father. Sturgis was a foolish, reckless man who thought nothing of putting the lives of those around him in danger."

Nate couldn't let that statement stand. "But surely there was good in him, too? If your niece and her mother loved him as much as they obviously did, then they had to see something in him worthy of that love."

"I'll allow that he *did* have a way about him, a certain charm and wit that most ladies found hard to resist."

From Dr. Pratt's tone, Nate could tell he didn't consider those good qualities.

Then his host shook his head and straightened. "How did we get started on this topic? It's *your* history I intended to discuss this afternoon."

Nate shifted uncomfortably, returning his focus to the chessboard. That was one topic he didn't want to discuss. "There's not much to tell, sir." He moved his next piece. "I grew up in fairly comfortable circumstances in the town of Plattisburg, Pennsylvania. I had one sibling, a younger sister. Unfortunately, she and my parents have all passed away so I have no family left to speak of."

Dr. Pratt's expression turned sympathetic. "I'm sorry. A man's life is so much richer if he has family around him to share it with."

Nate couldn't agree more.

But Verity's uncle wasn't through interrogating him yet. "Why did you come to Turnabout? I know you're a friend of Adam Barr's, but I figure it would take more than that to cause a man to pick up and move halfway across the country with little more than the clothes on his back."

This was getting into very uncomfortable territory— he needed to redirect the discussion. "I suppose we all have a few things in our past that are painful to look back on or that we wish we could erase." He met the man's gaze without blinking. "I just reached a point in my life where there was nothing left for me in Plattisburg and getting a fresh start somewhere else felt like a good idea." He allowed a touch of cynicism to color his voice. "As for the dearth of possessions I arrived with, it was everything I owned."

Everything he'd said was true, as far as it went. But it was time to change the topic before the man boxed him into a corner he couldn't maneuver out of. "Has your niece always been interested in medicine?"

Dr. Pratt's expression softened. "Almost as soon as she moved in here, Verity wanted to help me in the clinic.

She was always getting underfoot, asking for things to do. She would handle any household tasks my wife gave her but then would head right back to the clinic to see if I'd let her help me with anything. I finally gave in and decided to teach her a few simple tasks that would allow her to assist me."

It sounded as if Dr. Pratt loved his niece very much. It also sounded to him as if young Verity had been trying to replace her beloved father with her uncle.

"She was a fast learner," Dr. Pratt continued. "Never saw anyone take to it that quickly or at so young an age."

Nate had never doubted Verity was an intelligent woman—it was part of what appealed to him about her. But it seemed she had a natural talent, as well.

Verity appeared in the doorway just then, putting an end to their conversation. He noticed she'd changed out of her pretty new dress and into an everyday dress. But there was no touch of black to be found on this one either. He took that as a good sign.

"So who's winning?" she asked.

Nate sent a smile her way. "It appears your uncle currently has the upper hand." The doctor was a skilled player who was making him work to find any advantage he could. This game could potentially go on for quite some time.

Apparently Dr. Pratt thought the same thing. "I see my niece has some pails and a basket in hand. I believe that's her not-so-subtle hint that she's ready to go."

Verity gave him an affectionate smile. "Perhaps I *was* being a little too obvious."

Dr. Pratt leaned back and waved them on. "Why don't you two go on. We can finish this game another time."

Nate didn't have to be told twice. With a nod to his opponent, he stood and joined Verity.

She allowed him to take the pails from her, but held on to the basket. "Aunt Betty packed us some lemonade and a couple of pieces of gingerbread in case we feel the urge to snack while we are out."

"Your aunt Betty is a woman after my own heart."

Verity laughed. "Well, she's keeping an eye on Joy, and Joy is keeping an eye on Beans," she said. "So I think we can safely slip out now."

As they stepped outside, he lent her his arm to descend the porch steps. "So where do we find these dewberries your aunt is coveting?"

"There are some vines near the tree line out past the schoolyard. But they've likely been picked over already." She slid him a touchingly shy look. "There's another really great spot a little ways west of town, but it's too far to walk comfortably. However, Uncle Grover already agreed to loan us the use of his buggy, if you're of a mind to go for a ride that is."

A buggy ride with a pretty girl on a fine spring day—he couldn't think of anything he'd rather do. "So, where does he keep his buggy?"

Twenty minutes later Nate was maneuvering the buggy out of the livery's carriage house, Verity seated by his side.

Once they left the town behind them, Verity began pointing out landmarks of interest—the grove where she always harvested pecans in the fall, the meadow where she liked to take Joy for picnics, the pond where she and her uncle fished when she was a child.

He thoroughly enjoyed these glimpses into her life

and wondered if there would come a day when he could share them with her.

"I see you brought two pails along," he said. "Do you really expect us to fill both of them?"

She raised a brow at that. "Well, I certainly expect to fill *my* pail. Whether you fill up yours is entirely up to you."

"Oh ho, are you issuing a challenge, Mrs. Leggett?"

Her eyes were sparkling in a most attractive manner. "And if I were—are you planning to take me up on it, Mr. Cooper?"

"I do believe I am. As for stakes, shall we say the first one to fill their pail forfeits their slice of gingerbread."

She raised a brow. "High stakes indeed. I'll have to rethink my plan to go easy on you."

"Then we are agreed—no mercy from either quarter!"

She grinned but rather than return his verbal salvo, she pointed to an open area just off the road. "We're here. You can turn the carriage in over there."

He complied, then tied off the reins and hopped down. He quickly moved around the carriage to help her down, forcing himself to just offer her a hand rather than take her by the waist like he really wanted to.

"There's no need to tether Banjo," she said as she stepped down. "He's docile and won't wander far."

Nate reached inside the buggy to fetch the pails. By the time he turned back around, she was moving away from the buggy.

"Hold on there," he said. "Don't think I'm going to let you get a head start on me."

She laughed. "Don't worry, I can't start without my pail. I just wanted to sample a few before we get started." She put her hand to her chest in an exaggeratedly virtuous pose. "Just to make certain they're good enough for Aunt Betty's cobbler, of course."

"Of course." He quickly caught up with her and tucked her hand on his arm. "This ground is rough," he said by way of explanation. "One of us with a bad ankle is enough."

Nate was thoroughly enjoying this newly revealed playful side of her. If a new dress was what it took to bring it out, he hoped she had plans to purchase quite a few more.

He allowed her to "teach" him how to pick the berries—how to tell which berries were ripe and which were not and how to pluck them from the vine to do the least damage to the fruit. It was endearing to see her earnestness and her concern that he had a clear understanding.

"One of the things you need to be careful about," she said as they got started, "is to check the area around the vines for snakes, yellow jackets and other pests, like spiders." She gave a delicate little shiver on the last.

"Spiders?"

She turned to her berry picking. "Yes. I absolutely hate the things." Then she colored and glanced at him from the corner of her eye. "The truth is they absolutely terrify me—especially those daddy-longlegs type. I can tolerate them from a distance but if one gets near me—" She shuddered. "I suppose you think I'm a cowardly ninny."

"What I think is that you don't care much for spiders," he said drily.

She gave a little gurgling laugh at that. "You certainly believe in understatements, don't you?"

"Actually, it reassures me to know that you're not perfect."

She did finally meet his gaze. "Perfect? Now you're just being sarcastic."

"Not at all. You, Mrs. Leggett, are dauntingly accomplished. You are a good mother, you ably assist your uncle in his medical practice, you lead the Sunday choir, you agree to form a children's choir at the drop of a hat, and speaking of hats, on top of all the rest, you're a talented milliner. You have to admit, that is quite an impressive list."

She shook her head. "Thank you, but there are a lot of folks whose list would be much more impressive." She waved a hand in his direction. "Look at you. You can play the piano better than anyone I ever heard before, you've agreed to help with the children's choir, you can craft beautiful leather goods, and, most impressive of all, you had the courage to pick up and move halfway across the country to start a new life."

He'd been enjoying her praise—up until that last. Was that how she saw his transplanting himself to Turnabout? It made him feel more of a fraud than ever.

He turned back to the berries and for a while they worked in silence. Then he became aware that she was surreptitiously watching him with a touch of concern in her expression. So he plucked a berry and rather than tossing it in his pail turned to her. "I'm not sure of the etiquette surrounding picking dewberries. Are we allowed to eat as we go?"

She nodded solemnly. "Not only is it allowed, it is considered mandatory. One must taste the berries every so often, just to make certain they are worth harvesting." Then she grinned. "I've already partaken, and at the pace you're going, I can eat quite a few more and still fill my pail before you."

"Is that so? Well, my dear Mrs. Leggett, we'll just see about that." And he popped the berry in his mouth.

She laughed, then her expression took on a shy cast as she nervously tucked a tendril of hair behind her ear. "Actually, I was thinking it would be nice if you'd call me by my given name."

He was deeply touched, especially knowing that had probably been difficult for her to say. He gave a slight bow. "I'm honored. And would be even more honored if you would return the favor." Then, to lighten the mood, he gave her his best scowl. "But if you think that will make me go easy on you, *Verity*, you're mistaken. I still plan to win this competition."

She laughed and tossed a berry at him. With that, the mood lightened again. The friendly banter passed between them with the ease of longtime friends. He was called on a few times to slay spiders for her, though he noticed she had no trouble with the lizards, bees and various insects they encountered.

And if their hands and arms seemed to "accidentally" brush against each other with a remarkable frequency, well, she didn't seem any more interested in complaining than he did.

It was the most perfect afternoon he'd experienced since well before he'd gone into prison.

It took a while to fill their pails, partly because they ate liberally as they picked. But finally, all too soon, she held up her pail triumphantly. "Mine is full. I do believe I win."

He stroked his chin, keeping his expression solemn as he studied the contents of her pail. "Hmm, I suppose I shall have to concede." He gave an exaggerated bow. "My slice of gingerbread is hereby awarded to you."

She laughed. "Don't feel too bad. I had experience on my side." She peered at his pail. "And it looks like you were close. Perhaps if you'd eaten a few less…"

He grinned. "Guilty. But I didn't notice you being particularly restrained in that area yourself."

She raised a brow. "Remind me—who won this little contest?"

He laughed, then took her elbow again as they turned toward the buggy. This time it felt more natural and at the same time more special. Did she feel any of this? Or was it just him?

Suddenly she stopped beside a moss-covered log. "I think I have something lodged in my shoe. If you'll carry my pail back to the buggy and fetch the basket, I think I'll sit here and empty it." She grinned up at him. "And I might just let you have a bite or two of *my* gingerbread."

"With incentive like that, how can I refuse?" He took her pail and helped her sit, then straightened. "I'll be right back."

She waved him away. "No need to rush. This may take me a few minutes."

He'd just stowed the berry-filled pails and grabbed the basket when he heard her yelp. Startled, he whirled around and saw her pop up and begin shaking one arm frantically. Nate dropped the basket back into the buggy and sprinted toward her. He'd seen some wasps earlier and was certain she'd been stung. "What is it? Hold still and let me see."

But she wouldn't stop her frantic movements and he had to forcibly take her arm to still her. She was trembling so much that his concern doubled. What in the world had turned her into this shaky, hysterical person? "Tell me what's wrong."

Her only response was a near-hysterical "Get it off of me. Please, get it off of me."

Finally, understanding dawned. It took him a moment longer before he saw not one but two of the long-legged but perfectly harmless spiders clinging to her sleeve. He quickly brushed them away. "There, they're gone now." Apparently he'd been wrong to assume she'd exaggerated her fear of the things.

She finally stilled her frantic movements and buried her face in his chest, wrapping her arms tightly around him. Startled, he instinctively wrapped his arms around her. He could feel the frantic beating of her heart and he gently rubbed her back, whispering soothing nothings until her heartbeat slowed to something close to normal and her hold on him relaxed. She didn't pull away, though, just stood there in the circle of his arms, which was fine by him.

"I'm sorry." Her voice was low and embarrassed.

"I'm not." The words were out of his mouth before he could stop them, but he couldn't regret them.

She pulled slightly back, just enough to look into his eyes. And what he saw there took his breath away. Vulnerability. Need. Longing.

With a shaky hand, he stroked the soft curve of her cheek. "Sweet Verity." Her name felt so right on his lips.

She closed her eyes for just a moment and leaned into his palm. When she opened her eyes again there was a soft, shy invitation. Slowly he lowered his face to hers, holding her gaze, trying to attune himself to the least nuance of doubt or withdrawal.

Then their lips met and he was lost.

Chapter Fifteen

Verity was lost in a sea of emotions. Nate's kiss made her feel such warring sensations—both safe and wild, vulnerable and empowered, cherished and cherishing. Never, not even during her five-year marriage, had she felt this way.

She could lose herself in this kiss, this embrace, forever.

Then, abruptly, he ended it and pulled back.

She blinked, momentarily disoriented by the brusqueness of his action. She searched his face for some clue as to what he was feeling right now, why he had suddenly turned cold. His guard was up again, his expression suddenly distant, unreadable. The only sign that he had been affected by that kiss was a slight change in the rhythm of his breathing.

The smile he gave her was almost perfunctory. "I think it's probably time we head back to town."

That was it? No acknowledgment of that kiss they'd just shared? What was wrong? It felt like a very clear and very definite rejection.

Trying to disguise the sick feeling in her stomach and hoping the warmth in her cheeks didn't translate to heightened color, Verity nodded. Without waiting for him to take her arm, she turned toward the buggy. She didn't want him to see her face right now. Because she knew it would show how very flustered and confused and utterly miserable she felt.

She hadn't taken more than a couple of steps, however, before she stumbled. He had a hand on her arm before she could truly fall, and he kept it there as they walked in silence the rest of the way to the buggy. He helped her up with all the care he'd show a stranger, then moved around to the other side. In a matter of minutes they were on the road and headed toward town, all without another word.

Verity tried to figure out what had gone so terribly wrong on this afternoon that had seemed to be going so well.

The teasing banter they'd exchanged during the berry picking had been exhilarating and he'd appeared to enjoy it, as well. And even when she'd made a fool of herself over the spiders, he had reacted with genuine concern for her, never once making her feel silly or annoying. In fact, the way he'd held her, had done his best to calm and soothe her, had seemed to convey something more than mere friendship. And she was almost certain she hadn't imagined that tenderness she'd seen in his eyes when he'd caressed her cheek.

And, oh, how that caress had made her feel.

With her former husband, a man fifteen years her senior, she'd felt safe and comfortable. But there was nothing comfortable about the way Nate made her feel.

The sweet wonder in his gaze, the gentleness that came through the touch of those rough, work-callused fingers, had combined to make her feel as if she was safe, yes, but also cherished and desired, as if she was someone special, in his eyes at least. It had emboldened her to try to show him how she felt, as well.

But she'd obviously done something wrong. Had she misread his feelings? Or had her own unseemly boldness made him reconsider any affection he might have felt?

The ride back to town seemed to take forever. And for most of it she mentally berated herself. Why hadn't she held herself in check, squelched this impulsive display the way she had so many others?

Had she irreparably ruined her friendship with Nate?

Finally she could stand it no longer. She had to do something, had to try to do what she could to cut through this stiff silence between them.

"Nate, I'm so sorry. I shouldn't have—"

"Don't."

His sharp command, more growled than spoken, startled her into silence. Why was he so angry with her?

He clenched his jaw and raked his fingers through his hair with an angry, jerky thrust. "Don't apologize. You didn't do anything wrong."

Was he just being polite, trying to spare her feelings? "I don't understand."

He took a deep, defeated-sounding breath. "You think I'm a hero. But I'm not."

That again. "You're being too modest. You—"

But he wouldn't let her finish. "Verity, I *don't* deserve hero worship. Not from you, not from anyone. You don't know—"

It was her turn to interrupt. "Stop right there." Relief flooded through her. *That's* what was bothering him.

"First, you're not the best judge of what you *do* and *do not* deserve in the area of hero worship. The fact that you won't acknowledge what a courageous thing you did for Joy only proves that you are a genuine hero." She held up a hand to halt the argument she saw forming on his lips. "And second, what I was very clumsily attempting to convey back there had nothing at all to do with hero worship." If she'd left him with any doubts as to her feelings, surely she'd just settled the matter. Had she made the situation better or worse?

The muscles in his jaw worked for several heartbeats before he finally seemed to come to a decision. A decision he did not seem to be happy with. "That only makes it worse."

There was her answer. "I see." Everything inside her seemed to shrivel. "I'm sorry. I didn't intend to make you uncomfortable. Let's speak no more of it." Please let this ride be over soon. All she wanted was to lock herself in her bedroom and fall apart in private.

Abruptly, Nate steered the horses to the side of the road and pulled the wagon to a stop. The town was in sight but they still had a fair amount of privacy from here.

"What are you doing?"

He set the brake with a sharp, angry motion, then turned to face her. "I will not let you feel any guilt, or shame—" he waved a hand "—or whatever other negative feeling is rattling around in that mind of yours." His expression was fierce. "And don't try to deny it. I can see from the look on your face that you're second-guessing every word you uttered or gesture you made since we set out this afternoon."

She hadn't even been aware that he was watching her, much less that he was able to read all of that.

"I'll say again—you did *nothing* wrong. I treasure every moment of our time together this afternoon, more than you will ever know. But I realize now that you won't believe that, not without an explanation. So now I'm going to give you that explanation."

Seeing the dread in his expression, she wasn't really sure she wanted to hear what he had to say. "If it's something you'd rather not talk about, don't feel you need to tell me."

His smile had more grimace than humor to it. "Too late. I need to tell you this for myself as well as for you. There's something you don't know about me, about what I've done, where I've been."

She saw the guilt and something darker cloud his eyes, turning that beautiful blue to a murky, storm-cloud gray. "Whatever all of that is, it can't possibly be as bad as you're making out."

"Can't it?" The words were so softly uttered that she barely heard them.

His expression had such a poignant, bittersweet edge to it that she touched his arm, hoping he would feel something of her support, her faith in him. "Then tell me so we can put it behind us."

He reached up to cover her hand with his own and just stared at them for a moment. Then he gently disengaged and straightened. He turned so that he was facing her fully and met her gaze almost dispassionately. "Nine and a half years ago I robbed a bank. I've spent the majority of the time since then in federal prison."

Verity froze. She wasn't sure what she'd expected, but it wasn't this.

He was a bank robber.

Just like the man who'd shot and killed Arthur.

Just like the man who'd taken her little girl's daddy from her.

* * *

Nate watched Verity's instinctive recoil, the hand that shot to her mouth, the horror in her eyes. It was every bit as nightmarish as he'd imagined it would be.

Because back there, when he'd shared that kiss with her, he'd realized he loved her—deeply and completely. And that scared him as nothing had before.

Before he realized what he was doing, he reached a hand out. "Verity—"

She crossed her arms tightly over her chest. "Perhaps we should go." Her voice had a cold, lifeless quality to it.

Nate dropped his hand and gave a short nod. "Of course." He faced forward and set the buggy in motion again. Verity had moved as far from him as she could on the seat of the buggy, and she was so stiff she looked to be in danger of snapping in two.

This is what he'd done to the woman he loved. Why had he thought he could play with fire and not get burned? Or worse, get someone else burned.

Rather than going directly to the livery, Nate stopped the buggy in front of her uncle's home. "I'll let you out here so we don't have to walk from the livery with those full pails." He planned to climb down to lend her a hand, but she had scrambled down before he could so much as set the brake. As she reached in the buggy to retrieve the pails, he cleared his throat. "I'll be back to get Beans after I've tended to the buggy."

She froze a moment, then shook her head. "That won't be necessary. Wait here and I'll get him for you now."

That stung. She obviously wanted him entirely gone from her life as soon as possible.

Without waiting for his answer, she turned and marched quickly up her front walk. A moment later she was back with Beans in her arms. She set the dog on the buggy floor then straightened. "I'll give Uncle Grover and Aunt Betty your regards."

What else could he say? He nodded, but she had already turned and headed back toward the house. He watched her until she disappeared inside, but she never once turned back around.

He set the buggy in motion again. Had he made a mistake telling her? Would she keep his secret? What did this mean for his work with the church choir and children's choir?

And would she put the pieces together and figure out Adam's secret, as well?

He raked his fingers through his hair. He'd made a grand mess of things.

Beans, as if aware of his mood, whined at his feet. He scooped the dog up with one hand and set him on the seat beside him. He gave the animal a scratch behind the ears, not sure which one of them drew more comfort from the contact.

"I hate to tell you this, boy, but that may be the last time you get to play with Joy. I'm afraid I've made a royal mess of everything."

Because, if he wasn't mistaken, he'd lost any chance at all he had with Verity.

Verity tried to go through the rest of the afternoon and evening as if nothing untoward had happened. And for the most part she just felt numb.

She helped her aunt wash and store the berries.

She read a book to Joy, though later she couldn't remember what story she'd read.

She even organized the supplies in her tiny workroom.

When supper time finally rolled around, Verity did her best to keep up her end of the conversation, deflecting talk of the berry-picking expedition as much as possible.

At last the meal was at an end and the kitchen was cleaned. She took Joy upstairs and got her ready for bed, going through their nightly rituals of prayers and a lullaby.

When she tucked the covers up under Joy's chin, the little girl looked up at her with concern in her gaze. "Did you see a spider while you and Mr. Cooper were out picking dewberries?"

Verity gently brushed the wisps of hair from her daughter's forehead and attempted a smile. "Yes, pumpkin, I did. In fact, two of them got on the sleeve of my dress." She still remembered the sweet way Nate had held her after his "rescue" of her, the way he'd tried to comfort her and make her feel safe and not at all foolish. How could this be the same man who'd done something so awful, so disregarding of the hurt he was doing to others?

"I thought so." Joy's self-congratulatory words brought her back to the present. "Because you looked all dis-bob-u-lated when you got home."

Verity smiled at her daughter's mispronunciation of *discombobulated*, one of her aunt's favorite words. But the smile faded quickly. "You're a very smart little girl to figure that out, but I'm all better now."

"You don't look all better." Joy dragged her hand out from under the covers and patted Verity's cheek. "Don't worry, Mama, I don't think those bad spiders followed you home."

Touched beyond words by her daughter's love and

concern, Verity gathered her in a tight hug. "Thank you, pumpkin, I'm sure you're right." Then she let her go and tucked her back in. "Now, you get a good night's sleep and don't worry about me and the spiders anymore. Okay?"

"Okay." And the girl rolled over on her side and shut her eyes.

Verity knew from past experience that Joy would be sound asleep in a matter of minutes.

Pleading a headache, she bid good-night to her aunt and uncle then escaped to her own room to turn in early.

But not to sleep. Because the numbness she'd felt since Nate—no, Mr. Cooper—had driven away was wearing off. In its place was an aching sense of loss.

She sat on the edge of her bed and grabbed a pillow, hugging it to her chest and rocking back and forth.

She kept trying to reconcile the man she'd come to admire so deeply with the man who'd done that terrible thing he'd admitted to this afternoon.

He was a bank robber. A man who'd carried a gun into a place of business, a place where innocent people, people with families who loved them, would be present. And he'd tried to forcibly, maybe even violently, take what didn't belong to him.

There was nothing heroic about such an act. About such a man.

No wonder he'd felt so guilty whenever she used that word. Why hadn't she believed his protests?

When she thought about how she'd acted around him today—teasing him, *flirting* with him, throwing herself into his arms. And then letting him kiss her. No, more than that, she'd practically invited that kiss. What a besotted fool she'd been. She'd let herself be led by her emotions rather than reason. There'd been nothing reasonable about this afternoon, no thought about the consequences of her actions.

And look where it had gotten her.

She touched her lips. But for that moment—that moment just before he'd abruptly ended that kiss—it had been so sweet, so wonderful, so exhilarating.

No! She wouldn't think of that.

It had all been a lie.

But it hadn't felt that way.

Verity got very little sleep that night. At some point she began worrying about how she would act toward him next time they encountered each other. And given his involvement with the choirs, there would be no way to avoid him completely, not until Zella got back at any rate.

She supposed she could deal with his playing on Sunday mornings.

But to have him working with the children? That seemed wrong on a number of levels. It wasn't that she thought he would do anything to harm them—that thought was too ludicrous to even contemplate—but his influence over them would be questionable, and if his story ever came out, it would confuse the children.

Not that she would reveal his secrets. Even knowing what she now knew, she couldn't bring herself to expose him to such critical scrutiny. But for her peace of mind she'd have to replace him as her partner on the children's choir project, and she needed to do it before the next practice session on Tuesday.

First thing in the morning she'd have a talk with Mrs. Peavy. After all, she usually served as Zella's stand-in.

Just how had it happened that Mr. Cooper had ended up in that position this time, anyway?

Verity didn't get quite as early a start the next morning as she'd planned. She'd barely made it downstairs when Meechum Smith was brought into the clinic with a broken arm. It was a bad break and she'd worked beside her uncle for several hours to help him get the limb cleaned, set and splinted properly. By the time they'd completed the procedure, Mr. Smith was unconscious. So Verity had prepared a bed in the infirmary for him. She tried very hard not to remember the last patient who'd spent time there. Luckily his wife, Ellen, had accompanied him and she planned to spend the day with him, so Verity could make her escape as soon as he was properly installed there.

After cleaning up she was finally able to slip away. She trudged down the sidewalk toward the Barr home with a heavy heart. During the time she'd worked beside her uncle this morning, she'd been able to forget her world had been turned upside down yesterday. But as soon as she'd been dismissed it had all come flooding back.

She should never have let her emotions have sway over her. Much better to let reason be her guide. Her marriage to Arthur may not have been the fairy-tale romantic relationship she sometimes found herself dreaming of, but it had been comfortable and safe. If Arthur hadn't made her feel the same fluttery anticipation she'd felt with Mr. Cooper, neither had he made her feel this dark, aching sadness.

She would ask Mrs. Peavy to help her with the children's program and would use the time this was taking away from Mr. Cooper's business as the reason. And in few weeks or so, when Zella returned, he would step down from the Sunday choir music, as well. There would be no need for her to have any further interaction with him.

Which should have made her feel a whole lot happier than it did.

When she arrived at the Barr residence, Verity bypassed the front entrance and went around to the back. Buck, the Barrs' big, fierce-looking dog, raced up to greet her. But his wagging tail let her know it was friendly curiosity rather than aggression.

She gave the animal a pat on the head and then climbed the back porch steps. The kitchen door was open, leaving only a screen door as a barrier against insects and other unwanted intruders. She could see Mrs. Peavy inside, already busy at the stove.

Verity tapped on the door frame and called out a hello.

Mrs. Peavy glanced up and smiled when she recognized Verity. "The door's unlatched, come on in." She wiped her hands on her apron as Verity complied. "Can I get you a cup of coffee?"

Verity shook her head. "No, thank you, I'm fine."

"If you're looking for Reggie, she's out taking a walk with Patricia. But she'll be back shortly, if you want to sit and visit for a spell."

Verity shook her head. "Actually, it was you I came to see." She looked at the pots simmering on the stove and the pie ready to go into the oven. "But if you're busy, I don't want to interrupt your work."

Mrs. Peavy smiled. "Actually, I'm ready to take a

little break." She waved toward the table. "Have a seat and I'll join you in just a minute."

Verity pulled a chair out at the table as Mrs. Peavy slipped the pie into the oven. The older woman then moved to the counter, where she retrieved a small jar before taking a seat across from Verity.

"Well, now," she said as she opened the jar, "I hope you won't mind if I apply this liniment while we chat. I was just waiting until I got the pie in the oven."

"Not at all." Verity caught the familiar scent and it brought her up short. "Are you having problems with your hands?"

Mrs. Peavy nodded. "These old hands are beginning to show their age, I'm afraid. Some days are worse than others, but this liniment helps." She sighed as she worked the medication into her hands. "I was so glad to learn Mr. Cooper could play the piano and was willing to take over while Zella was away. I'm afraid my days of being her substitute have just about come to an end."

"I'm so sorry to hear that." For a number of reasons. Was this why Mr. Cooper had been asked to sit in for Zella rather than Mrs. Peavy?

"There now." Mrs. Peavy screwed the lid back on the jar and leaned back. "Much better," she said with a smile. "Now, what did you want to talk to me about?"

What could she say? Asking her to take Mr. Cooper's place was out of the question now. But there was something else she could ask. "Who will take your place as Zella's substitute now?"

Mrs. Peavy frowned slightly. "I haven't really given that much thought yet. But there are a couple of ladies here in Turnabout who could serve very capably."

"Like who?"

"Well, Maude Wick for one. And Viella Higgs. And of course, now we have Mr. Cooper." She gave Verity a probing look. "Why are you asking?"

Verity chose her words very carefully. "I was thinking I might ask someone to take over playing the piano for the children's program. Mr. Cooper's business is so new, it doesn't seem fair to ask him to close up two afternoons a week to help us out."

"I see." Mrs. Peavy tilted her head slightly, giving Verity a probing look. "Has he asked you to find him a substitute?"

"Oh, no. This was my idea." Though after yesterday she had no doubt Mr. Cooper would be relieved not to have to work with her any more than necessary. "It seems wrong to impose on him so heavily when he's barely settled into town."

"Well, you're a good friend."

Verity mentally winced at that far-from-accurate statement. But she was trapped, unable to reveal the true state of affairs without giving away the whole story. And she wasn't ready to expose him that way.

But Mrs. Peavy spoke up again, rescuing Verity from having to examine her motives for that last thought too closely.

"I'm afraid you're not going to have much luck with Maude and Viella, though. Maude's new baby is due in just a few weeks. And Viella's just moved her ailing grandmother in with her. That's why it was such a godsend to learn that Mr. Cooper was talented and available."

"I see." What did she do now?

"If you really think it would be best to let Mr. Cooper off the hook, perhaps I could—"

Verity quickly reached across the table and gently clasped the woman's knurled hands. "That's very generous of you, but please don't give it another thought. As I said, Mr. Cooper hasn't uttered one word of complaint. I'm likely making mountains out of molehills again."

She stood. "Now, I've taken up enough of your time. Please give Mr. Peavy and the Barrs my regards."

As Verity shut the screen door behind her, her mind was scrambling to figure out what to do now. The next practice with the children's choir was tomorrow, and she wanted to get this matter settled before then. She wasn't certain she could work so closely with him again, at least not without giving away her feelings to those around them.

Perhaps the solution was to not worry about getting another piano player. Perhaps they could do the entire program a cappella. She would need some help, but she could ask one or two members of the church choir to assist her. Of course that would mean going into explanations of why she wanted to make the change. She supposed she could always use the same excuse she'd given Mrs. Peavy.

The bell jangled as his shop door opened and Nate looked up hopefully. But it was Belva who had entered, not Verity.

He wasn't sure why he kept expecting to see her walk in. She'd made her feelings about him quite clear when he dropped her off yesterday.

Why in the world had he kissed her? If he hadn't given in to his own longings, they might still be friends at least.

Not that he could find it in him to truly regret that

kiss. Everything in him had responded to her—he'd wanted to cherish her and protect her and claim her as his own. For those few moments she'd made him feel as if he could scale mountains and explore oceans and slay dragons.

And now, not only did he no longer have the right to hold her, but he'd lost her friendship, as well.

"Well, now, don't you look like someone just mowed down your prized flower patch. What's ailing you?"

He summoned up a smile. "I've just got a lot on my mind today. What can I do for you? You're not planning to change the design on your saddle again, are you?"

She laughed good-naturedly. "No, I think we're all done with that. I just came by to ask you something."

"And what's that?"

"I turn twenty in two weeks, and that's when I get the inheritance Aunt Imogene left for me."

He already knew all of that from their earlier discussions. Hard as it was to believe, this young lady was about to become a wealthy heiress.

He figured she'd get to her question in her own time, so he followed her conversational lead. "So, are you planning all the things you're going to do with the money?"

She nodded, her face split in a wide grin. "Well, getting my horse is the first thing. And then I figure I'll do some traveling. But before I can do any of that, I need to get my house in order, literally."

"What do you mean?"

"Part of my inheritance is Aunt Imogene's home over in Tyler. I haven't seen it yet, but I understand it's big and it's in need of some work. There's a caretaker, but the solicitor is telling me he's elderly and ready to retire." She traced a circle on his worktable with a finger.

"Since I don't know very many people whom I would trust with that responsibility, I was wondering if you'd be interested in the position."

Nate leaned back and stared at her for a long minute. Was this the answer he was looking for? A chance to start over somewhere else.

But that felt an awful lot like running away. Was he ready to give up already? "Belva, I'm flattered that you'd ask me, but—"

"That was quick." She leaned back on her heels, disappointment coloring her all-too-readable face. "Is it because I'm a woman? Or because I'm younger than you? Or both?"

"Neither." He leaned forward and tried to explain things in a way she'd accept at face value. "I just moved here, just opened my shop. I want to see if I have what it takes to make a go of things. I'm sure you'll find someone else—"

"Please don't say no just yet, at least not until you've heard everything."

There was more? Ah, well, what could it hurt to hear her out? He folded his arms across his chest and leaned back again. "All right, I'm listening."

"Okay." She took a deep breath, then launched into her pitch. "The solicitor tells me it's a fair-sized place with a large house and a stable in the back. There's staff to handle the day-to-day things. It's the caretaker's job to manage them and to keep an eye on the overall well-being of the entire place. You'd have lots of say in how the place is run, a small cabin of your own on the property to live in, and I'm sure we could even find a place to set you up a workroom if you wanted to continue with your saddle making."

She paused for a breath and he took the opportunity to ask a question. "Why me?"

Her brow furrowed. "What do you mean?"

"Why ask me to take the job? You barely know me, after all. And I have no experience with the sort of work you're describing."

"You're my friend. And it would be good to have a friend with me when I start my new life."

Nate saw her vulnerability then, the lonely girl who was heading into a new adventure she wasn't sure she was quite ready to face alone. His resolve wavered. A young woman in need was definitely his Achilles' heel.

Belva apparently felt his indecisiveness. "You don't have to give me an answer today," she said quickly. "Why don't you take a few days to think it over?"

"All right. But Belva—" he leaned forward, shooting her a very pointed gaze "—I would be thinking of a backup plan if I were you."

She nodded, but from her optimistic expression he wasn't certain if she really took his words to heart.

After she had gone, Nate bent over his work again. Belva's visit had been a welcome, if temporary, distraction.

But it had also driven home one very disquieting fact.

That he seemed to be destined to always disappoint the women in his life.

Verity had returned from her visit with Mrs. Peavy to find their resident patient asleep, her uncle resting, and Aunt Betty teaching Joy how to prepare the dough for a dewberry cobbler. Needing something to occupy herself, she'd gone to her workroom. A half-finished hat sat perched on a wire form, waiting for her to complete it. But she decided she was in the mood to start from scratch. She grabbed netting and lengths of ribbon and silk flowers and went to work with almost manic focus.

But it was no use. She didn't find the sense of satisfaction and accomplishment she normally found when she worked on a hat. Instead, her thoughts turned to her own reprehensible lack of control. Ever since Mr. Cooper had appeared on the scene she hadn't been herself. She'd been acting impulsively and emotionally and without proper regard for consequences.

And look what it had gotten her.

She supposed she could understand why Mr. Cooper hadn't told her his history sooner—his idea of getting a fresh start probably included suppressing all traces of his past. Whether that was the ethical thing to do, however, seemed questionable.

If they hadn't kissed, would he have told her at all? Would she have been better off not knowing?

Because now he had turned her into a coconspirator in keeping his secret from everyone here, as well. Being the only one in town who knew his secret was...

She stilled.

No, that wasn't entirely true. Though Mr. Cooper hadn't said so, she knew there was one other person in Turnabout who had to already know of his past. The same man who had practically vouched for the newcomer to the rest of the townsfolk, who had, in fact, recruited Mr. Cooper for the church pianist job.

She set down her materials and began to forcefully roll down her sleeves.

Oh, yes, Adam Barr definitely had some explaining to do.

Chapter Sixteen

Verity entered the bank and went directly to the manager's office. She'd taken a circuitous route so she could avoid passing in front of either Mr. Cooper's or Hazel's shop. Cowardly and perhaps a bit foolish of her, but there it was.

To her satisfaction, Mr. Barr was alone in his office.

He looked up when she tapped on his door frame and greeted her with a smile as he stood. "Mrs. Leggett, hello."

She gave a stiff nod. "Mr. Barr."

"Please have a seat and tell me what I can do for you today."

She remained in the doorway. "Do you mind if I close the door first?"

There was a subtle shift in his expression from friend to businessman. "Not at all."

He waited until she was seated, and then took his own seat behind his desk again. "Now, what's on your mind?"

"Mr. Cooper."

His expression took on a wary aspect, as well it should. "What about him?" he asked.

"He told me some troubling things about his past yesterday afternoon. I assume you are aware of where he's been for the past nine years and why."

There was the barest flicker of surprise before he schooled his expression again. "I am."

"And yet you said nothing." She didn't bother to mask her disapproval.

He spread his hands. "It wasn't my story to tell."

"Perhaps not." Verity could feel all of her pent-up emotions starting to spill out, but felt helpless to stop it. "But, if I understand the sequence of events properly, it was you who encouraged him to move here, you who helped him get established, and you who convinced him to take Zella's place while she is out of town, even though you knew that it meant working with the children's program."

"All of that is true. And I stand by all of it." He gave her a steady, unapologetic look. "And I also stand by him."

How could he say that?

He studied her for a heartbeat, then leaned forward. "Mrs. Leggett, I know what happened to your husband, so I know Nate's story was difficult for you to hear. But do you honestly believe he poses any kind of danger whatsoever to the children, or to anyone in Turnabout for that matter?"

She shifted in her seat. "Not directly. Not deliberately."

He spread his hands. "Then?"

"These are *children*, children I have some responsibility for. What if they learn to trust him, to…to care for him? And then later they learn the truth about who he is." To feel betrayal, as she had.

He raised a brow at that. "Who he is?"

She waved a hand impatiently. "A bank robber, of course."

"That's what he *did*. It's not who he *is*."

His matter-of-fact tone and steady gaze were making her feel defensive. "You're splitting hairs."

"I disagree. Those are two very different things." He leaned back in his chair. "But, be that as it may, if it's the children's sensibilities you're worried about, it's been my experience that children might give the adults they encounter a token respect, but they only give their trust—and their hearts—to those who deserve it."

He held her gaze. "And for that matter, how would anyone else ever find out the truth, unless Nate himself chooses to tell them?"

She heard the underlying question in his tone and stiffened. "They won't hear it from me."

"Nor will they hear it from me. As I said, it's his story to tell, when and if he chooses to do so." Then his expression softened slightly. "You say Nate told you what he did. Did he tell you *why* he did it?"

The question caught her by surprise. "No, but surely you don't believe the end justifies the means? You, of all people, should have a stronger sense of justice than that." In addition to managing the bank, Mr. Barr was a lawyer.

"No, but the kind of man that you know in your heart that Nate is, the kind of man who would set aside his own safety to rescue a child in danger, must have had a powerful motive to take such a step, don't you think?"

She winced at this not-so-subtle reminder of what she owed Nate.

But he had one more question for her. "Don't you

believe in second chances, Mrs. Leggett? In leaving ultimate justice in God's hands, and in obeying His directive to forgive one another?"

"Of course. I just…" Verity let her words trail off, not sure how to finish the statement.

Then she stood. "Thank you, Mr. Barr. You've given me a lot to think about."

He stood, as well. "You're welcome." His gaze held a note of sympathy. "Despite what he did, Nate's a good man. I think if you'd just talk to him and give him a chance to explain, you'd agree with that, as well."

Verity nodded noncommittally, then made her way home at a slower, more deliberate pace than she'd used on her earlier march to Mr. Barr's office. She mulled over everything he'd said to her. Was he right? Would Nate's explanation of *why* he'd robbed that bank change her mind about him? She certainly wanted to believe she hadn't been *entirely* wrong about the sort of man he was.

Perhaps knowing the full story would bring her some peace with all that had happened. And she did owe him that chance.

But in her heart she knew that understanding his motives might help her look more kindly on him, might even heal their friendship, but it would never be enough to bring them back to that sweet, we-belong-together bond they'd shared ever so briefly.

That part of their relationship was dead before it had really had an opportunity to set down roots in their hearts.

And that made her ache deep inside for what might have been.

Later that afternoon, Verity took a deep, bracing breath and walked into Nate's saddle shop. When he looked up she saw the surprise in his eyes, quickly followed by a strange mix of hope and wariness.

It seemed a reflection of how she herself was feeling.

Nate set down his tools but didn't rise. "Can I help you?" His tone was guardedly polite. Not unexpected.

Beans had popped up from his nap beneath the worktable and was now staring up at her with a tail-wagging welcome.

She bent down to pat the dog and tried to keep her tone equally businesslike. "Aunt Betty made a cobbler with some of the dewberries we picked yesterday."

"I'm glad they served her purpose."

"Since you didn't take any of the berries for yourself, she wanted to make certain you got some of the cobbler." She straightened and lifted the basket she was carrying. "I have it right here."

"That was very generous of your aunt. Please tell her thank you for me."

"Of course." He was certainly not making this easy for her. "Where would you like me to set this?"

He waved to the counter. "Right there, if you don't mind."

She crossed the room and carefully placed it just so on the counter. She could feel his gaze on her the entire time. Did she have the courage to go through with this?

She turned and met his gaze.

"Did you come here just to deliver the cobbler?" he asked softly.

"No."

"Then what?"

She tightened her lips a moment, then leaned back against the counter. "It's a nice day. I thought, if you were ready to take a break, we could go for a walk."

This time there was no mistaking the flicker of hope in his expression.

Before he could say anything, she clarified, "It would give us an opportunity to talk without interruption."

For a moment Nate just sat there, studying her face, as if trying to read something there. Then he nodded. "Very well." He stood and reached behind him to untie the leather apron he wore. His movements were calm and deliberate, but she once more had that sense of tension simmering below the surface.

Nate hung the apron on a peg, then moved around the table to open the door for her. She was very careful not to brush against him as she passed.

He started to follow her out and then paused. "Do you mind if Beans joins us?"

"Not at all."

The silence between them held as they left the shop. He let her take the lead and she headed for the churchyard. As before, she led him through the entrance to the cemetery and around to the bench beside the oak.

Nate remained standing. Beans took the opportunity to sniff around what was obviously new territory to him.

While she was still trying to figure out how to start, Nate spoke up. "If this is about my continuing to work with the choir or the children, then I will make it easy—"

"That's not what I want to talk about." Was that a flicker of relief she saw in his face?

"Then what?"

She sat up straighter, determined to see this through no matter what. "I have two questions for you."

He seemed to brace himself. "All right. Ask."

"First—did you bring a gun with you when you robbed that bank?"

He clenched his jaw, but he nodded. "I did."

Her spirits dropped. How could he? Whether he intended to harm anyone or not, just by bringing a weapon to—

"But it wasn't loaded."

"Oh." Did that make it better? She wasn't sure.

"What's your second question?"

His tone was brusque. Was he in a hurry to get this over with, too?

She tilted her chin up. "I want to know why."

His guarded expression wavered for a moment, then returned. "Why?"

"Why did you rob that bank?"

A bitter smile twisted his lips. "Does it matter? You're not someone who believes that the ends justify the means, are you?"

Almost the exact same question she'd asked Mr. Barr. "No. But I want to understand. And the only way I can do that is to hear the whole story, complete with your reasons why."

Would he open up to her? And if he did, would it truly change anything?

She wanted to understand.

Nate thought about that for a moment. Would it do him any good to go through that whole sordid tale again, or would it only stir up those old wounds and still leave her unmoved?

It hadn't been lost on him that she was wearing mourning attire again—that solid black skirt and a drab gray shirtwaist. That was undoubtedly his doing.

He supposed he owed her that small satisfaction she'd asked for, regardless of the cost. But where to start? He raked a hand through his hair, trying to decide how much to tell her, or more to the point, how much of himself to reveal to her.

"That question is going to take me a little longer to answer than the first."

She shifted, as if settling more comfortably in her seat. "I have the time."

Nate glanced toward the graves that held the remains of her parents. "The other day you told me how your parents died." He had treasured the way she shared that part of herself with him. Would she feel even the tiniest bit of the same?

He turned back to meet her gaze. "Now I'll tell you about mine."

Her eyes widened a bit at that, but she merely nodded.

"My family was well-to-do. Not wealthy, mind you, but we didn't lack for anything and were able to enjoy some of the finer things of life." He hadn't realized just how good a life he'd had growing up, until he lost it.

"In addition to my parents, I had a sister, Susanna, who was two years younger than me. We were a relatively happy family, with a wide circle of friends.

"Then, when I was seventeen, my father made some disastrous financial investments and lost nearly everything we had. We were forced to sell our home and move to more modest quarters just to get by. We also let go all the servants except Leena, our housekeeper, who was elderly and almost part of the family. My mother, who always had a somewhat delicate disposition, not only had to take on more of the household work herself, but she cut herself off from many of the friends in her social circle."

Verity folded her hands in her lap. "That must have

been hard on all of you. But surely you don't mean you robbed a bank just to—"

"No, of course not." He waved a hand impatiently. "We were getting by well enough, even if it was without the luxuries we'd grown so used to. But my father felt a great deal of shame over what had happened and, two months after we moved, he hung himself."

He heard a small gasp and saw Verity's hand go to her throat. "Oh, Nate, I'm so sorry."

He took some comfort in her soft tone and use of his given name. At least, for the moment, she wasn't looking at him with loathing.

But she was waiting for him to continue. He skipped over the part of the story where it had been he who found his father's body, he who had had to shield his mother and sister from the gruesome sight, he who had had to deal with all the nightmare of official inquiries and paperwork. "Afterward, my mother took to her bed, leaving me and Susanna to deal with the day-to-day household things as best we could. Six months later she passed away in her sleep." It was Susanna who had found the body this time. He wished he could have spared her that at least.

"At the age of eighteen, I had sole responsibility for my sixteen-year-old sister, for Leena, who was staying to help even though we couldn't pay her, and for the upkeep of our home. All of that with no income and my only skill that of playing the piano."

"Is that when—"

He shook his head. He'd still had his pride, even then. "I got a job playing piano at a music hall. It wasn't much, and it wasn't socially acceptable, but it was enough to keep us going."

"That was resourceful of you."

"I thought, if I could just keep us together and make do for a few years, perhaps I could find a good, decent husband for Susanna and a viable position for Leena, and then I could strike out on my own."

"So what happened?" Sometime during the discussion she'd picked up Beans and now held him in her lap, stroking his back with gentle, even movements.

"Susanna got sick. And it was bad. Tuberculosis. She needed medical treatment that I couldn't afford to pay for. I tried every avenue I could, selling everything we owned that had any value, borrowing money until I was so far in debt it seemed I would never get out. And still it wasn't enough. I saw my little sister wasting away in front of my eyes. I thought, if I could just get her into a good sanatorium, one of those places that specialized in care for patients like her, then it would give her a fighting chance to get better."

"So that's when you robbed the bank." There was no question in her tone this time.

"I planned it all out, thought I had everything covered. Except I didn't plan for an off-duty policeman to walk into the bank just as I was making my getaway."

"What happened to your sister?" she asked softly.

This was the most difficult part, the part that had haunted him every day of his incarceration. "Leena, bless her heart, did her best to look after Susanna. At least my sister wasn't completely alone. But her illness got progressively worse. And because of her connection to me, a convicted felon, most of the so-called friends we had left shunned her. About a year after I went to prison I received word that she passed away. And I wasn't even able to go to her funeral." He clenched his jaw at the memory. "I know I got what I deserved, but Susanna deserved so much better."

He realized he'd balled his hands into tight fists at some point during the story. He forced them open, allowing his hands to hang loosely at his sides. "So there you have it, the whole sordid story." Had it made a difference? He couldn't tell.

"Thank you for sharing it with me." Her voice was subdued, but not unkind. "It makes things a whole lot clearer."

Regardless of how she now felt, there was one thing he had to ask of her. "I know I don't have the right to ask you this, but I'd appreciate it if you didn't tell anyone my story." He still had an obligation to protect Adam's reputation as best he could.

"I understand. And I assure you, I have many faults, but I don't gossip." Then she brought her hand up to fiddle with her collar. "Just so you know, however, I have already spoken to Mr. Barr."

He was hoping her mind wouldn't start down that path. "Adam? Whatever for?"

"I realized he had to already know your story since you and he were acquainted before you came here, and I wanted to confront him about it. He didn't give away any of your secrets, though. He merely told me to speak to you."

So maybe she hadn't already guessed Adam's secret. He needed to get the focus off his friend and back onto him. "So now that you've heard my story, where does that leave us? I mean, if you prefer to have someone else play the piano for the church service and the children's practice sessions, I'll understand. I can quietly step down without there being any awkwardness."

She'd started shaking her head before he'd even finished speaking. "I see no need for you to step down. You said you're here to start over, and I think you deserve that chance. Unless you do something to show me I'm wrong, I have no problem with proceeding as we'd planned." She paused, seeming to choose her words carefully. "As for where that leaves us personally, I'd like to think we can remain friends."

The slight emphasis she'd put on the word *friends* let him know there would be no repeat of that amazing kiss. But friendship was a start. He could be patient. Perhaps over time she would learn to trust him again.

She set Beans on the ground and stood, brushing her skirt. Then she glanced his way, a little frown wrinkle above her nose. "I have one more question for you, but don't feel like you have to answer it if you don't want to."

He braced himself, not sure what to expect. "Ask away."

"How did you end up as a saddler?"

That's what she wanted to know? Relieved that she was showing an interest in him beyond his crime, he felt a little more of his tension ease. "In prison, they like to keep the inmates busy. And they also make money hiring out the prisoners to the locals in the area, money that supposedly goes into the upkeep of the place." He gave a self-mocking smile. "Piano playing was not a very marketable skill, and I didn't know how to do much else of any real value. So I offered to work with a fellow prisoner who was a skilled leather worker. Mack taught me just about everything he knew about working with leather. And I found I enjoyed the work. Like with playing the piano, there is a real artistic component to the craft."

It was a bit anticlimactic to be talking about such everyday things after the charged conversation they'd just had. Of more concern was the question of whether she was really comfortable with putting his less than stellar past behind them now.

It seemed, for now at least, that she was.

But could he live with that? He longed to take her hand again, to have her look at him with the soft admiration and warm feelings he'd seen in her gaze yesterday afternoon, to have her feel comfortable teasing and being teased by him.

To be able to wrap his arms around her to offer her comfort when she needed it, or something more.

He should be glad that their friendship was restored.

But he was greedy and wanted more.

A lot more.

Verity, not wanting to talk to anyone, went outside to work in the garden when she returned home. Nate's story had broken her heart. He'd been through so much tragedy, so much heartache, and at such a young age. By her reckoning he'd spent nearly a third of his life behind bars. How had he managed to come out of that with his spirit intact?

No, the ends didn't justify the means, but he'd been desperate, and he did what he did not to save himself but his sister. She could understand such feelings. If it had been her and Joy in such a situation, there was very little she wouldn't do to somehow provide what her daughter needed to survive.

And, as Mr. Barr had pointed out, Nate had paid the price for what he'd done. Knowing what she knew now, she was certain they could return to their friendship and work together without any tension between them.

And perhaps, in time, they could be more than friends.

But she wouldn't rush it this time. She'd learned her lesson there, as well. Acting impulsively only led to disaster. Better to take slow, measured steps, to tamp down any temptation to be impulsive, just as she'd always done before Nate came along.

Because, yes, she was still very much attracted to him, but she also knew that simple attraction was not enough. There were certain qualities that she required of a husband for herself and father for Joy—qualities such as stability, reliability, caution.

Other things, such as how special he made her feel and how her pulse always quickened when he was near, were merely frivolous emotional trappings that were fleeting at best and that muddied the waters of how to build true, lasting relationships.

Relationships like the comfortable one she'd had with Arthur.

And if there was a piece of her heart that disagreed, that yearned for those frivolous emotional trappings, well, she'd just have to work harder to tamp that down, as well.

Chapter Seventeen

The Tuesday afternoon practice session with the children went well. She and Nate were able to work together without any awkwardness. If there was none of the shared glances and exchanges of banter that had crept into their conversations of the past few weeks, that didn't really affect the way they worked with the children.

And at the end of the session, she and Joy walked with Nate as far as his shop, just as they usually did. She even allowed Joy to go in and say hello to Beans, but cut the visit shorter than normal.

But she no longer went out of her way to see Nate between sessions. There were no invitations to lunch or supper, no taking Joy by to visit with Beans, no looking for chance opportunities to bump into him.

On Wednesday, when Verity delivered her latest millinery creation, Hazel confronted her. "Something's changed between you and Mr. Cooper. What happened?"

Now, what had brought that on? Verity wasn't even aware that Hazel had seen them together since Sunday, much less had an opportunity to watch them interact with each other. "I'm sure you're imagining things. Mr.

Cooper and I are just what we've always been—friends. Nothing more, nothing less."

"You might fool everyone else, Verity Magdalena Leggett, but not me. You and Mr. Cooper were well on your way to being something more interesting than friends up until this week. Now it seems like the two of you are merely colleagues." Then her gaze sharpened. "Did he do something to you?"

"No!" Verity was shocked that anyone would think such a thing of Nate. Then she took a breath and elaborated more calmly. "I admit I was temporarily taken with Mr. Cooper, perhaps even imagined myself developing tender feelings for him. After all, he saved Joy's life and he is an attractive man. But that's all it was—a passing fancy. One doesn't build a lasting relationship on such surface things."

Hazel crossed her arms. "I would hardly call his saving Joy a surface thing."

"Of course not. But you know what I mean. He's a nice man, but *if* I were to ever marry again, it would be to a man of unquestionable character and integrity. A man who is steadfast and dependable. A man like—"

"Mercy me, Verity, you already had all of that with Arthur. Don't you want some excitement and romance in your life?"

Verity felt the tug of those words on her heart, but resolutely tamped it down. "We're not all like you, Hazel. Some people prefer to live quieter, more conservative lives."

"Some people, perhaps, but you'll never convince me that in your heart of hearts, that's what *you* really want."

Verity decided this was a good time to change the subject. "If you're finished trying to orchestrate my social life, there was another reason I came in here this afternoon."

"Oh?"

"I've been thinking that I might want to open my own millinery shop one of these days."

"Oh, I think that's a fabulous idea! It's something you should have done a long time ago. So what can I do to help?"

"First of all, I'm still in the thinking-about-it stage, so don't start planning my grand opening just yet."

Hazel waved a hand airily. "I make no promises on that score."

Verity rolled her eyes, then turned serious. "I've always admired your business sense. You've built a successful seamstress business here and I figure the millinery business will be similar. So, I'd like to sit down and talk to you at some point about what sorts of things I will need to plan for and what the best way to go about setting this up will be. That will give me a better handle on when, or even if, I'll be ready to get started."

"Absolutely. And I suggest you also speak to Adam Barr. He has both the financial and legal expertise to guide you in areas that I'm not so adept at." Then she gave Verity an assessing look. "Do you have a place in mind to set up your shop?"

"Not yet. As I said, I'm still in the mulling-it-over stage."

"Then I have my first piece of advice to give you—lease a corner of my dress shop. It'll be perfect—we will basically have the same customers and I could use some help around here, someone to cover for me when I have to be elsewhere."

Verity had to admit it was a very tempting proposal. It would solve a lot of her worries about how to get started.

And it would be fun to work with Hazel. At the same time, though, she didn't want to take advantage of her friend's generosity.

"That's a very magnanimous offer. But you haven't taken the time to think it through—"

Hazel waved away her concerns. "I don't need to think about it—it's the ideal solution. And I assure you I plan to get every bit as much out of this as you will."

"Then thank you. That's definitely an idea to add to the list." But if she followed through on it, she'd be certain she paid her friend a fair lease price.

"You have a list?" Hazel asked.

Verity grinned. "I plan to start one. Now, as I said, I'm not ready to do anything right this minute, so let's talk some more about it after the festival. I just thought it would be good to begin thinking about some of the possibilities and obstacles now."

Hazel shook her head. "Obstacles are no fun. I plan to concentrate my efforts on the possibilities." Then she gave Verity a pointed look. "Besides, I'm sure you'll do enough thinking about the obstacles for the both of us."

Is that how Hazel saw her, as someone always looking at the negative side of things? That wasn't truly the way she was—was it?

Sure, she preferred cautious action over the impulsive, but that was how responsible people conducted their lives. That didn't mean she didn't know how to appreciate the positive aspect of things as well, though. Just look at the work she was doing with the children's choir, for example. She hadn't let any obstacles get in her way when she'd taken on that task.

Still, Hazel's comment stuck with her long after she'd left the dress shop.

* * *

"Very good, everyone." Verity smiled at the members of the children's choir. "I think you all have the first two songs down really well. Let's take a little break, then we'll start to practice that last song."

She glanced over to where Nate sat at the piano. The final song was to be sung a cappella, so he'd be helping her with the vocals rather than at the instrument.

Hazel's words from yesterday, about her needing some excitement and romance in her life, returned unbidden. Nate had been really good about respecting her wishes since Monday. He'd been polite and helpful but hadn't pressed her for anything more than friendship. Neither of them had made any mention of that kiss they'd shared Sunday.

And now they were going to sing together again.

Perhaps now that her feelings had changed, it would be different. Because singing was as much about emotion as it was about vocal skills.

But, just as before, singing with him was an incredibly moving experience. His singing voice seemed to resonate perfectly with something deep inside her, to fill up the empty places there, to complement and enhance her own voice. She couldn't help but meet his gaze as they sang. It was as if everything that stood between them melted away when they sang, as if the tight control she kept on her emotions, her very heart, were not proof against him when he sang.

When they finished, the last notes of the song seemed to hang in the air for a long moment as she felt powerless to look away from his gaze.

"I don't think we can sound like that, no matter how much we practice."

Fern's words broke the spell. Verity blinked and then turned to face the children. "Nonsense. All it takes is a little bit of practice." She could still feel Nate's gaze on her, could still feel that incredible tug of *rightness* she always felt when they sang together.

Please, let him look away so I can think. "Now we're going to break up into groups, just as we did for the first song, and Mr. Cooper will work with the first two groups and I will work with the other two groups. So find your corners."

She turned a bright, impersonal smile his way. "Mr. Cooper, let's plan to get everyone back together in about thirty minutes."

He nodded and turned away. And at last she felt free to breathe normally again.

Nate took Beans out for a walk after children's choir practice that afternoon. While the dog happily sniffed out various scents and fearlessly treed squirrels, Nate's thoughts turned to the subject that always seemed to be on his mind lately—Verity.

She had kept her word to consider him a friend—at least outwardly. He didn't imagine the casual observer would suspect anything had changed between them—including that kiss they'd shared, another thing he couldn't seem to get out of his mind.

Was Verity softening toward him? There'd been a moment, when they were singing together, that he'd seen something in her eyes when she looked at him. But it could just as easily have been his imagination.

The thing was, he couldn't blame her. After what he'd done, and how he'd let down his sister, he couldn't really expect a woman like Verity, or any good woman for that matter, to want him as part of her family.

But he was determined now to stay here and fight for his place in this community. He might have lost his chance to win her affection, but he could still find a home for himself here.

And if that was the best he could do, then it was much more than he'd had just a few months ago.

Besides, there *was* one woman he could help.

Calling Beans back to his side, he directed his steps toward the boardinghouse.

For a change, luck was on his side. He found Belva sitting alone on the boardinghouse porch, writing what appeared to be a letter. She looked up when he started up the steps and set down her pencil.

"Nate. What an unexpected surprise."

She made as if to rise but he waved her down. "Please don't get up."

She settled back down and he leaned his hip against a nearby support column. Beans trotted over to sniff at her shoes and she reached under the table to scratch his ears.

"I suppose I can guess as to why you're here. You've made a decision about my offer."

He nodded. "While I truly feel honored that you'd trust me to handle this job for you, I'm not going to take you up on your offer."

She leaned back with a resigned expression. "I'm more than a little disappointed, but I can't say as I'm all that surprised. It's pretty obvious that you've started forming ties here. I hope Verity knows how lucky she is."

Surprised by her comment, he had to smother a grimace. He decided it would be best to just let it pass.

"There *is* something else I'll do for you, however, if you like."

Her demeanor perked up. "What's that?"

"I'll travel with you to your new home when you get ready to move in, and I'll go with you to meet with the solicitors and help you take care of whatever business is entailed with claiming your inheritance. I'll also stick around to help you interview candidates for that caretaker position and I won't leave until you and I are both satisfied that you have the right man for the job."

She gave him a look that was a mix of surprise and hope. "Are you sure? That's going to take a lot of time away from your business here."

"I'm sure." It was what he would have liked for someone to have done for his sister if she'd been placed in a similar situation.

Belva grinned. "I sure as Christmas morning don't aim to talk you out of it. I accept." Then she held up a cautionary hand. "But I do have one condition."

"Which is?"

"That you let me pay you for your time."

"I don't want—"

She lifted her chin. "I insist. It would be the same wage I plan to pay the caretaker I eventually hire. As far as I'm concerned, you're temporarily serving in that capacity."

Realizing how important this was to her, he nodded. "In that case, I agree."

She offered him her hand to seal the deal.

He shook her hand, then reached down to rub Beans's head. "Have you told your aunt Eunice yet? Or are you waiting until your birthday?" She'd confided to him that, according to the terms of her aunt Imogene's will, she was to take possession of her inheritance on her twentieth birthday. And she was to tell none of her relatives about her good fortune until one month before the happy event.

Belva glanced toward the house, as if worried her aunt Eunice might suddenly appear. "I'm going to tell her right after the festival. It'll give her a couple of days to get used to the idea before my birthday rolls around."

"And how soon do you plan to leave?"

"My birthday is on Tuesday. I'd like to leave on Wednesday but can postpone it a bit if that doesn't fit your schedule."

"Assuming a replacement church pianist can be found, I can make that work." He would wait until after the children's performance on Saturday to tell Verity. Would she miss him at all? Or would she be glad to have him gone for a while?

Belva rubbed her chin. "As much as I'm looking forward to being on my own and starting fresh, I think I'm going to miss the folks here in Turnabout. Everyone has been so kind to me. It's been especially nice since I joined the choir."

He couldn't argue with her there. The town, and its residents, had lived up to everything Adam had said it would. And he had a particular fondness for the choir, as well. But he gave her a reassuring smile. "I'm sure the place you're moving to will welcome you just as warmly." Then he raised a brow. "And you can always come back to visit from time to time."

"Maybe I will," she said archly. "Especially if I had the right kind of incentive. Such as attending someone's wedding."

He ducked his head, ostensibly to scratch Beans behind the ears again. Hopefully she hadn't noticed any telltale sign of just how sharply that innocent comment of hers had cut him.

If she planned to wait on a wedding invitation from him and Verity before she returned, she might never see Turnabout again.

Chapter Eighteen

"So, how has it been, working with such a young choir group?"

The Saturday afternoon tea group was gathered once again in the Blue Bottle Sweet Shop. Verity's thoughts had been drifting, thinking of Nate and how it felt like a very long time since Thursday when she'd seen him last.

In fact, she found herself eager to get done here at the Blue Bottle so that they could go on to choir practice. Which was absurd, especially given that she had no intentions of relaxing her nothing-beyond-friendship stance with Nate.

So Abigail's question about the children's choir was a welcome distraction. "Actually, it's been a lot of fun." She meant that. "And quite rewarding. I'm thinking about seeing if they want to continue on as a choir after the festival."

"You mean have a full-time children's choir?"

Verity nodded. "We could even have them sing one hymn in church each Sunday."

"What a lovely idea." Janell set her teacup down.

"There may be other schoolchildren who would want to join in once we have the play behind us."

"All would be welcome," Verity agreed. "Of course, I'd have to see how Reverend Harper feels about it. And check in with Zella, too, since it would mean extra work for her, as well."

"Perhaps, if it's too much for Zella, Mr. Cooper would consider working with you on this." Hazel's tone was just a little *too* innocent.

Before Verity could say anything, though, Janell spoke up again. "You have to admit, he's done a great job these past few weeks while Zella is out of town."

Belva nodded. "Mr. Cooper does have a way of putting a body at ease. I imagine that makes him ideal for working with the children."

Verity still hadn't quite figured out what the relationship was between Belva and Nate. Just good friends? Or was Belva looking for something more?

She shouldn't be bothered by that thought since she no longer wanted anything more than friendship for herself.

But somehow, she was.

Later, as they left the Blue Bottle, Hazel fell into step beside her. "I've been thinking about ways we could arrange your hats in the fashion emporium to their best advantage," she said enthusiastically. "I'm picturing a set of deep shelves along the back wall, maybe three rows high, running two-thirds of the length. Depending on the size of your hats, you should be able to display around two dozen. What do you think?"

"I think you're being premature." But it did sound very appealing. "I told you we'd sit down and discuss it after the festival."

"It doesn't hurt to think about it some ahead of time,

does it?" She gave Verity a pointed look. "It also doesn't hurt to let you know I don't plan to drop the subject."

Verity rolled her eyes. "I never thought you would. But again, let's save this for *after* the festival."

Perhaps she would mention it to Nate, though, just to get his input. From a purely business perspective, of course. After all, he had recently opened a business of his own, so he might have some relevant insights.

The fact that it would give her an excuse to stay after practice and speak to him was just a pleasant side benefit.

Nate put his music away as the choir members drifted out after practice. Belva had paused just a minute to chat with him but then hurried off, saying she'd promised her aunt Eunice to lend her a hand with supper this evening.

It wasn't until he moved away from the piano that he realized Verity had remained behind when the others left. Was she actually going out of her way to see him?

"Do you have a minute?"

Apparently she was. "Of course. Is there something about one of the choirs we need to discuss?"

"Actually, I did want to ask you something about our practice sessions with the children this coming week."

Would she have anything to do with him once he was through acting as Zella Ford's stand-in? "I'm listening."

"We've got only two practice sessions left before the festival kicks off Friday night. They're doing well, but I thought it might be a good idea to have this week's sessions run for ninety minutes each rather than an hour. What do you think?"

He rubbed his chin. "That sounds like a good idea to me. The more practice they get in, the more confident they will be the day of the performance." And he wasn't averse to spending a little extra time with her, as well.

"And it won't be a problem for you?"

"I think I can manage the extra thirty minutes without any problem."

She smiled and gave his arm a quick, light touch. "Thank you."

Emboldened by that touch, he nodded toward the door. "May I walk you home?"

"You can walk me as far as your shop."

At least she hadn't refused altogether.

"There was one other thing I wanted to discuss with you," she said as they fell into step together.

"More choir business?" He had to physically restrain himself from taking her arm. She wanted nothing more than a neighborly kind of friendship.

"No, this is of a more personal nature."

His attention quickened at that. Discussing things other than choir was a step in the right direction.

"Remember I mentioned once that I'd like to open a millinery shop someday?"

"Of course."

"Well, I've been thinking that I should at least look into what all will be involved in such an undertaking so I'll know when, or even if, I'll be in a position to give it a go."

That sounded so like her. Careful to a fault. But at least she appeared to be moving forward. "That seems like a prudent approach."

"I thought so." There was just a hint of smugness in her voice. "Anyway, I mentioned this to Hazel and she's offered to lease me part of her dress shop to display and sell my hats whenever I get ready. I was wondering what you thought of that plan."

He was encouraged by the fact that his opinion still seemed to matter to her. "Actually, I can see a lot of really great advantages for you in such a setup. You'd have a place that was ready to move into with very little setup work required. The location is one that many of your potential customers already frequent. You and Miss Andrews could share the staffing duties, covering for each other as needed." He nodded. "It's ideal, really."

"So you don't see any negatives associated with going this route?"

It seemed that she was still looking for reasons *not* to follow through on her dream. "Well, I suppose there is always some potential for problems. For instance, if you and Miss Andrews had a falling out, things could get mighty awkward for your respective businesses. And you would need to make certain you both had the same understanding of how the money would be handled, how the floor space and display space should be divided and what the on-site responsibilities of each of you would be, especially in regards to each other's wares."

"Oh, my, that's a lot to think about."

"It is. But there's a way to manage the risk. You can save both of you a lot of headaches, and heartaches, by getting all of this down in a contract that you both sign. That way there won't be any misunderstandings down the road."

She sighed. "There's so much to consider. I hadn't thought of any of that. What if I miss some other key problem areas?"

He shook his head. "Verity, you're never going to be able to account for every possible catastrophe. There's just not much in life that comes with guarantees. But if you never step out in faith, you never have the chance to grab hold of the blessing."

She gave him a curious look. "Is that what you did, step out in faith?"

"Well, I'll admit that what I was stepping away from wasn't something I wanted to hold on to, so it was easier for me. I guess what you need to decide is, is that dream you have of having your millinery shop worth fighting for, worth facing the possibility of failure for? And you're the only one who can answer that question."

"I never thought of it that way." She was quiet for a long moment, then she met his gaze again. "I guess one of the things I'm struggling with is trying to decide how I will know when the time is right. Maybe I should wait until I have more money saved up."

He raised a brow. "Is that really what's holding you back? Money? Or is it fear?"

He could tell that remark hit home. They'd reached his shop by now and were standing outside it. He tried one more time to make her understand what he was trying to say. "I know you like to use a slow, well-thought-out approach to making decisions, Verity, but there is such a thing as overthinking a problem. At some point you have to act. If not, that's a decision in and of itself, isn't it?"

She gave her purse strings a little tug. "Thank you for your input—it has certainly given me something to think about. If you'll excuse me, it's time I headed home."

He watched her leave, fairly certain he'd made no dent at all in her examine-things-exhaustively approach to decision making.

And he certainly hadn't done anything to further his relationship with her at all.

* * *

Verity walked away, mulling over Nate's words. What he'd said sounded an awful lot like what Hazel had told her a few days ago. Both seemed to imply that she was overly cautious. To her way of thinking, there was no such thing—either one was cautious or not, it was a simple as that.

Yet there was a nagging little voice in her head telling her she was missing something, something important.

This was something she needed to think on more. Step out in faith, he'd said. Was that the something she was lacking—faith?

Perhaps her problem was that she thought too much. And perhaps didn't pray enough.

Chapter Nineteen

Nate arrived at the Tuesday practice session to find Verity already there ahead of him. She greeted him the same as always, without any apparent rancor from their previous conversation. Did that mean she had decided to take his advice? Or merely ignore it and move on?

The practice session went well. The children were able to run through all three of the songs with only a few missteps on the last one. It was great to see how well they were coming together, how eager they were to do a good job and how proud they were to have a part in the program.

At the end of the session, Miss Andrews came by with the smocks she'd made, and she and Verity helped the children try them on over their clothing.

Verity had them all line up side by side with the smocks on and made a big show of telling them how wonderful they looked. He saw several of the children stand a little taller under her praise.

When they were done, Verity collected the smocks from each of them, telling the children she would keep them safe and pass them out again the day of the performance.

Dismissing the choir members, Verity turned to him. "If you have a minute, there's something I'd like to discuss with you."

"Of course." Was she wanting to continue their last conversation?

"The children have been working so hard, I've been thinking I'd like to do something to reward them."

Of course she would. "Did you have something particular in mind?"

"Well, because many of the festival activities will take place on the school grounds, the town has canceled classes for Friday. I was thinking we could take advantage of that and have a group picnic down by Mercer's Pond that day. We could invite the members of the choir along with their families. What do you think?"

She certainly didn't mind making plans or undertaking large projects when it was for someone else. Why couldn't she show that same kind of spirit when it came to her own dreams?

But that wasn't what she'd asked him. "Wouldn't it be better to do that *after* the performance?"

She nodded. "I thought about that. But if we waited, that would mean doing it after church on Sunday, when everyone is likely to be tired from the prior day's festivities. Or waiting until the following Saturday, which feels like it would be too much of a delay." She grinned. "And besides, doing it on Friday lets the children know I'm rewarding their effort, not their performance."

That statement was so like her. She didn't just concern herself with teaching these kids how to do things, she concerned herself with their hearts and their spirits, as well. It was one of the many things he admired about her.

"Can I count on you to be there?"

He gave a short bow. "Of course. I'd never pass up a chance to attend a picnic." Or to spend some time with her. "What do you want me to do?"

"Just be there to help us keep an eye on the children. If everyone comes, there'll be a lot of them there. The Tucker family alone has ten children. And I don't imagine many of the dads will be available to come."

"I can certainly do that." He started to tease her about protecting her from spiders as well, but just in time he remembered where that had landed them last time, and thought better of it.

"Oh, and feel free to bring Beans," she added. "The children, especially one in particular, will enjoy having him there to play with."

He wondered if that soft smile that teased at her lips was due to her thoughts of her daughter or if perhaps she was beginning to warm toward him once more.

Friday dawned bright and sunshiny—the perfect day for a picnic. Verity had a large hamper filled to the brim with sliced ham, fresh-baked bread, cheese, apples, cucumber pickles, boiled eggs and a buttermilk pie. There was also a jar of lemonade. No one would go away hungry today if she could help it.

The children had all been enthusiastic at the idea of a picnic when she first announced it. She had also talked to the mothers, and every one of them had agreed to join in. They were going to have quite a nice turnout for their outing.

As planned, Nate collected her uncle's buggy from

the livery and pulled up in front of the house to pick up her and Joy. When he arrived, he hopped down to take the hamper from her, then whistled. "This is mighty heavy for just one meal."

Verity laughed. "I have a feeling it will be quite empty by the time we head home this afternoon."

"Bringing a big appetite with you, are you?"

She laughed again. "There's a lot of sharing that goes along with these picnics. We won't be the only ones eating from this basket."

He hefted it into the back of the buggy. "Then I guess I'd better be sure to get my share early."

He took the blanket Joy was carrying and tossed it behind the seat with the hamper. Then he took the little girl by the waist and swung her up in a wide arc, making her giggle and Verity wince.

Then he turned to hand her in. There was a moment's awkwardness as she remembered the last time they'd rode in this buggy. She could tell from the slight tightening of his jaw that he was remembering, too. But then she lifted her chin, smiled and offered him her hand. She refused to let anything spoil this outing. She and Nate had called a truce and she was ready to leave the past in the past. They were friends now, and as friends, could enjoy each other's company.

In a matter of seconds she was perched on the seat next to Joy.

Nate climbed up on the other side of her daughter and they were off.

With Joy sitting between them, holding Beans and Lulu in her lap, the remaining wisps of that momentary awkwardness disappeared. The little girl's happy chatter not only entertained them during the trip, but it successfully filled any of the silences that might have popped up between the adults.

They were the first ones to arrive, just as Verity had hoped. She spread their blanket in a prime spot that was in the shade of a large cottonwood tree and what she considered a safe distance from the pond itself. Then she spread a second blanket nearby.

Nate looked at the arrangement and then raised a brow in her direction. "Expecting company?"

She smiled and shook her head. "No, that's the community 'table.' Everyone will place the contents of their baskets there and then when it's time to eat, you can choose whatever items catch your eye."

"I see." He eyed the arrangement skeptically. "But it looks like that could get a bit messy."

She laughed, enjoying the chance to introduce him to their traditions. "Trust me. We've done this lots of times. Not everyone serves themselves. Three or four of the ladies will be in charge of filling plates—you just have to let them know what you want." She grinned. "This also takes care of the problem of some of the kids who have eyes bigger than their stomachs."

As she was speaking she'd moved her hamper to the community blanket. She wouldn't set the contents out until much closer to mealtime—no point in feeding the flies and ants.

Other families began arriving almost immediately. The children scattered to play while the adults staked a claim on a patch of ground to spread their cloths. They chose patches close together to make it easier for everyone to chat and visit with each other.

As Verity had predicted, Nate was one of the few men who had come. Most of the fathers were working or helping to get things set up in town for the festival. In fact, the only other man there was Stuart Draper, Harriett and Susie's grandfather.

Mr. Draper had walked with a pronounced limp ever since he'd gotten hurt in an accident over ten years ago. But he had a skill that didn't require the use of his legs and that endeared him to children. He was an expert at carving whistles and simple flutes from scraps of wood. At her urging, he had brought a couple of his creations for the children to play with, and also some materials to carve new ones on the spot.

In addition, several of the children had brought kites and there were balls and bats as well.

Once the picnic blankets were all arranged to everyone's satisfaction, the women were soon busy chattering away, comparing hamper contents, swapping news and generally socializing. While they visited, the children ran with great abandon around the meadow. Verity kept Joy in sight, making sure she didn't get too close to the pond, and not letting her stray too far from the adults.

Beans was also a big hit with the children. The dog was alternating his time between exploring, racing around the meadow with the children and letting himself be petted into a blissful stupor.

Nate seemed to take his role as a protector for the children quite seriously. Several times she saw him counting noses, and on the occasions when the count was not to his satisfaction, he'd march over to a section of the meadow that curved around the pond and then become hidden by trees. Sure enough, he'd reappear shortly with one or more kids in tow and send them back to safer— or at least more visible—ground. Apparently there were turtles and minnows to be found in the shallows there, and the children found it an irresistible attraction.

But he was more than a disciplinarian. He took time to play with them, as well. She saw him give one group lessons on how to skip stones, he played horseshoes with another group and worked to untangle a kite string for a teary-eyed youngster.

He even talked her into taking one end of a jump rope while he took the other, and together they turned the rope for nearly thirty minutes as the girls took turns jumping. It was so endearing—heartwarming really— to see him with the children.

When it was lunchtime, Mr. Draper blew on his loudest whistle, one that made a sound so shrill it actually startled a number of birds from the trees. But it served the purpose of getting everyone's attention, and the children came scurrying in from all directions. When everyone was accounted for and had gathered on the individual family picnic blankets, Mr. Draper offered up the blessing on behalf of the group.

Then it was momentary pandemonium as everyone tried to make food selections. But at last all the plates were served and things quieted in the meadow while everyone partook of the delicious food.

Nate, naturally, shared her and Joy's picnic blanket. She smiled as she watched Joy laugh at something he'd said to her. And then he casually slipped Beans a sliver of meat. It felt nice to have him there with them. It felt like…family.

Verity sat up straighter, trying to shake off that unexpected thought. Where was her resolve, her caution? The trouble was, she was having trouble remembering why all that mattered. He *was* a good man, deep down she knew that. As for the rest, maybe he and Hazel had been right. Perhaps it *was* time she stepped out in faith.

Nate looked up just then and caught her staring at him. Something of what she was feeling must have shown in her face, because his expression shifted from amusement to first uncertainty, and then something much warmer and deeper. They held each other's gaze without speaking, without moving, for three heartbeats.

And then Joy spoke up, asking for another piece of corn bread, and broke the spell.

Verity blinked and turned to her daughter. "I'm sorry, pumpkin, what did you say?"

Joy held up her plate. "I'd like another piece of corn bread, please."

Nate stood. "I'll get it." He looked down at Verity, his expression still warm and rather mysterious. "Can I get you anything while I'm up?"

She shook her head, and with a nod he walked away.

As she watched him saunter over to the food blanket, she began second-guessing herself. Should she have looked away? What message had he read in her gaze? What had she wanted him to see there?

Then she remembered they weren't alone. Had anyone else noticed anything untoward passing between them? Verity did her best to surreptitiously look around the gathering. As far as she could tell, no one was paying the least bit of attention to them.

Nate returned, the requested slice of corn bread wrapped in a cloth napkin. "Here you go," he said, handing it to Joy.

When he settled back down on the blanket, she felt a new tension strumming in him, something that seemed to tug at her, as well. It was almost like when they sang together—something inside him speaking to her and vice versa.

It was so real it amazed her that no one else could feel it.

Nate stood with his back against an oak and his arms crossed over his chest. Beans lay in the grass at his feet, panting. The dog had had a busy morning trying to keep up with the children and seemed to be happy just to stay with him for now.

From here Nate had a fairly unobstructed view of the meadow. Their picnic meal had ended a few minutes ago and, like Beans, everyone appeared to be moving at a much slower pace than earlier.

Several picnic blankets had been spread in an overlapping line under the shade of a nearby tree and many of the toddlers and younger children had been put down for their naps. Mr. Draper was keeping an eye on them, freeing the mothers to help with the cleanup or to take advantage of their temporary freedom to just visit.

Some of the older children were playing with the ball and bat well away from the picnic area, while several of the girls had claimed one of the blankets as a place to play with their dolls.

He spotted Verity among a cluster of women who were cleaning up and reorganizing all the leftovers. As if she felt his gaze on her, she looked up, smiled and then went back to work.

He was still trying to decide what to make of the look they'd shared earlier. The message in her eyes had been unmistakable. She felt something for him, something more than friendship. But was that emotion real and of the lasting variety this time? At least now he didn't have to worry about what would happen if she found out his secrets—she already knew them all.

It was frustrating that he couldn't do anything to resolve this right now, couldn't have a meaningful conversation with her among this crowd. And taking a walk alone together was also out of the question—she'd never leave Joy unattended, even among this crowd of motherly types. Perhaps, though, when he brought her and Joy home this evening, they could find some time to talk in private. It was definitely something to look forward to.

He saw Joy race up to tug on Verity's skirt, her trademark "can I please" expression in evidence. He pushed away from the tree, deciding to drift closer to the pair to see what was going on.

"But Mama, please," he heard Joy plead, "I want to see the bunny."

Verity shook her head. "I told you, pumpkin, I'm too busy to go with you right now. And besides, the bunny is probably long gone."

"You don't know. He might still be there."

"What's this about a bunny?" Nate inquired once he was close enough to join in.

Joy whirled around at the sound of his voice, a hopeful expression on her face. "Mr. Cooper, will you take me to see the bunny?"

Before he could answer, Verity spoke up. "Joy, I've already told you, you need to stay close to me."

Nate saw the mutinous expression form on Joy's face, and spoke up quickly. "I don't mind going for a walk with her. I've been meaning to take Beans out for a bit of exploring anyway."

Verity looked from him to her daughter. "I don't

know. Joy, maybe you should just stay here and keep me company while Mr. Cooper walks Beans."

"But what about the bunny?"

"Let her go." Nate tried to cajole a smile from Verity with one of his own. "I promise to keep a close watch on her. And we'll definitely stay away from the edge of the pond."

She held out for a moment longer, and then finally gave in with a loud huff of breath. "Oh, very well. I suppose it'll be all right. But Joy, see that you mind Mr. Cooper. No running off on your own."

"Yes, ma'am. Come on, Beans, let's go find the bunny."

Nate matched his steps to those of the little girl and dog at his side. He was so proud of Verity for overcoming her fears and letting Joy out of her sight in this setting. He knew it had been a big step for her. And it felt very good to know that it was putting her trust in him that had allowed her to loosen the reins.

"So tell me about this bunny," he said to Joy.

"Molly told me they saw a bunny last time they were out here."

"Is that right?" So this wasn't a recent sighting. No wonder Verity had expressed doubt that it would be nearby.

Joy nodded. "Molly said she got close enough to almost pet it before it hopped away." The wistful gleam in her eyes was sweet to see.

He needed to temper her expectations, but there was no point in dashing her hopes completely. "We'll certainly keep a look out. But bunnies are *very* shy. There's so many people here right now that I really don't think a bunny will come out of hiding today."

"But he might," she insisted stubbornly.

"I suppose." He couldn't bring himself to express any stronger doubt. "But I tell you what. If we don't see a bunny today, we'll come back another day with just me and you and your mother and see if we have better luck."

"Okay. But let's try to find him today."

Nate nodded in solemn agreement. They were reaching the section of meadow that wrapped around the pond and formed a pocket out of sight of the picnic area. He'd intended to turn back when they got to this point, knowing Verity would want to be able to keep Joy in sight. But he heard a ruckus coming from around the point and he could tell it was some of the kids from their party.

And they sounded as if they were in trouble.

When he rounded the corner, sure enough, three kids were standing at the edge of the pond. Well, two of them were, anyway. The third was actually in the pond and seemed to be in some kind of trouble. Nate didn't recognize any of them from the choir—they must be some of the family members.

"What's going on here?" he called out.

All three started and turned to face him.

"It's Davey," one of the boys said as he waved toward the kid in the water. "He's got his foot caught on something and we can't get him out."

The boy, Davey, stood in waist-deep water right beside a tree trunk that had fallen over the pond.

"It's starting to hurt something awful," Davey added.

Nate could tell the boy was trying not to cry but was right on the verge. His foot was probably caught on some kind of rope or net that was down in the silt or lodged in the underwater part of the tree trunk.

He glanced down at the little girl whose hand he held

and realized he had a problem. Verity wouldn't want him taking Joy that close to the water's edge, especially if he was going to have to focus his attention on someone else. He could take her back first, but he wasn't sure how badly hurt Davey's leg might be.

He quickly took off his jacket and spread it on the ground. "Joy, I need to go over there and help Davey. I want you to sit right here on this coat and not get up until I return. Do you understand?" Hopefully the jacket would serve as an anchor for her.

"Yes, sir. But then can we go look for the bunny some more?"

"I promise."

As soon as he reached the waterline, he turned to see how Joy was doing. She still sat where he'd left her, hugging her knees. She waved when she saw him looking and he waved back, then turned to the two boys who were unencumbered.

"What's your name?" he asked the largest of the pair.

"JJ."

"JJ, you see that little girl sitting over there?"

JJ nodded.

"I want you to keep an eye on her for me. Let me know if she tries to go anywhere."

The boy nodded, but Nate wasn't satisfied. He didn't completely trust Joy not to forget her promise if she saw some critter that she wanted to get close to.

He held JJ's gaze a moment longer. "It's very important that you watch her. Understand?"

The boy nodded again. Then Nate turned to the other boy. "And you are?"

"Irvin."

"Irvin, I want you to go back to the picnic area and

very calmly ask Mrs. Leggett to come down here. Tell her not to worry, but that Mr. Cooper needs her help with something. Do you understand?"

The boy nodded, but before he could take off, Nate grabbed his arm. "Remember, be sure to tell her not to worry." He wanted her here because of her medical experience if something should be wrong with the boy's foot. But he didn't want her jumping to the conclusion that something had happened to Joy.

When the boy nodded this time, Nate let him go. Deciding he'd covered all contingencies as best he could, Nate gingerly waded into the pond beside the trapped Davey. Then he very carefully felt under the water around the boy's foot. Sure enough, he found Davey's foot was tangled in a knotted length of rope that had wrapped itself around a limb under the water.

"I've found the problem, but it's going to take me a few minutes to get you free. Just hold on."

Nate tried loosening the rope, but it was too slippery to get a grip firm enough to work the knots.

Davey shifted position and let out a yell.

"Easy now. There are some jagged bits of wood down there." There was a real danger the boy could do himself serious injury if he wasn't careful. "Here, lean on me if you need to." Nate held out his arm, elbow bent, and the boy latched on. He let him balance like that for a minute and then helped him transfer most of his weight to the body of the tree.

That done, Nate reached for his pocketknife. Careful to position the knife in such a way as to not harm the boy, he went to work sawing on the rope. It was thick so it took several minutes, but at last it was done. As soon as the rope separated, Nate lifted the boy bodily, intending to carry him out of the pond.

"What's going on out here?"

Nate turned to see Verity striding toward them.

"You're just in time. Davey here had a little accident."

"So I see." Then she looked around. "Where's Joy?"

Nate's gaze flew to the spot where he'd left the little girl and his heart thudded in his chest.

Joy was no longer sitting on his coat.

Chapter Twenty

Nate looked around the area frantically but there was no sign of the child. He glanced toward JJ but the boy had hung his head and wouldn't meet his gaze. Obviously JJ had fallen down on the job.

He quickly set Davey down on the bank then turned back to Verity, remorse for what he had let happen, for what it would do to the woman he loved, nearly suffocating him. "She was just here. She couldn't have gone far."

He saw the blood drain from her face, saw the fear in her eyes. "What do you mean, you don't know? You promised me you would watch her."

Her words hit him like a knife to his chest. "I turned away to help Davey and when I looked back, she was gone. But I'm going to find her."

She glanced at the water with fear-filled eyes and he made a sharp movement.

"No! She didn't go near the pond—I would have seen her. She must have wandered into the woods, but she wouldn't have gotten far."

"I'm going with you to look for her."

"No. You need to stay here and check on Davey. Besides, if she slips past me in the woods and comes back here, you need to be waiting for her."

He turned to JJ. He knew the boy was feeling miserable for his lapse of attention. The kid needed a chance to redeem himself. "JJ, I need you to do something for me."

The boy looked up, finally meeting his gaze, guilt radiating from him.

"Go on back to the group and tell them what happened with Davey and with Joy. And then borrow that very loud whistle from Mr. Draper and bring it back here to Mrs. Leggett."

He turned to Verity. "If Joy does come out of the woods without me, blow that whistle and I'll know to stop my search and come back."

She nodded.

Without another word, he strode quickly into the woods. He called for Joy as he went, listening closely each time for a response. The longer it went without a response, the deeper the dread lodged in his chest. If something had happened to that precious little girl, he would never forgive himself.

Twenty minutes later he finally spotted her, curled up on the ground with her eyes closed. Was she breathing? He rushed over and dropped down beside her. The sweetest sight he ever saw was the sight of her eyelids fluttering open.

"Oh, hello, Mr. Cooper. You founded me." She lifted her arms up to him.

He pulled her into his lap, and struggled to get his voice under control. "Hello, Joy. Are you okay?"

"Uh-huh. But the bunny ran away."

He offered up silent prayers of thanksgiving that she was unharmed. Then he gave her a bear hug. "Everyone has been very worried about you. Especially your mother."

Joy wrapped her arms around his neck. "Is Mama mad at me?"

It was much more likely that it was him Verity was angry with, and he couldn't blame her. "Right now she just wants to know that you're all right."

When they finally cleared the trees, Verity was there, pacing. Her face was white and drawn and she was rubbing her arms. Several of the other women were there with her, keeping her company.

As soon as she saw the two of them step from the woods, she raced over and took Joy from his arms.

"She's okay," he said quickly.

"No thanks to you." Anger and betrayal blazed from her eyes.

"I'm sorry." It was inadequate, but what else could he say?

"I trusted you, trusted your word that you wouldn't let her out of your sight."

Her voice was low and controlled, but it thrummed with emotion, all of it sharp, all of it aimed at him.

"Please don't be angry, Mama." Joy wrapped her arms around her mother's neck. "He tolded me to stay on his coat but I saw a bunny."

Verity stroked her daughter's hair and he saw how her fingers trembled. "I'm not angry with you, pumpkin."

But the eyes-blazing look she shot his way let him know *he* wasn't so lucky.

It was going to be a very long carriage ride back to town.

Chapter Twenty-One

T he children took their places in line inside the church, fidgeting nervously as they waited for the signal to take the stage. Their performance would take place in just a few short minutes—all of their hours of practice and preparation coming down to this.

Verity went down the line, talking to each child in turn, doing what she could to ease their nervous fears, letting them know how very proud she was of each and every one of them. All the time the back of her neck tingled uncomfortably with the knowledge that Nate was behind her at the piano, watching her.

The children were to perform on the church steps and they were lined up down the center aisle, waiting for their cue to file out. The church doors and windows were all thrown wide open so that the music from the piano could clearly be heard by performers and audience alike. Which meant for the first two songs on the program, Nate would be inside the church, heard but not seen.

Which was all right by Verity. She still hadn't been able to forgive him for not keeping a better watch over

Joy yesterday. When she thought about her baby, alone in the woods for nearly half an hour, it just tied her stomach in knots. So many things could have happened—snakes, falls, even her finding her way back to the water's edge.

Even if Nate had been focused on helping Davey, he should have set one of the other children who was present to watch her.

No, the man was not to be trusted. He might have the best intentions in the world—trying to help his sister all those years ago, helping Davey yesterday—but his judgment was far from sound. If she'd needed a sign that he was not the kind of man she should try to build a life with, she'd gotten it loud and clear yesterday. And just in the nick of time.

Hazel finally stepped inside, signaling it was time. Verity pulled her focus back to the children and the program they were about to perform.

She led the group out the open doors and into the sunlight. They looked so cheery and hopeful in their bright green smocks. The children lined up in two rows, just as they had practiced, without any missteps.

Hazel stayed inside the church and positioned herself where she could see both Verity and Nate. She would relay any signals that needed to pass from one to the other.

Verity tried to maintain her composure as she turned to face the audience. By now, most of the town knew what had happened yesterday, and how she had reacted to it. Hazel had tried to talk to her, to tell her Nate deserved another chance. But Verity had simply walked away from her. She was done with giving him chances.

She could have forgiven him, maybe, if what he had

done had endangered her. But not her baby—that she could not forgive.

Pulling her thoughts away from her anger one more time, she gave the children a broad smile and then turned to the audience.

"Welcome, everyone, to the very first performance of Turnabout's new children's choir. They've all been working very hard these past few weeks, and once you've heard their performance, I think you'll agree that it hasn't been in vain. And now, without further ado, I present to you the Turnabout Children's Choir."

There was a small smattering of applause as Verity turned back to face the children. She raised her hands, then nodded to Hazel. The music started almost immediately.

Using the hand signals the children were now accustomed to, Verity counted the beats and the four youngest children stepped down one stair right on cue and started the song. They were a bit wobbly at first, but they gathered confidence as they went and by the end of their assigned verse they were singing with vigor. All the children chimed in on the chorus and then it was time for the next four to step down and sing their verse.

At the end of the number, the audience erupted in applause and Verity was happy to see the wide smiles on the faces of her choir. Once the applause died down, she signaled that they were to resume their positions, and they did so with only minor scrambling. Again she held up a hand to bring them to attention, then signaled Hazel. This time, when it was time to sing, the group sang out all together. There were two children who had their timing slightly off, but they caught up quickly and on the whole, that number was a success, as well.

The third song was the one Nate had taught her, the one that would be sung a cappella. The original plan had been for Nate to come on out here and help her direct it. But after waiting a few minutes, Verity realized he was not going to make an appearance.

She had a slight pang over that since he had worked as hard as she on this program and deserved some recognition for his efforts. But part of her was relieved as well that she would not have to face him in front of her neighbors.

Smiling at the children, she gave them the count. This time, when the younger group stepped forward to sing the first verse, she sang softly with them, helping them to carry the tune without the piano for help.

When the final note had been sung, the applause was louder than before and lasted longer. Verity had the whole group step down and take a bow.

And then it was done.

Most of the children raced off to join their parents, and several folks came up to offer Verity congratulations on how well the program had come off. Again she felt that slight pang of conscience that Nate was not present to get his share of the praise.

At one point, Joy tugged on Verity's skirt. "Why didn't Mr. Cooper come out to be with us on the last song like we practiced?"

"I don't know, pumpkin. Perhaps he was feeling a little shy. But you all still did a wonderful job."

"Is he going to walk with us through the festival? He told me yesterday at the picnic that he would and that Beans could come, too."

"Oh, pumpkin, I don't think so."

Joy gave her a solemn look. "Are you still mad at him because I got losted?"

"That's between Mr. Cooper and me." Despite her feelings, she didn't want to taint Joy's feelings toward Nate. She knew his fondness for her daughter was genuine.

She quickly changed the subject. "Why don't we go see what we can find at the festival? I hear they have a talking parrot that you can see."

That was sufficient to distract her daughter, and away they went. Verity did her best to see that Joy had a good time. They watched the other schoolchildren perform the play. They cheered for the contestants in the three-legged race and wheelbarrow race. They did indeed get to see the talking parrot, which Joy considered interesting but not very cuddly.

But Verity was just going through the motions. She wasn't able to lose herself in the spirit of the event. Twice she caught herself looking for Nate, without success, among the crowd, and she despised herself for it.

More than anything else, she felt a deep sense of loss and betrayal. And she wasn't sure which hurt the most.

Zella, who had returned to town on Friday, was back at the piano on Sunday. Verity looked for Nate and saw him sitting near the back of the church. Next to Belva.

Nate strode down the sidewalk toward the clinic, Beans at his heels. He'd done a lot of thinking, and a lot of praying, since the incident at the picnic four days ago. And he'd reached one significant conclusion. He couldn't—wouldn't—let things go on the way they were.

It was time he moved on.

He climbed the front porch steps to the Pratt home

and rapped on the door. It was the doctor's wife who answered his knock. To his relief, the look she gave him held more sympathy than animosity.

"Hello, Mr. Cooper. Are you here to see Verity?"

He removed his hat. "Yes, ma'am. If you don't mind, please let her know that I don't plan to take up much of her time."

"She and Joy are out back, working in the garden." The doctor's wife pointed to her left. "Just follow the house around that way and you'll see it." She gave him a look that was almost conspiratorial. "If you need time alone with my niece, just tell Joy I said she could bring Beans inside to feed him some scraps I have."

"Yes, ma'am, thank you." It seems he had at least one ally in this household.

Nate followed Mrs. Pratt's directions and found the garden easily enough. Verity was on her knees with her back to him, pulling weeds. Joy was nearby, rather inexpertly weaving a daisy chain. As soon as Beans spotted them he gave a yip of recognition and raced forward. Joy scrambled to her feet and met him halfway.

Verity was slower to react, though he thought he detected a certain stiffening of her back. When she stood and turned to face him, there was a guarded expression on her face.

"Hello, Mr. Cooper," Joy said. "I looked for you at the festival but couldn't find you."

"I'm sorry I missed all the fun, but I wasn't feeling up to it." Before the little girl could press further, he delivered Mrs. Pratt's message. "Your aunt Betty told me she has some food you can feed Beans if you want to take him to the kitchen."

"Yes, sir. Come on, Beans."

And with that, child and dog were off.

Verity watched her daughter go, ignoring him, until he heard the back door spring closed. Then she turned to him. "What are you doing here?"

Not exactly a warm welcome. "I came to let you know I'm going out of town for a while."

There was a flicker of something in her expression, but he couldn't tell if it was relief, surprise or curiosity. It certainly couldn't be regret.

When she didn't say anything, he continued. "I was wondering if you would allow Joy to take care of Beans for me while I'm away."

"I don't know—"

"Look, I know you're angry with me. And I probably deserve it."

"Probably—"

He held a hand up. "I'm not here to debate that point with you. But just because you no longer trust me is no reason to punish Joy and Beans. I'd like to know that someone who cares for the animal as much as I do, someone like Joy, will be looking out for him."

"How long will you be gone?"

He slid his fingers along the brim of his hat. "I'm not sure. Perhaps a month or more."

"That's quite a lot of time to be gone from your business."

Did she seem so disapproving because of the commitment she'd have to make with Beans, or was there another reason?

She hadn't asked for an explanation, at least not outright, but he decided to give her one, anyway. "I'm going to help Belva to get settled into her new place and to deal with some staffing issues. I'm not sure how long that will take, but I've committed to not leave her until I'm satisfied everything is running smoothly." The news about Belva's inheritance and her moving to her newly acquired estate had broke yesterday, so he wasn't betraying any confidences.

"I see." She tilted her head, studying him almost analytically. "But you *are* coming back?"

He saw no indication of whether she was hoping for a yes or no answer from him. "I am." That was part of the thinking he'd done these past few days. He'd come very close to telling Belva he'd take her up on her offer after all.

But in the end he'd decided he wasn't going to run away. Not from Verity. And not from his past. "But don't worry, I will make very sure that our paths don't cross any more than they must. You have no need to fear you will receive any unwanted attentions from me. You've made it clear you want me out of your and Joy's lives and I plan to honor that wish."

It hurt that she felt this way, but he couldn't let it define his life, who he was. He'd dealt with loss before. This was just a different kind of loss.

He felt his jaw tighten and he deliberately relaxed it. "I just have one last thing I want to say. I've made a lot of mistakes in my life, some of them really big mistakes. Those mistakes have been costly, to me and to those around me. I regret what happened Friday, and the pain it cost you, more deeply than you will ever know."

He put his hat back on. "Tell Joy goodbye for me. I'll come by to retrieve Beans when I return." With that he turned and walked away.

* * *

Verity watched him depart and tried to sort out the emotions she was feeling, without much success.

Deciding she needed a walk to clear her mind, she went inside to clean up. When she told Joy about Nate leaving Beans in her care, her daughter wasn't as excited as she'd thought she would be.

"But Beans will be sad that Mr. Cooper is gone," her daughter said. "And I will be, too."

"He won't be gone forever. He's coming back whenever his business is finished."

"But you said he would be gone for *weeks*. That's a long time. Me and Beans are going to miss him."

"I'm afraid it can't be helped." And with that unhelpful answer, she headed to her room before her daughter could press further.

As Verity changed clothes, she remembered what Mr. Barr had said, something along the lines of children giving their heart only to those who are deserving.

Verity had intended to take a nice long walk, but somehow she found herself standing in the doorway to Hazel's shop.

Hazel looked up and gave her a broad, welcoming smile. "Hi there, come on in. Have you heard the news about Belva? It's all anyone is talking about."

Verity joined her at the counter and nodded. "I have. I'm happy for her."

"You should have seen Eunice this morning at the mercantile. The poor woman couldn't decide if she was more happy for her niece or irritated that Belva had kept the whole thing secret from her. I, for one, have a new respect for Belva. Anyone who can keep a secret from a busybody like Eunice, while living under the same roof with her no less, is one clever, resourceful person."

Verity was able to smile at that. "It seems she was able to keep it a secret from everyone, not just Eunice."

"Except perhaps Mr. Cooper."

"Mr. Cooper?" Funny how she couldn't seem to get away from him.

"Yes." Hazel was obviously enjoying being privy to something Verity wasn't. "Haven't you heard? He's going to go with her to help her deal with the solicitors and make sure she gets settled in okay."

"I heard."

"Well, I imagine she gave him more than a few hours' notice when she asked him—don't you?"

Of course. So that was the bond the two of them shared—Belva had trusted him with her secret.

Hazel, apparently tired of waiting for a response from her, tried a slight change of subject. "I hear he went to see you this morning."

Verity grimaced. "Word certainly travels fast around here."

"Well? Was it just to let you know he was leaving?"

"That, and he asked us to watch over Beans while he was away."

"I hope this means the two of you have made up."

"Made up." Verity couldn't control the note of anger in her voice. "Hazel, we didn't have a lover's spat. He put Joy's life in danger. That's not something I can easily forgive."

"I know, but—"

"The subject is closed. Besides, there was something altogether different I came here to discuss with you."

Hazel didn't seem at all happy with her change of subject, but she didn't argue. "And what might that be?"

"I've decided that I'm not ready to open a millinery shop right now after all, so there's no point in us discussing it."

"If it's the money, I can—"

"It's not that." She grimaced. "Well, it's not *just* that. I've decided I want to spend more time with Joy. Setting up a millinery shop, even if I did it here with you, would take away from that. Maybe, once she starts school in the fall, we can talk about it again."

Hazel's lips were pursed in disapproval and her hands were crossed over her chest. "And when fall arrives you'll have some other excuse."

Verity was taken aback by her friend's directness. "You don't know that—"

"Oh, but I do." She waved a hand. "It's what you do. Any time, *any* time, you get close to achieving some long-held dream, you find a reason to back away. Like you're doing with your millinery-shop dream. And with the way you're pushing Mr. Cooper away."

Verity took exception to that. "Pushing Mr. Cooper away has *nothing* to do with anything but his trustworthiness. He promised to keep an eye on Joy, and because he broke that promise she wandered off. It ended well, but that was no thanks to him."

"Actually, according to what I heard, it was he who actually found her."

Verity made an impatient movement with her hands. "Yes, of course. But she was missing for twenty minutes. So many things could have happened to her."

"But they didn't. And what did he do to earn your

wrath—he turned his back for just a few minutes in order to help one of the other children."

She couldn't believe Hazel was actually taking his side in this. "With a child Joy's age, a few minutes is all it takes."

"You mean like that day a few weeks ago when she ended up in the street in front of my shop."

Verity felt as if she'd been slapped in the face. "I don't... It's not the same..."

Hazel's expression softened. "I wasn't trying to imply that you're not a good mother, Verity. I just wanted to help you see that it can happen to anyone, even the most vigilant of guardians. Even *you* can't keep your eyes on Joy every hour of every day."

Verity shook her head, refusing to accept that.

But Hazel wasn't ready to let it drop. "Yes, something could happen when you're not looking. Like with Arthur. And with your parents. But you've got to trust that God is in control."

Then Hazel straightened. "But, back to my original complaint. You've become quite adept at giving up before you reach the finish line. I'm not sure what it is you're scared of—failing, achieving your dream but being disappointed by it, or something else. Whatever it is, you need to take a really good, honest look at yourself and see what kind of example you're setting for Joy."

What did she mean by that? Surely—

Hazel stepped forward and wrapped her arms around Verity. "I love you like you were my sister. But it's a sister's job to say the things to you that no one else will."

Unsure how to respond to that, Verity merely nodded and took her leave.

Not wanting to pass in front of Nate's shop, she turned

in the opposite direction. Then turned on Schoolhouse
Road. She wasn't ready to return home yet. She needed
to be alone and do some prayerful thinking about what
Hazel had just said to her. And there was a nice quiet
spot in an open field just past the schoolyard that was
perfect for that.

How could Hazel, her very best friend, have said such
things to her? That she was being too hard on Nate. That
she was setting a bad example for Joy. That—

"Mrs. Leggett?"

She stopped walking and found herself confronted by
a young boy. She realized now that she had been passing
the schoolyard and all the children were out at recess,
which must be where he had come from.

Taking a closer look at the student, she recognized
him as one of the boys who'd been involved in Nate's
rescue of Davey.

"Hello, JJ. Is there something I can do for you?"

"I just wanted to say how really sorry I am for what
happened with your little girl on Friday."

His words caught her by surprise, but she smiled
down at him. "Thank you for your concern, JJ, but Joy
is fine now."

The boy swallowed, something obviously still on his
mind. "But I've been feeling real guilty about what happened, and I just wanted you to know."

"Guilty? JJ, I know you were there when Joy went
missing, but none of this is your fault."

"Yes, it is." The boy's Adam's apple bobbed twice,
then he drew his shoulders back. "Mr. Cooper, he asked
me to keep an eye on Joy while he was helping Davey. I
was supposed to let him know if she tried to get up. But
I was just so worried about Davey, and then he yelled

real loud and I just forgot all about watching her. I'm just so, so sorry."

Nate had assigned someone to watch Joy? Why hadn't he told her? Then the explanation jumped out at her— because he was trying to spare JJ's feelings, of course.

She put a hand on the boy's shoulder. "Thank you for telling me, JJ, and for your apology. It takes a really brave person to own up to something like that."

Some of the tension seemed to leave the boy and he offered her a shaky smile. "I just thought you ought to know, it wasn't Mr. Cooper's fault." And with that, he rushed back onto the schoolyard.

Verity slowly continued on her way, her head spinning with everything she'd heard today.

What if Nate had told her about JJ's role? Would it have made a difference? Or would she have railed at him, anyway? Was she, like Hazel said, afraid of achieving her dreams, to the extent that she looked for reasons not to reach for them?

What had she become?

And what had it cost her?

The next morning, Verity approached the saddle shop with some trepidation. She'd spent much of yesterday searching her heart and praying for both clarity and guidance.

So many things had come clear to her now, not the least of which was that she had been hiding behind this cautious, indecisive attitude for most of her life, and it had kept her from enjoying so many of the blessings God had in store for her. And even worse than that, she had been well on her way to doing that to Joy, as well.

She had also realized, with absolute clarity, that she

loved Nate, had loved him for a while now, and that she had been doing just as Hazel said, pushing him away out of fear.

But no more. She was ready to reach for that dream—even if she was too late, it was worth risking that disappointment to have a chance at that kind of happiness.

But some of her old fears returned as she wondered if she'd taken too long to come to her senses. He'd said yesterday that he was ready to let her go. Had he meant it?

She reached his shop door only to find it locked. The Closed sign hung in the window and all the shades were drawn. Well, that was to be expected since he'd be leaving today. But surely he hadn't actually gone to the station yet—the train didn't leave for another hour and a half.

Taking a deep breath, she knocked on the door.

Nothing. No light, no sound of movement.

Had she missed him after all?

She knocked again, louder this time. Still no response.

She couldn't let him go off for goodness knows how long without letting him know how she truly felt. She'd prefer to have that discussion in private, but if she had to have it at the train depot, or in the middle of Main Street for that matter, she intended to have her say.

From the corner of her eye, Verity saw that she had attracted some attention from a few passersby on the sidewalk. She also spotted Hazel standing in the doorway of her shop, giving her an approving grin.

Titling her chin up defiantly, Verity ignored her audience, raised her fist, and this time she pounded the door for all she was worth.

Chapter Twenty-Two

Nate had his bag packed and was ready to head to the train station. Trouble was, it was ninety minutes until the train was scheduled to pull in.

So what did he do with himself in the meantime?

If he had a piano here he could lose himself in music. If Beans were here, he could take him for a walk.

But since neither of those things was true, he was left to his own thoughts. And he'd had just about enough of his own thoughts lately.

An unexpected sound caught his attention. Was someone knocking at his shop door?

He considered ignoring it—after all, he was leaving town, so he wasn't available to do any repair or commission work right now. But then he thought better of it. Perhaps whoever it was wanted one of his stock pieces. Besides, it was a distraction, and that's just what he needed right now.

As he headed down the stairs, the knock came again, this time louder, more insistent. That didn't sound like a customer. He quickened his pace, making it to the door in record time. He turned the knob and yanked the door open, then froze as he saw Verity standing there, poised to knock again.

"Hello," she said feebly, looking suddenly shy and uncertain.

"Is something wrong? Is it Beans?"

She waved a hand in a feeble gesture. "No, no, nothing like that. I just needed to speak to you before you leave."

What was going on? When he'd met with her yesterday she'd hardly said anything at all, and what words she *had* uttered had been hard, unforgiving. He wasn't sure he could stand much more of that right now.

Then she looked at him with a vulnerability that snagged at his heart. "May I come in? I promise I won't keep you long."

Without a word he stepped aside to allow her to enter.

She walked to the center of the room, then turned to face him.

Whatever she had to say, she was being uncharacteristically dramatic about it.

"I made a couple of decisions last night," she said by way of opening. "Well, this morning, really, since it was well after midnight."

Where was she going with this? "Making decisions is a good thing," he said mildly.

She nodded. "I decided I'm going to take Hazel up on her offer and go into business with her."

Despite the tension between them, he was proud of her. He knew how much she hated taking risks, and this was a big one. This time he was able to give her a genuine smile. "So you're finally ready to reach out and try to catch your dream. I know it seems scary, but if there's anything I can do to help, from a purely business perspective of course, let me know."

"Thank you." The smile she gave him was every bit as warm as those she'd given him during that ill-fated berry-picking expedition. Was her excitement over her newfound business decision spilling over into other parts of her life?

Then he shut down that train of thought. He'd let himself be fooled by her softening attitude in the past. He couldn't let it happen again. So he pasted on a polite smile. "I'm almost disappointed that I'm going to be away while you're getting everything up and running."

"So am I."

It was getting harder and harder to ignore those wistful looks she was giving him. "Talk to Adam. He can help you get your business off on the right foot."

"I will."

She stood there silently, but he could tell there was something else she had left to say. Then he remembered she'd said she'd made two decisions. "Was there anything else?"

"Yes." She straightened and met his gaze with a straight-from-the-heart directness. "I couldn't let you go away without telling you how I feel."

Everything inside him stilled, waiting to hear what she'd say next.

"I've been a fool and a coward. You have an adventurer's heart—you're impulsive, you're willing to try new things, and you know how to make a game out of most anything. You're not afraid to take charge when necessary, but you can follow just as well. When you see someone who needs help or something that needs doing, you find a way to get it done. And you have the biggest heart of anyone I've ever met."

His pulse, traitor that it was, was ignoring his resolve to not read too much into her words. She could just be apologizing, nothing more.

But she wasn't through talking. "Yet, knowing all that, I ignored what my heart was telling me and looked for ways to push you away. Because you're not the kind of man I wanted to fall in love with—you're not predictable, deliberate or particularly cautious."

She took a step closer. "But as I said, my heart has a mind of its own, and it finally got through to me. I love you. You're not a safe choice, but you're the person I want to spend my life with. I know you have no reason to trust me, to return those feelings, but I had to say it to you because you deserved to know."

She loved him? Did she really mean that? Or would she turn on him the next time he failed her? "What happened with Joy—"

"Was no more your fault than her nearly getting run over by a wagon was mine." Her expression held regret and something else. "You could have thrown that back at me all the time I was blaming you, but you didn't."

"I couldn't. You already felt so guilty—"

Her smile wavered. "There you go, being all noble again, making me love you even more."

He still couldn't wrap his mind around those words, couldn't believe after her coldness of the past few days that she could mean those words.

Then he saw her expression shift, saw the hurt and disappointment behind the overly bright smile she pasted on her lips. "Well, I've said what I had to say. And as I said, I don't really expect you to return those feelings after all I put you through. I hope you and Belva have a nice trip."

She made as if to pass him and he stepped in front of her. "Verity, please don't say those words unless you mean them." The words felt as if they'd been torn from someplace deep inside him. "Because I do love you—deeply, completely, eternally. And I love Joy as if she were my own daughter. But I will never be those things you say you want. I will never be the safe choice. So it would be far better for you to never say those words to me again than to say them lightly."

She lifted a hand to stroke the side of his cheek. "You are the man I want—not some list of traits. I love you, not because you're a hero—which you are, by the way. But I love you because of the man you are. I love *you*. Today and forever."

Those beautiful words, the love shining from her eyes, the soft caress of her hand on his face all combined to erase the last of his doubts. His hand snaked up to close over hers and he gave her palm a quick kiss, his gaze never leaving hers. But he'd much prefer to kiss those sweet lips of hers. And when she lifted her face to him, it was all the encouragement he needed.

He pressed his lips to hers. And once more was lost.

Verity wrapped her arms around Nate's neck. Because of all they'd been through, and all they'd just promised each other, this kiss was much sweeter than the last one. Her heart was so full she thought it would burst from her chest.

And this time when the kiss ended, it was with mutual sighs. He held her against his chest a moment, stroking her hair, both of them comfortable with the silence, knowing that there would be time enough later to speak of the future they would build together.

For now she reveled in his closeness, in having his arms around her, in knowing he'd forgiven her and returned her love.

Why had she ever feared this?

Finally she pushed back, resting her hands on his chest. "You still have a train to catch."

He grimaced. "I wish now that I'd never agreed to go."

"You wouldn't be the man I love if you hadn't. Belva needs you right now."

He bent down and dropped a kiss on her forehead. "I expect you to be planning a wedding while I'm gone. Because I'll be wanting to walk you down the aisle when I get back."

She raised a brow and put a hand to her heart. "Why, Mr. Cooper, is that a proposal?"

Nate frowned. "Did I skip over that part?"

"I do believe you did."

He placed a finger under her chin and tilted it up. His beautifully intense blue eyes were filled with an emotion that set her heart aflutter all over again.

"Verity Leggett, will you do me the very great honor of agreeing to be my wife?"

She threw her arms around his neck again. "I thought you'd never ask."

Epilogue

Verity stood at the back of the church, accompanied by her uncle, her daughter and her best friend.

"Hazel, stop fussing with my dress. It's fine."

Her friend ignored her plea. "Hold still. I just want to make sure this bow is perfectly even." Hazel stepped back and then sighed. "You make an absolutely radiant bride."

"Thank you." And Verity felt radiant. And blessed. And so marvelously happy.

It was her wedding day.

It had seemed as if this day would never come. Nate had been gone for five very long weeks. They'd exchanged letters during that time, but it hadn't been the same as seeing him. Hearing his voice. Holding his hand. Kissing his lips.

He'd finally returned to Turnabout just three days ago and today they were getting married. Within the hour she would become Mrs. Nathaniel Edward Cooper. She definitely liked the sound of that.

Joy glanced up at her. "Mama, how come your bouquet is so much bigger than mine?"

She smiled at her ever-curious daughter. "Because I'm the bride and you're the flower girl."

Joy seemed to think about that for a moment. Then she looked up again. "Well, then, why can't I be the bride and you be the flower girl?"

"Because you're not old enough to be a bride yet." She gave her daughter a serious, conspiratorial look. "Besides, I have to be the bride so Mr. Cooper can become your new daddy."

That seemed to make everything okay for Joy. Her demeanor lightened and she nodded in satisfaction. "Oh, okay."

Verity turned to her uncle, stepping forward to adjust his tie. "Uncle Grover, did I ever tell you and Aunt Betty how much I appreciate you taking me into your home all those years ago, and how very much I love you?"

Her uncle patted her hand, gazing at her fondly. "It was our pleasure, my dear. You have brought so much joy into our lives." He glanced at the little girl standing nearby. "Both literally and figuratively."

There was to be a grand reception at her aunt and uncle's home after the wedding. Verity had tried to dissuade them but they had insisted.

She stood on tiptoe and kissed her uncle on the cheek. "Thank you for making me feel loved."

Piano music signaled the beginning of the ceremony and Verity's pulse jumped in anticipation. Hazel opened the door and signaled Joy to lead the way. Verity smiled as she saw that Joy had managed to slip Lulu among the flowers in her basket.

The little girl, her flower basket on her arm, headed down the aisle with her head held high, leading the way to where Nate waited for them both.

Then it was Verity's turn. She slid her hand onto her uncle's arm and together they walked through the door and into the church proper.

And there he was, standing tall and proud at the front of the church, watching her with those amazing blue eyes, waiting for her to join him.

His gaze was focused on her with enough love and pride to make her feel like the luckiest woman on earth. She was so blessed to have this man in her life.

Joy stood beside him, holding on to his right hand. The little girl's face was beaming with happiness. The sight of the two of them together, obviously already connected by a beautiful father-daughter love for each other, made her happiness complete.

When they finally reached the front of the church, Uncle Grover turned and kissed her cheek, then placed her hand in Nate's free one. In a completely impulsive, unplanned gesture, she reached down and placed her bouquet in Joy's flower basket then took her free hand. For a moment they stood in a circle there at the front of the church, the three of them joined together, a symbolic sign of the life they were embarking on today.

Nate smiled into Verity's eyes, loving that she was learning to be impulsive, learning to figure out when it was okay to follow her instincts.

He gave her hand a squeeze and she squeezed right back. Then Verity bent down to kiss her daughter on the cheek and released her hand. Nate, with great formality, escorted the little girl to the front pew, where Verity's aunt and uncle sat. He, too, kissed her cheek, and then seated her, bowed and turned to return to Verity's side.

His oh-so-wonderful wife-to-be welcomed him back

with a smile that held love and the promise of wonderful things to come.

He couldn't believe this woman, this sweet, intelligent, sometimes frustrating but always loving woman, was finally going to be his—his to cherish, to protect, to share his life with. She knew about all his scars, his dark secrets, his weaknesses, and she loved him anyway.

He had truly been blessed when God brought her—and the little girl he already loved as a daughter—into his life, a blessing he would spend the rest of his days thanking God for.

Then together, he and Verity turned to face Reverend Harper, ready to speak the vows that would bind their lives together from this day forward.

Vowing to love and cherish, for the rest of his life, the woman standing before him with the sweetest smile and eyes brimmed with love for him was the easiest promise he'd ever had to make. His "I do" was said loudly and with absolute conviction.

Hearing her speak those same vows in her beautiful voice and with that steady, unwavering gaze that was focused on only him both humbled him and filled him with pride.

At last he had found the place he belonged—right here at the side of the woman he loved.

* * * * *

SPECIAL EXCERPT FROM

❧

LOVE INSPIRED
INSPIRATIONAL ROMANCE

What happens when a tough marine and a sweet dog trainer don't see eye to eye?

Read on for a sneak preview of
The Marine's Mission *by Deb Kastner.*

"Oscar will be perfect for your needs," Ruby assured Aaron, reaching down to scratch the poodle's head.

"That froufrou dog? No way, ma'am. Not gonna happen."

"Excuse me?" She'd expected him to hesitate but not downright reject her idea.

"Look, Ruby, if you like Oscar so much, then keep him for yourself. I need a man's dog by my side, not some... some..."

"Poodle?" Ruby suggested, her eyebrows disappearing beneath her long ginger bangs.

"Right. Lead me to where you keep the German shepherds, and I'll pick one out myself."

"Hmm," Ruby said, rubbing her chin as if considering his request, although she really wasn't. "No."

"No?"

"No," she repeated firmly. "First off, we don't currently have a German shepherd as part of our program."

"I'd even take a pit bull." He was beginning to sound desperate.

"Look, Aaron. Either you're going to have to learn to trust me or you may as well just leave now before we start. This isn't going to work unless you're ready to listen to me and do whatever I tell you to do."

His eyebrows furrowed. "I understand chain of command, ma'am. There were many times as a marine when I didn't exactly agree with my superiors, but I understood why it was important to follow orders."

"Okay. Let's go with that."

"For me," Aaron continued, "following orders is black-and-white. My marines' lives under my command often depended on it. But as you can see, I'm having difficulty making that transition in this situation. We're not talking people's lives here."

"I disagree. We're very much talking lives—*yours*. You may not yet have a clear vision of what you'll be able to do with Oscar, but a service dog can make all the difference."

"Yes, but you just insisted the best dog for me is a *poodle*. I'm sorry, but if you knew anything about me at all, you'd know the last dog in the world I'd choose would be a poodle."

"And yet I still believe I'm right," said Ruby with a wry smile. Somehow, she had to convince this man she knew what she was doing. "I carefully studied your file before you arrived, Aaron, and specially selected Oscar for you to work with. I'm the expert here. So how are we going to get over this hurdle?"

"I have orders to make this work. How will it look if I give up before I even start the process?" He shook his head. "No. Don't answer that. It will look as if I wasn't able to complete my mission. That's never going to happen. I'll *always* pull through, no matter what."

Don't miss
The Marine's Mission *by Deb Kastner,*
available July 2021 wherever
Love Inspired books and ebooks are sold.

LoveInspired.com

LOVE INSPIRED
INSPIRATIONAL ROMANCE

UPLIFTING STORIES OF FAITH, FORGIVENESS AND HOPE.

Join our social communities to connect with other readers who share your love!

Sign up for the Love Inspired newsletter at **LoveInspired.com** to be the first to find out about upcoming titles, special promotions and exclusive content.

CONNECT WITH US AT:

Facebook.com/LoveInspiredBooks

Twitter.com/LoveInspiredBks

Facebook.com/groups/HarlequinConnection

HARLEQUIN

Heartfelt or thrilling, passionate or uplifting—Harlequin is more than just happily-ever-after.

With twelve different series to choose from and new books available every month, you are sure to find stories that will move you, uplift you, inspire and delight you.

HNEWS2021